STEPHEN COONTS'
DEEP BLACK: DARK ZONE

STEPHEN COONTS'
DEEP BLACK:
DARK ZONE

Stephen Coonts
and Jim DeFelice

WHEELER
WINDSOR
PARAGON

This Large Print edition is published by Wheeler Publishing, Waterville, Maine USA and by BBC Audiobooks, Ltd, Bath, England.

Published in 2005 in the U.S. by arrangement with St. Martin's Press, LLC.

Published in 2005 in the U.K. by arrangement with the Orion Publishing Group Ltd.

U.S. Hardcover 1-58724-888-3 (Hardcover)
U.K. Hardcover 1-4056-1104-9 (Windsor Large Print)
U.K. Softcover 1-4056-2091-9 (Paragon Large Print)

The text of this Large Print edition is unabridged.
Other aspects of the book may vary from the original edition.

Set in 16 pt. Plantin by Ramona Watson.

Printed in the United States on permanent paper.

British Library Cataloguing-in-Publication Data available

Library of Congress Cataloging-in-Publication Data

Coonts, Stephen, 1946–
    Stephen Coonts' Deep black — dark zone / written by Stephen Coonts and Jim DeFelice.
        p. cm.
      ISBN 1-58724-888-3 (lg. print : hc : alk. paper)
      1. Intelligence officers — Fiction. 2. Undercover operations — Fiction. 3. National security — Fiction.
4. Cyberterrorism — Fiction. 5. Large type books.
I. Title: Deep black — Dark zone. II. Title: Dark zone.
III. DeFelice, Jim. IV. Title.
PS3553.O5796D444 2005

                            2004026760

STEPHEN COONTS'

DEEP BLACK:
DARK ZONE

Authors' Note

The National Security Agency, Central Intelligence Agency, Federal Bureau of Investigation, National Security Council, and Marines are, of course, real. While based on an actual organization affiliated with the NSA and CIA, Desk Three and all of the people associated with it in this book are fiction. The technology depicted here either exists or is being developed.

Details of some actual security procedures and equipment have been omitted or changed in the public interest.

1

Charles Dean saw her first.

The beauty of her face sliced past his jet lag, shocking his eyes and reaching whatever primal instinct it is that makes a man react immediately to beauty. The bright glint of her smile stood out against her rounded cheeks like the chiseled perfection of a Michelangelo sculpture, their milky whiteness accentuated by the red-orange curls streaming back from her head like flames. The rest of her body was as beautiful as her face, but it was the face — her eyes, her mouth, her smile — that caught his attention, riveting him so that he stared through the window of the London bus. It captured him so completely that when the smile began to change to a frown he felt the woman's sadness. As her expression changed from frown to confusion he, too, became puzzled. And then he realized what was happening: the woman on the street was being robbed.

In the next moment he saw that his

partner — they were traveling covertly to the same destination, not sitting together — was rushing past him to get out of the bus. Dean got up as well, following, thinking that he had lost track of the stops and missed the one where they were supposed to get off and have breakfast. It wasn't until he reached the steps of the double-decker bus that he realized his companion, NSA Deep Black operative Tommy Karr, was running to help the girl.

The bus stopped just long enough for them to get out. Dean got to the sidewalk and started to follow Karr. The other op was a bear of a man and when walking seemed to lumber, but once sprinting he could move extremely fast. He was moving now, pulling far ahead, past the woman and closing on the thief. Dean chased them around the corner toward a narrow alleyway. Professional paranoia kicked in as Dean neared the alley; belatedly he twisted backward, checking to make sure he hadn't been followed. He slowed his pace to little more than a trot and turned into the alley, warily watching the sides to make sure he hadn't run into an ambush.

Karr and the thief were gone, but the woman stood a few yards away, hands on knees catching her breath. If anything, she looked more beautiful in her distress.

"What are you doing?" hissed a low voice at the side of Dean's head.

Dean went to the girl. Her hands were balled up in fists and her face white with anger.

"They stole my purse," she said between breaths. "I have my wallet in there. All my money. Keys."

"Are you all right?" Dean asked.

"I have my pictures and credit cards and everything."

A mild French curse tripped out of her mouth. Dean was surprised and then realized she had been speaking English with an American accent.

"What are you doing?" repeated the voice.

"Helping someone," he answered aloud.

The girl looked up at him. She was in her early twenties, younger than he'd thought.

"Just talking to myself," he told her. "Bad habit."

"They stole my bag," said the girl. "There were two of them — a short skinny one and a blond hunk."

"The hunk's not a thief," said Dean. "He's a friend of mine. He's trying to help."

"Oh." She unclenched her fists and curled her arms in front of her breasts, holding herself protectively. "Oh. Well, thanks."

The girl wore a knit top over her skirt; the top stopped just high enough to let her tanned belly peek out. It wasn't a belly at all; it was taut and tight, as if she were an athlete. She wore Nikes on her feet, black running shoes with red ripples up the middle.

"You have a mission, for cryin' out loud!" said the voice in his head. "You're not a tourist!"

Dean ignored the voice. Karr told him this would get easier to do; like much the younger man said, that prediction had proven correct.

"Which way did they go?" Dean asked the girl.

"Over that wall. Do you think he'll catch him?"

A thick hand and then a shock of golden hair appeared at the top of the wall as if in answer. Tommy Karr vaulted his six-eight frame over the wall, grinning and holding the girl's purse in his paw.

"Hey, of course I'll catch him," Karr said. "Pipsqueak like that? Give me a break." Karr stalked forward, pocketbook in hand. "Here you go, ma'am." He turned and winked at Dean. "Hey, Charlie. What are you doing in London?"

"Backing you up," said Dean.

"Thanks." Karr turned back to the girl, who was going through the purse. "All there?"

"Yes."

Dean saw the smile he'd seen from a distance up close now. Her eyes flashed and Dean realized the girl was going to kiss Karr; he felt a twinge of jealousy and even disappointment, wishing that he'd been the one to grab the thief.

"Aw, hey, it was nothing," said Karr as she kissed him on the cheek. Karr blushed a decent red — something Dean had never seen him do. "Saved you a trip to the police station. Come on, Charlie; you owe me a coffee from the last time you backed me up. Better make it breakfast," he added, starting to walk from the alley. "I just worked up an appetite."

"Let me treat you," said the girl.

"Sorry," said Dean. "We, uh, we have to talk business."

"Business before pleasure," said Karr. He laughed — Tommy Karr *always* laughed — and waved at her. "Forget about it."

"Well, at least tell me your name."

"Kjartan Magnor-Karr," said Karr. "But you can call me Tommy."

"Tommy?"

"The name's a long story. But it's easier to say than Kjartan, right?"

"I'm Deidre Clancy."

"Great. See ya around," said Karr. He jumped back into motion, trotting out into the street to hail an approaching black cab.

"That was an extremely foolish thing to do," hissed the voice in Dean's head as he and Karr settled into the back of the cab. The voice belonged to Marie Telach, who was the supervisor in what was known as "the Art Room," a high-tech situation room and information center at the headquarters of the National Security Agency in Fort Meade, Maryland. The Art Room connected field operatives such as Dean and Karr with the full range of NSA resources, including satellite data and real-time code breaking, to use the layman's term for cryptography. Dean and Karr were part of the small cadre of agents who worked for the Desk Three covert operations group, generally known by its code-word designation "Deep Black" — assuming, of course, that it was known at all.

Deep Black had been designed to bring the agency's technological edge to covert operations, and it certainly did that. Some of its gadgets bordered on science fiction. To take one example: while the communications system that the agents used had actually been perfected in the early 1990s, it was still at least a generation beyond the systems used by even the most advanced security teams, eschewing traditional earbuds for chip sets implanted near the ear. While there were some technical limitations with the coverage, a system of satellites kept them in instant contact throughout most of the Northern Hemisphere and a good portion of the Southern. The system included a wireless microphone, antenna, and controls integrated with the agent's clothes, usually in his belt.

Dean, a relative newcomer to Deep Black and by far the oldest field operative, was somewhat dubious about the technology. The communications system might allow the Art Room to supply an agent with up-to-the-moment intelligence all right, but it also let the people there interfere with what was going on. Telach's job was to supervise the specialists on duty in the Art Room, including the "runner" who fed information to the team during a mission. But Telach tended to act as if she controlled the field ops as well. Dean, who had seen the results of "input" from head-quarters during the final days of the Vietnam War, bristled at the idea that someone in a bunker several thousand miles away had a better idea of what to do than he did.

Karr, however, was used to Telach hounding him. He handled her as he handled nearly everything — with a joke.

"Hey, Mom," he said aloud. "What's up?"

"Don't give me one of your routines, Karr. You're lucky Mr. Rubens wasn't here. He'd've read you the riot act."

"What, he took off again? I thought he worked twenty-four/seven."

"I'm not in the mood for your smart-aleck answers today, Tommy. It's still pretty early back here. Now let's stick to the game plan from now on."

"Yeah, sure. The game plan was break-fast, right?"

Dean looked at the cabbie in the rear-view mirror. If he thought his passengers were "crackers," he kept the proverbial cabbie's silence about it.

"Breakfast?" Karr asked Dean.

"Good for me."

"We have time, right? The meeting hasn't been changed?"

"It's still at two," said Telach tersely.

"Well, there you go," said Karr.

"Tommy, I realize this is a routine assignment, but please, stick to the game plan from now on. Get breakfast, then take a quick look at the park and play tourist for a few hours. *Don't* chase any more purse snatchers."

"Shepherd's pie would hit the spot," said Karr. "Can you get that this early?"

"I'll settle for some coffee," said Dean as the cabdriver finally glanced in the mirror to see what the crazy conversation was about.

2

Mussa Duoar was not an unintelligent man, but he did not understand the equations or the mechanics of the computer simulation the engineer demonstrated for him. He only knew that the changing lines on the screen represented a three-dimensional wave rushing toward shore. As they reached the edges of the green trapezoid on the computer panel, they nudged the top of the scale drawn there, which represented fifty meters above sea level.

"The force of the explosion creates a series of waves that are amplified by the geography of the Channel," said the engineer in his rapid, Pakistani-inflected English. "You have the initial shock wave, followed by the Chunnel collapsing. As the energy waves radiate away at a rapid speed, they meet a series of underwater promontories which increase the effect, as we see in this set of equations. Interestingly, the angle is quite significant, due to the amplitude."

Mussa smiled at the engineer. *"Je ne comprends pas,"* he said in French.

The man blinked at him. Though he had come from Pakistan to France nearly three years before, he didn't understand more than a few words of the language. Mussa, who spoke Arabic, English, and several North African languages besides French, switched back to English. "I don't understand. Can you put this in words for a simple layman?"

"Of course," said the engineer indulgently. He had to speak very loudly, because the office was located in the upper floors of a printing factory in the city of Paris. There were advantages to this — the rest of the floor was empty and there were no workers nearby, save for the two men on Mussa's payroll guarding the door outside. But the incessant pounding of the machines below made it difficult to think, let alone hear someone else speaking. The sound was so loud that a gun could be fired here without being heard elsewhere in the building — Mussa had already tested this for himself.

"The explosion and collapse of the tunnel beneath the Channel is like the earth shifting across a fault line during an earthquake," said the engineer. "The speed and size of the drop represent a great deal of energy. That energy is transferred through the water as a wave. As the wave hits the shallow shoreline, it bounds upward. Think of it as a water balloon being squished from the bottom — the water has to go somewhere. The effect is a wall of water that rushes over everything. It's similar to a tsunami caused by an earthquake. In vulnerable areas like Japan and Alaska in the United States, waves have reached over fifty feet high and obliterated large buildings. The underwater geometry is different, but the size of the initial event should be larger and its effect more concentrated. Is that more understandable?"

"Very," said Mussa.

"It's a slight distortion, but the general idea is there." The engineer flashed a series of equations on the screen that he said demonstrated the importance of speed and amplitude in the simulation. His model was conservative, he said, based on an earthquake that would be measured at "only" 6.0. The blast they were contemplating should yield at least 6.3, if not more. Assuming that his calculations were correct and the Channel tunnel collapsed, the shock wave would be several magnitudes greater.

"I have a second set of simulations to demonstrate that," said the engineer, tapping on his computer screen. The man loved his simulations, Mussa thought; he spoke of the equations involved as a fanatical wine lover might talk about a wine.

"So you see, fifty feet of water, as a minimum. Assuming, of course, that the models and their assumptions are correct. I believe they are, but this is the thing one doesn't know until it happens."

The sudden note of doubt in the engineer's voice shook Mussa. "The bomb won't explode?"

"Oh, no, no, that's a given. That part we're sure of. I've told you that many times. That we're sure of. You've seen those equations many times. Many, many times. The tsunami. That's what I meant. And even there — something will happen. Something devastating and pleasing to God. I have dreamed of this effect for months. I've modeled it many times. I'm sure something will happen. Something brilliant. But will it be fifty feet? Seventy-five? One hundred? Those are things we cannot know."

A fifty-foot wall of water radiating through the English Channel would wipe out Belgium and the Netherlands, as well as much of the French coast. But as far as Mussa was concerned, all of that was simply a bonus to his actual goal — obliterating the Chunnel, which connected Britain and France. It was God's revenge: the infidels had dared to claim their tunnel superior to the one true God's decision to separate the lands; Mussa had been chosen to prove their folly.

The engineer's reassurance that the weapon would work relaxed Mussa, and he let the man prattle on. The engineer called yet another simulation up on his screen. He had spent considerable time on this — time that had cost Mussa dearly.

"Very similar to the fault line of an earthquake. Imagine a girder dropped in a swimming pool," said the engineer. "A wipeout, I think the Americans say."

The engineer brought up a new set of calculations that showed the best place for the device to be located: 8.342 miles from the start of the French side. Such precision would not be possible, the Pakistani admitted, but the closer the better.

Cherbourg, Le Havre, Calais, Dunkerque, Oostende, Knokke — overwhelmed with a flood that would rival the Patriarch Noah's. *Perhaps that was the one true Lord's actual intent,* thought Mussa. It was not his to know beforehand.

But the possibility was delicious, was it not?

Mussa turned to the window, gazing toward the Eiffel Tower in the distance.

Delicious horror. And it would come at the climax of his complicated plan for revenge: personal revenge for the death of his father, revenge on the nation that had discriminated against him and his family, and revenge on the race that had devastated his people. God was powerful.

"And when will I be paid?" asked the engineer.

Mussa turned around, pretending to be shocked. "I thought you were working for the glory of Allah."

"Always," said the engineer. "But I must also see to worldly concerns."

"You've spoken to Arno?"

"As you directed."

"And the brothers?"

"The brothers?"

Arno was Mussa's lieutenant and was doing much of the work on the Chunnel project; it was necessary that he be kept informed. The brothers were another story.

"I'm not sure I know what you're talking about," added the engineer. The man was very good with computers, but he was not a convincing liar, and so his confusion now

reassured Mussa that the brothers —
known to him as Said and Jamal, though
he doubted those were anything like their
real names — had not been contacted. He
did not trust them and had kept their operation isolated from his own concerns.

"I've done everything you asked," said
the engineer.

Mussa nodded. "Then you will be paid
promptly, by the grace of God."

"The sooner the better. And will there
be a bonus?"

"A bonus? Oh yes."

The engineer began to smile. As he did,
Mussa took a Glock 25 from his pocket
and put three bullets through the engineer's forehead. Mussa had not planned to
kill the man himself, but his greed dis-
gusted him.

3

William Rubens, the head of Desk Three and the number two man at the National Security Agency, got up slowly from his bed and took a deep breath. He held it, as he had been taught by his yoga teacher many years ago, then slowly exhaled. He repeated the process twice more; after the third time he stretched forward, hands together, and began the sunrise pose, the first yoga posture he had ever learned.

Rubens regarded yoga more as an interesting collection of ideas than tenets of religion, and his daily routines were more physical workouts than spiritual exercises. He did not believe that souls recycled through the universe, and the Indian theory of the body and its different energies and cycles seemed laughable to him. But the postures did send a warm surge up his spine, relaxing him in a way that sleep never seemed to accomplish.

Rubens had never slept well, and these days he slept as poorly as ever. It was not the tension of his job; he had dealt with that for a long time. A personal matter bothered him, which was unusual for Rubens. He liked to say that he had no personal matters, and it was not so far from the truth.

He finished his routine and went downstairs for his coffee. After he poured it, he put his right index finger on the small pad at the right of the secure computer on the countertop. With the fingerprint recognized, the computer proceeded through the first stages of its boot-up. When the screen flashed, Rubens pulled the keyboard out and typed in his passwords, allowing the computer to proceed, tying into the NSA system by a secure connection.

As he waited, he picked up the remote and turned on the small television across the room near the bread machine that he had never used. Rubens had probably as little love for the television as he had for baking bread (the machine was a present from one of his many and mostly annoying cousins), but he had come to appreciate the fact that it was important to check the mainstream news media every so often. The daily news summaries he received via e-mail could not communicate the impact of television's visuals.

He lingered on CNN only long enough to realize that the anchor was pontificating about a sports drug scandal. On Fox, a man in a rumpled gray suit declared that the time had come to invade North Korea. The text under the man's face claimed that he was a former CIA analyst. Rubens knew the man well enough to know that this was indeed true — and that the man's area of expertise had been European farm commodities. Rubens listened for a minute before deciding that the analyst knew as little about Korea as Rubens did about European wheat.

If there *was* a time to invade North Korea, it had been in the 1990s. Clinton had blown it, like much else — but that was all academic now.

Rubens flipped through a few more channels before turning his attention back to the computer. Once a cut-and-paste Xerox job, the daily briefing was now delivered to the upper echelons of the administration via e-mail with links to more detailed information available on SpyNet, an exclusive intranet service used by the government's "information" agencies, of which the NSA was one. Ruben scrolled through the e-mail quickly. It was all very low-level, and nothing piqued his interest.

A good thing. That meant nothing had blown up overnight.

He emptied his cup of coffee and picked up the black phone that sat at the side of the computer. The phone looked as if it dated from the 1960s, and it was in fact possible that the outer shell did. Inside, however, the phone held a state-of-the-art encryption device that rendered his conversations indecipherable to anyone who did not have a similar model. And in theory — much in the field of encryption was theory, for the most part impossible to definitively prove or, to put it more accurately, not worth the time needed to prove — only the person with the number Rubens dialed would be able to understand what he said.

"Art Room," said Marie Telach, picking up on the other end of the line. She knew it would be him, but the flat, neutral answer was part of her personality. The fact that she never deviated was a large part of the reason he had chosen her for her job, though lately she had shown alarming signs of being human.

A vacation would cure that, no doubt.

"This is Rubens. How is the Korean operation proceeding?"

"Lia is on her way to the airport. She'll be in Beijing in a few hours."

"Very good. And the other matter," added Rubens. "Tommy Karr and Charlie Dean?"

"There was a complication."

"A complication?"

The mission had been a routine milk run.

"Tommy stopped a purse snatching near the Courts after they landed in London."

Was that all? Rubens glanced at his watch. "Making the jump to police work, is he?"

"They're on schedule. The meet isn't for a while yet and everything looks fine. But I thought I should mention it because the robbery victim —"

"Please don't tell me it was a member of the SVR," said Rubens, using the Russian initials for the Russian Foreign Intelligence Service, *Sluzhba Vneshnev Razvedki,* one of the successors to the Cold War era KGB.

"No — it was Deidre Clancy, the daughter of our ambassador to Great Britain."

Rubens did not know Ambassador Alroy Clancy very well; he'd been appointed to the post largely as a reward for his service to the President's campaign committee. This was exactly the sort of complication Rubens could live with.

"He didn't realize who it was," added Telach. "He thought she was just another pretty girl. I expect you may hear about it at some point."

"I appreciate that, Ms. Telach. Anything else?"

"Nothing at the moment."

He looked over at his clock. "I'm off to my seven o'clock appointment. Keep me informed on the Korean matter. You can buzz me."

"Yes, sir."

The politically connected ambassador to Great Britain owing Desk Three, and by extension William Rubens, a favor: the day was starting out on a good note.

Twenty minutes later, Rubens parked his car in the lot of a suburban Maryland nursing home. He tried to force himself into an overtly cheerful mood as he walked the thirty feet or so from his car to the front door.

Overtly cheerful was a difficult act here. The home was a good one but far from lavish. The lower floors had the feel of a modest apartment house in a once middle-class neighborhood gone slightly to seed. The upper floors were more like hospital wards.

The truly grim floor was at the very top, where he was bound.

Rubens smiled at the receptionist — at this hour, the job was held by one of the uniformed security people, an older woman who worked here largely because her father was a resident — and passed on to the elevators beyond. Rubens was a regular visitor early Monday and Thursday mornings, known not only by the security guard and medical staff but also by the housekeepers and even one or two of the cafeteria personnel. They knew him not as William Rubens but rather as "the General's friend." The title was more of an honor than Rubens could have explained.

One of the nurses from the twelfth floor was waiting for the elevator, a tray of medicines in her hand.

"Morning," she said.

"Hello. How is he today?" asked Rubens.

The nurse grimaced before she spoke; the expression communicated much more than her words.

"Good days and bad days," she said.

"Yes. We all have them," said Rubens.

"Yes, we do, hon. Yes, we do."

As the General's days went, this one would actually be classified as a good one — when Rubens entered, the old man who had once been the head of the NSA was sitting upright in bed, staring toward his window at the side of the room. The view was of a gray patch of an old train yard, long since abandoned to junk cars and piles of broken furniture. The window was dirty and turned the scene even grayer. But the General undoubtedly didn't notice.

"Good morning, General," said Rubens. "You're looking good today."

Major General John Paul Rosenberg (Ret.) turned in his direction and nodded. Rubens pulled over the metal chair and sat at the side of the bed.

"I picked up a book on Mussolini the other evening, of all things," said Rubens. "A biography. The one by Fermi. I had never read it. I started thumbing through it and found myself engrossed."

The General did not acknowledge the statement. Rubens — who had indeed picked up a copy of the book — began telling the General about what he had read: the Italian dictator's childhood, his attraction to violence, his background. It was exactly the sort of conversation the two men might have had twenty years before, though then the roles would have been reversed. Then the General was trying to broaden Rubens' sense and understanding of the world, arouse his curiosity in things beyond math and art.

Military history and politics were special passions for Rosenberg, though when they talked about math and art, Rubens had found the General at least as knowledgeable as himself.

An odd combination, the General had said the very first time they had spoken — Rubens' second day at the agency, at lunch.

Odd to others but not to Rubens. He had loved math as a boy; its logic brought order to his life and channeled his imagination. Art was more a family birthright, passed down in the genes. He was descended from Peter Paul Rubens, the Flemish painter who lived from 1577 to 1640 and was so famous that people besides art historians knew who he was — albeit often because his name had become a euphemism for "fat."

Where many youths might turn to art as a relief from the rigors of school subjects like math, Rubens found relief in the other direction. His early years were nothing but art; he was saturated in it by the time he reached high school. The unemotional impersonality of numbers was a great comfort. Working on his doctorate had seemed more like a vacation than the rigorous exercise it was supposed to be.

The General had sent Rubens to MIT, where he'd obtained another doctorate, this one in political science. His thesis involved the intersection of information technology and foreign relations; part of it remained classified, though in Rubens' opinion this was now due more to inherent bureaucratic caution than any real need for secrecy.

MIT had been important for other reasons. He had taken a postgraduate seminar in foreign relations and technology there, studying with George Hadash, now the national security adviser. In some respects Hadash had taken over the General's role as career mentor, but the relationship was otherwise very different. Hadash, though certainly an intelligent man, had too many flaws. And the General — the General was not only Rubens' intellectual mentor; he was also a bona fide hero. He had proven himself under fire, first as a seventeen-year-old private in the Italian campaign during World War II and later as a colonel in Vietnam. He'd earned his way to Officer Candidate School at a time when Jews were, at best, a novelty in the officers' ranks, and if any man deserved the title "a soldier's soldier," John Paul Rosenberg did. From Rubens' first day at the NSA, he had viewed Rosenberg with awe and reverence, both well deserved.

Their roles now were worse than reversed. To the General's great credit, Rubens had used his intellectual gifts to broaden his knowledge in many ways. But the General's deterioration over the last year, due to the accelerated effects of Alzheimer's disease, had left him far emptier than the bright young man he'd set out to cultivate nearly two decades before.

"I'm hoping that the Mussolini book will explain something about his attraction to violence," said Rubens. "I can understand the attraction to power. We all want to feel important."

The General turned to him. "Marshall was very underrated. A hell of a man."

This was not the non sequitur it appeared on the surface, Rubens decided. Mussolini had been Italy's dictator during World War II. Marshall — George C. Marshall, clearly — had been the head of the Army and one of Roosevelt's top lieutenants during the war. And, as the General stated, one of the most underrated leaders in American history, or certainly one of the most forgotten. How many five-star generals won the Nobel Peace Prize? Yet Marshall didn't exist to most Americans.

Mussolini–World War II–Marshall. The connection was logical.

"An important leader," said Rubens. "FDR seemed to understand his worth."

"In Moscow, a difficult place to be."

Rubens waited patiently for more information, but none came. After more than a minute of silence, he prompted with a comment about the KGB — this often got the General going, if only on a tangent. But the old man had fallen completely silent. After another long minute, Rubens began talking about Marshall, asking about the relationship between Marshall and President Truman. But the General no longer acknowledged him.

Rubens stayed for twenty minutes, as he always did. Then he rose to leave. He was almost to the door when the General's daughter, Rebecca Stein, came in. She feigned surprise at finding Rubens there, though he knew the meeting could not have been by chance.

"William, how are you?" she said, holding out her hand to him.

"I'm very well, Rebecca."

"What a nice surprise."

"Yes," he said. "I'm sorry, I have to be on my way. Good-bye, General. I'll see you later in the week."

"Would you mind if we visited for a moment?" Rebecca asked Rubens. "I'll come with you. We can talk while you walk."

Rubens said nothing. He let her out of the door ahead of him, strolling toward the elevators neither slowly nor quickly.

"The competency proceeding," said Rebecca. "I've started — I mean, we're preparing papers."

"Yes, of course."

"You're going to, uh, uh," she said.

"Object? I have to. Your father wanted me appointed guardian."

"That's up to the court," said Rebecca.

Rubens didn't answer. Technically, she was correct. But the court was bound by state law to take the incapacitated person's wishes into account. Several years before, the General had specified that Rubens should look after his affairs if he became incapacitated. The document was in order, except for one small possible technicality: it used the term *conservator* rather than *guardian* in naming Rubens to look after the General's affairs. To a layman, the difference might have seemed insignificant, but under Maryland law the roles were subtly different; the conservator's powers were slightly more limited. At least technically, an incapacitated person with a conservator retained more rights — and, in Rubens' view, more dignity. The difference was mostly symbolic, certainly in this case — but the symbolism would have been significant to the General. And therefore it was significant to Rubens.

It was also a door for Rebecca and her lawyer.

"I know that there are, that you have objections," said Rebecca.

Rubens pushed the elevator button.

"My father merely filled out a form that the government told him to fill out," said Rebecca.

"Even if the agency had advised him on that matter, which I'm not sure that they did, the fact remains that he was free to do as he pleased."

"Oh, give me a break."

Rubens welcomed the sarcastic tone; he felt more comfortable dealing with Rebecca when she wasn't pretending to be nice. The door to the elevator opened. Rubens stepped inside. Rebecca did so as well.

"Dale Jamison told my father that he had to have someone from the NSA as his guardian," said Rebecca. "He was ordered to insert you. That's no more an act of free will than being robbed."

"Quite a comparison," said Rubens.

"A hearing will be very embarrassing for your agency, I can guarantee," said Rebecca.

Rubens took a long, deep breath — a yoga breath — before answering. He could be cruel, but it was not necessary; all he had to do was state the facts. "The General carefully considered the circumstances, and chose to nominate me to handle his affairs. I think that's significant."

The elevator opened. Rubens, thankful to be released, strode out.

"Mr. Rubens. Billy."

Rubens did not break his stride. He hated to be called Billy.

Still, he stopped when she touched his arm.

"We shouldn't be enemies," she said. "We want the same thing."

A lie, but he let it pass.

"I'm not your enemy," he told her. "But I have my duty."

"Because the agency wants you to do this."

"No, because your father asked me," said Rubens. "I owe it to him."

"I'm his daughter!"

Of the many possible responses, he prudently chose silence.

"Legally, I should be entitled to be his

guardian," continued Rebecca more calmly.

"Legally, if it is submitted to a court, then the matter will be decided," said Rubens. It was the mildest thing he could think of to say.

"Bill, please, be reasonable. I thought we were friends."

She gripped his arm gently, squeezing it like she might squeeze the hand of a baby. He wanted to believe that her motives and emotions were sincere. But he couldn't; if she had been sincere surely she would have made things right with her father long ago. The General had given her plenty of chances.

"I'm sorry. I didn't think any of this should go to court," said Rubens honestly. "The informal arrangement was fine with me. You've always been able to see whatever records you wanted. There's no need to do any of this."

"This isn't a matter of looking at bank records," said Rebecca.

And so, she was flushed from her lie. She wanted control — undoubtedly for financial gain. Greed, not concern, motivated her.

"I have to do my duty as I see it," said Rubens. "You'd ask no less if I were doing it for you." He resumed his stride toward the car.

4

Lia DeFrancesca got out of the vehicle with her light bag and waited for her escort, feigning considerably more fatigue than she actually felt. Her two-day visit to North Korea had been an utter and complete bore. It was North Korea, of course, and no undercover American operative could afford to take a visit to the world's most tightly controlled enemy state lightly. But it had been, in a word, dull.

As Deep Black assignments went, her job had been relatively straightforward: visit the North Korean port city of Hŭngnam while posing as a Chinese journalist. She was supposedly writing a story about the port, but this was merely intended to be a cover for passing along a business card from the Hong Kong industrialist who owned the newspaper. The high-ranking military people she had met with upon her arrival knew this, of course, and anticipated a successful business relationship in the future.

Which surely would be possible. But that cover was itself a cover for Lia's real mission — giving the phone number of a dedicated CIA line that could be used to set up a visit to China by one of the men who wanted to defect.

Lia had passed along the card within an hour of arriving. The rest of the time she'd pretended to be a journalist, accompanied by a Korean whose Chinese was rather limited, though if Lia were to complain the woman stood a good chance of being sent to a retraining camp from which she would not emerge alive. Lia's Korean was also limited; fortunately, the Art Room had round-the-clock translators to help fill the gaps.

Her keeper had taken Lia on a one-hour stroll around the city each day. She had seen a residential area that combined a 1950s-style apartment building (built in the 1970s) and much older traditional homes. She'd also walked through what appeared to be a factory district, though it was completely devoid of people and there was no smoke coming from any of the stacks.

On the way back to the hotel yesterday, Lia had seen a group of musicians with battered brass instruments pass nearby. Lia asked who they were and her minder explained that they were a band recruited to perform for workers in the countryside as they labored on nearby farms. The practice had been very successful after a flood in 1999, and the great leader Kim Jong Il had requested it be renewed.

The minder said all of that without taking a breath and then stopped speaking so abruptly that Lia thought she had suffered a seizure. They walked silently the rest of the way to the hotel.

Working in fields after harvest time? Only in North Korea.

The 737 that was due to take Lia back to China was visible beyond the terminal building at the airport. North Korean airports were all under military control, and the only airport that saw much "normal" civilian business was near the capital. The facilities hosted aircraft used for long-range patrols of the oceans to the east, but the base was not considered an important one and even by Korean standards appeared run-down. Flights from China came twice a week. The airline, Hwatao, was owned by a conglomerate that listed Shanghai as its home address, though Lia knew from her brief that its stock was split between a general in southern China and two brothers from Taiwan — an interesting example of the intertwined interests of free and communist China.

"Du bu qi," said her minder, using Chinese. The words meant "excuse me" or "pardon" in Putonghua, the official Mandarin dialect of northern China. Lia's cover called for her to use Putonghua, though she was more comfortable and familiar with Cantonese, which she had first learned as a very young child after her adoption in America. The similarity between the two dialects sometimes got in the way, as her brain tended to blur them.

"What is it?" replied Lia in Chinese. She looked back toward the car, thinking she had left something inside.

"A comrade wishes to speak to you," said the minder. "Those men will escort you."

Lia spotted two soldiers walking toward them from the terminal building.

"Why?"

"Oh, routine," said the minder.

"A fee?" asked Lia.

"Zaijan," said the minder without answering the question. "Good-bye."

"Yes, good-bye, and thank you," Lia told her.

Fee was a euphemism for a bribe, which tended to be customary.

Lia gripped the handle of her overnight bag tightly. She had no weapon on her. Her only link with the outside world was her communications system, which was powered by circuits and a battery built into her belt. She clicked it now, making sure it was on. "A fee," she muttered under her breath, just loud enough for the Art Room to hear.

"We briefed you on that," answered Jeff Rockman, who had just taken over as her runner. "Pay it and come home."

The men carried AK-47s that were perhaps twice as old as they were. Several paces behind them was an officer; he was a few years older and shorter than Lia.

"Nu xing shenme?" asked the man in Korean. He was a lieutenant.

"He's asking your name," said the translator in the Art Room as Lia hesitated.

Actually, he was asking her family name, Lia realized, and the implications were very different. She felt her body tense.

"Why?" Lia answered sharply in Chinese.

"Come this way, miss."

"Wo xing Wang," she told him, saying that her family name was Wang. She then asked what was going on, as she was due aboard the flight waiting out on the tarmac.

The officer's face flushed. He stamped his right foot and pointed in the direction of the building. *"Jepjjok!"* he thundered. "That way." The two soldiers flinched.

"I am on important private business," she said.

North Korean officials tended to back off when she spoke firmly and with implied authority. But the young lieutenant was too full of himself — or maybe too worried about losing face in front of his men — to do that. "You will come now or be dragged away," he told her.

Lia struggled against her instinct to lash out. She probably could deck the lieutenant and wrestle one of the weapons from one of the soldiers. But there would be no escape after that.

I played it wrong, she realized. *I should have been more submissive, more in character. He needs to feel superior.*

Lia bowed her head forward. *"Mianhamnida,"* she said in Korean, giving an apology. "Yes, I am going."

The officer said something in Korean that she did not understand. The translator back in the Art Room apparently did not hear it or thought it unimportant to relay.

There was a subtle etiquette involved in

the bribe exchange. The official would not be merely after money. While China was North Korea's strong ally, there was a great deal of resentment among most Koreans toward their large northern neighbor. China's historic domination and long occupation of the Korean peninsula caused deep animosity, which could not be erased over a period of only fifty years. Many Chinese — and this would especially apply to anyone associated with the Westernized and hence "decadent" Hong Kong area, where Lia's credentials as well as her travel arrangements declared she was from — were viewed by the Koreans as greedy, soft, and worse. The fact that she was a woman, alone, young, and single, didn't help the situation, as it only lowered her status in the eyes of the official, at least partly canceling any connection she had to the higher-ups in town. Lia and her briefer had played out different scenarios on how to offer the bribe, which of course wasn't referred to as a bribe but an "official fee for expediting important matters." Lia had to be the one to suggest it, once the official pointed out a problem.

She followed down the hallway toward a small room at the side of the building. The room smelled of fresh paint. The walls were bright white and there were six overhead incandescents, unusual in a country where power was severely rationed. In the middle of the room sat a large table, the folding sort often used at banquets. The four chairs next to it were heavy metal affairs with vinyl cushions. Lia walked toward the table but waited to sit until instructed to do so — an important point her briefer had emphasized.

Outside, she heard the sound of the 737's engines being spooled up.

"I hope my papers are in order," she told the officer in Korean. "My time here has been wonderful and productive. I have met with many important people."

She continued on with a standard formula about how helpful the local officials had been and how indebted she was to Korea's great leader, Kim Jong Il. She stuck to the official cover that she was a journalist; the officer would know and probably care nothing about the business arrangements.

The phrases did nothing to soften the officer's grimace. He requested her travel documents. Lia hesitated, worrying that the officer intended on taking her place on the plane himself, a contingency she had not considered until now. But she had no choice but to hand over the small sheaf of papers.

As she did, she mentioned that she hoped all of the proper fees had been paid. The lieutenant did not take the hint. Nor did he seem all that interested in the documents themselves. He pushed the papers to one side and stared at her.

"My superiors would not wish me to be late arriving in Beijing," she said in Chinese. She wanted the Korean translation — she thought it likely now that the officer did not speak Chinese very well, if at all — but the Art Room had gone silent. Possibly they had decided to communicate as little as possible, which was standard procedure when a field op was in a difficult situation.

And this definitely qualified. The aircraft engines seemed to kick up another notch.

Lia decided to turn her communications system on and off, in effect flashing her runner back home. But as she reached for the belt buckle, one of the guards grabbed her arm. His fingers dug into her bicep. It took all of her self-restraint to avoid turning on the man and taking him down.

Could I if I have to?

Absolutely. She could have his rifle in a breath, club his companion in the stomach

— no, the head or neck — then bring the gun to bear on the officer.

And then?

The officer said something in Korean. Lia did not catch it all, but the words she understood were ominous: he called her a tasty plum.

The Art Room translator started to supply the words, but Lia didn't wait. "My employer wishes me home on time," she said in Chinese. "And unhurt. I do not work for a mere newspaper," she added. And then, switching from Chinese to Korean, she asked if she had to pay a customs tax: *"Gwanserui neya hamnikka?"*

Her sharp and quick tone conveyed her anger and emotion quite clearly, just as her snapping open the purse showed she was willing to pay for her freedom.

The lieutenant leaned forward, eyes locking on hers. He told her in Korean that she was not in China. As the translator began translating in her head, Lia placed her hands on the edge of the table and leaned forward.

"I'm in a hurry," she said in Korean. The phrase sounded like *"ku-p'haiyo"* and under the best of circumstances would not have been considered particularly polite.

"You're going too far," hissed the Art

Room supervisor, Marie Telach. "Relax. He just wants money. And to see you cower. Let him have his ego trip."

Lia stared at the Korean officer; the lieutenant stared back. Finally he started to smile and then laugh. He raised his head, looking at the guards. Lia, though still angry, began to relax.

"I'm sorry," she said. She launched into the standard apology again, blaming the stress of travel for her rude behavior.

The lieutenant nodded. The documents, he said, were good, but she had neglected to get a stamp.

"Then that must be taken care of," said Lia, relieved that finally they had come to the endgame. "How much is the fee?" she asked in Chinese. "I understand that it is very important to pay properly for the trouble a visitor brings."

As the Art Room translator began giving her the words in Korean, Lia saw the shadow of one of the guards moving from the corner of her eye. She started to spin toward him and was caught off-guard by the hard shock of the other man's fist against the other side of her head.

Her breath caught in her throat as she fell forward, fists flailing but catching

51

nothing but air. She tried to get up but lost her balance and spun down toward the floor, pummeled into a cocoon of numbness.

5

The autumn air had a slight chill to it, and Dean zipped his windbreaker as he walked along the lake, feigning interest in the nearby pelicans. Buckingham Palace lay almost directly ahead, though the park's trees and rolling terrain hid it from view. His interest in the palace was in keeping with his cover; to authenticate the person he was supposed to meet — and vice versa — he had to ask about the palace and its tours. The contact was to give the hours for tours backward: 5:30 to 9:30.

Karr was somewhere behind him, a hundred or so yards away, wandering around the park near the lake. St. James Park was once a marshland, and despite its well-kept gardens and elaborate lawns, it did not take all that much imagination to picture the park wild. Tourists and office workers lolled through it, pausing to stare at the birds or admire the flowers, then wandering off nonchalantly, as if they had no cares in the world. Dean tried willing himself into a similar mind-set; his mission was a simple one and could have been accomplished by a clerk at the embassy — or so Karr said. All they had to do was meet a messenger, get something from him, and bring it home.

They had no idea what they were getting and only the vaguest description of the man: He would wear a brown beret and would stand at the crown of the bridge for a moment before descending to meet them ten yards "farther on" from the base. They would then authenticate each other with the prearranged phrase.

Simple enough. But in his short stint with Desk Three, Dean had learned that nothing associated with the NSA was simple. Dean gazed at the water, then turned abruptly and began walking. He glanced at his watch; he was right on time.

Two small girls ran past him. *They must be schoolgirls,* he thought, then wondered why they were out of school in the middle of the day. A middle-aged woman followed. She looked as if she were going to say something to him; he smiled. He didn't know if his contact would be male or female, but he doubted he or she would have children along. That might be the ultimate cover for a spy, Dean thought — kids.

The path before him was empty. He turned back toward the pond, stooping low to see one of the brightly colored birds. He had to make contact along this side of the path and wanted to stay within a fifty-yard stretch where it was easy for Karr to watch him. So he became a bird-watcher, inordinately interested in the red feathers of the nearby fowl.

When he rose there were more people ahead. He strolled forward slowly, forcing a smile on his face.

Come on, he thought to himself. *Come on.*

Tommy Karr rubbed his chin as he leaned against the iron fence, watching Dean from the corner of his eye. Their contact was running at least five minutes late. Delays were an inevitable part of the business and did not in and of themselves signal trouble. Nonetheless, delays tended to complicate matters even when they were caused by nothing more dangerous than a traffic jam. The rendezvous point had probably seemed like a good one to whoever had chosen it — Karr suspected the messenger but did not actually know — but in point of fact the park was not well suited for an exchange. The woods on the other side of the lake provided easy cover for a surveillance operation; Karr had gone through them earlier and found none, but a jogger could easily trot down the nearby path and vanish in the woods. Karr had also planted a small video camera on a tree near the path — the camera was about the size of a large marble and called a video fly, *fly* being a takeoff on *bug*. Signals from the fly were relayed to a small transmitter that uploaded them to an orbiting satellite and from there to the Art Room. But it would have been impossible to cover every possible position where a trail team might hide. Just as bad, there were policemen at both ends of the path and others who would eventually notice Dean pausing on the pathway; sooner or later someone would get nosy.

Not that they hadn't covered that contingency, at least to an extent. At ten minutes past, Dean would walk to the very far end of the arranged area, cross over the bridge, and then loop back. When he reached the far end of the area he would look impatiently at his watch and begin playing the worried companion, wondering where his date had gotten to. That act could take them through another fifteen minutes; they'd then swap positions for five minutes before bagging it. Karr didn't know what the reset procedure was or even if there was one. If the messenger failed to show, they would go back to being tourists, take in some of the sights, and wait for further instructions.

Something cracked sharply in the distance. Dean spun abruptly around. Karr, unsure what was going on, pushed upright from the railing. Then Dean started to run, and Karr did, too. Only after his first two steps did he realize the crack had been a gunshot.

Dean ran toward the bridge. He knew the crack belonged to a rifle — it was difficult to identify a specific weapon from the sound of a shot fired in the distance, but the sound was so familiar to him that he had no trouble guessing it was a Remington Model 700 or some military variant. He also knew it had not been aimed at him, for if it had it surely would have struck him; the rifle was once the weapon of choice among snipers, preferred for its accuracy.

A man somewhere past middle age lay sprawled in the middle of the bridge. He'd been taken down with a shot in the precise middle of his temple.

It was the messenger — his brown hat lay on the pavement. He'd only just reached the middle of the bridge.

Dean glanced around. The woman he'd seen with the two girls earlier was looking at him in horror. There were two, three other people nearby.

"Call the police," he said. "A bobby. Quick! Go!"

Dean turned to judge where the shot would have come from, then pointed in that direction. "There! Call someone — have the police go there."

There was no need for an ambulance, and so he didn't suggest it. But he knelt down and opened the man's sports coat as if checking him for more wounds and making him comfortable.

In reality, Dean was looking for whatever the man was supposed to pass him or at least an ID. He found nothing. Dean leaned down as if listening for a heartbeat and rifled through the man's pockets. There was a hotel room card with a magnetic strip, some change; nothing else. He pocketed the card, then looked up to see one of the little girls staring at him. He pretended to try to resuscitate the dead man with CPR.

A hand on his shoulder sent a shock through his body. Dean spun around to find Tommy Karr.

"Our package?" asked Karr.

"Don't see anything," said Dean.

"Nothing?"

"I don't think so."

"ID?"

"Can't find any."

"We want to blend into the crowd," said Karr, standing up. For once he wasn't smiling. "Come on. He's dead, Charlie."

"I know that."

"Well, let's go."

"We can't just leave him."

"Yeah, we can. Come on."

Dean started to get up, but it was too late to fade away. One of the policemen who'd been on foot patrol through the park came running up, radio microphone and a whistle in hand.

"The shot came from over there," Dean told the officer. He pointed across the lake. "From over there somewhere."

"Please remain where you are," said the policeman, pulling his radio microphone up. "Please wait. If you took anything from him, I advise you to lay it on the ground quickly."

"I didn't rob him."

"I didn't say you did, sir. Please don't move. There will be questions. You, too, sir," he added, pointing at Karr.

Dean belatedly realized he'd made a serious mistake.

6

Rubens stared at the large screen at the front of the Art Room. "When did you last hear from her?" he asked.

"It's over ten minutes now," answered Telach. "She was in this room here."

The red dot from Telach's laser pointer moved through the boxes on the schematic of the airport terminal building, skimming across the lower left-hand side of the screen. Their information on the layout of the terminal was sketchy, based largely on Lia's observations when she had arrived a few days before. The building was only one story and not very large, and they knew exactly where Lia was thanks to the small implant of a radioisotope in her body. They also gathered that the belt controlling and powering her communications system had been removed, since the signal and feed had died without being turned off. As a security measure, the communications gear only worked when close to the implant in an operator's skull.

"It's nearly eleven o'clock their time," said Telach. "Nighttime."

"I see that," answered Rubens. He glanced at Lia's runner, Jeff Rockman, who was sitting a few feet away, staring at his computer screens. His head slumped forward and his face looked like the color of a bleached bone.

"You're sure she was struck?" Rubens asked.

"No doubt at all," said Telach, though the question had been directed at Rockman. "The blows were pretty loud. The plane took off five minutes later."

"No indication that they knew she was an agent?"

"As I said, we think the officer was looking for a bribe."

"And Lia didn't give him the money?"

"She tried. He just seemed — she didn't act submissive at first. . . ."

Telach's voice trailed off, but Rubens could easily picture what had happened. Lia had run into a young officer who expected to be treated as a god. Suddenly confronted by someone who didn't cower at his sneer, either he or his minions had lost it.

The man wouldn't have been assigned to the airport because he was a genius or a stellar officer. And in his eyes, women — even Chinese women — would be lower than animal dung. Hopefully he was smart enough to realize that killing a foreigner would cause him difficulty.

Not much to pin one's hopes on.

"She could be dead," blurted Rockman.

Rubens glared at him. "Let us remain calm. We will watch the situation as it develops and respond accordingly." It was a cold reply but the correct one. The Art Room needed to operate with quiet detachment. "Contact the terminal manager," Rubens told Telach. "The civilian. Have the call come from someone from the airline who noticed that she wasn't aboard the plane, looking for her. Then the military people there, then the people in town. Everyone she's spoken to since she landed."

"Everyone?"

"Everyone in Korea if you have to. I want it clear that people are asking about her. Don't blow her cover; be judicious."

"Yes, boss," said Telach. She nodded to Rockman, who began arranging the calls with the translators.

"Have the Russian plane move in," said Rubens. "Have them just fly in. I want them there."

"Just go there? It's nearly an hour from the border and they won't be able to get fuel."

"Just go. We're paying them enough, aren't we?"

"They'll just take off if she doesn't show up."

"Have them wait as long as they can. Get Fashona in place."

Rubens could send in an extraction team from South Korea, but that would blow the entire operation. More important, if that was actually necessary it would probably be too late.

He had to get Lia back, at all costs. But it was critical to do so in a logical, calm manner — and his job now was to communicate that to everyone else. The matter was as under control as it was going to get for the time being; he had to signal confidence by moving on to the next problem.

"What is going on in London?" he asked Telach.

"The police brought Dean and Tommy to the station for questioning."

"Was the victim our messenger?"

"We believe so. He had a brown beret. But he didn't have anything with him, not even a scrap of paper. And neither we nor the police have an ID." Telach punched the

63

control unit on her belt and the screen at the front of the Art Room flashed with a grainy video image of a man with a brown beret walking along a park path. She watched the sequence intently, then jabbed her thumb hard on the controls to stop it a few frames before the man was assassinated.

"That's the messenger?" said Rubens.

"Yes," said Telach. "Whoever shot him was in the bushes on this side of the park. It's about two hundred and fifty yards away. Well planned. Probably escaped through the fence there, into that apartment complex."

"What's Johnny Bib working on?" asked Rubens.

"His team is slated to review the Biowar file," said Telach, referring to a mission Deep Black had recently completed. The Biowar mission had taken the Deep Black team around the globe to Thailand and Burma (or Myanmar, as the dictators there preferred), where they had stopped a designer virus. "They're in the process of setting up interviews with scientists so they can get background information on the virus biology before proceeding."

"Give him the information about the two Web domains, the sites on the World Wide

Web that were supposedly used to send messages. Tell him to find out what he can about them."

"We already had the information checked on. It was authentic," said Telach.

"Yes. But I want Johnny Bib to look at it."

"Yes, sir."

Rubens glanced at his watch. He had a meeting at the White House he couldn't miss — just couldn't miss. And yet he couldn't leave the Art Room now, not with Lia's fate unknown.

"Should I alert the embassy in London?" Telach asked. "To get Dean and Karr out?"

"Yes. Suggest to Tommy — no, better make it Dean. Tell Dean to call the embassy. As soon as the call is placed, alert them there and get someone to pick them up. No sense having them waste more of the day with the police."

By "them there" Rubens meant the Central Intelligence Agency.

"Lia's moving!" said Rockman from his console.

Telach went over quickly. Rubens followed as well. "Moving or being moved?" he asked.

"Impossible to tell."

Rubens looked over the runner's

shoulder at the terminal building schematic on the computer screen. Lia's position was marked by a small green dot that moved to the right along one side of the building. The dot stopped near the area they had identified as the reception area — but not quite inside.

"Still no audio," said Rockman.

"Did you get through to anyone there?" asked Rubens.

"The civilian manager," said Rockman.

"He assured us there was no problem," said one of the translators nearby. "But of course he would say that."

"Keep making the calls," said Rubens. "Prudently, please. Polite concern, nothing more. They are very sensitive, and at the moment they have what we want. Where's the Russian plane?"

"On its way," said Rockman. "We may have to bribe the people at the terminal again."

"Do it." Rubens looked at Telach. "Whatever it takes, Marie."

"Thank you," said Telach.

Rubens wanted to stay, but the meeting was far too important.

Surely his boss could handle it. Rubens' place was here.

"We have the terminal manager back,"

said Rockman. "He says there was a mix-up in papers, but she is fine."

"Tell him there is another plane on the way. Imply very strongly that she must be on it. No — state that directly. And there will be no repercussions so long as she is. And alive."

"Go," said Rockman to the translator. The runner looked at his screen — the words were being translated there by a special program — then held up his thumb.

"I'm going to the White House," Rubens told Telach. "Keep me informed."

Traveling to the White House with his boss, Vice Admiral Devlin Brown, meant a quick helicopter ride rather than the more tiresome car caravan down to D.C. It also meant a few minutes of uninterrupted conversation, a rare occurrence in a typical workday.

"I saw the General this morning," said Rubens as the helicopter, a specially equipped civilian version of the Sikorsky Blackhawk, lifted off.

"How is he?" asked Brown.

"Very bad," said Rubens.

"A shame. A friend of mine's mother had Alzheimer's. She was very violent toward the end."

"He's not that, thank God. Not in his nature, I think."

"A feisty old bird like him, not violent?" There had been several directors between Brown and Rosenberg, but many tales about him still circulated.

"I don't know if he was so much feisty as determined," said Rubens. "If you crossed him, I would imagine then it might seem like uncomfortable."

"I hope you stick up for me as well when I'm packed on the top floor of a nursing home."

"His daughter has gone ahead with her threat," said Rubens. "I expect the suit will be filed any day. I'm to talk to the attorney about it tomorrow."

"She really is a piece of work, isn't she? Very greedy. How much is his cousin worth?"

"Fifteen million, in that neighborhood." The General stood to inherit everything his slightly older cousin owned when he died. The cousin was also in a nursing home and suffering from Alzheimer's; physically, he was in somewhat worse shape, and not given very long to live.

"If we make it clear that she can have access to the money, will she drop the suit?"

From Brown's point of view — and the

NSA's — the proceeding wasn't about the General at all. The General had a vast store of personal papers and other effects, presumably containing a great deal of information about the agency. It was rumored that he had been working on a memoir before he got sick. Rubens' protests to the contrary, General Rosenberg *was* a feisty old bird, and it was very possible that he had recorded his thoughts on a wide range of agency projects. The agency had a series of confidentiality agreements and the resources to legally prevent anything he wrote or said from being published, and there was no question it would move to do so if necessary. However, discretion was always the better part of valor as far as the NSA was concerned, and heading off a potentially messy — and public — confrontation was infinitely better than arming the men in black with subpoenas and sending them to confiscate a moving van's worth of uninventoried papers, notes, tapes, and computer disks.

But in this matter, Rubens was *not* acting on the agency's behalf.

"I don't know that there is a basis for compromise with her," said Rubens.

"She's that much of a witch, eh?" asked the admiral.

"Stubborn. Like her father," he answered.

"Is his care adequate? Perhaps we could arrange for him to be moved to the facility she suggested. Mount Ina, was it?"

The facility in question was a private nursing home where care cost about ten thousand dollars a month. It was an excellent facility, and if the decision had been his, Rubens would have gladly moved the General — and footed the bill personally, if necessary. But the General had expressly forbidden it: his cousin was there, and whether the General stood to inherit his money or not, he hated him. In fact, if he were in his right mind, he probably would have denounced the inheritance somehow or given it away to a charity — preferably one his cousin couldn't stand.

"Have you thought about moving him?" asked Brown when Rubens didn't answer his question.

"Yes."

"You'd pay with your own money, wouldn't you?"

"For the General there is nothing that I would not do. He would, however, have felt betrayed if I offered it. He did not take charity. But from an objective point of view, his care now is as good as is possible.

The people who watch him are decent people. They are genuinely concerned. That would appear the most important thing."

"Do you need additional legal help?"

"I believe the lawyer I retained will be sufficient," said Rubens. "And a lawyer from the NSA would only help Rebecca make her case."

"Keep me informed," said Brown, turning his attention to the papers he'd brought along.

Despite the fact that the two NSA officials were running ten minutes ahead of schedule, Secretary of State James Lincoln and his two aides had beaten them into the Oval Office. Lincoln was holding forth on the importance of rewarding France for its steps over the past year to align more closely with American Middle Eastern policies — a relevant if not uncomplicated point, given the President's pending visit to France at the end of the week.

"Ah, there you are, Admiral. Billy, hello," said President Jeffrey Marcke, swinging upright in his chair. "Secretary Lincoln is just reminding me that the French helped with our Revolution."

Lincoln's smile seemed a little pained.

71

"Maybe Admiral Brown will tell us about John Paul Jones," added the President. He loved to tweak his advisers, and Lincoln was an easy mark. "Didn't the French give him a ship?"

"The French have been interesting allies throughout history," admitted Lincoln. "But they are coming around. They're trying to make up for their miscues before the Second Gulf War. Better late than never."

"Billy has a château in France, don't you?" said the President, changing targets.

Rubens winced internally but tried to act nonplussed. "To be more precise, the château is my mother's."

"It overlooks the Loire near Montbazon. Heck of a view," said Marcke. He had been there when he was still a senator, a few years before. "But if I recall, William, you don't particularly like the French."

"I try not to let personal opinions cloud professional judgment," said Rubens.

Jake Namath, the head of the CIA, appeared at the doorway, followed by the deputy director of the CIA for operations, Debra Collins. George Hadash, the national security adviser, was right behind them.

"Gentlemen, Ms. Collins. Please sit

down," said the President. "The Secretary of State and I have been discussing French history. Mr. Rubens has come to talk about something slightly more recent, with unfortunate implications for the future. William, you have the floor."

"In the late nineteen-fifties, the French shifted their nuclear weapons program into high gear," Rubens said, launching into his brief. "They began refining plutonium and shifted to that as a basic weapons material after working with uranium. In 1960, they exploded a sixty- to seventy-kiloton weapon in Algeria near Reggane in the Sahara. Within roughly a year's time, there were three more explosions. These were billed as tests, although at least one was a hastily arranged detonation to keep a half-finished weapon from falling into the hands of the so-called mutineering generals."

Rubens glanced at Hadash. The revolt of the French generals was not well known outside of France and Africa, and even some of the histories that reported it confused basic information such as the dates and locations. Rubens and Hadash, however, knew it all very well: Fifteen years before, Hadash had devoted an entire week of his seminar at MIT talking about it. In his opinion, it not only represented Europe's last attempt to hold on to African colonies; it also showed the futility of military insurrections in an industrialized democracy.

That was Hadash's view. Rubens had written a rather long paper arguing that it did not.

He'd gotten an A-minus.

"There was at least one other warhead close to completion at the time," continued Rubens. "This was the so-called *Chou* weapon — *chou* as in the French word for cabbage or kale. It was also apparently a reference to the small size and shape of the bomb."

In this case, *small* was a relative term; the weapon weighed roughly several hundred pounds. At the time, American intelligence believe it was similar to the American W-9, which had been developed several years before as a warhead for artillery shells. Its yield was calculated at anywhere between forty and ninety kilotons. Little Boy, which was exploded over Hiroshima, had a calculated yield of "only" fifteen to sixteen kilotons, with some sources figuring it as low as thirteen.

At the time, American officials — not to mention the French — feared that the unfinished warhead had been confiscated by the mutineers. That turned out not to be the case — it had in fact been spirited away by a junior officer and placed in a desert storage facility. After the mutiny, the unfinished bomb was moved to a nuclear storage facility that became an underground dump for radioactive materials. The weapon wasn't forgotten, but the program that it had been part of received a low priority for a variety of reasons and it remained in storage.

"Wasn't its plutonium very valuable?" said Collins.

Rubens frowned but answered her question. "Of course. But in the immediate aftermath of the mutiny there was a certain amount of slippage in information and priorities, and there is some question of whether the technology the French had would have been well suited to safely reworking the warhead. In any event, there was an entirely new regime in place with different aims for their weapons. Even at the highest estimate, this would have already begun to seem like a rather small yield, certainly compared to American and Soviet programs. The captain who had moved it happened to die in a car accident before the mutiny itself was fully suppressed, and so he wasn't around to, shall we say, advocate for the warhead."

"And we know where it is?"

"We've known since the mutiny, and tracked it since 1982," said Hadash. "William did a paper on it for me."

The fact that Hadash remembered the paper pleased Rubens — though he feared that his former professor might share the fact that it had yielded another A-minus.

Come to think of it, A-minus was the *only* grade Hadash had ever given him. He would point that out.

"The NSA had a program called Seed Finder during the early Reagan years," said Rubens. "By that time the French had misplaced the weapon — on paper only — at least twice and located it again. Their estimates of its size and bulk in the nineteen-eighties — well, their calculations were incorrect. They clearly underestimated its potency."

The NSA had "contracted" with the CIA's Special Collection Service — in some ways the predecessor to Desk Three — to place sensors at the site to help evaluate the warhead and judge its potency. A CIA officer had lost his life in one of the operations, and two agents (foreign employees of the CIA) had also been killed before the sensors were successfully planted.

"The sensors are regularly checked and updated," said Rubens. "Two weeks ago, a change was detected."

"The warhead is gone?" asked Collins.

"Part of it," said Rubens. "Although a portion of the bomb structure remains."

The unfinished bomb's nuclear "kernel" consisted of several disks of refined plutonium, which were designed to be compressed by a special girdle of high explosives to create a nuclear explosion. At least one of the disks was still in place, because the French monitoring system had not detected the change.

"How could they miss it?" asked Lincoln.

Rubens was tempted to say it was because the French were arrogant and pompous imbeciles who couldn't see past their noses — but he merely shook his head.

"Their technology is not particularly effective. And they have underestimated the size of the material from the beginning. The error is compounded greatly over time," Rubens pointed out. "I must say, our technology frankly has some drawbacks as well — the units in place must be checked in person, and it may have been moved at any point over about six weeks between inspections."

"I think what you need to address," said the President, "is how the material is likely to be used."

Rubens nodded. "There are two possibilities. One is as a bomb. There would be enough material to construct a weapon with a yield of sixty kilotons, more likely less, possibly more, depending on the state of the plutonium and of course the design of the bomb. The material could be inserted into a properly prepared bomb; anyone with access to the plans from the time should be able to construct a high-explosive shell to set it off. Anyone without access to that could engineer a solution. In neither case is it easy, but it's certainly do-able. More likely, in our opinion, the plutonium could be used in conjunction with other radioactive materials to create a number of dirty bombs."

Rubens turned to his theory that the material had been stolen by a private criminal organization with the idea of selling it on the open market. It did not appear to have been sold already — or at least the NSA detection net had not spotted it in the Middle East.

"Our best guess is that it is still somewhere in Algeria. Alternatively, it may be in France."

"France?" asked Collins.

Rubens didn't think so himself, but a radiation counter on a ship to Marseilles had some anomalies that were still being investigated. The ship had docked in Bilbao, Spain, after visiting the French port — and there the anomalies had disappeared.

"Either there was a problem with the device, which is not unheard of, or the material was carried into France. As you know, it can be somewhat easier to move things into Europe than the Middle East," added Rubens. This was because the Arab and northern African countries were covered by a network of American, Israeli, and NATO sensors. Scrutiny at European ports was not nearly as intense.

"We have some additional information from an eavesdropping source in Morocco," added Rubens. "It ties the ship to a charity used by different terrorist groups. It's circumstantial, however."

"Which means you have no real information," said Collins. She was angry because Rubens hadn't shared the information about the missing material privately before the meeting. The fact that Hadash had ordered him not to — a fact that neither Rubens nor Hadash would volunteer anyway — was beside the point.

"That's true," said Rubens. "It's merely a suggestion, not hard data."

"Are you pursuing that source?"

"We're working on it," said Rubens.

The "source" was actually an eavesdropping device in Morocco. As luck would have it, the battery that powered the device had died twenty-four hours before; Rubens was scrambling to plan a mission to replace it.

"We want to locate the bomb and raise the issue with the French," said Hadash. "The difficulty is how to do it. We don't want to give away our intelligence-gathering methods."

Or embarrass the French too severely, thought Rubens, *given their recent trend of cooperation with America.* The French had only recently woken up to the fact that Islamic fundamentalism posed at least as great a threat to Europe as it did to America. Now that they were finally cooperating, they had to be handled delicately.

"How long would it take to make this into a bomb?" asked Namath.

"Impossible to know for certain," said Rubens. "Weeks rather than days. Months most likely. But it could even be years."

"So it could have already been constructed?"

"Very possible," said Rubens. "As I said, the most likely use is as a dirty bomb, and that could be put together relatively quickly."

"The French have to be notified," said Hadash. "We need their help tracking it down."

"I believe they'll help us," said Lincoln. "But they'll ask us to share information. And if we want help, we'll have to do so."

"The NSA concurs," said Brown. "My suggestion is that we indicate we came by the information via an intercept."

"What if they want more?" said Lincoln.

"I don't think mentioning the monitoring project would help one way or the other," said Namath. "And that's what you're worried about. Intercepts — we can be vague."

"In the past the French haven't taken much seriously unless they have very strong corroboration," said Lincoln.

"Telling them we're watching over their shoulder isn't going to make them cooperative," said Hadash.

"I agree," said Lincoln. "But they may not take an intercept very seriously."

"They may not," admitted Rubens.

"Well, let's take the chance that they will," said the President. "They've been shaping up. Their cooperation in Africa over the past few months has been very useful. How many terrorists have been arrested?" he asked Namath.

"At least a dozen."

"And now we'll reciprocate," said Marcke. "Since we'll be there on Friday, I think State might bring this missing warhead up at a high but informal level, and refer the French to Admiral Brown. He can take it from there."

"That sounds reasonable," said Lincoln. "Since we're on the topic of Europe, I have some concerns about some of the alerts that the NSA recently passed along concerning high-level Americans being targeted there. That was the phrase used in the Philippines last year just before an attack on one of our ambassadors. I want to issue an alert to embassy personnel."

"That's premature," said Hadash.

The debate zigzagged from there, Lincoln worried for his people, Hadash trying to put it in perspective. Brown took Lincoln's side; the CIA people took Hadash's. Rubens said a few words backing up his boss, but the alert system was not under his jurisdiction and, frankly, he didn't care much for it. Besides, Lincoln was operating on emotion rather than logic; he wasn't going to be mollified by technical arguments about the worth of the data.

"What we need is more information," said Marcke finally. "Admiral, let's find out what's going on."

"Absolutely," said Brown.

"I have to protect my people," said Lincoln. "Let me tell the embassy staffs *something*."

"I think if you want to discourage unnecessary travel by close dependents, that would be in order," said Hadash — very likely offering a face-saving compromise because he would be in Europe with Lincoln and didn't want him grouchy the whole time.

"All right," said Lincoln. "I will."

As the others filtered out, the President asked Rubens if he was feeling OK.

"Yes, sir. Why?"

"You look a little tired. You should get more rest. Take a vacation."

"Yes, sir."

Marcke smiled at him. "I'm serious."

"I will. As soon as I can."

"If I didn't know you hated France so much, I'd suggest you come with us."

"The only thing wrong with France is the French, Mr. President. I'm as ambivalent about the French as they are about us. But I wouldn't want them to be blown up by a nuclear weapon."

"We'll make sure it doesn't happen, William. Not on our watch."

7

Dean looked up from his seat as the door opened. He'd been in the police interrogation room now for nearly two hours, repeating the same story at least a half-dozen times. It was a short story, at least: it relayed exactly what he had seen at the park and included the outlines of the cover he had been supplied with. With the exception of his cover — businessman in town for a conference, taking a stroll with a friend he'd chanced to meet — it was all absolutely true.

It left out a lot, but it was true.

"Who is it that you know at the embassy?" asked the chief inspector, the older of the two men who'd been questioning him. His name was Lang and he smelled of cigarettes. Dean noticed that his fingertips were stained brown. Every so often he excused himself, probably to grab a smoke.

"I don't know anyone," said Dean. "I just called the number you gave me."

"The embassy sent someone to speak to

my superior," said the detective. "It was all very unnecessary."

"I didn't mean to cause any trouble," said Dean. "I've answered all your questions and told you what I saw several times. You can't think I had anything to do with shooting the man."

The detective gave him a look that suggested the contrary. He slid a pad of paper down on the table.

"A place where I can contact you, both here and in the States," he told Dean. "Include address and phone number, if you will."

Dean wrote down the name of the hotel Desk Three had reserved, then added his home address and phone number. The chief inspector took back the pad and looked over the information so slowly that he seemed to be checking each letter against some master file in his brain. Then he got up and waved the pad at Dean, indicating that he should follow.

When he got downstairs, Tommy Karr was there, talking to the desk sergeant about the best place to get "real" shepherd's pie and a pint. As Dean walked up, the policeman had just mentioned a place near Waterloo Station — a major train station on the other side of the Thames —

and Karr acted with exaggerated surprise, as if authentic British beer could not be purchased anywhere near a railway. They chatted on for a few more minutes, Karr oblivious to Dean or the embassy representative, who was waiting for them nearby. The representative was a young man in a business suit whose close-cropped hair and posture screamed military.

Karr finished kibitzing with the sergeant, pointing at the policeman as if he were a drinking buddy before walking away. "Later," he told the sergeant, strolling over to the man from the embassy. "Say, can I get you to give me a lift? I just got some good pointers on places on food. It's a little past teatime, but I'm hungry. Charlie, you grab some grub, too."

"Actually, sir, the ambassador wishes to speak with you," said the escort.

"You oughta be a salesman, or maybe a politician," Dean told Karr as they walked to the embassy car. "You have that hail-fellow-well-met act down cold."

"Just getting some local intelligence," said Karr, bending himself into the backseat of the embassy's Ford. Dean slid beside him.

"I'm guessing you're a Marine who was

ordered to dress down for the occasion," Karr said as the driver put on his seat belt.

"Lieutenant Dalton, sir."

"Charlie was a Marine," offered Karr. "Back in the old days. Who was it you fought, Charlie? Barbary pirates?"

"From Tripoli to the Halls of Montezuma," Dean said drily.

Karr smiled. Dalton glanced in the mirror. Dean realized he'd balled his fingers into a fist, tensing in anticipation of the questions: "Where did you serve?" "What was your rank?" "What did you do?"

It felt so long ago now that talking about it was an effort, one he didn't feel like making. But the young man said nothing.

Dean reached into his pocket and took out the room key that he had snatched from the dead man. Without saying anything, he held it out so Karr could see.

Karr grinned. "They thought it was yours?"

"The first policeman made me empty my pockets in the park. Good thing we didn't check in."

"Ah, you would have come up with something," said Karr.

Dean wasn't sure about that. He'd never been a particularly good liar, and he certainly couldn't joke and josh the way Karr did. He remembered the words an older commander had once used to describe him on a fitness report or something similar: *taciturn by nature.*

He'd seen it as a compliment then. Now he wasn't so sure.

"Semper fi," the lieutenant said as he left Dean and Karr in a waiting room upstairs in the embassy. "Good luck, sir."

"Thank you, Lieutenant," said Dean. "Semper fi."

"Nice furniture, huh?" said Karr. He dropped back into a frail-looking antique chair against the wall.

"What are we going to do now?" Dean asked.

Karr shrugged. "We give the Art Room time to sort this all out, Charlie. Relax. You're too wound up."

"I should be more like you, right? Water off a duck's back."

Karr chuckled. Dean knew by now that the op actually was much more serious, much more focused, than he appeared. Under his "What, me worry?" veneer and his corny sense of humor, he was calculating several steps ahead. He was a sharp, truly bright kid who also happened to be immensely big. Dean thought Karr had learned to pretend to be goofy as a boy growing up. Bright kids usually didn't fit in by showing how smart they were; they had to adopt some sort of act, like class clown. And yet nonchalance was definitely part of Karr's personality. The op would laugh in the face of a hurricane and probably honestly think getting soaked was interesting.

The door opened. A man in his early thirties stuck his head out into the hallway. "Karr, what are you doing in London?"

"Stephens, you Anglophile you." Karr jumped up and walked to the man. As he came close, he reared back and started to throw a punch with such force that Dean thought he would knock the man through the wall. But he pulled his fist back at the last second, stopping it a half inch from Stephens' shoulder.

"I knew you weren't going to hit me," said Stephens, whose posture and closed eyes suggested the exact opposite.

"You're awful trusting for a spook," said Karr.

"You're awful obnoxious for an NSA clown." The man turned to Dean. "You're Charles Dean?"

"Yes."

"Nice to meet you. I feel sorry for you, if you have to work with Tommy Karr. He ever tell you how he came to be called Tommy?"

"I've never asked."

"Don't. Come on inside. I have a million questions for you, though I'm sure you won't answer most of them."

Just then there were footsteps on the nearby staircase; Dean and Karr turned to see a young woman and an older man descending. Dean recognized the woman's skirt before her face came into view — it was the girl they had helped in the street.

"You," she said as she came into view.

"Well, hey, hello," said Karr.

"Oh my God. These are the people I told you about, Daddy." The girl came over to them. "What are you doing in the embassy?"

"Lost my passport," said Karr, patting his pockets. "Would you believe it? Dumb of me, huh? Lose my head if it wasn't attached."

The girl frowned, clearly not believing him. She looked to Dean. He nodded solemnly, but her frown only deepened.

"Thank you for helping my daughter," said the ambassador.

"Anytime," said Karr. "Pleasure was mine."

Stephens stood awkwardly to the side.

The ambassador nodded at him, then tapped his daughter's arm to get her to follow as he went back to the stairs.

"Whoa," said Stephens inside. "You know the ambassador's daughter?"

"I know her purse better," said Karr. He recounted what had happened.

"Wow. I wish *I'd* saved her purse," said Stephens.

"Start out with something like her keys, then work your way up," said Karr. "Now where's the encrypted phone? I think we're supposed to call home and get yelled at."

8

Mussa Duoar smiled at the waiter as he placed the large cup of coffee down on the small table at the café on boulevard Saint-Germain near the heart of Paris.

"*Merci*," he told the man, thanking him in French. "How long would it take me to get to the Seine from here?"

The accent in the reply, though clipped, cinched it for him.

"You are from Algiers, yes?" Mussa asked, this time in Arabic.

The man stared at him for a moment. "*Oui*," he said. The French word was followed by a flood of Arabic, asking Mussa how he knew and if he was Algerian as well.

"No," said Mussa, speaking again in French. "I came from Egypt many years ago, probably before you were born."

Mussa was barely thirty and the waiter twenty at least, but he liked to play the old man. It was not so much of an act, he calculated; his experiences had aged him in many ways. He began telling the man about Cairo — a very beautiful city, he claimed, and one he longed to return to.

Perhaps it was beautiful, but Mussa had no claim to it; he had been born in Algeria just as the man had. Mussa's father had worked against the French and been executed, rather cruelly, nearly a decade after the struggle for independence — a revenge killing ordered by a member of the foreign service, Mussa had learned nearly five years before. Though an infant at the time, his father's death had shaped Mussa's life in many ways.

Soon it would be avenged. But there were other matters to deal with now.

"Tell me about yourself," he told the waiter. "Have you been in France long?"

The man nodded. Something about his gesture — the way his head drooped at first, perhaps — told Mussa more about his attitude toward his adopted land than his words. As the waiter related how he had come to the country several years before, where he lived, how he studied, Mussa watched his face and gestures for the unspoken story — the disappointment and emptiness in his new life, the missing core of connectedness to the community, the doubts about himself and who he truly was. Mussa knew this story very well; it was his business to know.

He did not ask the man outright if he was an observant Muslim. Instead, Mussa mentioned a place in his *arrondissement,* or quarter of the city.

"Yes, I know that place. It is right across from the mosque," said the man.

A few more questions and Mussa learned the man's attitude toward the local teacher at the mosque. As the waiter spoke, his spiritual thirst began to betray itself. His words came more quickly; there was tension and yearning in his voice. Here was a soul in search of salvation.

"A bright young man like you," said Mussa finally, "should mix with others of potential." He took a business card from his pocket — it belonged to a pharmacist in a town twenty kilometers away, pinched from the counter — and wrote an address on the back. "The mosque here has a very good set of such people."

The waiter took the card eagerly, stuffing it into his pocket, then went back to the kitchen to get another order. Mussa took a sip of the coffee, then glanced at his watch. Paris was an hour behind London; the job there would be done by now.

He took another sip of coffee, then left

some change in the plate along with the euros for the bill. He got up and got into his car, trolling slowly through the narrow streets as he made his way to his next appointment in the Marais.

Driving through the Jewish quarter of Paris amused Mussa. He found the small plaques dedicated to the dead killed by the Nazis — and the few who resisted them — quaint in a way. As a devout Muslim it could not be said that he *liked* Jews; on the contrary, he hated them quite probably as much as the thugs who had planted the bomb in the synagogue he was just passing soon after the Germans took over the city. But he did not find them much of a threat, surely not in France. In Israel it was certainly a different story, but here in France it was more sensible — and profitable, surely — to hate the French. This white woman with her dog, slowing him now as she crossed the street near the Musée Picasso: he hated her with her upturned nose and her snooty expression. Their eyes met and a frown came to her lips as she saw a dusky face in the big BMW.

All his life, Mussa had seen such frowns. Soon he would have his revenge, striking a blow that would resound through Europe.

A man was waiting for him around the

corner from the museum. The man was not in Mussa's employ but a Yemeni whose interests overlapped his own. Mussa pulled over to the curb and made as if he were asking directions. The man came over and, after pointing vaguely to the north, bent down to talk.

"The brothers are ready to strike, but they need more material," said the man.

"The material is not easy to obtain," said Mussa. "My technical adviser had commitments that could not be avoided."

"They need more material according to the plan you outlined."

The material they needed was plastic explosive. Mussa had supplied them with a new type that he had manufactured himself; the material was slightly more powerful than the American C-4 and somewhat more stable, but it was expensive and difficult to manufacture. He needed his own store for the Chunnel project. Still, the brothers' "project" was an important one and he would have to find them more material.

"They are devout," said the man. "And ready."

"It is important that they act when I tell them," said Mussa. "Vitally important."

"An hour here, a half hour there — what is the difference?"

"The difference is everything," said Mussa sharply.

"Then they will do as they are told," said the other man.

"I will find what they need," said Mussa. "They are wise enough to follow the instructions explicitly?"

"We have been over this."

"Explicitly? The number of packages is very critical."

"Explicitly," said the Yemeni, a note of surrender in his voice.

"It will be done, with God's will." Mussa saw someone on the street and raised his voice. "And where can one find good knishes?"

The Yemeni was used to Mussa's provocations. "Around the corner and to the left."

"I'll tell the rabbi you sent me," said Mussa, putting his car into gear.

9

The words came at her from somewhere above, blurring together like a murmur that sounded more like a hum than a sentence.

"Mianhamnida mianhamnida mianhamnida . . ."

Lia bolted upright, consciousness flooding back. Her head quickly began throbbing.

Where was she? What had happened?

"I am intensely sorry," said a man's voice in Korean. "Very sorry."

She glanced down. She was sitting on a couch, wearing different clothes, baggy trousers and a blouse much too big for her. Army clothes, a uniform of some sort.

What had happened to her? She felt dazed. She'd been smashed in the head, beaten, and for a few moments had blacked out.

More than a few moments?

"Where am I?" she asked in Chinese.

"I do not understand," said the man in Korean. He said something else; Lia had

99

trouble deciphering. When he finally stopped speaking, she answered haltingly in Korean that she was thankful for his kindness but was OK now and could be left alone. The man responded with something else she couldn't understand.

The pain in her head moved from the back to the front. It felt as if a large vibrating sander was being pulled back and across her skull.

The man was telling her about an airplane. He paused finally and asked if she was all right.

"*Wo hen hao,*" she replied automatically in Chinese. "I'm fine," she said. "I'm all right."

The man shook his head at the obvious lie.

"*Gonghang?*" she asked in Korean. "Am I at the airport?"

"*Ne.*"

Yes. She was still at the airport.

Lia blinked, pushing her hand over her eyes, squeezing her eyelids closed. When she opened them, he was gone.

She knew who she was; she knew she was on a mission to North Korea and that it had gone reasonably well. But she didn't know what had happened since she arrived at the terminal.

She did, though.

Oh yes, she did.

Her body ached; her legs felt as if they had been pummeled. Her neck hurt and her cheek and eye felt swollen.

That wasn't the half of it.

She knew.

Rage surged in her, then fear, then rage again.

Out. She had to get out.

Out.

Where were her clothes and her suitcase? She needed her belt — it enabled her com system.

Lia got up and took a few unsteady steps toward the closed door. The pain seemed to run to the right side of her head, as if it were water that might slosh around under the effect of gravity. As she reached for the doorknob she sensed that she would find the door locked; she was surprised to find it wasn't.

The hallway was empty. As Lia stepped out, she realized that she had no shoes on. She continued anyway, padding across the cold concrete. There were two other doors along the hall; when she reached the far end she entered the reception area of the airport. Across from her was the small metal desk the local authorities had been using as a customs station when she arrived. There was no other furniture in the room.

The terminal had two small windows next to the doorway on the right; the door led out to the tarmac area. Her pain increased as she walked toward it, and she felt her eyelids pressing down from above, weighted by the pain and the fatigue from her struggle.

Struggle? Was that the word for what had happened?

Struggle. A nice euphemism.

Something seemed to smack against her forehead as she reached the door. Lia froze, almost dazed again, then realized she was hearing the sound of an aircraft landing — not a jet but a twin-engined turboprop with its loud, waspy roar. She pulled open the door and stepped outside. An aircraft had turned off the runway and was heading toward the terminal.

"Is that my plane?" she said in Chinese, though there was no one to ask except herself.

This was just as well. The words came out in the Cantonese she had first learned as a girl.

Lia remembered a lesson she'd had as a five-year-old with Dr. Lau, a Hong Kong native who'd come to America many years before. Trained as a medical doctor, Lau had never practiced medicine in the United States; he made his living mostly by giving Chinese lessons to his well-heeled Connecticut neighbors. Lia had been adopted by an American couple as a baby; they'd done as much as they could to teach her about her culture, even starting her on Chinese as a three-year-old. Dr. Lau became a family friend as well as an instructor, visiting often until he passed away when she was in high school.

The lessons with Dr. Lau seemed more real to her now than the aircraft taxiing toward her. Just as she took a step back it curled around sharply and stopped a few yards away. Lia began walking forward, ignoring the engines' roar. She had just about reached the wing when she realized someone was shouting behind her. She turned and saw that the man who'd been with her in the room earlier had run up behind her and was holding out a plastic bag to her. It didn't look familiar, but she took it anyway.

When Lia turned back around she saw that a door had been opened at the side of the plane. A small set of stairs folded out from the bottom half of the door to the tarmac; a man in a blue uniform stood at the base of the steps. Lia walked toward him, feeling herself tilting sideways, pushed down by the pain in her head and the rest of her body as she walked toward it.

The man said nothing as she climbed inside. Another man stood near the aisle. There were a dozen seats in the plane, but no other passengers. Lia went to the second row and sat down.

Why did the plane come?

Where am I going?

The bag — where is the bag?

It was in her hand. She opened it and saw that her clothes were in it. She stared at them for a while; when she finally looked up, one of the men was standing over her with a cup of tea.

You're Chinese, she reminded herself, pushing her head down in a bow of gratitude. *Stay in character.*

As she thought that, she noticed the symbol on the tag of tea, which had been left draped over the side of the cup.

On the tag was the Chinese character *jing:* Quiet. Silence.

A message?

Lia fingered the tag, then took a sip of the tea, contemplating the bitter taste.

10

Karr frowned at Stephens when he failed to leave the room with the encrypted phone. "Come on now. Play by the rules," he told the CIA officer.

"OK," said Stephens. "But maybe I've bugged the phone."

"I wouldn't put it past you." He waited until Stephens had left the room, then got up from the chair. "Come on, Charlie."

Dean had just sat down in one of the swivel chairs in front of a row of computer terminals on the other side of the room. He seemed reluctant to get up.

"Jet lag get to you?" Karr asked the older man. "Come on, we'll walk it off."

"Where are we going?"

"Avoiding a half hour of trading put-downs with Stephens," said Karr.

"Is he supposed to debrief us?"

"He's probably supposed to try," said Karr. "Don't worry. He won't get in trouble if we walk. He was parked here after some problems in Georgia. Basically he was shell-shocked and they go easy on him."

Karr led Dean down the hallway to a back set of stairs and then out through a side entrance. When they reached the driveway, Karr threw the guards a salute and strolled out onto the sidewalk. It was past 6:00 p.m. and starting to get dark. He took a moment to get his bearings, then started toward what he thought was the nearest tube, or subway, stop, Bond Street. He'd only taken a few steps when, turning to see if Dean was keeping up, he spotted an empty taxi.

"Yo, cab!" he yelled, more like a New Yorker than a Londoner. He paused at the window, telling the driver that he wanted to find the best steak and kidney pie in the city. When the driver asked if he was a crazy Yank, Karr replied cheerfully that he was.

"And a hungry one. I was going to have fish and chips, but I think I need something thick against these ribs. I'm in your hands."

Inside the cab, Karr reached to his belt and clicked on the communications system. A woman's voice, raspy with a cold, reverberated against the bones of his skull.

"Where have you been?" demanded Sandy Chafetz, their runner back in the Deep Black Art Room. "Why did you turn the com system off?"

Karr did what he always did when a runner asked a stupid question — he ignored it.

"Hey, Charlie, you got that room key?" he asked, digging into his pocket for his handheld computer and a small attachment that allowed him to send video directly from the unit. Snapping them together, he took the key from Dean and panned it for the camera.

"Got it?" he asked Chafetz. Karr liked Chafetz — she was a lot easier on the eyes than Rockman — but she wasn't quite as sharp as the other runner, nor was she as good at marshaling resources. Karr thought this might be because she was a little too chummy with the "backbenchers" — the analysts and mission specialists assigned to various duties who worked behind her in the Art Room. You had to whip some of those guys to get them to give you information that didn't need to be translated from geekese.

"I have it," she told him. "We're analyzing it now. What hotel is it?"

Karr laughed. "Jeez Louise, if I knew, I

wouldn't be asking." He handed the key back to Dean and then leaned forward. "So, driver, where's this restaurant you're taking us to again?"

"Over in Covent Garden," said the cabbie.

"It's not a tourist trap, right?"

The driver began to protest. Karr laughed at him, then glanced at Charlie Dean. "You going to fall asleep? Your eyelids are just about glued together."

"Long day."

"The good ones always are," said Karr.

"A hotel called the Renaissance," reported Chafetz. "On Holburn."

"Holburn." Karr leaned forward. "You know what, driver? We're going to have to make a detour. Do you know a place called the Renaissance Hotel? It's on Holburn? That's near Covent Garden more or less, right?"

"More or less."

"You can just drop us off there. But give me the address for that steak and kidney pie before you drop us off."

Dean waited for Karr to tip the driver, then followed him past the three doormen and into the hotel. The Renaissance had once been an insurance company's headquarters but now was a well-appointed hotel perched between the business, legal, and theater districts, catering to visitors of all three. The floors were rich marble, the wall panels thick wood. They took a right at the door; the desk was straight across, but Karr just gave one of his waves toward the receptionist and went directly to the elevator. Apparently he was following directions from the Art Room, which could communicate with each field op separately or together on a conferenced channel. When the elevator arrived, the two men stepped in; they were alone in the car.

"Put that door key in the slot on the right," Karr told him. "See that? The Renaissance floor?"

Dean pushed it in. A light blinked next to the slot and the elevator began moving upward.

"Pretty fancy place," said Karr.

"Maybe we should get a room," said Dean.

"Never sneak the bill past Rubens. We're lucky we don't have to stay at Motel 6."

The elevator stopped on a private floor, where guests who had reserved the premier-tier rooms had their own lounge and other facilities, including a spa and a concierge on twenty-four-hour duty. The latter stepped forward now, apologizing that the lounge had closed for the evening.

"Thanks," said Karr. "Just wanted to impress my friend. Definitely worth the extra freight."

The concierge grimaced momentarily but then turned to Dean and assured him that the guest services were top-notch. Karr played up the stereotypical noisy Yank routine, stepping over to the room on the right and looking around. The concierge offered to give Dean a tour; Karr answered that it wasn't necessary and led Dean back to the elevator.

"What was that all about?" asked Dean as they headed to the tenth floor.

"We needed to insert the card into a reader so the Art Room could scan it," he explained. "I was just killing time until they got everything worked out. It works like an ATM card. The whole system is computerized, which lets the staff downstairs change the locks by just punching a few keys. Fortunately, it also allows the Art Room to open doors for us. Tenth floor, room one-oh-one-one."

People thought of the NSA as an agency of snoopers and eavesdroppers. From what Dean had seen, it was more like the biggest club of hackers in the world.

They found the room quickly. While Dean played lookout, Karr retrieved a small fiber-optic device and a long wire from the bottom of his belt — a telescoping video camera, equipped with a miniature fisheye lens for checking out a room that might be booby-trapped. But as small and thin as the device was, he had trouble pushing it under the door, which was fitted very closely to the threshold.

Just as he finally got it, the Art Room warned Dean that the elevator was arriving.

"I'll slow them down," said Dean, striding quickly down the corridor toward the elevator foyer. He got there as the door opened, paused a second, then turned the corner just in time to "accidentally" plow into one of the guests.

Unfortunately, it was a nine-year-old girl, and he just barely managed to grab her before she fell. She looked at him, panic-stricken.

"Hey, watch it!" shouted the father.

"I'm sorry," said Dean to the girl. He lowered himself to eye-level. "Are you OK?"

The girl started to cry. She turned; her mother gathered her into her arms. Both parents looked at him as if he were a masher.

"I'm sorry," said Dean, still holding her.

"Let go of her," said the father. He stood perhaps five-seven to Dean's six feet but nonetheless looked as if he wanted to fight. He had an Irish lilt to his voice.

"It was an accident," said Dean, letting go of the girl. "I'm sorry."

"Be more careful next time," hissed the man. He put his hand on his wife's shoulder and pushed her along to the hall. Dean turned and watched them walk down the hall.

Karr had disappeared.

Dean ducked back in the vestibule where the elevators were, pressed the button, and waited. Two older women were in the car when it arrived; he got in, saw that the lobby button was already lit, and stood toward the back. When the elevator arrived, he walked out, then pretended to check his pocket and realize he had forgotten something. He twirled around, pulling the card key out of his pocket and playing with it as he waited for the elevator.

He wasn't as good an actor as Karr, he thought. But he could play a part if he had to.

Back on the tenth floor, the hallway was empty. Dean walked slowly, hesitating when he reached the room; the door was closed. Rather than going in he started walking again.

"Karr?"

"He's in the room, Charlie," said Chafetz. "Before you go in, post a video fly in the wall sconce or something. There aren't any video cameras in any of the hallways and we can't see what's going on. Tommy didn't have a chance."

Dean slipped a fly — a tiny bugging device roughly the size and shape of a dime — out of his pants pocket and wedged it carefully at the top of the lighting fixture.

Inside the room, Karr knelt in front of the fake wardrobe, which hid a large television set and a set of drawers. To the right of the drawers was a safe; the Deep Black op was using his handheld computer to listen to the tumblers on the safe. With a handkerchief on his hand, he pushed down the handle and pulled the door open; the safe was empty.

"I figured." Karr closed it, spun the combination, then returned the dial to the number that had been set when he began. "Check the loo, would you? The WC?"

Dean went into the bathroom. The soap had been opened, but nothing else. A hotel bathrobe hung on the hanger behind the door; it didn't look as if it had been used, and its pocket was empty. Dean went to the wastepaper basket, which had a wrapper and some tissues. He examined the wrapper: it was for candy, a fancy piece of glossy paper with a shiny picture, the sort of thing you put around a one-cent piece of flavored sugar so you can charge twenty cents.

A small striped box sat at the bottom of the basket. Dean took it out and looked at it; it had the name "Hediard" on it. The word *Paris* was in the logo.

"Hediard," said Dean.

"You talking to us, Charlie?" asked his runner.

"There's a box. It has an address. Twenty-one place de la Madeleine, Paris. It may have been for candy."

Chafetz corrected his pronunciation, then told him that Hediard was a very fancy gourmet food shop.

"In Paris," she added. "Oo-la-la. Treats for the sweet."

"Message on the phone," said Karr out in the room, pointing to the blinking light. "Want to listen in?"

"Take a second," said Chafetz.

While the Art Room worked on that, Karr opened the bureau and looked for something — anything — in the drawers. They were empty.

"Here you go," said Chafetz, piping the phone message in over their communications system.

"Waterloo at eight," said a male voice. It had a foreign accent — maybe French, maybe Italian, maybe anything; Dean couldn't place it. There was a time stamp on the message; the call had been made fifteen minutes before 2:00 p.m., undoubtedly when the occupant was en route to the park.

"What's it mean?" Dean asked.

"Waterloo train station," said Karr. "You think that's tonight or tomorrow?"

"If it's tonight, we ought to get moving."

"Yeah." Karr groaned. The drawers were empty, as was the dead man's suitcase. There were no papers or anything else that might vaguely relate to the man's identity or mission here.

"The room was registered to Gordon Kensworth," said Chafetz. "We're checking the credit card data now."

"Sounds British," said Karr.

"Maybe. The address he registered with doesn't wash," added the runner. "What a surprise."

"I found this," said Dean, handing Karr the candy box and wrapper.

"Sweet tooth," said Karr. He looked at it

115

for a minute. "So he was in Paris, or knew someone who was. Better put it back where you got it." He looked at his watch. "We have about twenty minutes to get to the train station, which is about twenty less than we need. Leave the room key on the desk over there. They'll add ten pounds to the poor guy's bill if we just toss it away."

11

Patrick Donohue thought he recognized the man in the hotel from the park. His first impulse — the instinct he always fought against — was anger, not surprise, and he'd felt an urge to wrestle the man in the hallway. He'd controlled it, of course, but the girl deserved the real credit. She acted completely naturally, crying out and falling back tearfully when she bumped into the man, the perfect cover for Donohue. He vented his anger, appearing to be just another overprotective parent, before continuing down the hall. He acted exactly as a guest would, and the credit truly belonged to the girl.

He stopped at a door across from the entrance to the stairs. Donohue put his hand in his pocket as if looking for his card key. As soon as he was sure the hallway was clear he pushed the woman and child toward the stairwell and quickly followed.

"Down," he hissed.

The prices he charged anticipated complications, and by all rights he ought to take this one in stride. And yet as they descended the first flight of stairs Donohue realized he had lost some of his equilibrium. He'd always fought to control his anger, but now it was closer to the surface. Why should he react with anger rather than surprise? Why should he react at all?

He'd probably been mistaken about the man. Surely he was — he'd seen a few faces through his scope, generic American faces, as he waited. This was just another generic American face. Not the same one.

He was losing his edge. He would have to retire soon, very soon.

Donohue thought of this the whole way down the steps. He led the woman and the girl out of the stairwell and down the thickly carpeted hall to the bar, which was nearly empty. He walked to the far end and out the door, turning left and then left again onto Holborn, the main street, walking toward the tube entrance around the corner. The woman had learned not to question him and followed along silently, herding the girl with her.

It wasn't until he passed the tube entrance that Donohue had calmed his mind sufficiently to stop and, after making sure that they hadn't been followed, consider the situation without emotion.

Survival was the first priority. The man in the hall had clearly not recognized him in any way.

Nor had they been followed. So the question was whether to go back and attempt to complete the assignment or simply walk away.

The fee for searching the room was relatively minimal, and thus walking away was easy. But it might also sour the relationship with the Arabs. They were unpredictable about these sorts of things, easily offended on ridiculous matters.

The search had clearly been an afterthought. Only when Donohue called to say that the job was done was there a question about computer disks that might be in the room. To Donohue, this suggested that someone had searched the body soon after the hit: very possibly one of the policemen in the park or a member of the crowd. But it also implied a certain uncharacteristic sloppiness, which concerned him. The information about the assassination had been vague, and while certainly enough to identify his victim it lacked the usual details his employer — Mussa Duoar — was known for. Mussa hadn't supplied them himself, of course — he had had one of his many minions, an Egyptian if the accent could be trusted, do it. Donohue had only dealt with the Egyptian once before, and it was possible that he was merely prudently limiting the intelligence to what was necessary for the job. However, there was a touch of — what was it? Vagueness? Haste? This worried Donohue, for it potentially exposed him to trouble.

He was being overly cautious. Jumpy even. Using the woman as a cover — truly unnecessary.

What would he do next, see ghosts? The room should be searched. He shouldn't succumb to paranoia.

"Let's try this again," he told the woman. "Come."

Donohue left the woman outside the door but took her daughter inside with him. He knew as soon as he opened the closet that the room was sterile. Nonetheless, he searched anyway.

"Check the drawers there, quickly," he told the girl.

"Why are you wearing gloves?"

"No questions, girl. Do what I say."

Nothing. An empty suitcase. He checked it carefully for secret compartments, but it was the sort of thing you picked up from a street vendor for ten pounds or so, the fabric thin and the stitching so poor it was bound to fall apart on its first trip.

The dead man's room, Donohue decided. He should have been told.

Sloppiness then. Mussa's people were slipping. He would charge double for his time.

"Quickly, girl. Close the drawers and come with me."

Outside, they walked to the end of the block and turned into the tube station, descending the escalator and proceeding to the right, mingling with the sparse crowd. Donohue said nothing. The woman's eyes hunted around as they always did. She reminded him of a pigeon, pecking and poking on the sidewalk for food.

"You were very good this evening," he told the girl as the train finally arrived. "Very good."

He took her arm gently and nudged her toward the open door. The woman went in behind them, glancing at him to see whether she should sit with him or not. He smiled and even leaned his body close to hers, as if he were relaxing.

"We'll get some dinner," he told her. "Then you can go back to the hotel."

"The plane is early in the morning," said the woman.

"There's plenty of time."

They took the metro two stops to Oxford Circus. Donohue knew of a good restaurant there, run by a Frenchman who'd found it easier to overcharge the English for food than his fellow Parisians. Donohue ordered a bottle of one of the house wines; the woman required no encouragement to drink and kept at it after the waiter brought another bottle. Her daughter seemed to sink farther in her seat as the meal progressed. She picked at the salmon he'd ordered for her and didn't eat her vegetables. Donohue found himself sympathizing with the girl. The trip had none of the allure for her that it did for her mother, whose head was easily turned by fancy talk and the appearance of luxury. She had no story she could share with her friends upon her return home. Nine-year-olds, even those from the poor sections of Dublin, were not particularly impressed by fancy hotels or flying first-class or walking in a park. The mother hadn't even taken her to Buckingham Palace as he suggested in the morning; she'd had a massage at the hotel instead, leaving the girl to sit on the nearby chair and read a magazine.

Donohue's mother had been similarly distracted and self-absorbed, and watching

the child stare blankly at her plate reminded him of many similar dinners he
had had, albeit at home and with much
plainer fare on the plate.

Sympathy was not one of Donohue's
stronger character traits, and it did not last
long. The woman began babbling about
how beautiful London was, and his disdain
for her quickly crowded out everything
else.

"It *is* beautiful," he said. This section of
the restaurant was empty and no one was
close enough to hear. "We'll get a chance
to do more touring tomorrow."

"Tomorrow? I thought we were going
home."

"I think we should stay another few
days." He put his hand on hers. "Why not?
You don't have any commitments, do
you?"

Her face flushed as she shook her head.

He paid for dinner in cash, choosing a
moment to leave when there was no one between them and the front of the restaurant.
He left 20 percent of the bill as a tip —
slightly on the generous side, but not so
much that it would cause him to stand out
particularly. He made it seem to the
woman that he had just had an impulse to
stroll around a bit before leading her back

to the hotel, meandering over to Blackfriars Bridge and crossing. At this hour the bridge was not heavily traveled and they saw no one else on the walkway. A gang of teenagers crowded near the bank as they reached the far side of the Thames, but that worked to his advantage; he nudged the woman's elbow to steer her to the right, making a point of gazing in their direction and frowning.

"They won't bother us," said the woman as they turned down the steps and onto the darkened path. "We're just tourists."

A foolish thing to have as your last words alive, he thought, taking the silenced pistol from his pocket.

Donohue shot the woman in the side of the head once, then turned to the girl. Her eyes gaped at him as he fired, but he had seen such expressions before.

Two more shots for each, insurance.

He dropped the pistol from the Millennium Bridge at midspan and continued up to Victoria Street, where he caught the underground and began making his way to Paddington and from there to the airport.

12

Dean stepped onto the long escalator at the foot of the tube station, relieved to be out of the tunnel. Something about the depth of the thing bothered him. He didn't have a phobia and he didn't feel as if the walls were crushing in — but he *did* feel uncomfortable. The London subways may have saved thousands during Nazi bombing in World War II, but the long trip downward made Dean feel like he was in a mausoleum.

"To the right, and smile," said Karr, just behind him. "We're on camera."

Surveillance cameras were placed throughout the station. They were used first of all by the local police authorities to help cut down on crime, pickpockets especially. But they were also routinely used by the intelligence agencies; Waterloo was the British terminus of the Chunnel, and an access point to the Continent for "those of dubious purpose," as the MI5 briefing paper Dean had seen put it. The cameras were not a secret, though there were a number that were rather inconspicuously placed and moved around every few months. Professional spies and terrorists could be assumed to make note of where the cameras were and avoid them as much as possible.

Which naturally led Karr to suggest they check all of the "shadows" — areas where the video cameras couldn't quite reach. Guided by the Art Room, they walked through the shop area on the concourse outside the platforms to the commuter trains. They split up and took opposite sides of the terminal. Dean got the half on the right and found a spot near the escalator down to the Eurostar entrance where someone could linger without being seen. He worked out in his mind how a meet might go down — "Gordon Kensworth" would come in, having checked his message, be trailed along and then contacted as he passed the newspaper stand at the center.

Or perhaps he would have told Dean and Karr to call the hotel, check the voice-mail message, and they would be contacted.

Either way, someone would be watching. Unless they knew Kensworth had been killed.

There was a woman standing near the

spot as Dean passed by, looking as if she were watching one of the schedule screens posted above the heads of the crowd but definitely checking the crowd carefully. Dean walked past, went into a nearby shop that sold coffee and snacks, then browsed in the flower shop across the way, checking surreptitiously to see if the woman was still there.

She was. She glanced at her watch, then leaned against the nearby rail, trying to look nonchalant.

"I think I have her," he muttered.

"Funny, I think I have *him*," said Karr.

Chafetz told them to watch their respective suspects. Neither changed position over the next few minutes.

"What do you think?" Karr asked Dean over the conferenced communications circuit at 8:10.

Dean took out his satellite phone — it looked like a regular cell phone, without the thick antenna usually associated with the devices — and used it as a cover to talk over the communications system. "I say we page Kensworth at eight-fifteen. See what happens."

"We will," said Chafetz. "Be ready."

The woman Dean was watching looked to be about thirty. She had short hair and a slender build, though her shoulders seemed a little broader than he would have expected, which Dean interpreted as a sign that she worked out a lot — as Lia did.

He missed her.

He reached in his pocket for change and approached the newsstand. The announcement sounded as he did: "Passenger Gordon Kensworth, please pick up the beige phone. Gordon Kensworth."

The woman started to move. Dean dropped a ten-pound note on the counter near the register — far too much for a copy of the *Guardian* — and followed her as she crossed toward the commuter platforms. He paused in front of the entrance, looking at the blue sign with the line information; as he did, the woman walked inside toward the tracks, turned right, and then walked along the platform.

Dean stepped out of the way as a group of commuters hurried through. He sidled right and saw that the woman was angling back toward the concourse. Dean spun around, nearly knocking over a pair of nuns as they tottered toward their train.

"You're being followed," said Karr cheerfully as Dean got back out into the terminal. "Maybe you got the right person after all."

Dean continued along the side, watching for the woman. She came out at the far end of the platform and walked toward the street entrance. He pulled out his cell phone and pretended to dial a number.

"Want to hand off?" he asked Karr.

"Nah. Keep doing what you're doing. The woman should stop ahead and ask you what's up. Throw out the identifier we were supposed to use in the park."

Dean had to quicken his pace as she neared the entranceway, but he still lost her by the time he reached the street.

"Left, left," said Chafetz. "We can see you in the security camera network. Go left."

As Dean started in her direction a flood of visitors just off one of the commuter trains came out onto the walk. He tried sliding through, but there were too many of them. By the time he made it past, the woman had disappeared. He continued past the bus stop, angry at himself for having blown such an easy assignment. As he turned the corner, two men stepped from the shadows so close to him that he barely saw them as they grabbed for him.

"Buckingham Palace," was all Dean could get from his mouth as the men tried to grab him. They weren't being gentle; as one launched a fist at him Dean ducked and started to fight back. He managed to push the closest one to the ground, then whirled to face the other, who made the mistake of swinging against him. Dean ducked and plowed into the puncher's midsection, upending him like a bull tossing a matador. Someone jumped him from behind; caught off-balance, Dean struggled to shed him and finally managed to get him off him and to the ground. But as he staggered back a fourth thug emerged from around the corner.

"Tommy, where are you?" said Dean out loud.

"Just hold it," said the man. He took a step forward — then flew to the sidewalk as Karr answered Dean's question in person. One of the men who'd been on the ground threw himself at Karr and was sent flying into the wall headfirst. As another started to get up, Karr grabbed the back of his shirt and threw him clear across to the other curb.

There were sirens in the distance, and blue lights were flashing up the street.

"Police!" yelled one of the men on the ground.

"You have nerve yelling for the police," said Dean.

"No, Charlie, they *are* the police," said Karr, holding up an ID that had fallen in the fight.

13

By the time the aircraft landed, Lia felt more like herself. Not well, not normal, but more the person she was.

That person had been worked over fairly hard. Her head pounded and her arms and legs were so sore they felt as if they'd been put in a compactor and compressed. Her right cheek and eye felt swollen.

The two men in the airplane said nothing as the aircraft turned and came to a stop. One of them opened the door to the cabin and went down. The other looked at her expectantly. Lia steeled herself, taking a long breath before rising. She reminded herself that she must speak Putonghua; she reminded herself that she worked for a newspaper owned by a rich businessman and a military official; she reminded herself that she was Lia DeFrancesca and she *would* get through this.

It was dark outside, and if there was a building nearby it was unlit. Lia's feet were bare, and the steel treads felt cold on her feet. The muscles in her legs began to cramp. Lia forced herself down onto the blacktop. She took a step and remembered her bag of clothes.

She needed the clothes — the belt that would activate her com system was in it.

I should have put the belt on.

I'm losing it.

Lia turned and started back up the steps. The attendant appeared in the lit doorway; he had her bag in his hand. She walked up and took it. As she did, the look on his face told her something was wrong.

Run!

There was nowhere to go. When Lia turned back around she found the other attendant waiting at the bottom of the steps.

"This way, miss," he said in English.

She stared at him, confused — honestly confused at first, then realizing that she should play it that way.

"This way," he repeated, still using English.

Lia bowed her head slightly, then in Chinese told him that she begged his pardon, but she could not understand.

He said nothing for a moment, then pointed to the left.

I am Chinese, she reminded herself.

What would she do if, not having been adopted, she'd been born in China and grown up there? What would she say? How would she act?

"Excuse me," she said, still using Chinese, "but where am I going?"

The man pointed and started to speak, telling her in Russian that she was to walk around the aircraft as he asked.

Russian?

You're in Russia. Of course. Russia. Just over the border probably.

Safe?

Lia walked in the direction the man pointed. There was a car there, its motor running. Two tall men in uniforms flanked the doors, snapping to attention as she approached. The car door was already open, but the interior light was not on. After she got in, the two men did so as well, one climbing in next to her.

Lia felt her pulse thumping in her neck. The man told the driver something. She thought he was speaking Russian — she *knew* he was speaking Russian — but she couldn't decipher the words.

I speak Russian, she reminded herself. She'd begun studying Russian as a sophomore in high school, but for some reason the meaning of the words wouldn't come.

Sand and grit covered the carpet on the floor. The throb in her skull increased. She wanted to do something to relieve it, but she was paralyzed.

She looked at her bag. She thought of getting dressed or at least reaching into the bag and pushing the switch on the belt that activated the communications system. But all she could do was stare at the bag as they drove.

God, am I afraid?

If it was fear, it was a kind of fear she had never known. It gnawed at her fingers and the left side of her body, the side near the Russian. She felt the swollen parts of her face sagging downward.

I am not going to cry.

The idea shocked her. She took a slow breath, narrowed her focus.

I will get through this.

Lia pulled her arms up across her chest.

What if she was a prisoner? What if the Koreans had decided somehow to sell her to the Russians? That sort of thing used to happen all the time during the Cold War.

She'd be interrogated. She needed a plan.

Her first strategy would be to stick to her cover story. She'd speak Chinese, ask for her "boss" to be called.

135

The Art Room would be tracking her using their locator system, which utilized satellites to pick up a special radioactive isotope embedded in her forearm.

What if her cover had been blown, though?

If that was the case, then the Russians would be very interested in her. Deep Black had helped foil a coup some months before. They would be *very* interested.

Did I tell the Koreans who I worked for?

The thought that she might have betrayed her country shocked her. That was the worst humiliation, she thought. The very worst.

I was a coward.

Nonsense. She hadn't told anyone anything. She had said nothing. She had fought her attackers.

What if she'd been drugged and couldn't remember? Bits and pieces were jumbled in her mind — she wasn't thinking clearly and might not be remembering correctly.

She couldn't remember anything, could she?

I am a survivor, not a coward.

What kind of mealymouthed word was that? *Survivor?*

Don't second-guess yourself. Focus on what is in front of you.

The words seemed to rise from the seat behind her. The voice was hers, but the words weren't. She knew them well and knew when she had heard them. They came from her father, her adopted father, Bill, teaching her to play the piano before an orchestra when she was in junior high.

"Focus on what is in front of you."

"I am, Daddy. I am."

The vehicle stopped. Lia realized there was a plane nearby — she could hear the loud rumble of an idling jet engine. The man next to her opened the door and got out. He told her in Russian to follow. She hesitated as if she hadn't understood, then pulled the handle of the car door on her side. It didn't open. The Russian reached his hand toward her. Her pulse quickened and her fingers began to tremble.

Lia looked at the door and realized it was locked. She reached for the lock and pulled it up. The Russian's hand grazed her side as she did. It was a gentle touch, merely meant to encourage her, but she yelped involuntarily.

Outside of the car, a sprinkle of rain hit her face. A plane sat a few feet away. It had no lights at all, not even in the cockpit, but the three engines at its tail were rumbling. Lia saw a shadow at the rear of the plane immediately below the tail; she took a step toward it and realized a stairway folded down from below the tail.

The engines rumbled and she found herself ducking almost to the ground and she went to the plane, hands out in front of her like a chimpanzee as she climbed up the ladder.

The plane was either her way to safety or her way deeper into hell. She thought of running into the darkness beyond the aircraft, but what good would that do? She'd be found sooner or later, and by then the airplane would surely be gone, possibly taking her only chance with it.

Lia tried to relax the muscles in her shoulders and arms as she climbed into the body of the plane. It was an ancient airliner. Mildew mixed with the scent of jet fuel inside. There was no one else aboard.

The door was pushed upright from below. Lia turned, wondering if she was supposed to lock the door. There was a bar at the side; she pulled it down and there was a loud click.

A second later, the plane began to roll. Lia scrambled to get into a seat. Pain thundered through her skull as the aircraft accelerated and then lifted upward.

The cabin lights flickered on when the

airplane leveled off. There were only twenty or so rows in the aircraft; Lia sat in the last.

A curtain separated the passenger compartment from the forward cabin and cockpit area. She moved up one row and then another and another, debating with herself whether to go forward into the cockpit or not. Surely the plane was being flown by someone sent to rescue her. But she remained afraid, and her thumping heart prevented her from getting up again after she reached the third row from the front.

The curtain parted. A short balding man with a thick black beard and mustache entered the passenger area, grim-faced behind his glasses.

"Fashona," she said.

At first, the word seemed to come from someone else. Then the information flooded into her brain.

Ray Fashona. A Desk Three associate who'd worked with Lia and Tommy Karr and Charlie Dean in Russia.

Fashona!

She tried to shout it, but her voice would come only as a whisper. "Fashona!"

"Hey," he said. He walked past her down the aisle to the back where the boarding ramp was located. She got up, and when he returned she threw her arms around him. "Fashone."

"Come on, Lia, you know I *hate* being called Fashone. It's Fashon-*a*," he said. He put his hands on hers to let him go, but she wouldn't. "Tommy started that. He thinks it's funny. He thinks *everything* is funny."

"Oh, God, Ray," she said. "Oh, God. Thank God."

"Yeah. Him and Rubens. He paid those Russians who picked you up a fortune to sit on their butts for the last two days in case something got messed up. They had to dump a bag of money at the airport to — supposedly. I think they probably just pocketed it."

"Oh, God, Ray. Thank you. Thank you."

"Look, I gotta go fly the plane. The Russians' idea of an autopilot is a two-by-four against the yoke, you know what I mean? Come on up front with me."

"OK."

She released him and followed him to the cockpit, where she sat in the first officer's seat. He fished around near the center console and came up with a headset for her.

"Better snap yourself in," he told her. "Lot of turbulence. We're going to land on

Hokkaido, the northern island of Japan. From there I don't know what the Art Room has in mind."

Lia leaned her head back gently against the seat, hoping that the soft cushion might ease some of the pain in her head. It didn't.

But it was going to be OK.

"Hey, you sure you're all right?" Fashona asked. "They said you had a tough time."

"Yeah."

Fashona turned and looked at her. "You don't sound like yourself."

"Well, who do I sound like?" she said sharply.

"Now you sound like yourself," said Fashona, turning his attention back to the controls.

She closed her eyes, hoping for sleep and praying that Fashona and his aircraft weren't a dream.

14

"Who is Gordon Kensworth?" asked Rubens as he paced in front of the Art Room.

Sandy Chafetz looked up from her console a few feet away. "We're working on it. The credit card account belongs to someone else completely, a Vefoures in France. It may be a phony — the account seems to have been dormant for a little over two months, and then was used to pay for the fare from France and rent the hotel room."

"Why was he worth murdering? What else would he have given us?" asked Rubens. He meant the questions rhetorically, but Chafetz ventured an answer, suggesting that perhaps the people whose message system he'd stumbled onto resented it.

"That would go without saying. But it would have been easier to deal with him in France," said Rubens.

There were other questions, many other questions — one of the Web sites had been compromised by French intelligence two or three months before and didn't seem to have been used since.

So many possibilities, thought Rubens. He had to winnow them down.

Rubens leaned over and looked at the monitor where Dean's and Karr's positions were marked. The police had taken them to a station near Waterloo. A long string of charges were being prepared to punish them for beating the daylights out of the surveillance detail that had attempted to question Dean. So far, neither man had said anything.

The police hadn't revealed why they were watching Waterloo Station, and the Art Room, so far moving very cautiously, hadn't been able to figure it out. It could be something simple: pickpockets were on the upswing in the city, and the police had been taking plenty of heat over it.

Even if that was the case, eventually the police would connect Dean and Karr to the earlier murder investigation and have even more questions.

Should he blow their cover now and get it over with? Call up MI5 and say, "Help"?

Two of my men were in London to pick up a list of computers used by terrorists operating in France. We didn't tell you because we thought

you might tell the French, who would in-
advertently tip off the terrorists.

Not particularly flattering for anyone,
but it was the truth.

MI5 would feel obliged to get involved.

And the French?

Very complicated.

He could call the embassy again.
Whether that would work now, though . . .

"Ms. Chafetz, tell me about that incident
earlier, the one where Tommy Karr ran
down the purse snatcher," said Rubens.

"Marie actually handled that herself,"
said the runner. "I didn't come on duty
until just afterward. This was a pretty routine assignment."

"They got off the bus and ran after the
thief," said Telach, coming over. "Tommy
vaulted over a wall and caught the guy as
he was trying to go through the bag."

"The ambassador's daughter was unhurt?" asked Rubens.

"Yes."

"But she was in danger."

"Well, it was a purse snatching."

"Get me the U.S. ambassador."

"Not MI5?"

"Please, Marie."

"With the time difference —" She
stopped midsentence. "Yes, sir. Right away."

"Fashona's on final approach to Hokkaido!" said Rockman on the other side of the room. "They're touching down in Hokkaido right now. She's safe. Thank God."

"I believe we can take some credit as well," said Rubens drily. "Make sure the doctor meets the plane, as we discussed."

15

Sometime during college, Alroy Clancy had found he could get by on four or five hours of sleep a night. The ability had come in handy at law school and then during his days as a plebe in a corporate law office; by the time he put law on the back burner to concentrate on real estate development at twenty-eight it seemed incomprehensible that anyone could sleep for longer than six hours.

It still seemed that way. The American ambassador to Great Britain did not have a "usual routine," but midnight nearly always found him in his study catching up on international news. He generally worked until about 2:00 a.m., rising again at 6:00. One of the very few benefits of being a widower was not having to worry about disturbing his wife when he came to bed or rose.

Clancy began reading some of the mainstream press stories analyzing the President's upcoming trip to Europe. As usual, the media had half the facts wrong and a tenth of the analysis right. The *New York Times* editorial writers were particularly perverse, claiming that France's recent trend toward a greater alliance with Washington had made the world a more dangerous place. As he shook his head and flipped the page, his phone rang. At this hour, it was likely to be America, and so he picked up immediately.

"Mr. Rubens of the National Security Agency on the line for you, sir," said the night operator. Clancy insisted on a live person answering his phone; the only time someone dialing the embassy got a machine was from 2:00 to 6:00 a.m.

Clancy punched the flashing light on the console next to his desk. "Mr. Rubens, good evening," he said.

He expected that Rubens would be apologizing for the trouble earlier or at least calling to give him a heads-up on what had happened. But instead, the number two man at the secretive spy agency told him he needed a favor.

"I have a bit of a difficult situation. Two of my men have been taken into custody by the London constabulary," said Rubens.

"With the police? Your department

seems to do that a lot. We just bailed out some of your men."

"It happens that these are the same ones. I'm afraid I can't go into the details of the situation, but I need them removed from custody expeditiously."

Clancy didn't know Rubens very well, but he had a reputation of being something of a prig and a snob. His tone now confirmed that — he made it sound as if Clancy worked for him.

"What details *can* you go into?" said Clancy, consciously putting a sharp edge on his voice.

Rubens explained that the men were following up a lead from the earlier incident and apparently blundered into a sting by the police.

"What I need is a pretext for them to have been in Waterloo Station that has nothing to do with their actual mission," said Rubens. "One that would avoid presenting details and yet be very persuasive. The incident involving your daughter earlier suggested an idea to me. Since it's known that they have a connection to the embassy, then we might say that they were watching for her, perhaps going to make a reservation with Eurostar or check —"

"My daughter? What does my daughter

have to do with this!" Clancy didn't have to force any edge into his voice now — no one took advantage of his daughter.

"She has nothing to do with this," said Rubens, his tone still haughty. "However, if my people were to say that they were watching the station prior to her expected arrival there — even if that arrival didn't occur — that might just be enough to satisfy all concerned. A simple phone call to you verifying the fact, and the entire matter would be dismissed with nothing more than a few hard feelings."

"My daughter Deidre is not to be involved in any of your department's operations."

"Of course not. That isn't what I'm suggesting," said Rubens. "I'm saying that if my men were to say that they were merely following up on the earlier incident involving your daughter, a pretext might be found that would satisfy everyone."

"How does lying to the British government cover all concerns?" Clancy slammed down the phone. He got up and walked over to the antique table at the side of the office, where a decanter of bourbon sat behind a small row of glasses. He took three small ice cubes from the bucket and then poured about a finger's worth of bourbon into a glass. After a birdlike sip, Clancy turned around to see that his daughter had entered the room and was standing across from him near the doorway.

"Deidre? I thought you went to bed."

"I thought I'd hunt you down for one of our conferences," she said. "What were you yelling about?"

"Nothing."

"I heard my name taken in vain."

"Oh, that was nothing."

She was dressed in sweats, her generation's version of a long flannel gown and eminently more practical.

She'd grown to look very much like her mother, he thought; a bittersweet blessing.

"Well, come in," he told her. "Sit down and let's hear about the job at the Musée Rodin."

"It's not a job; it's a fellowship."

She closed the door and came over. He pulled over one of the chairs for her, then got another so he could face her without the desk between them. They used to have these 1:00 a.m. talks all the time when she was in high school and home from undergraduate school. They called them conferences, and the sessions could last until daybreak. While more than a few had been difficult and even, for him at least, a bit frightening, he missed them greatly.

"Was there a problem about the purse snatching?" she asked.

"Oh no, don't worry about that."

She frowned, and Clancy wondered if he seemed too dismissive.

"Tell me what happened again," he said, sipping his drink. "The guy grabbed the purse and ran?"

She recounted the story. The two men who came to her aid — Rubens' men — had sprung from nowhere and saved her life, as she put it.

"You shouldn't be traveling alone," said Clancy when she finished. "There's just been an advisory about families traveling. This could have been a terrorist attack."

"I'm *fine*."

"I know you're fine. It's not you," he said quickly, "it's more me, my job. The ambassador is a target. You really should have an escort. Especially when you go back to Paris tomorrow. London is bad enough. But Paris?"

"I thought we were going to talk about the museum and the fellowship."

"We can. We will. I just don't want you to take any risks."

"I won't."

"I can get someone from the embassy to

travel back to Paris with you. What do you think?"

"Why?"

"Because there's an alert out about travel."

"I'm sure that's to places like Africa or Egypt, not Paris."

"France was specifically mentioned," said Clancy. "We can find a nice young woman. She'll blend in. She'll be your friend."

"Every time someone hears something in a bar, the entire State Department starts acting like nervous hens."

"That's an exaggeration." He tried turning it into a joke. "We're skittish roosters at least, aren't we?"

She rolled her eyes with an exaggerated smile.

Just like her mom.

"Someone to go back to Paris. Just on the plane," he said.

"What if I take the Chunnel?"

"You really want to take a train?" Once he was in overprotective mode, Clancy couldn't help himself. "Trains can break down."

"Planes can't?"

"The Chunnel then."

"I'll tell you what — make it the hunk

who recovered my pocketbook and I'll consider it," she said.

Clancy was not yet comfortable with even mild sexual innuendo from his daughter — would he ever be? — but he pretended to be and managed to ignore it. "What about one of the Marines?"

"They're too . . . Mariney."

"Mariney?"

"You know what I mean."

"One of our own security people. A young man?"

"The hunk who grabbed my pocketbook. I never thanked him properly."

"Fine. Consider it done. Now tell me about the museum. Rodin. Why sculpture? Why not painting?"

16

Dean repeated the story for the two British policemen. As he had each time, the detective in shirtsleeves took notes, recording nearly every word Dean said.

The other man stifled a yawn.

"We went to the train station because we were going to go to the London Eye," said Dean. "I got turned around, and I went outside to figure out where I was. I thought someone was following me, and I was right. When I turned the corner, I was jumped from the side. I started defending myself. I nearly got clobbered."

"All right then," said the man who'd looked bored. He got up. "I'm going to go get a bit of tea. George?"

The detective in shirtsleeves shook his head. "And you?"

"I'd take coffee," said Dean.

As soon as his partner was out of the room, the detective asked Dean if he had any other detail he might want to add.

"Not at all."

"You really do want to cooperate, chap."

"I don't know what I'm to cooperate about."

"Don't you, though?"

Dean stared at him; the policeman stared back. When the door opened, Dean looked up. Instead of the other detective, it was Chief Inspector Lang — the man who had been involved in the murder investigation.

The man in shirtsleeves jumped up. "Chief Inspector."

Lang grunted and sat down. He had an overcoat on — and still smelled of cigarettes.

"What happened?" asked Lang.

Dean repeated the story.

"And the friend that you just happened to meet went to the station with you?" said Dean.

"We both wanted to go on the London Eye."

"That's across the street and down the block away," said Lang.

"I didn't know that at the time."

"Come now. Who do you work for?" he asked. "The CIA, yes? Or are you FBI?"

Charlie gave an exaggerated sigh and looked toward the other detective. "You should call the number on the card I gave you. We make gauges for home boilers. You probably have one yourself."

"Have you seen the inside of our prisons?" asked the man.

"Are you threatening me?"

"Come on now," said Lang. "No need for any of this. Are you CIA or not?"

"Do I look like I'm CIA?"

"You do realize this is a murder investigation?"

"I didn't murder anyone."

"You came close," said the other detective.

Lang frowned. He shook his head at the man. "Why don't you take a break?"

"Maybe I will." He got up and went out.

"I would appreciate your cooperation," Lang told Dean.

"I am cooperating."

Lang drummed his fingers on the table. "We have an MI5 agent on his way over," said the chief inspector, rising. "We'll leave it to him."

Dean leaned back against the chair after the detective left. He was the one who should be yawning. He hadn't slept now for nearly two days.

Was the reference to MI5 a bluff?

There seemed too much disgust in the policeman's voice for that. And besides, guessing that they were spies wasn't exactly going out on a limb.

"Lang, let's make a deal," Dean said aloud. "Let's talk."

"No, Charlie, no," said Rockman from the Art Room.

"Come on. Let's talk before your spymasters get here," said Dean.

The door opened a moment later. Lang practically sprinted into the room with the other two inspectors trailing along.

"MI5 is not our master," said Lang.

"Before we talk," Dean said, "my partner comes in."

"We can't do that," said one of the other detectives.

"Sure you can."

"What if we did do that?" said Lang. "Then what?"

"We'll decide when I see him. You have nothing to lose, right?" added Dean. "As soon as MI5 comes I leave anyway."

Lang frowned.

"Look, I know the police were embarrassed because four of them couldn't beat up an over-the-hill Yankee tourist," he added, "but you have a murder case you're trying to solve, and holding me isn't going to help you do that."

"Bring the other American in," Lang told the others.

In the Art Room, Rockman leaned against his computer screen, practically yelping to Rubens.

"Dean wants to cut a deal with them," he said. "I tried to stop him."

"Yes. I heard," said Rubens. "As usual, Mr. Dean is a step ahead of us in assessing the situation. He's made the proper decision here. Don't interfere."

Rockman shook his head reluctantly, but Rubens saw what Dean was doing — trying to draw information out of the policeman, who would no longer be available, much less cooperate, once MI5 arrived.

Which would be any moment now.

Rubens reached to his belt for the remote control device for the communications system.

"Charles, this is Rubens. Can you talk?"

"Uh," replied Dean, more coughing than talking.

"That's fine. You've made the right decision, but be careful."

Dean snorted.

"Yes, I realize I'm stating the obvious," Rubens continued. "Nonetheless, they could hold you in connection with the murder, or simply charge you with assault. I daresay you would find either inconvenient, as would I."

"Well, howdy-hey," said Karr as he walked into the room. Dean was sitting there, arms folded across his chest. And here was bad news — Lang, the chief inspector from the park murder case, was sitting at the table with the other two policemen. "So what's going on?"

"Charlie is going to blow your covers," said Rockman in his ear. Karr thought it would have been nice for the runner to have told him this in a place where his reaction wouldn't be as conspicuous, like the interrogation room he'd just been sitting in all alone.

"They know we're spooks," said Dean.

"I do feel pretty spooky." Karr sat down, trying to work out what to say.

"I know you both work for the CIA," said Lang.

"Come on. Do I look like I work for the CIA?" said Karr. "I can chew gum and walk at the same time, right?"

"They're sending somebody over from MI5 to talk to us," said Dean.

"I get those confused," said Karr, still trying to psyche out what Dean was up to. "MI5 is internal intelligence and MI6 external? Or is that backward?"

One of the younger detectives told him

that MI5 was "tasked with internal security in the British Isles." He summarized their duties, sounding more than a little as if he had memorized a recruiting video.

"Sounds pretty good," said Karr. "Can we join?"

"I believe it is open only to British subjects," said the man.

"We really don't have time for fun and games," said Lang. "Who do you work for?"

"Let's just say the American government and leave it at that," said Dean.

"Why were you there?" asked Lang.

Karr looked at Dean, unsure exactly how the older man intended to play it.

"Question for you first," said Dean. "How'd you know to go there?"

"It was an anticrime task force," said the detective in shirtsleeves.

Karr laughed. Dean played it cool — very cool, thought Karr, watching. He stared at Lang, letting him know it was a test.

Points, Charlie, thought Karr.

"Old-fashioned police work," said Lang. He smiled depreciatingly, then took a pack of cigarettes from his pocket and began turning it over in his hand. "Luck. The woman in the park who was nearby when it happened thought she recognized him from her hotel. It's a high-class place and his clothes were less than the standard. He was also British, and didn't quite fit with the Asians and Americans who generally stayed there. We weren't sure, but we checked and found his room."

Dean nodded.

"And how did you know?"

"Same way we knew to meet him in the park," said Dean. "This was a backup meeting place, so we thought we'd see if an assistant or someone would be there. I saw the girl, thought maybe she was his backup, and followed her."

"That girl is a policewoman," said the detective in shirtsleeves indignantly.

"When did you set it up?" asked Lang.

"We didn't," said Dean. "It was set up for us. We're just messengers. We go to a place; then we go."

"What were you supposed to get from Kensworth?"

"Haven't a clue."

"Why did you think she was meeting him?"

"It was pretty obvious she was looking for someone. I was right — I just didn't realize she was working for you. Or Scotland Yard, or however you divvy that up."

Good gambit, Karr thought to himself — Dean had made what seemed an offhanded comment as an opening for the police officer to talk about his operation, subtly turning the tables. Lang volleyed back by ignoring the question.

"Why were you meeting him?" asked Lang again.

"Haven't a clue. That's the way it works."

"And how did you know to go to the station?"

"How we know everything," said Dean. "I just told you."

"You didn't go into his room? Say, a little before eight?"

"We know that room was opened," blurted the younger policeman.

Dean started to shake his head. Karr touched his arm. "We'd better come clean if we're coming clean," he said. "We were there. For about two seconds. We heard the message and then we went."

Lang nodded.

"Now it's our turn," said Dean. "Who's the dead man?"

"Gordon Kensworth."

"Is that his real name?"

"Wouldn't it be?" asked Lang.

"Were you watching the room?" asked Dean.

"We had only enough men to watch one place," said Lang. "The station seemed more important."

"The MI5 agent is Chris Wolten," said Rockman. "You've met him before. He's on his way upstairs."

"Is this an MI5 case or your case?" asked Dean.

"The murder is our case," said Lang.

"When did Kensworth rent the room?"

Dean had a solid technique, Karr decided — he asked questions he knew the answers to, both so he could validate what Lang said and so he would appear to know a little less than he actually did.

"He checked in yesterday."

"When did he get to London?" Dean asked. "Do you know?"

The inspector hesitated but then said the day before yesterday. In the morning he'd taken the Eurostar — the high-speed train that crossed beneath the English Channel via the Chunnel.

"Where was he before that?" asked Dean.

"We don't know. We don't know what his real name is yet. From what the hotel people tell us, he was English."

"Ask if he's in their identity database," said Rubens over the communications set.

"Is he in your identity database?" said Dean.

"No. He's not a criminal. And we haven't been told that he's a terrorist or a spy."

"Are you sure he's not one of yours?" said Dean. "Not an agent for MI5 or whatever?"

"I don't believe he's in Her Majesty's Service," said Lang drily.

"Whose service is he in?" asked Karr.

"You are the ones who were dealing with him," replied the detective inspector. "Don't you know?"

There was a sharp rap on the door. Chris Wolten entered.

"My God, it's not Kjartan Magnor-Karr, is it? The smartest man in the CIA?" said Wolten.

"I'm not that smart," said Karr cheerfully. "It's just my IQ."

He appreciated the fact that Wolten assumed he was with the CIA rather than the NSA, and didn't correct him.

"He beat a civil servant to a pulp," said one of the junior policemen.

"Really, Tommy?"

"I have a pretty bad temper. Especially when my buddy's been jumped on by four guys."

Wolten turned to Dean. "And you are whom?"

Dean hesitated — a play for the chief inspector, Karr thought, sharing his disdain for the intelligence dandies. Nice touch.

"Charlie Dean," said Karr. "My good buddy. Chris Wolten here is a liaison between, uh, different government interests."

"Yes, I am a liaison," said Wolten. "Chief Inspector?"

"I suppose you can have them," said Lang.

"Have they told you anything?" Wolten asked Lang.

"Nothing of interest."

"Oh, anything they say is of interest, Inspector. Come along, gentlemen."

"*Chief* Inspector," said Lang.

Rubens realized that the tiny bits of new information Dean had extracted — Gordon Kensworth had come to Britain from France via the Chunnel; someone else had snuck into his room not long before or after Dean and Karr — were like seeds. Some might sprout; some might not. As Karr bantered with the man from MI5 on the way out of the building, Rubens punched his communications line to connect with Johnny Bibleria's phone and get

165

his team of analysts and researchers to work on the new information.

Johnny Bib replied in his usually bizarre way, commenting on the number of tubes and length of the Chunnel train tunnel beneath the Channel — 3 and 31, respectively. These were prime numbers and to Johnny, who was by training a mathematician, they had significance bordering on the mystic. Calling Johnny Bib an eccentric was like saying that Einstein had written something about the speed of light, but Rubens was willing to put up with Johnny Bib's nonsense because he was a true genius when it came to providing the obscure insight necessary for truly important intelligence work. The NSA had amassed history's greatest collection of genius cryptographers and code breakers. It had mustered experts who could look at a pattern of telemetry and know what sort of system they were looking at without actually bothering to "read" the details of the transmission. The agency even had savants who could tease significance from seemingly random changes of electrical current. And then there was Johnny Bib, who could not only do all of that but also suggest where the key that tied it all together would be found.

Why?

It would be easier to figure out what Mona Lisa was smiling about. Rubens knew only that the cryptographers and others who worked with Bib worshiped him as a god — a rare honor for a mathematician.

But dealing with Johnny Bib was never easy.

"I don't like it," Johnny told him.

"Like what?" asked Rubens.

"The tunnel is one hundred fifty feet below the seabed," said Johnny Bib. "Not a friendly number."

"Please pass the information along to your team and see if it helps," Rubens told him.

"Yes. Have you given any thought to that other matter we were discussing?"

"Which matter?"

"Complex Fibonacci function," said Johnny Bib.

It was a classic math problem involving a progression of numbers — and a problem that, as far as Rubens knew, could not be solved. Johnny Bib had brought up a conjecture about a possible solution some months ago. To get him out of his office, Rubens had agreed to think about it.

"I haven't had time to consider it, unfortunately," he said.

"I really think that we're on the right trail."

"Perhaps. Concentrate for now on Eurostar. See if you can work backward from that somehow with this Kensworth. Passenger lists, maybe some connection or something. You know the routine."

"All right," said Johnny Bib, clearly dejected.

Rubens started to click off, then had an inspiration. "The train schedules probably work like a Fibonacci series."

"How so?" asked Johnny Bib, his voice perking up.

"You don't see it?"

Johnny Bib thought for a moment. "Connections in the series?"

"Precisely," Rubens told him. "But that's just the start."

"Yes. Yes, of course it is." Johnny's mind was already racing; he sounded short of breath.

Fibonacci had begun his inquiry into number series by wondering how many rabbits could breed in a year; the answer was found in an interesting series where each new number was the sum of the previous two: 0, 1, 1, 2, 3, 5, 8, 13, and so on. What that had to do with the fact that the dead man had come to England from

France Rubens couldn't imagine, but if that was what Johnny Bib needed to start his inquiry, he was more than willing to go along.

"Let me know what develops," said Rubens.

"Ambassador Clancy is holding for you," Telach told him.

"Clancy?"

"I think he wants to apologize."

"Too late," said Rubens. But he made the connection anyway.

"I can do that favor for you," said Clancy. "I have a condition, though. I want to arrange an escort for my daughter. She has to travel to Paris tomorrow. There's been a fresh alert put out and I'm concerned. As her father. I realize it's a lot to ask."

How convenient, thought Rubens, especially since he was probably going to have to send one of his team to France anyway; now they had the prefect cover.

Well, not perfect but certainly usable. And perhaps Clancy would be more cooperative in the future if the need arose.

"Mr. Dean should be available," said Rubens.

"Not Dean. The young man. Tommy something or other. He looked like a football player."

"Tommy Karr?"

"Yes. I think that was his name."

"It's too late to help with the police," Rubens told the ambassador. "But we may be able to arrange for Mr. Karr to escort your daughter. It may take a little time for me to set up, however."

"How much time?"

"It should be in place by morning."

"I appreciate it."

"Yes," said Rubens, killing the connection.

17

Denis LaFoote watched from the rented car as the Americans came out of the station, following the government man to a Ford parked up the street. LaFoote did not know for certain that the man belonged to the British intelligence service, but the tags on the car showed it was an official vehicle and that was a very logical guess. LaFoote started his own car and pulled into traffic behind them, following until they got onto M4, a major highway leading out of the city. At that point, LaFoote decided that he could no longer keep up without making it obvious that he was trailing them. He'd taken far too many chances already; his best bet now was to go back home and start from scratch.

His stand-in's death had been a terrible shock. He'd feared he was being followed or watched, but he thought he had managed to throw them off. Hiring the man had been prudent, but LaFoote hadn't thought it would be a matter of life and death.

How had they found him? What mistake had he made?

He'd used his friend Vefoures' credit card to buy the tickets back and forth between Paris and London. That must have led them to him.

Or perhaps the phone? He had checked the line for a bugging device with his old methods — had they been superseded?

Of course. In twenty years — of course.

Still, it was the logical risk, the least amount of exposure. And now it seemed clear to him that it must be Ponclare.

He tried not to jump to conclusions. Ponclare was, clearly, in the best position to order the murder, but it might not be the intelligence chief.

It had been several years since LaFoote had been in England, and the seventy-two-year-old belatedly realized that he had gotten lost — he wanted to be on M25, the highway that formed a circle around the city; instead he'd somehow managed to get back onto M4 and misinterpreted a sign for Heathrow Airport as being for Gatwick Airport, which was near his hotel. He pulled off the road to consult a map; as he unfolded the paper a police car pulled off behind him.

LaFoote tried to see the man in his

mirror as he approached. It might be a routine traffic stop, he thought — or perhaps it was another assassin. He had a small pistol in his belt beneath his coat, his old Mab PA-8. There was only a second to decide what to do.

Instinct told him to leave the gun hidden and roll down the window. He did so.

"Hello," said the policeman.

"Bonjour," said LaFoote. "How can I help you, sir?"

The policeman leaned down against the car. He smiled indulgently, then told LaFoote that he couldn't park at the side of the road, especially in the direction he was facing — LaFoote had gone off on the right side of the road, which was in the opposite direction of the traffic. Or would have been, had there been any traffic.

"Oh, *oui, oui,"* said LaFoote. He explained that he was lost.

The policeman took the map from him and, after turning it around a few times, found where he was and showed him how to get back to the highway. "It'll be easy from there. Don't worry, old fella; my granddad gets lost all the time."

LaFoote forced a smile to his face as he took the map back. Somehow he managed not to strike the officer as he pulled out, though the seventy-two-year-old Frenchman was sorely tempted.

18

A Navy aircraft was waiting for Lia after she finished with the doctor. It was a P-3 Orion, a large four-engined aircraft generally used for long-range spying missions. Thoroughly impressed, Fashona told her it meant Rubens was pulling out all the stops for her.

Lia shrugged. Beyond tired, she followed Fashona across the apron where he had parked his aircraft and nodded when a Navy chief petty officer came out from the plane and asked if she was Ms. DeFrancesca.

"We know you've been through a helluva time, ma'am," said the chief. "You're in Navy hands now. We'll take care of ya. Flying you direct back to the States. Not a care in the world. Leave the worrying to us."

Lia forced herself to smile for him. Though in his thirties, he came off considerably older, ancient even — the wise old man of the sea, she thought. She climbed up the stairway to the aircraft's rear compartment. The Orion — it was due back in the States for an equipment overhaul — boasted a large array of electronic sensors operated from consoles in the fuselage; the interior looked more like a high-tech computer lab than something that flew around the borders of hazardous airspace. The chief led her to a small lounge, insisted on giving her a blanket, and then went to "grab some grub." She found his doting father routine a bit much to take — another sign, she realized, that she was coming out of the fog that had descended on her in Korea.

It *was* like a fog, wasn't it? She saw it through a haze. There were bits missing — the end. How had she escaped?

She couldn't remember all of the assault. Just being punched.

Maybe she hadn't been assaulted.

I was assaulted.

Raped.

That was the word. Better to use it. Better to face it.

The doctor and nurses hadn't, actually. They had a kit and they had pills, but they hadn't actually said "rape," had they? They hadn't even said "assaulted," or "attacked." As if you could avoid the reality by not naming it precisely.

"Here now, ma'am," said the chief, appearing with a tray. A covered bamboo basket sat in the center; it was the sort used as a steamer and held two trays. At the top was a fish dish; below were some small dumplings and fussily cut vegetables. The chief had also found chopsticks — and a bottle of Sapporo beer.

"Nice airline," said Lia, trying to joke though her heart wasn't in it.

"Like I said, ma'am. Navy'll take care of you. Not a care in the world for you."

"Thank you," she said. And then she started to cry.

19

The British intelligence officer was polite — more than polite, under the circumstances — but Dean sensed the resentment beneath the surface. They were mucking around in his backyard and hadn't had the decency to tip him off about it. That was the way he saw it.

Wolten drove them to a large house about twenty miles outside of London that MI5 used as a kind of guest cottage. He used the word *cottage,* but the building looked about the size of the White House. There was a fire going in the study off the entrance but no sign of whoever had started it.

"So, chaps. Who was Gordon Kensworth?" asked Wolten, going to a sideboard and pouring himself a drink.

"Don't know," said Karr. "How long have you guys been following him?"

"We haven't. Drink, Charles?"

Dean passed. He leaned back in the leather club chair and felt his eyelids droop.

"Tommy?"

"Just a beer," said Karr.

"Bitters OK?"

"If that's what you're calling beer these days."

"We used to call it beer," said Wolten. He reached down into the cupboard. "But all the nasty business with the Germans caused a change in vocabulary. Now, how long have you been after this Kensworth chap? He's not a Russian, is he? Bosnian?"

Dean drifted off while Karr and Wolten danced. He started dreaming about Lia, wondered where she was, how she was. Then he looked up and saw Karr standing over him.

"What?" he said, struggling to open his eyes.

"Time for bed, dude." Tommy Karr's laugh made the old floorboards shake. "Come on. We need to get some sleep. They'll be hooking us up to the electrodes in the morning."

"I heard that," said the British agent from the other room.

Two rooms had been prepared for them upstairs. Karr put his finger to his lips as they walked up the steps — then announced very loudly that the whole place was bugged and Dean shouldn't think of saying anything. Dean wouldn't have had the energy even if he'd had the inclination. He collapsed face-first on the bed, still fully dressed. Somehow he managed to kick his shoes off before falling into a deep slumber.

20

Johnny Bib got up from his desk, took three steps to the side — precisely three — and placed his pencil into the sharpener. Working on a problem without a sharp pencil was a waste of time. He had seen this proven over and over. He had a theory that the type of pencil was also critical — but working out the various permutations would require considerable research, and he didn't care to spend the energy. It seemed better to just muddle through with a variety of pencils, such as those he had collected in the cup at the front of his desk, marching on through time like the point on a Euclidian line.

The metaphor wasn't exactly right, was it? Points did not march. Someone — a mathematician — might imaginatively trod over the points, but they wouldn't get up and walk by themselves. Not in Euclidean space, at least.

Johnny considered this as he went back to his desk. The metaphor wasn't right; the numbers weren't right; the conclusions were nonexistent. Kensworth did not exist in the time and place called London, and this person named Vefoures was a French pensioner who also didn't seem to exist, at least not lately.

Which told him something. But what?

Johnny Bib had been working on this question since nine or ten in the morning, and it was now past five in the evening. If there was an answer — and surely there must be an answer — he couldn't see it.

Perhaps some music would help. Johnny Bib sprang from his chair as the thought occurred to him and went back over to the credenza — three steps — and turned on the stereo. He selected the Thelonious Monk disk and went back to his seat, hoping to be inspired.

Inspiration did not knock. William Rubens did.

"What do you have for me, Johnny?" asked the Desk Three director, leaning in the open doorway. "Anything?"

"Numbers," said Johnny Bib. "Vefoures' bank account. Very nice digits: five-four-five euros."

"Only five hundred and forty-five euros?"

"Lives on a pension."

Rubens went over to the table in front of

Bib's desk, where the data the rest of the team had been sorting through had been carefully assembled. Johnny had sent most of them home for a break; the relief team had taken a break for pizza and would be back in a half hour or so.

"Nothing at all?" said Rubens.

"Little," said Johnny Bib.

"You've checked the servers on the Web sites?" Rubens asked. He was standing over the pile of information on the disk arrays in the servers, so obviously he knew the answer as well as Johnny. Johnny therefore declined to answer.

"The list we were given — did they check out?"

"There are only two computers. One was compromised by the French several months ago. The other is off-line and has been for the last day. Nothing of note."

Rubens pulled over one of the two laptops on the table and tapped into the team's dedicated computer. The NSA had used a special program to infiltrate computers used as servers in a network. The program could read what was stored on the disk arrays that fed into the computer and in fact could reveal just about everything on any drives accessible from the local network. The trick was to do it without being noticed, which at times could be complicated.

"The computer that's off-line — where is it physically?" asked Rubens.

"We're not sure," said Johnny Bib. "Clearly, it's part of another network."

"And you can't trace it?"

"We are working on it. It doesn't appear to have been used in a while. We think they swapped computers every three to six months. It fits other patterns."

"This model here. What does it do?"

"Predicts ocean wave patterns," said Johnny Bib. "It had been erased. Most likely it was put there by a geology student. They say it relates to earthquakes and tsunamis. I doubt that was used."

"But it's in the area of the computer that was hidden from the local user."

Johnny Bib looked at his boss. Rubens could be so linear at times. Just because the program was there *now* didn't mean that it had been there when the terrorists or whoever had hijacked part of the computer started using it. It had clearly been erased, probably before the computer was taken over. It was difficult to tell without having the physical disk. And even then, it might not be knowable.

Of course it would. If you could come up

with the right formula.

The drives had been accessed remotely and used for several purposes. One was to store programs and information that had mostly been erased and overwritten; the simulation was among the few things that remained more or less intact. There was a collection of photographs and a fractal generating engine that were probably both part of an encryption program. The computers had also been used to redirect requests on the Internet, making it difficult to trace where a particular query or e-mail, say, had come from.

Johnny Bib's team had been able to recover a list of Web sites that the two computers were used to access, looking for similarities. Statistically, the most common hits were of a weather site. Though this was perhaps to be expected, the analysts had nonetheless checked the weather site carefully in case it was being used to pass messages. One of Johnny's team members believed the forecasting systems might be a sophisticated means for encrypting data; so far, they hadn't been able to come up with a plausible model on how this could be true.

"Why was the page with the Paris weather updated ninety-seven times on the seventh and the twelfth?" Rubens asked. "Every other day is ninety-six times."

Johnny Bib looked up from his desk. "The actual site?"

"Yes, the site. Not the computer that accessed it. The actual Web site."

How he had missed that? And with a prime number as a clue, no less.

He all but grabbed the file out of Rubens' hands. "We're trying to figure that out now," he told his boss. "Right now."

It was some measure of Rubens' dread of the process that he showed up at the attorney's office a full half hour before the appointed time. The lawyer, a specialist in elder care law, had been recommended by Rubens' personal attorney, whose own expertise did not extend to that area. Used to law offices that were nothing short of palatial, Rubens had been shocked the first time he came here. Located in a two-story building that had only recently been converted from a house, the lawyer's office consisted of two rooms. The waiting room featured an L-shaped couch covered in corduroy so worn that the couch's support springs showed through. Across from it sat a desk that Rubens supposed a receptionist was meant to use, except that he had yet to see or speak to one.

The door between the reception area and the lawyer's office was as thin as it was flimsy. Even if she'd had a quieter voice, it would have been impossible not to overhear her talking with the people inside — clearly a violation of lawyerly ethics as well as common sense, thought Rubens as he sat down.

And yet his personal attorney called Ellen McGovern one of the best elder law practitioners in the state.

McGovern certainly had a steady stream of clients. The couch sagged with three middle-aged women, each wide enough to fill a cushion by herself. A young man in his early twenties hovered by the door. Rubens folded his arms protectively and tried to smile as he declined an offer from one of the women to share her bit of the couch.

Rubens tried very hard not to overhear the story unfolding inside, but he would have had to stuff his ears with wax not to. A woman in her sixties had been granted custody — it sounded more as if she had been stuck with it — of her two grandchildren when they were two and three. She'd raised them for ten years, then had a stroke that left her paralyzed. Who should take care of them now? A foster family appointed by the court? A nephew and niece who had volunteered? The grandmother?

As dire as the circumstances seemed, Rubens realized they weren't all that far from the tangled arrangements that had governed his own childhood — albeit with the great difference money might make. He pretended not to have heard anything as the people left. Everyone seemed to be engaged in a similar conspiracy, the women on the couch casting their eyes on the carpet as each one was called in and exited in her turn.

"So, Mr. Rubens, how are we this evening?" asked McGovern when it was finally his turn. He checked his watch as he sat; amazingly enough, it was only five minutes past the appointed time.

McGovern pushed a small box of cough drops toward him as she pulled out the file. "Want one?"

"No thank you."

"Diet?"

"Hardly."

McGovern laughed, then reached for the cough drops.

"How is the General?" she asked, turning to him.

"As poor as he's been," admitted Rubens.

McGovern nodded. She swung around in the chair, facing him. "Do you mind if I speak, well, still as a lawyer, but maybe one who's taking a broad look at things?"

"Don't you always?"

She smiled and reached to her head, poking a strand of her long hair back behind her ear. Rubens decided that she had been pretty in her youth. There were glimmers of it left in her forty-something-year-old face. But it had to poke through considerable fatigue. The brown knit sweater and gray pants she wore did little to define her body, and she gave no evidence that she cared to have it defined. Her desktop was covered with photos beneath a layer of glass; Rubens surmised that the children there were hers, though there were no photos of a husband and she did not wear a wedding ring.

"Alzheimer's is a very difficult disease," she told him. "It's very hard for a patient's family to deal with, extremely frustrating. People want to make their peace with someone and they're prevented from doing so. That's not easy to bear."

"Rebecca had her chance a long time ago."

"I meant you."

"Me?"

"When someone we're close to — someone we love and respect — is sick, our judgment clouds. This case, the whole procedure really, when it goes to court it's going to seem very . . . antiseptic at best."

"I realize that. I'm doing what I have to because the General asked me to. I'm doing what's right."

"If the court disagrees, can you deal with it emotionally?"

"I don't know," answered Rubens, surprised by the question and by his honesty. Not many people had ever bothered to inquire about his feelings.

"That's an honest answer." McGovern slid back in the chair. "What do you think Rebecca's motives are?"

"Greed."

"Not guilt?"

"Perhaps a little guilt at neglecting him. And causing him so much trouble when she was younger. Guilt, I suppose, yes. But mostly greed. She wants the cousin's money. And may even think, despite the fact that I've given her copies of all his bank accounts, that he has more squirreled away."

"Not love, though?"

"No."

"You think she's your enemy." McGovern

did not phrase it as a question. "Is there something I should know? No personal reason for a grudge?"

"Not in the least." Rubens sensed that she didn't believe him, but it was the truth; he had no grudge against Rebecca — except for the fact that she had broken her poor father's heart.

That was personal, perhaps. But that wasn't what the lawyer meant.

"OK," said McGovern. "Fair enough. I just want to make sure we know precisely where we're coming from."

She dropped into her standard lawyer speech, telling him again that she was representing him, not the NSA and not the General. The court would have to appoint a lawyer to represent his interests. "It almost certainly will be one of three people," added McGovern. "They're all very good."

"Yes. You said."

McGovern picked up her box and fished out another cough drop. "Rebecca's counsel has insinuated that they might ask for a jury. That's very unusual, and I expect that it's part of a plan to pressure you. Because your agency is against publicity, they think you'll be pressured to stand back."

"They think the agency is running the

show," said Rubens. "Are they going to tell the judge that?"

"Oh, they already have. Indirectly, maybe, but you don't have to read too deeply to pick that up."

"Will the judge believe them?"

"I don't know. I suspect that may be one of the reasons he's interested in meeting everyone tomorrow."

"Tomorrow?" said Rubens. "Already? You said not until next week. Don't they have to file their papers?"

"First of all, the papers have been filed. Second of all, this isn't a hearing. It's very informal. The judge is Jack Croner. Do you know him?"

Rubens shook his head.

"He's good. You'll like him. Very easy-going, very informal — a non-judge judge, if there is such a thing."

"That's good?"

"In this kind of case, a lot of times it is, yes."

"Why didn't you tell me?"

"I *am* telling you. His office called a little while ago. I would expect a hearing perhaps the next day, or the day after that. These proceedings move very rapidly, unless there's a reason to slow things down."

"And you said it was all right to meet tomorrow?"

"I said I would get back to him. But I am inclined to agree if it's all right with you. You have to remember, Mr. Rubens, that the schedule is not going to be one hundred percent in our hands."

Actually, it wasn't in their hands at all.

"What's going to happen?" Rubens asked.

"I suspect that the judge will subtly suggest that everyone ought to shake hands and come up with a good solution without starting a food fight," said McGovern. "And then he'll look around the room and go from there."

"There won't be an agreement. Then what happens?"

"He'll appoint a lawyer and order an examination."

"Quickly?"

"Probably. Croner likes to move ahead. He might even decide by the end of the week. Unless the General's lawyer moves for a jury. That's very unusual, and I doubt it would be done under these circumstances. But it's not my call. Now, if the suit happens to be withdrawn or there seems to be a meeting of the minds —"

"That's not going to happen."

McGovern got up. "Remember, I represent you, not the General," she said.

"He wanted me appointed guardian."

"He specified custodian. We're claiming that it's reasonable to assume he would have extended the responsibilities. It's possible the General's attorney may not agree. And we know Rebecca already doesn't. I have to get going, I'm afraid."

"Yes, well, so do I. Thank you," said Rubens. He waited while she pushed some files into a briefcase.

"Alzheimer's is a terrible disease," McGovern said as they walked to the door.

"Yes," said Rubens. "But I've been speaking to the doctors. There's a great deal of work being done. It's always possible that there'll be a cure."

"Are you hoping for a cure?"

"Hoping? Yes." He held the door open for her. "Do I expect one? No."

21

The smell of strong coffee woke Dean early the next morning, but when he went downstairs he found no one around. He followed his nose to a room toward the back of the large house. A silver pot filled with fresh, hot coffee sat on a round wooden table in the middle of the room; he took one of the cups next to it and fixed himself a cup.

The room was fitted out like a library, with upholstered chairs scattered in front of a wall of shelves. He began to browse, starting with the leather-covered tomes in the shelves nearest the coffee, moving through Thackeray and Dickens to George Eliot and D. H. Lawrence. After the novels he came to a history section, where leather-bound classics gave way to newer hardcovers. The books were not grouped in any particular order; Winston Churchill's history of the Second World War sat next to Gibbon's *Rise and Fall of the Roman Empire*. Next to them was *Suddenly We Didn't Want to Die*, an account of the U.S.

Marines during World War I.

Dean picked it out of the bookcase. The first pages caught his attention — especially the picture that showed a Marine as a young man after the war. He was still a kid but squinted toward the camera with some deep knowledge in his eyes. The book was written simply, but every word jumped off the page at Dean, pure truth and emotion.

When Tommy Karr found him nearly an hour later he was forty-something pages deep, riveted by the account of a burial detail and the horrors of burying bodies several days after the battle.

"Looking to score points with the hosts?" Karr asked, pouring himself a cup of what was by now cold coffee.

"Reading about U.S. Marines," said Dean.

"U.S. Marines?" Karr bent down and took a look at the book. "Hey, my great-grandfather was there."

"He was a Marine?"

"Belleau Wood, right?"

"You had a great-grandfather in the Marines?"

"Gee, Charlie, why do you say it like that?"

"Just asking."

"Fifth Marines, Fourth Brigade." Karr smiled, then chugged the coffee and poured himself another cup.

"I thought you were Swedish."

"Or something. Half. Decent coffee," added Karr. "Probably better when it was hot, right?"

"When are they coming to interview us?" Dean asked.

"They're not. They gave up," said Karr cheerfully. "The coffee is their way of telling us to sod off."

Karr put his finger to his lips, then held it up and twirled it around. "Back to London for us."

"How?"

"Chris left us a pair of bikes. Come on. You can take the book, as long as there are no bugs in it. Mail it back when you're done. I doubt they'll miss it."

Karr wasn't kidding about the bicycles, but they were meant to be ridden only as far as the train station, which was two miles away. Once they got there, Karr took out his PDA and scanned both the platform area and their things for bugs — and was so suspicious when he didn't find any that he scanned again.

"Maybe they trust us," said Dean. "We *are* allies."

"Nah. That's a reason *not* to trust us," said Karr. He pointed to the belt that activated the communications system and shook his head. Dean was only too happy not to bother turning on the system.

They didn't speak again until after they arrived in London nearly an hour later. Karr scanned the restroom in the train station and then slapped on all of the faucets.

"Your plane leaves at five from Heathrow," Karr told Dean.

"We're splitting up?"

"Rubens has loaned me to the State Department." Karr chuckled. "I get to play crossing guard."

Dean waited for the explanation, but none came.

"Get to Heathrow by three if you can," Karr said. "I should be back in the States in a few days. As far as I can tell, we're not being followed and there are no bugs in here. Outside in the station, they have a regular surveillance system. You can turn your communications gear back on whenever you want."

Dean nodded, then went over to use one of the stalls. By the time he finished, Karr was gone.

Dean circled around the train station, then went out on the street, checking to see if he was being followed. Finally he decided that he hadn't been and turned on the communications device.

"Charlie, where have you been?" asked Telach immediately.

"Somewhere out in the country. I just came out of Paddington train station."

"I know where you are," said the Art Room supervisor. "Why haven't you signed onto the communications system?"

"Tommy thought we were being followed."

Telach made an exasperated sound and turned him over to Lief Johnson, who had taken over for Rockman as his runner.

"There's an express train from Paddington to the airport," said Johnson. "You have to go back into the station and turn left."

"I know where the train is," said Dean. "My flight isn't until five tonight."

"We may be able to get you something earlier."

"Don't bother," said Dean, spotting a taxi.

Chief Inspector Lang looked as if he'd neither slept nor changed since Charlie had last seen him — but then again, the same could be said for Charlie.

"I'm on my way to the airport. I came to give you my phone number," said Dean. "And to get yours."

"You know why the man was murdered?"

Dean shook his head. "I assume it had something to do with us, but we don't even know who he was."

"You don't know, or you're not allowed to say?"

"I don't know. I'm not sure I'd be allowed to say if I did, but I don't know."

"The hotel room was registered to Gordon Kensworth."

"It was an alias. It doesn't check out. The room was reserved with a different name and account. Vefoures. I assume you know that by now. . . ."

Lang didn't answer. Dean had dealt with American cops occasionally as a gas station owner. They always were skeptical when you first met them. If you got past that, they could be fairly cooperative, often helpful, and even once in a while sympathetic — but it sometimes took a lot to get past that first hurdle.

Dean glanced at his watch. He wasn't sure how long it would take to get to the airport, and it was now past two o'clock.

"When I know more, I'll give you a call,"

he told the chief inspector. "I don't have to work through the channels, if that's what you're worried about."

"Are you interested in finding out who he really was?"

"Yes," said Dean.

"Come along then."

"Charlie, you have an airplane," said his runner over the communications system as he started down the steps.

"I'll take a later flight."

Lang turned around.

"Talking to myself," said Dean. "Bad habit."

"Do it myself," said the detective. "No one talks back at least."

"I wouldn't listen if they did," said Dean, trotting up behind him.

Outside, the detective paused to light a cigarette.

"Want one?" he asked Dean.

"No thanks."

"I didn't think you were a smoker."

"I don't hold it against anyone."

"Neither do I."

Lang led Dean to his car, a five-year-old compact with a dent in the door. As they drove, Lang told him that a missing persons report had been filed that answered the murder victim's general description.

He had a hunch that this was their man and was going to find out.

"Family member is over in Brixton. Do you know where that is?"

"Couldn't guess."

Brixton was in London, but it wasn't a place most tourists visited. The area mixed immigrants and hard-luck old-timers with a few dollops of working-class families trying to make ends meet. The flat they went to belonged to one of the latter, a Rose Pierce, who lived with her three tots. Her older brother Gordon Pierce, who had been staying in the room at the front for the past three months, hadn't come home the night before.

Rose's lip began to quiver as soon as the chief inspector showed his credentials. She led them back to the kitchen, hands trembling as she poured water into a kettle for tea. Dean took the pot from her and put it on the stove, then sat down at the small table. It was made of metal, the sides chipped and dented.

"I sent my kids around to my neighbor Eileen so's we could talk," said the woman.

"If you could tell us about your brother," said Lang, his voice soft and gentle, "it might help."

"Have you found him?"

"We don't know." He had a picture in his pocket, but it wasn't particularly nice, and Dean guessed that Lang wanted to spare the woman the heartache of seeing it if he could. "It's possible."

Fighting back tears, Rose told them that her brother had been out of steady work for most of his adult life; he'd been a miner in Cornwall years ago, been hurt and unable to work. The story of his accident was elaborate and hard to follow — he'd been bonked on the head, but the doctors were unable to find any real damage, not even enough to qualify for what the woman called a proper pension. Lang took notes dutifully, though Dean could see he didn't believe the brother had been disabled.

"He'd been a housepainter, on and off. At his age, not too many employers would take a chance. And he looks older than he was. That doesn't sit well."

"How old was he?" asked Lang.

"Fifty next month. The years wore him down. A few days ago he said he had a new job, something he couldn't discuss," continued the woman. "He left. He was gone for a whole night, didn't see him the next day, yesterday, or last night."

Lang frowned as if he didn't quite believe this, either, and asked her for details. But she didn't have any. Dean fit the missing time neatly into a sequence — the man was hired for the job, taken to France, then reintroduced into London.

"He came home from the pub that night, the last I saw him, and he had a few quid on him. He gave me a ten-pound note and said there'd be more. Bloody hell, that was unlike him. Not the generosity — Gordy was always a generous man. But to have money. That was mighty odd."

The detective took a few notes, changed the subject to ask about her brother's schooling, and then came back to the job he'd spoken of, making it seem as if it were an afterthought.

"Do you think someone hired him at the pub?" asked the detective.

"The pub? No. He got odd jobs sometimes in the morning."

"Would he have gotten paid in advance for an odd job?"

"Not usually."

"Which pub?" asked Dean.

The woman looked at him, surprised by Dean's accent.

"I'm an observer from America. Learning," he added.

"Kind of old to learn," she said.

"Never too old to learn something useful," said Dean.

"It was the Golden Goose, around the corner and down the block."

"Would you happen to have a photo of him?" asked the detective.

The woman's lower lip began quivering again as she got up from the table. The picture showed Kensworth — in life, Gordon Pierce — ten years before, hair already white, face well lined.

"It might be good if you could come over to the station with me," Lang told her.

She nodded once, then burst into tears.

22

Deidre Clancy had begun to feel foolish the moment her father said he had succeeded in getting "Mr. Karr" as her escort back to Paris. She'd mentioned him as a joke — completely and totally and utterly a joke — but her father tended to be literal minded, and once he set his course it was impossible to get him to deviate.

Which didn't mean that she didn't want to see the handsome man who'd retrieved her purse, just that she wanted to see him under some circumstance other than as her minder.

Now she bristled as she waited for him in the car, torn in all different directions. They had tickets on the Eurostar and had been instructed to show up an hour before departure. They were running very late; depending on traffic they might not make the train at all. Deidre hated to be late; it was a trait she shared with her father.

Finally Karr materialized, strolling from the doorway with a casual air, a backpack over his shoulder. He turned back and yelled something to one of the people inside, waved, and laughed. The driver held the rear door for him; Karr bowed his head as if it were all a joke and slid in.

"Hey there," he said. "Fancy meeting you here."

"We're running a little late," she said.

"You don't think they'll hold the train for you?"

Clearly he thought she was a spoiled brat — or even worse. As the car wended its way through traffic, Deidre watched out the window, annoyed at the entire situation. Meanwhile, Karr leaned back in his seat and seemed to doze. Then about halfway to the station he sprang to life as they bogged down in traffic.

"OK, let's go," he said, opening the door.

"What?" she asked.

"Pop the trunk."

Before she or the driver could say anything else, Karr had jumped from the car and was at the trunk. He grabbed her bag as it sprang open, then swung around to her side. She got out.

"This way, quick," he said.

She headed toward the curb, hesitating as she reached it because she'd forgotten to close her door.

"Come on, let's go," said Karr, looming over her. He gave her a gentle push and she started running, unsure what was going on.

"Left," he told her, walking behind at a pace that wasn't quite a trot. "Into the tube."

She stepped to the side at the doorway. He slid a ticket into her hand as he passed, walking quickly through the gate and then onto the escalators. He kept up the same brisk pace and they arrived on the platform just as a train was pulling in. They hopped in.

"Two stops," he said.

"Are we being followed?" she asked.

He didn't answer. The train was crowded; they had to stand near the door. Deidre squeezed toward him as the train stopped to take on more passengers. She reached toward her carry-on bag, but he shook his head.

It wasn't until the train stopped that she realized that they were at Paddington train station. He was out of the car so quickly that she had trouble keeping up; not until they made it upstairs did she point out that the Eurostar train for Paris left from Waterloo.

"Really?" Karr grinned and didn't stop walking.

"We're going to the airport?" she said when she saw the sign for the shuttle over to Heathrow.

"Very possibly," said Karr. "But we'll have to see how it plays."

They made the shuttle just as the doors were closing. Karr produced two tickets for the conductor.

"Are we being followed?" Deidre asked finally.

"Not that I know of."

"Why are we going by airplane instead of taking the train?"

"I like to fly," said Karr.

"I don't like this."

"Which?"

"I don't like being kept in the dark like this. What's up? Why are we changing plans?"

"For one thing, you bought the ticket in your own name, and you did it a few weeks back," said Karr. "So anyone interested in you had plenty of time to figure out where you'd be."

"I thought you said I wasn't being followed."

"You're not," he told her. "But I am."

LaFoote had nearly lost the American agent at the embassy; he'd had to circle on the bicycle at a distance until the car finally left. Luckily, he'd guessed not only that the man would be in the car but also that at some point he would abandon the vehicle, for either a second one or the tube. The retired French agent had spent nearly fifty pounds on the secondhand bicycle and felt a twinge of regret as he tossed it to the side before entering the tube station. But at least he'd made the train, getting in a car behind the American and the girl.

Given that some sort of mistake he had made had allowed his meeting to be compromised, LaFoote felt vindicated that he had at least managed to guess correctly that the government agent would return to the U.S. embassy. He hadn't managed to get onto the shuttle for the airport. He considered hiring a car but decided instead to fall back on a second plan — he'd go to London Airport instead, where he knew he could catch a flight to Paris. He might not beat the Americans — there were three flights over that they could take before he'd land — but he had a friend who worked for Air France who could watch the terminal for him. LaFoote called her from London and described the pair to her.

"Fred Astaire and Ginger Rogers," said his friend, who like LaFoote had worked as a spy some decades before.

"If Fred Astaire had blond hair and was over two meters tall, yes," LaFoote told her.

"I think you're getting paranoid," said the runner in Karr's ear when he finally made it to the restroom at the back of the airbus en route to Paris.

"Paranoia is healthy," Karr told him. "It's an old guy. He was on a bike."

"I really think you're hallucinating," said Johnson.

"Could be. You have my rentals ready?"

"I scrounged up two stiffs from the embassy in Paris," said Johnson. *Stiffs* was Johnson's favorite term for CIA officers; Johnson had worked at the CIA and was not particularly fond of his experience there.

"Good. Talk to you then."

Out in the cabin, the pilot was flashing the Buckle Up sign and preparing to descend.

"Did I miss anything good?" Karr asked Deidre as he sat down.

"Two little green men flew by the wing in their flying saucer."

"See? Now you're getting the hang of it," said Karr. "Sarcasm can be a very handy quality."

"So why would someone follow you?" asked Deidre.

"They want my secret to a long life," Karr told her. She seemed to be warming up a bit; maybe she wasn't the stuck-up rich kid he'd taken her for. "I'm actually over two hundred years old, you know. I fool a lot of people."

"Do you always turn everything into a corny joke?"

"Only when I'm awake. Although some people say I talk in my sleep, too."

"We're watching the gate for you," said Johnson after the plane landed and rolled toward the gate. The Art Room had infiltrated the security system at the airport and was monitoring the video cameras. "So far you look clean."

"Uh-huh," murmured Karr.

"What?" asked Deidre.

"Talking to myself. You'll find I do that a lot."

"Do you answer back?"

"Oh yeah. That's what keeps it interesting."

Karr spotted one of the CIA people drifting beyond passport control, but if anyone else was looking for him they were being extremely subtle. Karr led Deidre toward the queue for one of the shuttle buses into the city, then turned and went over to the taxi line, staying there for about five minutes — long enough, he figured, for the Art Room and the CIA officers to pick out anyone following him. Then he got Deidre and tugged her toward the rental car counter, where the Art Room had already reserved a car for Mr. Greene of London. Karr flashed the proper credit card, paused to negotiate an upgrade, and then went outside into the lot.

His shadow didn't show up until he was on the highway into the city — an old guy in a Renault, reported the CIA agents, who wanted to know what to do.

"Just tag along," Karr said. "I'll drop D here off at the embassy and then have a chat with Grandpa. Find me a dead end somewhere."

"Who are you talking to?" Deidre demanded.

"If I told you, I'd have to kill you," said Karr.

"*Stop.*"

"My phone has a mike in it," he told her. He pulled it out and waved it in the air. "I'm talking to our trail team."

"I don't believe you."

"Suit yourself," he said, sliding it back in his pocket.

"I'm D?" she said. "That's not much of a code word."

"Sorry. I'm not very creative when danger's breathing down my neck."

"Grandpa is the danger? Doesn't sound very threatening."

"That's just his code word. Besides, guy with a cane? Could have a machine gun there."

"Are we really in danger?"

"Nah. Nothing to worry about." He turned and smiled at her. "So you live in Paris?"

"I go to school here, yes."

"College?"

"Postgrad. Art history."

"Good field," said Karr, who had no idea if it was or not.

"I like to think so."

"I'm going to drop you off at the embassy," he told her, moving to the right lane as the exit approached. "They'll take care of you. I want you to stay with them, all right?"

"I really don't want to be taken care of," she said. There was something plaintive in her voice.

"Yeah, I know," said Karr. "But I do have to figure out who this is. I think he's tracking me, not you, but until we're sure, better safe than sorry. Promise?"

She didn't answer.

"Listen, if you don't promise, I'm going to have to hand you over to the Marines and have them put you in the brig."

"I promise."

"All right. No fingers crossed or any of that stuff, right?"

"Please."

Karr had concluded that the person following him was either a British agent or the person who had used the dead man to contact him. He hoped the latter. Still, he couldn't take any chances with her.

"So why are you being followed?" Deidre asked.

"If I knew, I wouldn't have to grab him."

"Can I come?"

Karr laughed. "No. Sorry."

"I won't get in the way."

"Well, I know it seems like it's fun and games. And it is." Karr laughed. "Maybe next time I'm in town. Looks like a nice place."

"You've never been to Paris?"

"Oh, I've been here once or twice," said Karr. "Never as a tourist, though."

"I'll give you a tour."

"Yeah?"

"Sure."

He turned down the Champs-Elysées, the main boulevard in the heart of the city. It was choked with traffic — which was fine, since it locked his trail in place. The embassy was a few blocks away.

"I wasn't kidding," she said when they reached the embassy. She reached into her purse and took out a small notebook. "I'd love to show you around."

"Really?"

"Yes."

"Well, great."

"Call me," she said, writing down her phone number and tearing off the page. "Please."

"Sure," said Tommy, grabbing the page and then getting out of the car. "That Marine there. Run to him now. Go!"

LaFoote drove past the embassy, trying to avoid the stare of the French policeman near the entrance. He turned left and then took a quick right, paralleling the compound. He saw a parking spot opening up on the side street to the left and turned in quickly, parking there, and got out.

Having thought over the matter, he'd decided his best bet was to contact the agent directly. The embassy was likely to be the safest place in the area to do so, but he wanted to make sure that he wasn't being followed by whoever had shot his messenger in London.

A small Fiat passed within inches of him as he waited to cross the street. LaFoote jerked back, a jolt of fear reverberating through his body.

He hadn't felt that in years. It took him a second to gather himself, his throat suddenly dry. Until now he'd been driven mostly by his anger, without much thought for his own safety. Now the realities of being over seventy settled in. He wasn't quitting — he would *not* quit even if it meant his death — but he must pace himself.

And above all he must be careful; he had no backup. In the old days — not the *good* old days, just the old days — in Africa he'd have at least two men covering his back in case of a misstep. Here it was all on him.

LaFoote had never been in the American embassy in Paris, not even as a young man. He'd dealt with plenty of Americans, however; while he found them almost incurably naive and optimistic, they had also been extremely honest. At the time he did not value such a quality. He did now.

LaFoote stopped at the corner of the street, unsure exactly what to do next. Besides the French policeman at the front entrance, there were guards immediately inside the wall. He surveyed the area, then decided to approach the policeman directly for advice.

Just as he stepped to the curb something hard grabbed him from the right side and dropped him to the pavement. As he gasped for breath, the face of the blond American he'd been following loomed above him.

"What do you say you tell me why you've been following me," said the American in heavily accented French. "Or one of us is going to be in a lot of trouble."

"I think," gasped LaFoote. "I think I'm having a heart attack."

"Then you'd better talk quickly."

LaFoote coughed. He'd had the wind knocked out of him and his back hurt from being thrown down, but he wasn't having a heart attack. Despite his tough words, the American loosened LaFoote's collar and helped him up. He took a small handheld computer out of his pocket and slid it over him.

"Is that a stethoscope?" asked LaFoote in English. He fumbled over the word *stethoscope* for a moment before guessing it was the same in English as in French.

"Nah." The American chuckled, as if that were the funniest joke in the world. "You speak English?"

"Some."

"Better than my French, huh?" The American laughed again. "You feel all right?"

"I think."

"You sent Gordon Kensworth?"

"*Oui*. Yes. That was not his real name. I regret that he is dead."

"Let's go somewhere we can talk."

23

Lia's flight arrived in Baltimore at 7:00 a.m. Two NSA security types — unofficially known as "the men in black" because they habitually wore black suits — met her in the terminal and drove her to NSA headquarters at Fort Meade, Maryland. Take away the security barriers and high-tech sensors and ignore the electronic surveillance doodads scattered around the campus, and Crypto City could be the home of GE or IBM. The big black buildings at the core of the complex looked like big black boxy buildings at the core of many corporate complexes. A huge parking lot surrounded the central buildings and looked no different from the lot around a suburban mall — though here it was a very bad idea to block the handicapped parking zone without authorization. The men in black were under orders to blow up suspicious vehicles.

Lia sat in the back of the car as the two security men drove her through the main gate. She didn't bother acknowledging when they told her they'd take her bag inside for her. She merely got out and walked into the main building, eyes pinned to the ground.

She went to the medical area, even though she'd already heard the results of the tests she'd taken in Japan. She was OK — that was how the nurse put it. OK.

Right. OK.

"Take these pills. Here's a shot."

"What's the shot for? And these pills?"

"You have to take them."

"Why do I have to do anything?"

"You want to."

"No, I don't want to."

"I know it's terrible."

"You don't know anything."

Lia remembered the conversation now and felt embarrassed for getting angry. It wasn't the woman's fault. She was trying to be sympathetic.

So was the NSA doctor, a woman internist about Lia's age. Lia said nothing, following directions mechanically, nodding or grunting in answer to the questions. Finally, exam and tests over, she went downstairs into the restricted area used by Deep Black, making her way to a small lounge the ops called the squad room that was used to debrief missions. A half-dozen upholstered chairs were set up in a circle. A small credenza for coffee, tea, and soft drinks sat on one side of the room; opposite it was a media center with a large flat-screen video panel on the wall. A rolling cart held laptops that interfaced with the dedicated Desk Three system as well as the rest of the NSA and government. There were also small digital video cameras for recording mission reports.

Lia took one of the laptops and sat down, deciding to check the news on the World Wide Web before starting her report. She surfed aimlessly for a few minutes, bringing up pages on the MSNBC Web site devoted to entertainment and then love and lifestyles. These were things she never looked at, and now she looked at them with an odd fascination, as if she had found an alternate universe.

"Ms. DeFrancesca, I didn't expect you back so soon."

Startled, Lia nearly dropped the laptop. William Rubens was standing above her.

"I'm OK," she said.

"I'm on my way up to my office. Can we talk later?"

Lia shrugged.

"Your report can wait a few days," he

added. "You might just take some days off now. Relax."

Rubens had established the policy of "fresh reporting" following a mission and was ordinarily a stickler for following procedure. He was trying to be nice.

"It'll only take me a minute," she said, getting up for one of the recorders.

It took her over an hour, though the report itself ran less than three minutes, once recorded. She described how she'd gotten into the country, her contact, the minder, the officials, the airport. She mentioned the attack and the people who had been there in the barest number of words. She had to do it twice; without hearing or seeing her first version she decided it had been too emotional and erased it.

The second version was nearly identical, in word and tone.

Report finished, she hand-delivered it to the Desk Three operations personnel director, Kevin Montblanc, an NSA lifer who acted as the Deep Black den mother. Montblanc's walrus mustache drooped at the corners of his face as he asked if she was all right. Despite her repeated protests that she was "fine, Kev, just fine," he told her she should — she *must* — see a counselor.

"I *must*, huh?" she said finally, walking out of the office.

Rubens had just gotten off the phone with Montblanc when Lia showed up in his office.

"You've refused counseling," he said as she sat down. "Why?"

"Because I don't need it."

"It's customary."

"Oh really? This happens a lot?"

"Ms. DeFrancesca. Lia."

"Don't start that crap with me."

Lia had always been a prickly person to deal with. She was the only woman on the team — in fact, one of only two who had ever passed the qualifying course. She'd also proven herself in the field, but Rubens sometimes wondered if she was worth the trouble.

Not today. Today he felt sympathetic. He held his chin in his hand and considered what he should say next.

Besides LaBlanc, Rubens had spoken to the medical people upstairs as well as in Japan. The preliminary tests showed that she wasn't pregnant and hadn't been given any sexual diseases. Her right eye was swollen, and there were bruises on her legs and arms. But the physical injuries were minor, considering.

"I could order you to get counseling," he said finally.

"You might as well order me to get a lobotomy."

"How much time off do you want?"

"None."

"None?"

"I was just on vacation. I want to work."

"You should get some rest."

"Screw rest," she said.

Rubens got up from his desk and began pacing around his office. She was as cranky and feisty as ever. A good sign?

"You can send me. I'm OK," she told him. "I know there's a mission you need a woman agent for. Marie told me."

"That can be done by anyone."

"All the more reason not to worry, then," said Lia. "I'll get better makeup for my black eye."

Maybe that *would* be the best thing for her, Rubens thought. The mission itself was indeed straightforward. And Lia — Lia was Lia. She needed to be in action, to taste it.

But this wasn't like getting up off a horse after you fell. If she were a man, would he send her out?

"Lia, for the record, let me state that I urge you to get care. You know we have plenty of people who can help," he added.

"Help me do what?" She put her hands on her hips, face tilted forward — she could have been a gunfighter daring him to draw.

"I would feel better if you went to counseling."

"Do we have another mission? Because I'm bored. I'm not sitting around knitting for a month until some dope of a doctor decides my inkblot test is normal."

It was her right to be difficult, wasn't it? Just as it was the General's right to name his guardian and not live where his hated cousin lived.

"I should order you to see a psychologist," Rubens told her stubbornly.

"You need me too much. Where am I going?"

"All right," he said finally. "All right."

He began telling her about Morocco.

24

Karr chose a café several blocks away, a small place tucked down an alley where his CIA shadows would be able to watch his back. He found a booth and slid in.

"You are very good," said LaFoote. "I would almost believe that you chose this place at random."

Karr laughed and took out his PDA, activating the bug sweeper; the place was clean.

LaFoote ordered a glass of wine. Karr ordered a fresh lemon juice, *citron pressé*, an old-fashioned French drink that came with a large vaselike pitcher of water and a much smaller one of sugar syrup. He'd never had this before and fussed over it — all the while waiting for the two CIA men to check in by phone with the Art Room and report that he hadn't been followed. Finally, they did just that.

"So tell me about computers," Karr said to the old Frenchman. "I'm interested in servers that are hijacked by terrorists and used to pass messages. Where can I find a list of them?"

"My friend Vefoures was an important chemist," answered the man. "And three weeks ago he disappeared."

Karr didn't know quite how to respond.

"Computers — how do you say that in French?" said Karr.

"He worked for the government for many years, always in secret. And then after he retired, he was called back several times. Most recently in January, by someone who said they were connected with the DST. But my friends at the DST knew nothing about it. And then, three weeks ago, he was no more."

"No idea what he's talking about," said Johnson, Karr's runner in the Art Room. "*DST* is the French abbreviation for *Direction de la Surveillance du Territoire,* one of the French intelligence groups under the Interior Ministry. Counterterrorism, industrial espionage, whole bunch of things."

Karr already knew that; he'd brushed up against a DST agent six or seven months back out in North Africa.

Nasty encounter, that. Guy had *no* sense of humor.

Karr took the small cup of sugar water and poured a bit more into his tumbler of *citron pressé*, fiddling with the do-it-yourself lemonade. "Takes the edge off, huh?"

"Can you help me?" asked the Frenchman.

"I think there's a basic misunderstanding here," said Karr. "There was a matter of computers. Someone passed along some Web addresses to a third party, who forwarded them to my boss. There were supposed to be some more. A meeting was arranged. Things went off-track. Somebody got shot. I don't know anything about a chemist."

A few more drops of sugar water, and the *citron pressé* would be almost drinkable, Karr decided.

"My name is Denis LaFoote. For twenty-eight years I was an agent with the foreign service and then the Interior Ministry and the DST, the Directorate of Territorial Security. It is similar to your CIA and FBI. I served many stations. You can check me out."

"I will."

The Frenchman's face blanched. "Not with Ponclare. Not in Paris."

"Why not?" said Karr.

LaFoote shook his head.

"Ponclare?" asked Karr.

"Head of the division responsible for Paris security, and has an overlap with some technical departments," said his runner. "Pretty high up."

"He is an important person in the directorate," said LaFoote. "More important than his title makes him seem. They rearranged everything some years ago, and now they play shell games with the bureaucracy. Politics — it is all politics. He is a bureaucrat, not like his father."

"Where do these computers come in?"

"While he was working, my friend received two e-mails from odd sources. I believe the word is *domains?*"

"Domains, sure," said Karr.

Domains were a type of computer network; they were common to many people as the portion after @ on an e-mail address. They corresponded to a set of physical computers, which was how the NSA had checked them out in the first place — and why the agency was interested.

"My friend kept the e-mails," said LaFoote. "When he disappeared, I checked them and found the addresses themselves did not exist. Then I did some more work. I had a friend with the government check and was told that they were suspicious, but he refused to give any other details."

"Suspicious how?"

LaFoote shrugged. "I'm not a computer

expert. The person who got this information for me was the son of a friend, a very good friend. The son is not quite the man the father was, but what young man is?"

"What part of the government did he work for?"

"*Direction Centrale de la Police Judiciare.* It is, how would you say, the public face of the Directorate for Territorial Security? They are connected. I cannot totally trust them."

"Why not?"

"I am not sure of them. For now, let me leave it at that. I don't want to prejudice you — I'm interested in the truth."

"You promised more Web sites or domains."

"No, more information. That was what was said on the call. And that's what I'm giving you. I have no information on computers. That's not what I wanted to talk to you about."

"You probably ought to tell me the entire story from the beginning," said Karr, "because it's not really making any sense to me."

As patiently as he could, LaFoote told the American about his friend Vefoures. He realized that the man would not care much for the details of their friendship, how they had served together in the army immediately after World War II and how they had both nearly married the same girl; he omitted these details and many others as well, sticking to the important facts. He put himself into the younger man's shoes and tried to anticipate what he would like and need to hear.

Some years in the past, Vefoures had helped develop a replacement for a chemical explosive several times more powerful than Semtex, the plastic explosive originally manufactured in Czechoslovakia but now fairly common throughout the world. Four or five months before, he had been called back into service by the DST — or by someone who claimed to represent the DST — and, after a few weeks, disappeared. The French secret service did not want to provide any information when LaFoote tried to find him.

"Did not want to, or could not?" asked Karr.

"Either one. I am not sure. It would look the same to me, would it not?"

"How do you know what he was working on?" the American asked.

"I know. We were very close friends. But of course without knowing how it was made, my information would be worthless, no?"

The American's eyelids flickered up in a way that suggested it wouldn't be if Vefoures wasn't supposed to be doing the work at all.

"Plastic explosive is pretty common," said Karr.

"This is more powerful and easier to shape. The focus — how exactly would I say that?"

"Focus?"

LaFoote's English was good, but his technical knowledge of explosives was not, and so he had trouble explaining what he believed was the most important quality of the material. There was a way to formulate and construct it that allowed its explosive force to be intensified — in the layman's terms that were sometimes used, it could be made into an explosive lens that magnified the effect just like a lens magnified light. Of course, like a lens, it did not actually alter the inherent force, merely taking advantage of the fact that explosions had wavelike properties.

"So why is this all significant?" asked the American.

"By arranging explosives in a certain shape, you can intensify the blast."

"Really? How?"

"You are smarter than you seem, aren't you?" asked LaFoote. "You are trying to seem as if you don't understand, but you do."

"I'll take that as a compliment." The American grinning at him — yes, he was one of those who pretended to be a joker, LaFoote realized. But he was very serious inside. He understood fully what LaFoote was saying.

A very good operative: such a man would have made a good partner in Africa when he served.

"The material might also pass by a standard detector without being picked up," said LaFoote. "I don't know about such details. There are many things about it that I don't know — as I said, I am not a technical man. I am just looking for my friend."

"And someone wants to stop you."

"It would seem."

"The DST?"

"It would seem."

"How'd they know about the meeting?" asked Karr.

"I used Vefoures' phone to call your embassy. They must have tapped the phone. I had checked the line with equipment I thought would be good — there must have been something I missed."

"I'm not sure why you'd contact us," Karr said.

"There was an NSA listening station in Morocco when I was younger. And one in Eritrea. Good men. We occasionally co-operated."

"I would have thought you'd call Central Intelligence."

"They are close with the DST, and military intelligence."

"And you think they killed your friend."

"I cannot trust the DST," said LaFoote. "They are riddled with traitors."

"How do you know?"

"I know."

"Ponclare?"

"I do not say he is a traitor." LaFoote chose his words carefully.

"You trust me?"

"Perhaps."

Karr laughed.

"There are two reasons you should be interested," LaFoote said. "First, the explosives are so powerful that a trunk of two hundred pounds would be the equivalent of a two-thousand-pound bomb. Or, to put it another way, the amount in a small device, say the computer that you have in your pocket or a cell phone, could blow a hole in an airplane skin."

"What's the second thing?"

"The second is that my friend bought a one-way ticket to New York City, which he was to use next week."

25

They spoke English in London, but Dean found the accents at times made it as indecipherable as Russian or Chinese. When the bartender ran down the list of beers the Golden Goose offered, Dean found himself pointing to the tap. He ordered a Marston, the same as Lang, and then listened as the chief inspector grilled the bartender about Gordon Pierce. Dean thought the detective was much too aggressive and adversarial; all he did was make the bartender defensive. The man finally told the chief inspector not only that he didn't have to answer any questions from a copper but also that they should feel free to drink up and leave.

Dean touched the policeman's sleeve. "Gordon was my wife's cousin-in-law," he said to the bartender. "We'd just like to know what happened to him, that's all. I'm from the States. My wife is upset, you know? So's her cousin."

"I could tell you were from the States, mate. What's it to me?"

"We thought it was going to be a holiday. My wife is Rose's cousin. Rose isn't taking it well."

"Pity," said the bartender, without any sympathy. He walked to the other end of the bar to serve another patron.

Lang lit another cigarette. Dean sipped his ale. That's what he got for trying to be a liar.

It was just past six; the bar was not very crowded, and more than half of the dozen booths and tables were empty. According to Rose, her brother would generally come here around four or five and stay until ten. Dean thought a stranger would have been more than a little obvious, as they were.

"Rose doesn't have a sister."

Dean turned to his right, where a short-haired woman in her forties had just put an empty pint glass on the bar.

"I know. My wife's her cousin. And actually a second cousin, once removed, but they don't have much family, and we wanted to see a friendly face in a foreign country. It's her uncle Tommy's daughter, Lia," he added, using the first names that came to his mind.

The woman scowled and pushed the glass farther in.

"You should go to see Rose, if you're her

friend," said Dean. "She's not taking it well. She really could use, uh, moral support. And we have to leave."

"She works hard, that girl," said the woman.

A waitress came over to take and refill the glass. The young woman glanced furtively at Dean but said nothing.

"Gordy was a drinker," said the woman who'd been talking to him. "He truly was. Gave his sister quite a lot of heartache."

"Maybe the mining accident had something to do with that," said Dean.

"Ah." The woman took the glass from the waitress, then turned to face him. "You don't believe that bull, do you?"

"I try to believe the best in people."

She took a long gulp of the beer. "He was a Frenchman. Older. Past your age by quite a sight. He didn't talk much, but he'd been in the night before and a time or two before that, I think. Gordy called him 'Reynard,' the Fox."

"Was that his name?" asked the detective.

"Was I talking to you?" snapped the woman.

The inspector reached into his jacket for his police credentials, but the woman waved them away. "I don't need to be talking to the police and wasting my time with an investigation."

"That sort of attitude will get you in trouble," said Lang. He put his credentials away and picked up his cigarette.

"I think anything you said that might help would be good for Rose," said Dean. "I don't think there'd be police involved."

"I've told you all I know."

"Was there anyone besides the Frenchman?" Dean asked. "Anyone watching him? Or other strangers?"

"Nah," she said. She took her beer and went away.

"Charlie, this is good. Try for a better date," said Marie Telach over the Deep Black communications system. "Anything more substantial, even just the first day he showed up, would be useful."

"Excuse me," Dean told the woman at the bar. He left his beer and went to look for the gents', a small room at the far end of the hall. He locked the door with the eye hook and leaned against the sink.

"Marie, are you there?" he said.

"We're always here, Charlie," said the Art Room supervisor.

"Gordon Pierce was approached by a Frenchman a few weeks ago. I don't know his name yet."

"We heard through your microphone. That jibes with what Tommy found out in Paris."

"What did he find out?"

"We'll go through it when you get back."

"Tell me now."

"Charlie, go on back and talk to that woman. See what you can find out."

"Tell me now or I'll go to Paris and ask Tommy myself."

"A former French intelligence agent set up the meeting. He says he sent it because he wanted to get our attention on another matter."

"Like what?"

"It had something to do with explosives. It may be big, or may not be anything. We don't have the whole story. We hope to by the time you get back."

"What was his name?"

She hesitated, then told him. "Denis LaFoote. He used to work for or maybe is still working for French intelligence. We're still working to verify that. He was a friend of Vefoures."

"All right."

"How long were you planning on staying in the pub?"

"As long as Lang does. Why?"

"Mr. Rubens wants you to help back up

another mission," added Telach. "As soon as you're done there, go directly to Heathrow. You'll be flying to Spain."

"What happened to my ticket home?"

"We told you earlier. Don't worry about the travel arrangements. Just do as we say. Go to Spain."

Dean thought to himself that maybe Karr hadn't always been such a kidder — maybe it was simply in reaction to having these people talking in his head all the time.

"We want you to fly to Madrid and meet Lia," added Telach. "She's leaving in a few hours. We'd like you to meet her in Spain. We'll have a full cover for you with new identity details and documents waiting. We're still pulling everything together."

"Some fresh clothes would be nice."

"On their way. We'll find a hotel room for you to shower in and shave."

"How is Lia?"

"Lia's Lia. She wanted to do a night parachute drop into Oujda."

"Where's that?"

"Northern Africa. Don't worry. Mr. Rubens wouldn't allow it. It's completely unnecessary — just Lia being Lia."

Dean heard someone outside the door.

"So this Frenchman — did he kill Pierce?" Dean asked.

"Unlikely. The theory here is that he sent Pierce to make contact and then would have approached you. His message was intercepted, but we're still working everything out. Please get to Heathrow as soon as you can."

Dean flushed the toilet, then ran the water over his hands. There were no towels; he had to wipe his hands on his pants. Lang sat morosely at the bar, his beer almost done and the ashtray now full. The woman who had been talking to him had taken her drink and was sitting in a booth with a friend.

Dean slid in next to her. "Does the name LaFoote mean anything to you?"

She shook her head.

"Vefoures?"

She made a face.

"The stranger was French?" Dean asked.

"Maybe. He had an accent."

"Did he say his name?"

"Mate, if he did, it's lost in the sands of time."

Dean asked a few more questions but couldn't pin her down on the exact date the man had appeared. The more questions he asked, the less sure her memory seemed to become. Finally he gave up and went back to the chief inspector.

"Come on," Dean told him. "I have some news. I'll tell you what I know if you give me a ride to the airport."

"Charlie, you don't have to share," hissed Telach in his ear.

Dean reached to his belt and turned off the communications system.

"When's your flight?" asked Lang as they walked to the car.

"As soon as I get there," said Dean. "Pierce was hired to meet us by a French intelligence agent. Or a former agent. We're still checking it out. He didn't have anything to do with the murder. My guess is that whoever shot Pierce thought it was him."

"What's his name?"

"Don't know yet. He knew Vefoures. He's looking for him."

"Did he see who killed Pierce?"

"Don't know."

"You don't know much."

"True."

"Should I trust you? I've seen how well you lie."

"Sometimes people need a reason to be nice."

Lang didn't say anything else until they

were a few miles from Heathrow.

"I arrested the owner of that pub two years ago for running guns to the Protestants in Northern Ireland," he told Dean. "They're all dirty there. Your French agent probably picked the place on purpose."

"Maybe. Or maybe he was just looking for a bar in a poor neighborhood where there'd be people who'd like to make some easy money."

"When we check Pierce's background, are we going to find out he's a spy?"

"I doubt it," said Dean. "But I honestly don't know."

"You have my card," said the chief inspector as they drove up to the terminal.

"And you have my number."

"Is it really your number?"

"It's my house," Dean told him. "If I ever get back there, I'll give you a call."

26

Karr gawked at the sights as he leaned against the rail on the third deck of the Eiffel Tower, a thousand feet above the ground. The sun had only recently started to climb up over the horizon, and it looked to Karr as if he were standing above it as well as the city. He'd actually never been to the tower, and despite the fact that he had traveled around the world, he was impressed.

The fact that Deidre had wrapped her arm around his as the first gust of wind hit them off the stairs didn't hurt, either.

The American embassy had arranged for a VIP tour for Ms. Clancy and guest before regular hours, and a member of the French Interior Ministry had personally escorted them. There were some advantages to being the "guest" of the daughter of an ambassador, Karr realized — especially if Dad was stationed a country away.

"Isn't it spectacular?" Deidre asked.

"Blows me away," said Karr.

"Come on. Be serious."

"I am."

She began pointing out the sights. They moved slowly around the platform and then put a few coins in the stationary binoculars.

"Breakfast?" Karr asked after the timer ran out a second time.

"Sounds good."

She was still holding his arm when they reached the ground. Karr slowed his pace to match hers as they walked down through the park. They had breakfast at an outdoor café a few blocks away, sitting next to one of the outdoor heaters to ward off the lingering chill from the night before. Karr fumbled his French after Deidre ordered; he finally resorted to English. The waiter smirked and disappeared.

"He thinks you're French," Karr told her. "And I'm the ugly American."

"You're not ugly."

"Well, thanks. Neither are you."

"So how long have you been a spy?"

"Who says I'm a spy?"

"What's it like?"

"Just like the movies," Karr said. "James Bond, double-oh-seven. I drive cool cars. Things blow up. Women throw themselves all over me."

"I'm sure," she said coolly.

"I've been offered my own television series," he said, trying to make light of his faux pas, "but I'm holding out for a feature film."

"I wonder who will get to play me," she shot back.

In the silence that followed that remark his satellite phone started buzzing. He pulled it out and found himself talking to Chris Farlekas, the Art Room supervisor who had spelled Marie Telach.

"Hello, Tommy. We have an update for you on your chemist. Your com system is off."

"Yeah, I know."

"Can you talk?"

"Oh, I suppose, if I don't have to say too much."

"All you have to do is listen."

Karr glanced at Deidre, who was concentrating on her meal. "Mind if I take this?" he asked.

"Go right ahead."

Most of what the Frenchman LaFoote had told Karr yesterday had checked out. Vefoures was a chemist and had worked for the government; though they didn't have any details on his projects, he worked in the areas that would have involved explosives.

"So what didn't check out?" asked Karr.

"The French government doesn't have any project going concerning plastic explosives that we can tell. Certainly not the DST. And if they did, they'd use someone else — there are plenty of younger people still working for the government that were involved in this project. He'd been out of it for a while. His last job was for a company in Tours, France, about two years ago. It was contract work. They're out of business."

"Maybe it was somebody else."

"It's a theory we're working on," said Farlekas. "He did contract work here and there. We think you should go to Vefoures' house, but be careful. Whoever took out Pierce may realize that they missed the man they were gunning for."

"No sign he's being followed?"

"We had one of your CIA friends track him last night. Clean so far."

"Hmmm. He thinks his former employers were involved," said Karr, choosing his words carefully because of Deidre.

"French intelligence?"

"Yup."

"Doesn't make sense that they took out Pierce. They would have gotten LaFoote directly."

"Unless somebody made a mistake. Or there's something we don't know yet."

"Granted. Can you pick up the chemical sniffer?"

"Already have."

The sniffer was an electronic device about the size of a tourist guidebook with a long wand attached via a thick cord. The wand could be "tuned" to look for specific chemical compounds with the addition of a memory card and a set of electronic circuits about the size of a Post-it. Somewhat similar though less sophisticated devices were just coming into use at airports where security teams screened luggage for explosives.

"How's the date going?" added Farlekas.

"Who says I'm on a date?" Karr smiled as Deidre blushed. "But I will say that having breakfast with the most beautiful woman in Paris is a great way to start your day."

27

A touch of gray, a fresh razor — Mussa
Duoar prided himself on never looking the
same two days in a row. It was a small thing,
a knack, and yet a very necessary skill. He
could vary his voice, offering any number of
accents in French, English, and Arabic; he
was especially fond of tossing a few Greek
words into his patter. Many people thought
he was really Greek, and he took that as a
great compliment.

Of course, these tricks were nothing
without the real tools of his trade — the
false IDs, the credit cards, and the endless
succession of phones. Mussa had worked
hard to build up the network that sup-
ported him. It stretched throughout
France to Germany and down to Africa.
Morocco was especially important; without
his people in Morocco to send information
for him, where would he be? And Algeria,
his birthplace, was invaluable in many
ways. But then, every node was important.
He might take the cell phone he had just

received from Wales and use it to call Germany, sending a message to someone in the café a block away in Paris. From there the message might travel back to Germany, around the web, to a young man in the Czech Republic, who would then call a friend in Morocco, who would receive only a one-word message. The chain would then flow in reverse — impossible to track, even for him. Money, identities, weapons, suggestions from sponsors in the Middle East flowed through Mussa's network. It morphed constantly, changing shape, gaining branches, losing itself in detours. He thought it like a garden that needed constant tending — this plant to be pruned, this to be fertilized.

And always there was weeding.

The Irishman whom he had used to kill the chemist's friend was useful in that regard. But he had other qualities that made him difficult to work with. Mussa did not mind the brutality — surely this was a trait of the profession, not to be lamented but rather praised. It was Donohue's unmasked contempt that made him hard to stomach. Mussa had worked with Irishmen before; the peace in Northern Ireland had flooded the market with highly trained talent. As a rule, they were good at their particular specialty and close-mouthed. As long as they were paid promptly and as promised, there were rarely problems with their work. Their religion and their propensity toward drink — genetic, Mussa believed — were regrettable but not fatal. Donohue himself seemed not to drink, but he compensated by being more obvious in his contempt than most of his countrymen.

If he had not been so much better than them at what he did, Mussa would have cut off their relationship long ago.

"There you are," said Donohue, appearing around the corner in the restaurant and sitting down.

"Bonjour," said Mussa. "Hello."

"Yeah. What is it you wanted?"

"Relax. Sit. Have some lunch."

"I've told you, I don't like meetings. They make no sense. They invite the police and busybodies."

Mussa had just the opposite view — phones, e-mail, letters, all could be intercepted and recorded without one's knowledge. Meeting someone in person was much safer. And it had the value of being more effective.

With most people.

"The police are never a problem for me,"

said Mussa. "There are ways to persuade them."

"You've never been in jail."

Best to change the subject, he decided. "Your other job went well?"

"Your stooge gave me next to no information."

"Now, now, it must have been sufficient. I've heard you did an excellent job. And you were paid."

"Yes."

The mention of money usually mollified him, but it seemed to have no effect today.

"I have another small task, similar to the last," said Mussa. "This time in Paris."

"I don't do Paris. I stay out of France."

Mussa was aware of Donohue's rule. It was not so peculiar as it seemed — a professional assassin needed to have a place where he might feel less on-guard, and men such as Donohue often declared one country, or a part of it, "off-limits." It was useless to argue with them about it: even though geographic safety was illusionary, the idea was nonetheless an important emotional factor, and emotion could not be broken by logic.

Money was another story.

"Would the payment of a million euros persuade you?" asked Mussa.

The look on Donohue's face showed that it would. But the Irishman was no fool; his brow immediately knit and his face pitched forward in a frown. "For that, you'll want the President or Prime Minister."

"Hardly." Mussa pushed the newspaper forward casually, his finger pointed to a name at the top of a column. The name was that of Monsieur Jacques Ponclare — the head of the Paris section of the Directorate of Territorial Security.

"You're joking," replied Donohue.

Mussa ignored the objection. "I have access to his schedule. It will be an easy affair to arrange, but the timing is critical."

"This is *considerably* more difficult than anything I've done for you. Or your friends."

"That is why the price is so much higher."

"Twice your figure, or no deal."

"Too much. I could use someone else."

"Go ahead."

The waiter approached. Mussa ordered an octopus salad for two. Donohue made a face at the word *pieuvre* — octopus — and Mussa relented and ordered a veal chop for him instead.

Neither man spoke as the waiter left, then returned with a bottle of mineral water.

"Twice what you said," insisted Donohue when they were alone again. Mussa did not speak.

Lunch arrived; the Irishman remained. That, Mussa decided, was a good sign.

"So, have you considered my proposal?" he asked when he was finished.

"Twice what you said."

Mussa sighed. The assassination was very important to him, as it would avenge his father's death and there would be no opportunity for a second try if things went wrong. Perhaps the funds could be found — but agreeing to the outrageous price would make him feel as if he were going against his nature, as if he were surrendering to the assassin, a mere employee.

"What if we split the difference?" asked Mussa.

"Twice."

"Let me contemplate it," said Mussa, giving in, though he was not willing to admit it. "I will contact you in the usual way. In the meantime, a retainer for your time will be provided, as long as you stay on call for the next week."

The idea of a retainer had obviously not occurred to Donohue, and he surrendered a rare smile. "Good food," said the

Irishman, pushing away from the table. "I'll see you around."

"*Au revoir*," said Mussa, savoring the last morsel of octopus. If revenge tasted this sweet, surely it would be worth the price.

28

Dean had never thought much about showers until Vietnam. He'd gone weeks without taking any on his first tour as a sniper; when he finally came back the water seemed to spark across his body, a light electrical jolt enlivening nerves he didn't know he'd had.

The shower he had at the Hilton Barcelona didn't quite approach that one, but it was close. The bed wasn't bad, either.

The Art Room had managed to insert a suitcase in the luggage at the airport for him with fresh clothes. Whoever had packed it had included three large candy bars, and while Dean ordinarily didn't eat chocolate, he opened one in the taxi on the way to the airport in the morning to pick up Lia. He found himself reaching into the bag for a second one as the driver slid around the traffic near the terminal entrance.

Lia's flight had stopped in Frankfurt and was running a few minutes late as Dean arrived at Terminal B. A few minutes ordinarily wouldn't make much of a difference, but their flight for Casablanca was due to take off in less than forty-five minutes; she had to get over to Terminal A for the next plane. Casablanca was just the first leg of the journey; once they landed they had to grab a puddle jumper for Oujda in eastern Morocco, where their target was.

Lia would be doing most of the work when they got to Oujda. She had to go into a building and replace a miniature bugging device planted in a women's room. The building was used as a communications center by a loosely knit terrorist network; the site was disguised as an office for an Islamic charity. This cover, however, provided a vulnerability, because the building was shared by other charity organizations, which would give Lia a pretext for visiting. She would arrive just after the office person she was supposed to see had left for home — she always left around four — excuse herself to go to the restroom where the bug was located, replace the unit, then leave.

Dean would back her up. Depending on the situation, he might take a look around the office of the fake charity group. The NSA was interested in collecting possible bank account numbers to track money the organization spread throughout the world. But that task was secondary to Lia's. He wasn't to do anything that would make them suspicious, let alone tip them off to the bug.

Missing the plane now would set everything back by at least a day and possibly a week, depending on the schedule of the charity organization they were using as a pretext for entering the building. Morocco might be nice, but Dean didn't particularly want to spend a week there, especially that close to the Algerian border. He pulled out his satellite phone and leaned against the wall in a hallway, pretending to use the phone while he spoke to the Art Room.

"So where is she?" he asked Rockman.

"They're just taxiing up now," Rockman told him. "You should be able to just make it. Wait out in the main terminal. Don't sweat the schedule. It'll work out."

Lia clutched her carry-on tightly as she headed down the hallway, cleared through Customs quickly with the help of the timely arrival of an airport manager — undoubtedly at the Art Room's prompting. She noticed Dean approaching on her left and quickened her pace toward the other terminal.

"What's up?" he asked, falling in beside her.

"Nothing."

"How was the flight?"

"Lousy."

"We're running late."

"Really? I hadn't noticed."

"They update you on the situation?"

"Pretty much."

"How was Korea?"

"Garden spot of the world."

"That what happened to your eye?"

An urge came over her suddenly: turn and run out of the terminal, take a taxi into the city, go to a hotel — any hotel — and quit, just totally quit.

But she didn't. She quickened her pace, following Rockman's directions in her ear as they made her way to the other terminal building.

"We're supposed to be on that plane," said Dean to the clerk at the boarding gate.

The man looked up from his terminal. "Oh. Hold on. There's some sort of computer glitch."

"You sure?"

The clerk glanced down. His terminal was working again.

"Lucky thing for you," he said. He found them in the computer and called over to the plane, which had experienced problems of its own and hadn't pulled away yet.

"Nice to have friends in high places," said Dean as they walked down the tunnel.

"Right," said Lia.

Dean had known Lia long enough to realize she wasn't the effusive type, but he expected a bit more of a hello. He stowed his bag in the overhead rack and sat next to her. Lia kept her head turned as if there was something interesting to see through the window.

"Hey," he said softly. He reached to touch her shoulder gently; she jerked away.

He felt as if he'd walked in on the middle of a movie that was hard to follow. They'd spent a week together on the Maine shore after their last assignment — long, languid days steering a friend's sailboat offshore and cool nights in the seashore village near the borrowed house. He'd loved the unhurried rhythm and casual intimacy.

"Are you OK?" he asked.

"I'm fine, Charlie Dean," she said. "Just fine."

"That's a good makeup job on your eye."

"I suppose you're an expert on makeup."

"I've had a few black eyes in my day. What happened?"

"I walked into a door. What do you think?"

"You're all right?"

"Peachy."

All right, he told himself. *Give her some space.* He turned and leaned his seat back, closing his eyes as if there were actually a possibility he could relax enough to nap.

29

The chemist's house was a small brick building close to the road and bordering on a large farm. The field of sunflowers had been harvested very recently, perhaps that morning, and Karr found that the smell tickled his nose in an unpleasant way. He started to sneeze as LaFoote unlocked the door to let them in, and then stood in the foyer sneezing.

The sneeze probably saved their lives.

As Karr reached for a handkerchief, he saw a thin thread strung across the bottom of the doorway to the left. He grabbed the Frenchman, pulling him down just as the back of the house exploded, showering them with debris. Karr pulled the old man with him as he crawled out. Just as he reached the path there was a second explosion, this one much louder and so violent that it rolled them into the nearby roadway. A fireball shot into the air. Large pieces of wood and stone began falling around them; a piece of brick about the size of a fist bounced off Karr's shoulder, and an even larger one flew by as he got up.

LaFoote was breathing all right, but he was dazed, and it took Karr a good two or three minutes to get him back to full consciousness. By then, Telach had started screaming in Karr's ear, asking what was going on, and there was a siren in the distance.

"I think there was an explosive rigged to ignite the gas main," said Karr, speaking to LaFoote as well as the Art Room. "Or something. There was a thread on that inner doorway."

"It wasn't booby-trapped last week," said LaFoote, coughing.

"All right, time for us to retreat if we can," Karr said.

"Why?"

"Because my French isn't up to an eight-hour workout with the police," said Karr. "Come on."

30

Mussa's phone rang just as he was about to board the airplane. He hesitated before answering — if he used the phone, his self-imposed rules called for him to dispose of it, and that would mean that he would have no way of communicating before evening.

However, if he did not answer it, he would have lost whatever opportunity this information provided. So he pulled the phone from his pocket and stepped aside.

"Yes?" he answered cheerfully.

"The farmhouse has exploded."

Mussa knew which farmhouse was being referred to — the chemist Vefoures' — but was nonetheless surprised. Of course, being surprised and showing it were two different things.

"A shame," said Mussa. "We should do something for the family of the man who was sent to disarm it, though I suppose his carelessness was to blame."

"It wasn't him. He hadn't gotten to it yet."

Hadn't gotten to it?

Mussa took a moment to stifle his anger. He had asked — directed — that the bomb be disabled within a few hours of learning that Donohue had done his job in England. The delay was inexcusable, though of course there would be some nonsensical excuse.

Another sign of corruption and seduction, the weakness of the West corroding Islamic values. When Mussa was young, orders were carried out promptly. Now, underlings worked on their own schedule.

"It was to be dismantled in only a few hours," said his caller, sensing his anger.

"These complications are unfortunate and unwelcome," said Mussa.

"No one was killed," said the caller. "The police are there. One of our friends made sure to get close enough for information."

"The bomb did not go off by itself," said Mussa, barely keeping his calm.

"No. We have additional information. Someone saw a friend of the chemist, a Monsieur LaFoote, at mass the other day. You had asked about him the other day."

LaFoote?

But the Irishman Donohue had already killed him. Even if one of Mussa's network

267

had not verified the shooting, he would have been confident that it had been carried out. Another man might have missed or botched the job, but not the obnoxious Donohue.

"LaFoote set off the bomb?"

"It seems possible."

"You are sure it was LaFoote?"

"Yes."

"Have you watched his house?"

"Not since you said it was unnecessary."

LaFoote had been poking around into the chemist's disappearance, raising trouble with the DST. He had even gone so far as to try to get American intelligence interested. Mussa had enough sources within the French intelligence agency so that he did not have to worry about problems from that quarter, at least not for the time being, but the Americans were a different matter entirely. Fortunately, the fool had made a call from Vefoures' phone two or three weeks ago. When Vefoures was first approached to work for them the phone was tapped with an automated device that worked only when the call was placed; it had been a surprise to find a call had been made, and Mussa's people had had some difficulty figuring out what was going on. Mussa, of course, had concluded it must be this LaFoote, who until now had only been an annoying ant, if that. And Mussa might not have been concerned, except that a number of CD-ROMs containing data on the explosives had been taken, apparently by Vefoures before he was killed. The data on them was supposedly technical — but who knew?

Interestingly, the disks had not shown up in England.

LaFoote back at the house — perhaps the disks had been there all along? The house had been searched but must be searched again.

And this LaFoote — even an ant could be annoying.

"Prepare information on Mr. LaFoote for a friend. Precise information," Mussa told his caller. "And this time, be sure that it includes photographs."

"It will," said the caller.

"Have Vefoures' house searched again."

"We have been over it twice. There are no CD-ROMs or anything that might —"

"Have the house searched again," said Mussa. "And this time they may take whatever they find, including the money — but the search shall be thorough. And there will be an additional reward if you find the disks."

"I will do it myself."

I'll bet you will, thought Mussa, pushing the button to end the call. As much as he disliked greed, it remained a most useful motivator.

31

Johnny Bibleria paced around the conference room, walking the perimeter at a rapid pace. Every so often he glanced up at the numbers on the white board at the front of the room.

"Nothing is related," he repeated. "Nothing."

They were missing something basic.

"What information would make a murder worthwhile?" Rubens had asked him. It was an excellent question, Johnny thought — but not the sort that a cryptologist should ask. It wasn't even something for a mathematician to contemplate. The answer involved morality or at least judgments separate from numbers. A mathematician needed a sequence.

Johnny stopped his pacing. He thought he saw part of a Fibonacci sequence in the updates of the weather site.

No.

Johnny Bib took one of the pens from the table and stepped toward the board.

The key must be the change out of sequence, but the numbers were merely a digit or two off. He made a grid based on the days of the week, ran the numbers in a line, put them backward . . .

Maybe it was like a pointer in a codebook. Use this page . . .

If it *was* a pointer, then they could see who had accessed the site and follow that person to the relevant Web page.

Except that they didn't have a record of the visits to the sites.

Johnny went back to the board. They were watching for another change on the weather site, hoping to see who accessed it and where the computer went from there. But that meant they were reacting, waiting. And there was no guarantee that they would be able to find anything useful if it *did* change.

There had to be a pattern *somewhere* that he could detect, surely.

32

It sounded absurdly easy when Rubens out-lined it — walk into the restroom, remove the old package, put in a new one.

But in real life, the fifty feet down the hall to the steps that led to the lavatory were treacherously long. Lia's legs trembled beneath her long, African-style skirt. The muscles in her thighs and calves felt weak and her mouth horribly dry.

There were soldiers posted along the walls and at the steps. Each man had a French-made FAMAS assault rifle, a smallish, odd-looking weapon nicknamed the bugle (or *le clarion*). Lia pulled the scarf a little farther down around her face but found herself staring at the weapons as she walked by, wondering if the guns were safed or ready to fire. It took all of her self-control to wrest her gaze back toward the carpet on the floor.

She started to slip on one of the steps as she descended. She grabbed the railing, just barely keeping herself from falling off the step.

I can do this, she told herself. *I'm just going to the bathroom.*

Two more soldiers stood outside the women's room near the bottom of the steps. She put her hands on her scarf, hooking her thumbs beneath the fabric — it wasn't an attempt to feign modesty or even hide her identity but rather to keep her hands from jerking wildly out of control.

I can do this. It's the easiest thing in the world.

An attendant sat inside, an old woman in a black chador who jumped as Lia opened the door.

The old woman began speaking in Arabic. Lia didn't wait for the translator to explain, nor did she attempt one of the rudimentary phrases she'd memorized on the plane. She walked directly to the last stall and closed the door.

"You were supposed to give her change," said Sandy Chafetz, her runner. "You get towels."

Lia didn't answer. She had no intention of leaving the stall now that she was inside. She knelt next to the commode. There wasn't enough room to see what she was doing, and so she slid her fingers along the floor until they found the bolt cover. Sure of where it was, she withdrew her hand and reached to the pocket of her dress, removing what looked like a small lipstick holder. She twisted the two halves, then pushed them together. The device was designed to provoke a response from the bug beneath the bolt cover. If she got a beep from the device, she would know that it had not been tampered with.

That, of course, was how it was supposed to work in theory. Lia thought that a really clever engineer could come up with a way to defeat it — the Desk Three people did that all the time. She felt herself leaning her head back as she reached in.

Nothing.

Run. Run now!

She put her hand back in the space behind the toilet, reaching farther.

Still nothing.

Get out!

Her hand trembled. A tiny beep sounded as she pulled it back.

"You're good to proceed," said Chafetz.

Lia took out a small medicine bottle with an eyedropper and placed it down on the floor, where she carefully unscrewed the top. The bottle held a strong solvent, which she needed to loosen the bolt cover. The scent was somewhere between rubber cement and ammonia; Lia coughed so hard she nearly lost the dropper.

The compact. She could use the mirror to see what she was doing.

As Lia reached into her pocket, her knee brushed against the bottle of solvent. Its contents spewed on the floor in front of the toilet.

Her hand trembled as she tried refilling the dropper from the nearly empty bottle, but she got no more than a half of the plastic tube filled. During the mission briefing they'd told her it would take at least four full eyedroppers of the solvent to remove the glue holding the bolt cover in place.

Lia applied what she could, trying to work the few drops around the base as if the dropper were a paintbrush. She got a little more from the floor, but most of the liquid had burned into the grouting around the mosaiclike floor tile. Panic surged in her chest, turning her esophagus to fire.

Almost too late she realized she was going to retch.

She got the top of the commode up just in time. Tears ran from her eyes; she gripped the porcelain lip with her hands, wanting to die.

33

Dean turned the corner behind the building, walking down the narrow alley toward a neighboring street. Two- and three-story brick apartment buildings nudged against one another on the left, crowding out much older structures that seemed as if they'd been made entirely of sand and glued into place. The charity building dated from just after World War II and was one of two nearly identical buildings lining the short avenue. The offices the terrorists used were on the second story at the corner, two floors over the restroom where Lia was.

The bug Lia was "servicing" was in principle a sophisticated electroacoustic receiver, sometimes called a concrete microphone. It worked by picking up minute vibrations in the building's concrete and metal structure; those vibrations were transmitted to a larger pickup unit outside, which then transmitted them back to the NSA for interpretation. Plumbers in the United States sometimes used a less sophisticated version to listen for leaking pipes in concrete foundations and structures. Theirs couldn't filter out various conversations or be tuned to pick up certain areas of the building's skeleton — but then again, Deep Black's couldn't have found a leaking faucet a few feet away, much less heard a conversation there. The device had been placed in the women's room not because it was difficult to detect there, but because the steel grid in the concrete carried the vibration from the room down in that direction. The bug could be easily defeated by heavy vibration devices — a simple vibrating sander against the wall would do the trick — but only if the targets knew to do so. And these didn't.

In fact, thought Dean, the people in the office were extremely confident that they were safe here; they had the windows wide open. Dean watched from across the street as two shadows flitted across the space. He crossed the street, listening to the voice above. There were at least two people inside and so there was no question of going in, but he put a small audio fly below the window. The fly was low-powered; its battery would last only a few hours, transmitting voice information to a small unit he tucked into a wall around the corner, and from there back to the Art Room.

"Good," said his runner as Dean crossed back. "They're talking about food or something."

"Maybe they'll go to dinner soon. Let me know if they leave," Dean answered.

"Will do."

Dean walked down one of the connecting alleys past the apartments, crossed near some smaller row houses — they were more like shacks — and then around to the street across from the charity building, pretending to look at the wares spread out on the sidewalk and in general playing the interested but distracted tourist.

A man dressed in traditional white desert garb stood nearby, a microphone in hand, talking rapidly. The translator back in the Art Room told Dean he was a native entertainer, telling what were supposed to be humorous stories, though judging from the bored expressions of the few people watching him the stories weren't very funny.

"The real entertainment is inside the medina," added the translator. "And not until much later."

Dean glanced at his watch. Lia should have been out by now.

"How we doing?" he asked the runner under his breath.

"She's working on it, Charlie," said Chafetz.

Dean walked down the street to a vendor who sold small morsels of charcoal-broiled fish. The translator told him how to ask for it, but Dean found it easier now simply to point, holding out a five-dirham note — a bit less than fifty cents at the current exchange rate. The man worked silently, scooping up a bit of the fish and placing it on a piece of bread. Dean took his change — two dirhams and fifty centimes — and nibbled at the food, walking slowly back toward the building.

"How is she doing?" he asked when he reached the corner across the street from the building.

"Everything's fine," said Telach. "Relax, Charlie."

"I'm going inside," he told the Art Room supervisor.

"There are still two people in the office. We can hear them very clearly."

"I'm not going into the office. I want to check on Lia."

"It's not necessary. She planted a video bug in the hallway. We can see all the way to the top of the stairs. Just relax."

"I'm going inside," he insisted, crossing the street.

34

"Lia?" said Chafetz.

Go away, Lia thought. *Leave me.*

The attendant said something in Arabic, harsh words, as if she were yelling at Lia for messing the stall.

"She's asking if you're all right," the translator told Lia. "Tell her this."

Lia had to listen to the phrase three times before she could attempt it; her voice stuttered as she spoke. The attendant asked if she was sure.

"Pregnant," whispered Lia under her breath. She wanted the words to tell the woman — it was the perfect excuse, wasn't it?

The translator, however, either didn't understand or couldn't hear.

"Pregnant," Lia tried again, slightly louder and coughing.

The attendant came to the door and knocked.

"I'm pregnant," Lia said in English. And the translator finally caught on, supplying a line about how Lia was expecting.

Men.

The woman began clucking sympathetically, offering a stream of advice. Lia moaned in agreement. She was ready with a cover story about her English: her identity was supposed to be Chinese, but she usually spoke English because most of the people she worked with did. But the woman didn't ask.

The woman also didn't move away from the door. While the metal stalls went all the way to the floor, there was enough of a crack at the opening for the woman to see through.

Lia couldn't think of anything to say to get her to go away. With her brain seeming to move only in slow motion, she wiped her face, hoping the woman would eventually run out of steam.

"A cloth for my face," said Lia finally, this time in Chinese. The translator relayed the Arabic words back and she repeated them. Lia waited until the woman went back to the washbasin, then rose and went to the stall. She opened the door just a bit.

"You can tell her you're sorry," said the translator, offering words. But Lia didn't need any; the woman nodded and handed her a wet towel, calling her daughter and telling her about her own trials. Lia listened for a bit, offering a weak smile and finally handing back the towel. She retreated back into the stall, closing the door. The woman went back to her post by the door.

Her stomach still queasy, Lia pushed herself to the floor. She clawed at the bolt cover; it broke from the floor with a loud snap. Lia coughed several times and then reached down to retrieve the old bug. It was two inches long but only three-eighths of an inch thick, a slightly misshapen pen top. She pulled out the replacement and slid it in, then reached for the transponder device to activate it.

It was gone.

Lia locked her mouth against the bile rising in her chest. She was going to do this.

As she slid her head down to get a breather, she saw the device sitting near her knee. She snatched it up, thankful that she hadn't crushed it by accident. She twisted it, then put her hand over the bug.

It beeped softly.

"Very good," said Chafetz. "We're getting data. Go."

Lia stood up, the old bug in her hand. She felt calmer now, not in control but calmer: she'd had a crisis but gotten over it.

This wasn't her, the nausea, the fear.

Maybe she *was* pregnant.

The idea literally shook her. The old bug slipped from her hand into the toilet. She was supposed to bring it out with her — it was worth several hundred thousand dollars and would be good as new once the battery was replaced — but there was no way, just no way . . .

She flushed the toilet. The water rolled up the sides of the bowl so quickly she thought to herself that it was going to go over the lip of the toilet.

But it didn't. As it receded, she saw that the bug didn't go down. It spun around in the water, mocking her.

Lia closed her eyes and flushed again. This time the water barely stirred in the bowl; the tank hadn't had enough time to refill.

She forced a slow breath from her lungs, pushing the air out from the bottom of her diaphragm, exhaling as carefully as she could, forcing herself to calm down or at least be patient, be more patient.

The third time, the water seemed to explode downward, and the bug went with it.

Lia fixed her skirt and took a breath. It was all downhill from here. Lia pulled open the door and stepped out, only to find one of the guards pointing his gun six inches from her face.

35

Dean trotted up the steps, glancing at his watch as if he were impatient — not exactly a difficult act, under the circumstances. He strode to the door of the charity office, feigning surprise when he found it locked.

"Ms. Yen?" he said, using Lia's cover name. "Ms. Yen?"

He turned around in the hall.

"Where is she really?" he said under his breath to the runner.

"Down the stairs on the left, past the guards," said Chafetz. "Charlie, Marie's having a fit. You shouldn't be in there. Really, Charlie. Lia's on her way out."

Dean carried two small Glocks as hideaway weapons. He reached for the one under his shirt, pulling it out and palming it against his stomach. He called again for Lia, using English and then a phrase supplied by a translator in the Art Room who he guessed was Norwegian, since according to his cover story that was his nationality.

Dean went down the steps and turned, sliding his hand and the small gun into his pocket. There was only one guard there, and though he looked at Dean suspiciously he did not challenge him. Dean went to the man and asked in English — he broke it up, trying to duplicate what he imagined a Norwegian would make it sound like — if the man had seen a young Chinese woman. The guard did not understand his English but began speaking French; as the Art Room scrambled to get the proper translator into the circuit Dean figured out that the man was saying she was downstairs. He played the grateful companion, pointing at his watch and complaining in English and very poor French about how late the girl was. He thought this might be a universal male complaint, but it failed to elicit any sympathy from the Moroccan. Dean thanked him and then started down the steps. As he did, the guard yelled at him.

"He's telling you to stop," said the translator, finally on the line.

"Faites attention!" yelled the man.

"He's yelling at you to watch out, to stop!"

Behind him, Dean heard the soldier fumbling with his gun.

Lia felt as if her face had been shorn from her body, as if she were just the small bit of flesh and bone around her eyes and nose and mouth — no skull, no body, no stomach. She neither thought nor felt anything for a moment, and then an idea occurred to her:

This is what death feels like.

The lessons of her Chinese teacher when she was five came back to her. The sound, more primitive than the writing of the words: *mmmm goi.*

Excuse me. The first phrase she had learned.

"Excuse me. This is a ladies' room," she said in Chinese, and then she turned to English. "Why are you here?"

The translator started to tell her how to ask who he was in Arabic.

"Why are you here?" she said in English.

The man lowered his gun a few inches until it pointed toward her breast.

Lia's left hand moved without her directing it to, jerking up to slam the top of the bugle-shaped rifle away. The rest of her body flew forward and the man landed against the floor, the gun clattering away and a strange sound shrieking from his lips.

To Lia, it seemed as if she were still standing back by the stall, watching it all unfold, watching her fist slam hard three times against the bridge of the man's nose, shattering it with the first blow, watching her knee as it punctured his rib. She watched as her body jumped back, saw herself scan the bathroom — the old woman had fled.

Lia scooped up the assault rifle and started for the door.

Dean was just about to spin and fire at the guard when he heard the scream.

It was a woman's scream, but it wasn't Lia's. He looked down the steps, then back toward the soldier. They both started in the direction of the shouts. An old woman in black dress appeared, yelling and cursing in a dialect so obscure even the Art Room translator couldn't decipher a word. Dean ran past her, then tried to stop as the door to the women's room opened and Lia appeared, a French assault rifle in her hand.

"You OK?" he asked.

"I'm fine, Charlie Dean," she said, walking past him up the steps.

36

Karr scanned the ruins of the chemist's house with the night-vision binoculars, a commercial pair that used light amplification technology rather than infrared rays to see. The police had left for the night, roping the area off with crime scene tape but otherwise trusting that it would not be disturbed before they returned in the morning.

"Ready?" Karr asked LaFoote.

"You're sure we'll know if the police are coming?"

"Oh yeah. A little birdie'll tell me. Come on."

Karr wasn't lying, exactly. Fifteen minutes before, just after the last policeman had gone home for the night, Karr had walked to a point on the other side of the hill, obscured from LaFoote as well as the nearby farmhouses. There he had taken a small black robot aircraft from his pack. Called a Crow, it had been designed to look like a bird from a distance. The aircraft, which could be controlled by Karr or the Art Room, provided real-time video of the area. Under other circumstances, Karr would have tapped into the video feed himself via his PDA. But he didn't want to share any more of his bag of tricks with LaFoote than absolutely necessary.

"Nothing coming for miles," said Rockman in his ear.

"Let's move out," Karr told LaFoote — and the Art Room.

The explosions and the fire that followed had destroyed the roof and gutted much of the interior of the house, but a good portion of the brick walls remained upright. The police theory — shared with Karr via a small boom mike — was that a leaking gas pipe in the kitchen had exploded because of some random spark.

The theory made *some* sense, but it failed to explain the extraordinary damage near what had been the refrigerator — clearly where the bomb had been set. That explosion might have damaged the gas line running beneath the kitchen in a crawl space, causing it to explode a few seconds later. Or perhaps there had been another bomb set on a delayed fuse.

Whatever the exact sequence of events, the bomb had blown through the floor and the crawl space, disturbing dirt that hadn't been touched in a hundred years. Karr's chemical analyzer picked up some traces of complex compounds used in explosives, but not as much as he expected; he had to slide the probe around in the dirt before he got strong readings. These were consistent with Semtex.

"Truck coming," warned Rockman.

Karr got up and found LaFoote, who was looking through what had been his friend's office. The office's walls had been battered; one had crumbled entirely and the other leaned toward the front of the house at a thirty-degree angle.

"Truck coming," Karr told LaFoote. "Turn off your flashlight."

"How do you know?"

"I told you. Birds talk to me," Karr said.

The pair squatted down behind a metal desk, watching as the headlights swept briefly across the front corner of the building and then back onto the road.

"Clear," Rockman told Karr.

"OK. What are we looking for?" Karr asked the Frenchman. "Papers?"

"*Non*," said LaFoote, opening the bottom drawer of the desk. He glanced in for a moment, then started to close it. Karr stopped him.

"What's all this?"

"Old soccer clippings," said LaFoote. "He was a fan."

Karr riffled through the yellowed papers. That's what they were.

"How about bank statements? Where'd he keep them?"

LaFoote shook his head — a little too quickly, Karr thought.

"You wouldn't happen to know his account numbers, would you?" asked Karr.

"Of course not," said LaFoote.

"We've got that already," said Rockman.

"You know where he banked?"

"There is only one bank in town," said the Frenchman. "You think you can trace payments?"

"Possibly I could get someone to trace his accounts," said Karr. "So what, the bank in town?"

"There's nothing there," said Rockman.

"He had another account," said LaFoote.

"Where?"

"I don't know the name."

"France?"

LaFoote kept his lips pressed together.

"Ah, come on. You can tell me. We're partners, right?"

"Austria."

"Austria's tough," said Rockman. "We're

going to need account numbers."

"So what was the bank?" asked Karr.

"I can't remember the name. But I have a copy of a statement."

"Where? Here?"

"*Non.*"

"Austria, OK, Vefoures took two train trips there four and five months back. Used his credit card," said Rockman. "Good going, Tommy."

"Yeah, but you know, I really need to know the name of the bank," said Karr, talking to LaFoote. "And an account number. I mean, if we're going to work together, we have to be kind of up-front with each other. You know?"

LaFoote nodded. "I'll get it for you. It's not here."

He opened another drawer of the desk and pulled out a small but solid-looking crowbar. Tommy looked through the drawers himself — there were no financial papers that he could see — then went to find LaFoote. The Frenchman had walked to the room at the front of the house and begun using the crowbar as a pick against the front wall near the corner. As in the other room, the two outside walls were intact, the interior ones badly battered. The wall that separated this room from the front hallway was about two-thirds gone.

Karr laughed as the Frenchman hacked at the wall. "Mad?" he asked.

"Non." LaFoote took a mighty chop at the wall, the edge of the crowbar chipping off a piece of plaster.

"If you hit it too hard it'll fall on us," Karr warned.

"The brick is far from the wall," said LaFoote, swinging again. "It won't fall."

"Car — two cars," said Rockman.

"Hold on, partner, hold on," said Karr, dousing his flashlight.

LaFoote took another swipe at the wall, breaking through part of the plaster, then ducked down just as the car lights appeared. The cars passed by quickly; the Frenchman started to rise.

"No, no, hold on," Karr told him. "Wait. Give them time to go where they're going."

"They're stopping, Tommy," said Rockman. "I think you'd better get out. Coming back," he added. "Go on. Get out of there."

"No time," said Karr. He pulled out his pistol and glanced at LaFoote, who had taken out his own weapon — an old revolver.

"We don't fire unless we absolutely have to," Karr told him. "And if we do, I want you to go through that window and run like hell," Karr added.

"I'm not running away."

"It's all right. I'll be right behind you."

37

When they reached the airport, Lia got out of the cab and went into the terminal, leaving Dean to deal with the driver.

The young man in the restroom apparently had wanted to rob her, not rape her. If the old lady was to be believed, he was an Algerian, not a local.

"Probably bribe her into keeping her mouth shut," Chafetz had said. "She'll be well off for a few months. Assuming he recovers."

Lia wasn't in much of a mood to add her own cynical comment. Maybe the old woman thought the slime had only wanted money; Lia knew differently.

Someone grabbed her shoulder. Lia spun, ready to deck him. Only at the last instant did she realize it was Dean.

"Hey, our flight's this way," he said.

He had a look in his eyes that she had never seen there before.

Pity?

She began walking in the direction of the

airplane gate. Dean hurried to keep up.

"Hold on a second," he said, grabbing her again.

"What do you want?" she said harshly.

"I wanted to talk to you for a second."

"What?"

"Get on the plane by yourself. I'm going to go back and get into the office and look around. I couldn't earlier because someone was there."

"What?"

There were people around. Dean stopped speaking, waiting until a pair of Moroccans passed.

"I'll catch a flight in the morning," said Dean.

"You think it's a good time to go back?"

"As good as any. There'll only be one guard, if he's not busy taking his friend to the hospital."

"Well, let's go then." Lia started back toward the terminal entrance.

"No, you take the plane."

"Let go of me, Charlie Dean," she told him as he grabbed her. "I'm not letting you go in there alone."

They locked stares. The taste of her stomach rose into her mouth, but she pushed her teeth together hard, steeling herself against it.

"All right," said Dean finally. "Let's talk to the Art Room about it and get something to eat."

"No, first we figure out how we're going to do it, then we tell the Art Room," she said. "Let's get a taxi."

38

Karr watched the two men approach the house. Both had military-style night-vision goggles strapped to their heads. They also wore dark clothes, and the bulk of one of the men in the shadows made Karr think he was wearing a bulletproof vest. One carried a submachine gun, probably an MP-5N; the other had a small backpack but no gun in his hand.

They came into the house through what had been the front door. Karr had a clean, easy shot on the first man in, the one with the gun; most likely he could get the second man as well. But that would leave whoever was in the other car, as well as seriously complicating the situation.

Then again, he might not get such a clean shot again.

Karr held off. The men passed through the house into the back.

"They're looking over the kitchen," said Rockman, watching the feed from the Crow. "Checking out the bomb crater. All right. Now they're going into the office."

Karr didn't need the play-by-play; the house was so small that it was obvious where they were.

LaFoote stirred next to him. Karr tapped the old Frenchman on the shoulder and held his hand to his lips.

The Frenchman nodded — then sneezed.

39

Rubens took his eyes off the screen at the front of the Art Room long enough to glance at his watch. The meeting with the judge about the General was due to start in forty minutes; he had to leave in ten minutes or risk being late.

So be it. It was just an informal session, after all. And his lawyer would be there.

When Rubens glanced back at the screen, it was blank.

"What's happening?" he demanded.

"I'm losing some of the communication bandwidth," said the man flying the Crow from a piloting bunker on the other side of the underground complex. "One of the satellites has a power glitch and we may blow some of the circuits. I had to shut down the feed as a precaution."

"No!" thundered Rubens. "Visual now, whatever the consequences! Show us what's going on with Tommy! Now, damn it."

Rubens never, ever raised his voice in the

Art Room, and if he'd said half a dozen cusswords during his entire NSA career, it was news to the staff. Everyone stopped what they were doing.

"Yes, sir," said the pilot, and the image snapped back on the screen.

40

Dean took the napkin and sketched the basic layout on it for Lia, diagramming the alley and the charity building.

"You could stand right at this corner here and watch the office," Dean told her. "You'll be able to see everything."

"And be run over by anyone who comes up through the alley in a truck," Lia told him. She reached into her travel bag for her PDA and pulled up the photos of the area they had been given as part of the earlier briefing. "I can get up on the roof from this fire escape," she said, pointing. "I'll have just as good a view."

"OK," said Dean. She seemed a little more herself, he thought. "I saw a place at the eastern end of the medina where we can rent bikes. We can stash them so we can use them to get away if we need to. We could use them to get to the airport if we have to."

"It'll be closed by now."

"You can't pick the locks?"

"That would get us in more trouble here

than if we killed someone," said Lia. "They don't like thieves."

"So what do you suggest? Hire a cab?"

She didn't answer, instead turning the PDA toward him. "How are you going to get into the window? There's nothing to climb on."

"It's only one story up. There are some crates behind the building in that alley there," he said, pointing at his napkin. "We can bring them over."

"They'll hold you?"

"I hope so."

"I should be the one who climbs in."

"You can't have all the fun," he told her.

Something flashed in her eye — relief? But if so, it turned into a scowl.

"I should go," she said.

"If the crates won't hold me, OK. Otherwise, this was my idea; I get to take the shot."

"All right. Listen, did the Art Room tell you I puked?"

"No."

"Yeah, well, I got sick in the women's room. I threw up. I think it was the solvent, because it smelled wretched."

"You all right now?" Dean asked.

"Yeah, I'm OK."

Dean stared into her face. "You told

them back in the Art Room?"

"I didn't have to. They could hear me. I spilled solvent all over the place. Junk."

"That's what did it?"

"I'm *fine,* Charlie Dean. I just wanted you to know. In case they pointed it out. Like I was sick or something."

"Yeah, all right."

"I'm fine."

"I didn't say you weren't."

41

Karr steadied himself in a crouch as the two men approached. They were talking, but he couldn't make out what they were saying.

There was another sound — a cat, mewing.

Something creaked in the room. The cat mewed again.

The man without the gun appeared in the opening. Karr didn't have a shot on anything but his chest, which was protected by a vest.

The cat screeched. Something fell across the room as it ran off.

The man started laughing and cursed. The two men went back to the office.

"He's got an Arabic accent," said the Art Room translator. "He's saying he would have killed the stupid cat if he'd seen it. The other one said maybe it was the cat that caused the explosion. They were laughing."

"They're going under the desk — looks like there's a strongbox there," said Rockman.

One of the men used his gun to get it open. They started exclaiming happily; Karr didn't need the translator to tell him that they had found a whole wad of cash.

"Tommy, we're having trouble with the Crow and the satellite system that's controlling it," said Rubens, cutting in. "We're going to lose its feed and the ability to control it in a little under two minutes. We can either fly it down the road and have you recover it later or self-destruct it as a diversion. I can see you. If you want me to self-destruct the Crow, move your left hand. Otherwise, move your right. You have ten seconds to decide."

Karr thought about it. The problem with using it as a diversion was that he couldn't predict what the men might do. An unexplained explosion might give them more reason to hang around.

"Very well," said Rubens when Karr moved his right hand. "We'll have it land in a field and we'll give you the GPS point."

"They have the strongbox — they must have wanted the money," said Rockman. "Looks like that's all they got from there, money. It's — ah — feed from the Crow's gone. Hang tight, Tommy."

The two men started back toward the

front of the house but stopped as the car lights flashed on and off. A truck passed by; as soon as it was gone they left, the car quickly driving off.

"Where'd the cat come from?" Karr asked LaFoote as soon as he was sure they were gone.

"Meow," said LaFoote. He put his hand to his mouth and this time the mewing seemed to come from the other side of the house. Then he picked up a small piece of debris from the floor and tossed it across the room, timing his screech perfectly so it sounded as if the cat had been startled and run off.

Tommy laughed.

"I learned a few things in my day," said the Frenchman.

On the third slap at the wall with the little crowbar enough of the plaster gave way so that LaFoote could reach inside and take out the small box Vefoures had hidden there. The box contained three CD-ROMs with information Vefoures had copied from his work computers. Vefoures had hidden them there soon after he had begun work. He'd had a bad premonition of what would happen to him.

Or perhaps a guilty conscience.

"Let me take a look at them," said the American.

"How do I know I can trust you?" LaFoote asked.

"Heck of a time to start worrying about trusting me," Karr said with a grin.

"Are you going to help me find my friend?"

"That's why I'm here."

The American reached out his hand. It was an easy, self-serving lie, LaFoote knew; he had told similar ones many times in his own career.

"I'll give you one disk," he told him. "And then you do something for me."

"Like what?"

"You find my friend. Then you get both."

"What happens if I find him and he doesn't want to see you? Or if he's dead?"

"He may be dead, yes," said LaFoote. He felt his voice tremble slightly, but he knew it was probable, if not certain. "If he is dead, you will get the disks. No matter what he says, you will get the disks."

"What about that bank statement?"

"I'll get that, too."

"Where is it?"

"With an acquaintance."

The American was huge — he could

grab the disks from LaFoote without much of a fuss — but LaFoote knew he wouldn't attack him.

"All right. I trust you, even if you don't trust me," said Karr. "One disk tonight. The rest when?"

"When you find my friend."

"Having all the disks might make that easier."

"No. This is just about the explosive he was working on."

"All right. One now. Two later." The American smiled and put his hand out for the CD-ROM. "But I need that account number. Right?"

"That I will get. It can't be done right away. The papers are not in my possession."

"Let's go where they are."

"No. They're safe. Don't worry. I'll retrieve them tomorrow."

"I never worry," said the American.

The Crow had set down in a field a half mile away. Karr had the Frenchman stop the car on the shoulder, then told him he'd be right back.

"Nature calls," he said, reaching into the back for his knapsack.

As he walked toward the Crow — its

landing site had been recorded by a Global Positioning System — he talked to Rockman about the CD-ROM and what to do next. The Deep Black safe house in Paris had a computer he could use to send the disk's data back to the Art Room.

"Why didn't you take the other two disks?" Rockman asked.

Karr chuckled. "Was I supposed to deck him?"

"Maybe."

"I think he's more useful to us if he's friendly," said Karr. "If I go back to Paris, can you get somebody to watch LaFoote?"

"One of the CIA agents from Paris is standing by at the train station," said Rockman.

"Just one?"

"It's the best we could do, Tommy."

"All right. Remind him the old guy is sharper than he looks, OK?"

"He's not *that* sharp."

"He's sharper than you think. He's just been out of it for a while, so he's not up on the technical stuff. But he'll pick up a shadow if the guy gets sloppy."

"We'll use the bug you set. And we know where he lives."

"While we were waiting for the police to leave he was telling me about his mother and some other relatives," said Karr. "He was staying with someone in Paris."

"Second cousin. We already checked it out. He used his apartment for the last two weeks, on and off. We have it under control, Tommy."

"What about that DST guy in Paris, Ponclare? LaFoote thinks he was involved."

"He's just paranoid," said Rockman. "Theory here is that Vefoures got paid a hunk of money from some terrorists to help them make explosives, then took off for parts unknown. Bought new ID, blah, blah, blah."

"How do you explain the explosion at his house then?"

"Vefoures booby-trapped it before he left."

"What, and left his money there?"

"You're assuming it wasn't counterfeit."

"Well, sure. But the house wasn't booby-trapped last week."

"It's possible LaFoote was in on it and Vefoures double-crossed him."

"Ah, you're overthinking it. I trust the old guy."

"He was a French agent in Africa, Tommy. Those guys weren't exactly the most ethical people in the world."

"Well, who is?"

"He thinks Ponclare is dirty because he forced him to retire," said Rockman. "We don't know why he was forced out. It may have just been a budget cut."

"What else do you have on Ponclare?"

"Career bureaucrat. Second generation. Decent record, blah, blah, blah. His father is more interesting. He was a legend in the French foreign service *and* the foreign legion. Dealt with the Algerian uprising and the mutiny by the French generals against the government in the early nineteen-sixties. If he was alive, I'd think he was behind the whole setup."

"Like father, like son."

"It's a nice saying, but I've never seen it play out in real life," countered the runner.

"Man, you're in a bad mood today," said Karr.

"Just skeptical. That's my job."

"I'll upload the disk as soon as I get back to Paris with it," said Karr. "Did you get plate numbers on those cars?"

"Looks like the plates were stolen, because the car types don't match. The registrations are from the south of France, pretty far from where you are. We're still sorting that out, but it doesn't look like it's going to lead anywhere. We had a lot of trouble with the Crow," he added. "Satellite they were using to control it crapped out. Rubens is pretty furious about it."

"As well he should be."

"He actually cursed."

"Really? Well, there's hope for him yet."

"I think Marie almost had a heart attack. You're about ten yards away from the Crow," Rockman added.

"Ughhh," said Karr, stepping in a mud hole that came halfway up to his knee. He had to back up and then circle to his left before he could get to the downed plane. The miniature aircraft had flipped over when it landed and broken one of its wings. He pried the busted stub off from the body, then got the other wing off and removed the tail, fitting everything neatly into his sack.

"Hey, your Frenchman's got a cell phone," said Rockman, who was monitoring a fly Tommy had left in the car. "I thought you said he was a technophobe."

"I just said he wasn't up on spy gadgets. Everybody in Europe has a cell phone. Who's he calling?"

"Hold on."

Karr zipped his pack back up and looked upward at the stars. For a fall night, it was fairly warm, and in the clear sky he could see dozens of constellations. When he was a boy he'd thought about becoming a scientist and astronaut, maybe going to Mars. He might do that yet.

"Girlfriend — no, no, wait — it's a sister of Vefoures. They know each other pretty well."

"Old flame?" Karr asked.

"Hold on, huh?"

Karr folded his arms, still gazing at the stars.

"He told her he's still looking for her brother, and not to worry. She was concerned, blah, blah, blah. He's off the phone. I'll get into the account and check it out."

"Have fun," said Karr.

"You need anything else?"

"Train tickets back to Paris would be handy. I'm a little short on cash."

"We'll see what we can set up. You may have to hit an automatic teller at the station."

"Make sure Dad's got some cash in the bank then," said Karr. "I don't feel like walking."

LaFoote looked at his fingers as he waited for the American agent to return. They were old fingers. Even in the dim light he could see the age spots and the

315

gnarled knuckles, swelled with mild but chronic arthritis.

He'd been ready to shoot the man in the house. The American's restraint had stopped him — the right move. He was wise beyond his years, the American: a jolly bear but a smart one.

A jolly bear. In LaFoote's day, that would have been the American's nickname.

This was still his day, for a few weeks anyway.

The American opened the door. The car lurched on its shocks as he got in.

"So what do you say?" Karr asked LaFoote.

"I don't say anything."

"That's just an expression." Karr rocked around in the seat. "I have to go back to Paris and send the information on the disk back, see if it's of any use." He scratched the side of his head, as if he were trying to get an idea out. "If you gave me the other disks, they might help."

"*Non.*"

"Your call."

"Yes, it is my call."

"So what do you want me to do next?" Karr asked.

"You trace his bank accounts and phone records."

"Which you've already tried to do, but couldn't."

LaFoote knew it was a guess, but the American said it very smoothly.

"Yes, of course. You have more resources than I have."

"What about your friend Ponclare? Should I ask him to help?"

"Monsieur Ponclare is *not* my friend."

"Figure of speech," said Karr. "Why do you think he was involved?"

"His organization contacted Vefoures."

"You're sure?"

"No," said LaFoote. "It may have been a trick to get Vefoures to cooperate. But my friend thought it was the DST."

"And it wouldn't make sense just to ask Ponclare?"

"If you ask him, he will know you suspect him," said LaFoote. "And you won't be able to trust whether he's telling the truth."

The American nodded. "If this was something the government wasn't involved in, who would it be? Terrorists?"

"Vefoures would never work with terrorists. Never."

"Assuming he knew they were involved."

"Yes. That is true."

"Maybe he didn't."

"Perhaps not."

"Maybe the Russians then, or the Chinese. Or even the Americans. Would he work with any of them?"

LaFoote wanted to say no; he felt he had to defend his friend. But the honest answer was that he might, and so LaFoote admitted it. "More them than terrorists."

"Well, maybe we'll figure it out from the information on the disk," said Karr. "Take me to the train station."

LaFoote put his car in gear and got back on the highway. "When will we meet again?"

"Whenever you want," said Karr. "Come with me to Paris."

"No, I have other things to do. Including retrieving the paper with the account."

"Maybe I should come with you."

"*Non*," said LaFoote. "That is not necessary."

"I didn't say it was necessary. It'd be convenient."

"I have personal things to do," insisted LaFoote. "I am quite capable of taking care of myself."

"Sure. But do you think you're going to go on being lucky?"

"I don't understand."

"Somebody gunned for you in England, and your friend's house blew up. You just missed getting fried two times. That to me is lucky."

"The house was booby-trapped," LaFoote said. "Not for anyone specific. You heard them; they thought the cat blew it up. And whoever tried to kill me in London thinks I'm dead."

"For now."

LaFoote considered what the American was saying. He knew that the man had his own agenda; that went without saying. But there was no benefit to the American that LaFoote could think of if he came to Paris.

And what if he were to die? It was a legitimate concern.

"I can't go with you, because I have things to do," said LaFoote. "But if anything happens, go to the church."

"To church?"

"In every town, there is one man who can be trusted to keep his word. In my town, it happens to be the priest."

Karr laughed. "That's not true of all priests?"

"*Non*," said LaFoote. "Especially in France. I will meet you in Paris tomorrow evening, at Gare du Nord — the train station. Nine p.m."

"I'll be there."

42

The words *judge's chambers* inspired a certain awe in most laymen, and Rubens was no exception. But when he showed up at the courthouse a few minutes late for the meeting, he was shown to an office that was, to be charitable, plain. The walls were in need of a good coat of paint, the curtains on the lone window seemed as if they had been bought at Wal-Mart, and even the American flag in the corner looked a bit worse for wear. At the center of the room sat a long Formica-topped table in front of a plain metal desk. A man in a pin-striped shirt sat at the desk, sleeves rolled to the elbows, tie loosened, salt-and-pepper hair gently mussed. This was Judge Croner.

"Mr. Rubens. Please, sit down. I'm glad you could come," said the judge. "We've only just been introducing ourselves."

Rubens nodded at the others and sat next to his lawyer, which happened to put him across from Rebecca. He was surprised to see that she had a frightened expression on her face.

It made her look younger. Not prettier — she was pretty to begin with — but definitely younger.

Her husband sat next to her: a chubby, pasty-faced accountant.

The judge began speaking about the mechanics of the legal proceedings in general terms, repeating things McGovern had told Rubens the other day and when they had first met. He was speaking in generalities, and Rubens got the feeling that Croner was watching their reactions, sizing them up so he could see how to proceed.

Rebecca's attorney interrupted as the judge began talking about what the medical examination would most likely entail. The case was straightforward, said the lawyer. Everyone would agree that the General was incompetent and that someone had to be appointed to see to his needs. This should have been done ages ago. The daughter was the natural candidate.

Rubens wanted McGovern to object — *he* was the natural candidate, the one the General had asked for. But she said nothing as the other lawyer continued. Rubens felt his anger rise as Rebecca's counsel declared that — *"with all due respect"* — other interested parties had their

own agendas. As important as those interests might be in their proper sphere, they
were of no relevance here.

The comments were, of course, directed
at Rubens, though he was not named.
Rubens finally found it impossible to not
speak out.

"That's simply not true," he said. "My
interests are the General's and the General's alone. He is my friend."

Ellen put her hand gently on his. Her
touch caught him by surprise and he
stopped speaking, even though everyone
was looking at him.

"I don't mean to insult you, Mr.
Rubens," said Rebecca's lawyer. "But you
can't deny that your employer has sent you
here."

Ellen squeezed his hand, speaking before
he could. "Mr. Rubens does work for an
important government agency, as did the
General. We're all aware of that. But of
course that's no more relevant here than
the fact that Mr. Paulson and I are attor-
neys."

It wasn't the strongest argument,
Rubens thought, but at least she was
saying *something*.

The other lawyer began talking about
"special employment requirements of the

government agency involved" and how these would skew Rubens' judgment even if he hadn't been ordered to come. Under other circumstances, Rubens might have been amused by the way everyone at the hearing was avoiding naming the agency or talking about what it did. But he wasn't amused now at all. He wanted to shout at them that it was the General who was important — that brave and intelligent man whose world had been reduced to a white room twelve by fifteen feet, whose brilliant mind was now a trampoline for delusions.

"Mr. Paulson is an eloquent lawyer," said McGovern finally, once more squeezing Rubens' hand. "I think the General would be well served if he were his counsel."

Why the concession? wondered Rubens. She should be attacking, not retreating.

"I quite agree," said the judge, who'd been silent all this time. "But of course he's not. An attorney will have to be appointed to represent Mr. Rosenberg's interests — should I call him General? He is a general, yes? Is that how he likes to be addressed?"

"He's actually a very humble man," said Rubens, though the judge was looking at Rebecca. "He introduces himself as 'Mr.,' but those of us who've known him for a long time, usually we call him General. I suppose other people would use that as well."

The judge nodded, but it was Rebecca who had the last word: "That would be fine, I think. I always just call him Daddy."

Where he'd taken his time before, now the judge spoke quickly, laying out the steps that he would take. The first and most important was to appoint a lawyer to represent the General. A medical assessment would follow, probably fairly quickly, but of course the General's lawyer would have an important say on the timetable. Everything from here on out would hinge on the General's court-appointed legal representative. Interested parties would always be welcome to add relevant information, but the law directed the judge to work in a certain way and ultimately he would be the one to make the decision.

That was the opening for Rebecca's lawyer. Rubens remained calm as the attorney suggested that a jury trial might be appropriate.

"An interesting point," said Judge Croner. "Of course, the General's attorney is going to be the one speaking for him, so from this point onward that would be a matter for him to propose."

As a courtesy to the interested parties, added the judge, he would of course keep them abreast of the timetable for the proceedings. He would certainly work with the General's counsel, whom he intended to name by the end of the day.

"Who would that be?" asked Rebecca's lawyer.

"Naturally someone with experience and the high recommendation of the Bar," said the judge, parrying the question gently yet firmly. He was not to be interfered with, despite his easygoing manner. "As I said earlier, a medical examination would proceed promptly thereafter. I would hope that the General's counsel would be prepared for a formal hearing by the end of the week. Ladies and gentlemen, thank you," said the judge, tapping his hands on the table and rising to dismiss them.

"So, what did you think?" McGovern asked as they descended in the elevator.

Rebecca, her husband, and their lawyer were in the car as well, and Rubens felt constrained to say he thought the judge was "a very nice fellow."

"Very sharp," said Ellen.

Was she talking to the other attorney or to him? Rubens said nothing until they were out in the parking lot and the others had walked off in the other direction.

"Is that timetable normal?" he asked.

"A little fast but not all that unusual. In a lot of instances, these decisions have to be made very expeditiously because medical care is involved. We could have a hearing on Friday and a decision right after that. Does it seem too fast?"

"No, I guess not."

"The fact that the General is who he is will also push Judge Croner to get things settled very quickly," added McGovern. "That's why he tried to solve things without a formal process."

"How did he try to solve things?" Rubens asked.

"Oh, that's definitely what he was doing. If they had made more of an opening, he would have sounded them out in detail."

"I'd appreciate it if you were more . . . forward," Rubens told her.

"How so?"

"You could have defended me. I'm not representing the NSA."

"That was obvious."

"How? The judge doesn't know me. When their lawyer said I was, you should have jumped right in. You did speak up, don't get me wrong, but it was a little late."

"Frankly, I would have preferred not saying anything at all," she told him. "I only said that to keep you from talking. The fact of the matter is, Mr. Rubens, you're not on trial. Neither is Rebecca. This isn't that sort of proceeding. The real way to think about this, if you want to think about it, is to pretend you're just watching. The judge invited you in as a courtesy. And the same with Rebecca," she added before he could object. "The hearing is about the General and *his* competence. Not yours."

"It's about who watches his affairs."

"It's about *his* future. Didn't you tell me *his* wishes should be honored? Isn't that what's important?" She touched his arm. "I'm sorry. I'm lecturing. Forgive me."

Rubens pursed his lips.

"What you said about what to call the General, that was better than any brief," she added. "It was very eloquent."

"It was just what I felt."

"That's why it was eloquent." She glanced at her watch. "It would have been better if it didn't come to this, but now that the process is under way, things will have a momentum and logic of their own."

"Why would it be better if it didn't come to this?"

"Don't you think that? These sorts of disagreements don't do anyone any good."

Yes, actually, he *did* think that. Why was he being so argumentative?

And why did he feel as if he were the one on trial?

"I may be somewhat busy over the next few days," Rubens told McGovern. "But you can call the number I gave you at any time, day or night."

"Days will be fine. I'll see you, Mr. Rubens."

43

As soon as Dean put his foot on the edge of the crate he heard it crack. He grabbed the ledge and pulled himself upward as the box collapsed in a heap.

"Too late to switch places with you now," he whispered to Lia over the communications system.

He thought he heard her growl in response.

Dean balanced precariously on the narrow ledge as he pulled the handheld computer out to scan for a burglar alarm. There wasn't one, and the two halves of the window were held together by a simple latch at the middle, which was easily undone by sliding his knife in through the crack. He used the knife to swing the far window away, then leaned over to peer inside. Besides making it possible to see into the dark office, Dean's night-vision glasses could detect beams from infrared devices used on alarm systems. There were none, and a second scan with the PDA failed to turn up a motion detector or more sophisticated bugging device.

"I'm in," he told Lia as he swung inside.

"I can see that."

"They don't have a PC."

"Smart of them," said Lia.

The group that had rented the office claimed to raise money for a service that trained nurses. It did actually do this, and in fact donated more than a hundred thousand dollars every year to schools in Egypt, Pakistan, and Iran. But such international operations provided a pretext for passing information among a host of individuals and countries.

While terrorists typically went to great lengths to keep their communications secret, experience had shown that offices such as these in friendly countries often had surprisingly lax security. It wasn't a case of hubris so much as human nature: if a threat wasn't imminent, it tended to be ignored. Dean's briefer had predicted there would be no alarm systems or other common safeguards, and so far it appeared as if he were right.

However, there wasn't a terribly lot to protect here: no computers and only two lateral files at the side of the office. Both were locked. Dean used the handheld computer to check for electronic security devices — he didn't particularly want to blow himself up trying to get a bank statement. When he found none, he took out the lock pick and went to work on the lock.

Dean had taken a two-day course in the fine art of jimmying locks after joining Deep Black, but he hadn't had much time to practice since then. The lock stayed stubbornly set.

And then he heard someone in the hall.

"Charlie, people coming your way," said Lia. "I can see them turning on lights."

No kidding, he thought, hiding behind the desk.

44

The garage was located in a warehouse that dated from the 1950s, a steel-fabricated structure whose sides were covered with dents and dimples, along with the faded splatters of a dozen paint jobs. It sat next to a rarely used railroad spur; when Mussa had first found the building the railroad had been an important part of his planning, but as it turned out he had used it only once. That was the way it went with such things, though — one might plan carefully and consider all of the alternatives, but in the end life made its own demands.

From the time he had bought it three years before until just six months ago, the warehouse had been part of Mussa's business empire and main source of income. To call it an empire was aggrandizement; Mussa arranged for the exporting of automobiles from Europe to Africa. This involved several phases: obtaining the cars, preparing them for transit, and actually shipping them. The warehouse was involved in the middle phase. As a rule, the vehicles Mussa obtained were mechanically perfect; he rarely procured one more than twelve months old. However, his customers in Africa and the Middle East required certain modifications, new serial numbers on engine blocks being among the most critical. Generally, he changed the exterior color as well. Other modifications tended to be done to order — armor, secret compartments, and certain types of electrical equipment, including cell phone jammers, had become almost *de rigueur.*

The car export business had been lucrative, though not without its liabilities. Surprisingly, its greatest liability had been its effect on his conscience. While Mussa could justify his thefts intellectually — he was taking vehicles from heathens — there was a part of him that objected. In fact, the objections had grown greater as his wealth increased.

Two years before, he had heard an imam suggest that guilt was merely faith speaking. Mussa still remembered that talk; in many ways it had helped set him on his current path.

But even the most righteous man must live in this world. Driving across the crumbling macadam toward the plant at the back of the old factory area near Marseilles, he felt pride at all he had accomplished, and even greater pride at what he would achieve in just a few days.

Sparks from a welder's torch inside the garage ended his brief reverie of self-congratulations.

"Non, non, non!" Mussa shouted, jumping from his car and running inside. The van was up on a lift, its undersides being reinforced and prepared for the extra springs. The five carefully fashioned explosives for the bomb assembly sat less than ten meters away.

Mussa's emotions ran so strongly that he couldn't even sputter a curse or an explanation; all he could do was point at the crates.

"Idiots!" he managed finally, speaking Arabic rather than French. "Idiots! Don't I pay you enough not to kill yourselves?"

Heads down, the workers took the van down and began moving it to the far bay. They were running behind schedule, but Mussa decided not to chide them further; they would undoubtedly perceive any urge now to move faster as a contradiction of these orders, and besides, past experience showed that they were just as likely to react by slowing down as speeding up once he left their sight.

There was a more effective strategy.

"Listen to me for a moment," he said loudly. "Listen. Stop what you are doing and listen."

The half-dozen garagemen came over to him.

"I will return tomorrow to gather everything. If everything is in order and the van properly loaded, everyone who has worked on the project will receive an appropriate bonus," he said.

The faces lit up with smiles. Mussa was not an ungenerous man, and all of those here had benefited from his bonuses before.

"Tomorrow, then," he added, looking around. "It is understood?"

He strode from the building before the heads stopped bobbing. Outside he checked his watch, then got into the car. Three kilometers away, he pulled off the road and took one of the cell phones from his bag.

Donohue picked up on the first ring.

"You're late," he told Mussa.

"It couldn't be helped. Have you considered my proposal?"

"Twice what you said."

"I would be willing to take your price if we can add another matter at your usual fee," said Mussa.

"I don't do package deals."

Mussa sensed a bluff.

"There was an error in your previous assignment. I am not blaming you, but it is a matter that needs correction. I am willing to pay to fix it," continued Mussa, "as clearly someone on my side erred, but it must happen very soon."

"I don't do package deals."

"Well then, that is that," said Mussa. "Perhaps in the future we will have occasion to be of use to each other."

He hesitated before hanging up — just long enough, as it turned out.

"What are the details?" said Donohue.

"The details will be forthcoming in the manner you specify," said Mussa. "The time line is critical. Which will be explained."

"If it has to be done on an expedited timetable, the scale changes."

Mussa decided he could concede on that point. Getting rid of LaFoote was important: it was the last loose end that needed tying up. If Donohue didn't do it, someone less dependable would have to.

"Well, of course. That is to be expected. And expenses will be covered," added Mussa, suddenly feeling generous. "Reasonable ones, of course."

"That's already figured into the fee. But the sentiment is appreciated."

The line clicked off. Pleased with himself, Mussa dropped the phone out of the car, then backed up to make sure he crushed it with his tire as he got back on the highway.

45

Lia adjusted the elastic band at the back of the night-vision glasses, twisting it so that it held tight against her hair. Most of the other ops loved the device, which looked like wraparound sunglasses and was only slightly heavier, but she could never get it to sit right on the bridge of her nose.

A light came on in the office where Dean was. Lia slipped the setting on the small, boxlike A2 rifle she held in her hand to burst fire; she could get three bullets almost instantaneously into the target, which was marked out with a cursor in her glasses. They'd picked up the gear at a small shop in town; Desk Three had literally hundreds of weapons and equipment caches stashed around the world.

"There's one man inside the room with him," she told the Art Room.

"We know," said Sandy Chafetz in the Art Room. "We can hear him. He's saying something to the other man — the person in the office is the manager and the other is

338

a guard. He needs to retrieve something."

"Where is Charlie?" asked Lia. The Art Room would be watching his location via an implanted radiation device accurate to within a few inches.

"Behind the desk," said Chafetz. "The big desk on the right."

Probably the manager's desk, Lia thought. If he came back to get something, that's where he was going.

"Diversion coming, Charlie," she said, grabbing the small grenade she had clipped to the collar of her shirt. She pulled the pin and threw the grenade over the roof of the nearby charity building. The grenade was a miniature "flash-bang" — a special grenade that exploded with a very loud boom and a flash of light, often used as a diversionary tactic during hostage rescue operations. The grenade exploded in midair with a loud *whap*.

"All right, Charlie, your move," Lia whispered.

When Lia's grenade exploded, one of the men in the office began to shout and ran out into the hallway.

The other leaned forward over the desk from the front, pulling open the top right-hand drawer.

Dean, no more than two feet away, tensed his leg muscles, preparing to spring.

"He's right over you, Charlie," Lia whispered. "Shoot him."

The desk creaked under the man's weight. The second grenade seemed louder, and the man jerked back but then reached again for whatever it was he wanted. A second grenade exploded outside and the man in the hall yelled, apparently for him to come.

"He wants him to hurry," said the translator. "He's the guard and he's worried about being away from his post."

The man on the desk took something from the drawer and ran out.

"Lia — can you see what he got?" Dean whispered. His voice felt hoarse.

"You're OK?" she asked.

"I didn't see what he took."

Lia saw a shadow moving through the building. She froze, paralyzed — she had wanted to follow, she had to follow, but she couldn't.

What held her back? Fear?

Fear.

No, she told herself. She had to stow the A2 or it would attract attention. She went into the shadows at the side of the roof and grabbed her backpack rather than the A2's case — there was no time to stow it away properly, and she certainly didn't want to be without it. Her hands trembled as she climbed over the side to the drainpipe and shimmied down ten feet before dropping to the ground. She ran across the alley and made it to the side of the building just as a guard crossed on the street. The manager was behind him, carrying whatever it was he took from the office.

"Lia — give us the feed from your glasses. We'll enhance it," said Chafetz. The feed had to be enabled by the operative because the signal it transmitted to an overhead satellite network was easily detected.

Lia clicked the button at the back of the glasses. She increased the magnification as well, watching the man as he walked to a small Fiat across the street, the guard looking around warily as he got in.

"Charlie, he's getting in a car," said Lia.

"Yeah, I'm coming. Wait."

"You see what he's carrying?" Lia asked her runner.

"We have an image. It's a phone coupler device — it's an old-fashioned modem, used to put on telephone handsets. You see a laptop?"

"I didn't, no."

"I'm going to follow him," said Dean. She heard him grunting, wrestling with something.

"How are you going to follow him?" she asked.

"On the bike. Describe the car."

"Blue Fiat. Can't see the plates. Just starting, driving west. Don't come out on this block — the guard is watching."

"Right. OK, good."

Lia's heart felt as if it were trying to stomp through her chest. She took a breath, then headed back toward the roof to retrieve the case she'd left behind.

The bicycle Dean had appropriated was an old single-geared type and, while sturdy, would not be confused with a racer. Dean huffed as he turned back toward the road where the car had headed. He had only a vague idea of the roads in the area, and the runner's directions weren't particularly helpful.

"Just tell me where there are pay phones around," Dean said, pedaling furiously. He hit a rut and nearly did a header.

"Why do you think he's going to a pay phone?" asked the runner.

"Well, for one thing, you'd never look for a data call from one, right? And I'm going to bet you've checked over phone lines in this city a million times for some connection with these guys and come up empty."

For another — he was taking a wild guess and couldn't think of anything else.

"Take a right," said Chafetz. "Then a quick left — there's a new set of stores near there."

Dean took the turns, slowing as he started to run out of breath. He saw a man walking on the street ahead with a briefcase and a small box shaped like a dumbbell — the phone device he'd seen in the office.

"I see him; he's on this block," said Dean, pedaling past. "He's going to one of the phones."

"Charlie, this is great," said Telach, breaking in. "But we need more time to map the pay phones out so we can intercept the call."

"He hasn't dialed yet," said Dean, watching as the man pulled a laptop out and booted it up. It took almost a minute for the laptop to run through its start-up routine; as it did, the man got the phone device ready. "Looks like he's almost ready to call," said Dean finally.

"We still need another minute," said Telach.

Dean swung the bike around without looking — and nearly got flattened by a bus he hadn't even heard. He rode back in the direction of the man, who was just putting down his briefcase.

"Hey!" Dean said.

"No, speak French," said Chafetz. "Tell him you're lost."

A translator jumped on the line and gave Dean a few phrases, telling him how to say that he was lost and he was looking for the medina.

The man responded by pulling out a pistol.

"Sixty seconds more," said Telach.

"English? Do you speak English then?" said Dean.

The man lifted the pistol.

"Why are you holding a gun at me?" said Dean.

"Get out of there, Charlie!" yelled Chafetz.

The man said something in Arabic.

"He says go or die," said the translator.

"*Oui*, OK. Yes, yes, I'm going," said Dean. He held his hands out at the man and gestured again that he would go. He grabbed the bike and started to back up — then seemed to lose his grip and drop it.

The man said something in Arabic.

Charlie grabbed the bike and turned around, pushing the pedals in earnest now.

"We've got it covered," said Telach. "Good going."

"Give me directions back to Lia," Dean said.

The drainpipe pulled away from the house as Lia grabbed it to climb back up, so she decided it would be easier to go around to the next building and climb up the fire escape. When she reached the second floor she saw that someone was near the window, and waited for a few minutes until deciding she could pull herself up on the other side without being seen. Lia did the same on the third floor, scrambling onto the roof.

She retrieved her gear, unloading and stowing the gun in its case and then pulling the strap over her rucksack. As she rose, there was a noise on the roof behind her. Lia swung around, not sure if it was Dean; a shadow appeared across the way near the fire escape ladder, then disappeared. Lia sprinted after it, pulling a small Glock handgun from her waistband as she crossed the roof. She reached the edge in a few bounds and bolted over the side, jumping down the ladder to the next landing, where the figure had just descended. The shadow tried to escape through the window, but Lia grabbed hold, pulling it out and sticking the pistol in its face.

The face of a nine-year-old-boy, shaking like a leaf, eyes like acorns.

She stared into them, saw his fear.

Is that how I looked to them? Is that how I look to everyone, now?

Lia pushed the boy away, then went down to the street. Dean was waiting on his bike.

"What were you doing?" he said.

"Making mistakes," she told him brusquely, brushing past.

46

Rubens sat in one of the empty seats in the Art Room's theater-style layout, staring at the screen saver on the computer monitor in front of him. A multicolored object floated across the screen, morphing into different forms as it came to each edge of the viewing area. The changes seemed random but were actually determined by a pair of complex mathematical formulas whose results only *looked* random when viewed over a short period of time. If you stared at the screen long enough a pattern would begin to emerge.

Intelligence gathering worked like that. Seemingly random bits of information had to be stitched together from a wide variety of sources to reveal themselves as something generated by a purposeful formula. This was, in Rubens' opinion, the reason that those trained in mathematics and cryptography were so good at intelligence work: they knew there were formulas behind what others saw as unrelated information flitting through the universe.

But there was also a danger that truly random events might be misinterpreted as being part of a nonexistent pattern. Or worse, unconnected strands might be erroneously connected, leading the analyst in the wrong direction.

Was that happening now? The man Dean had followed had used an antiquated analog coupling device to send a very short piece of information to a computer bulletin board in France. The technology was so old — it dated from the mid-1980s — that under other circumstances the NSA wouldn't have bothered paying any attention.

Ninety seconds after the transmission, the weather site on the World Wide Web that Rubens had discussed with Johnny Bib had been rewritten, two minutes ahead of normal schedule.

According to Johnny Bib, the change was doubly significant — not only was it outside the normal pattern of updates, but it also didn't alter a temperature as the other ones had. Instead, it involved a forecast three days ahead.

The change was subtle: "cloudy" became "thunderstorms." At the regular update time, the old prediction was restored.

Surely this meant something . . . or was it a simple programming mess-up?

The potential intersection of the two Desk Three missions — one to find missing atomic material, the other to find a chemist who might have made explosives for terrorists — was both tantalizing and frightening.

But was it a pattern or a non-pattern, meaningful or random noise?

"Boss, Lia and Charlie are clear. You want them back here?" asked Telach.

"No. Have them go to France. Tell them . . ."

He paused, not knowing exactly what to tell them.

"Have them go to Paris, spend the night, relax a little," he said.

"Relax?"

"If nothing specific develops, they can back up Tommy Karr. Let's let Lia catch her breath for a few hours. Contact Tommy — I want him to see if he can get more information from Monsieur LaFoote on the Web sites that were used to transmit instructions. Why wasn't his friend suspicious? Or was he? What else does he know about the e-mails or domains? See if he can find out what computer his friend used to go on these sites, that sort of thing. And check if there were others."

"He did already try. I'm not sure how technically competent the old guy is, let alone how much he really knows. Tommy worked him over pretty well while they were watching the police search the house. There are two more CD-ROMs, and possibly some information about an account that Vefoures had that we haven't been able to track down on our own. Otherwise — well, you know Tommy. He's everybody's best friend. I don't know that LaFoote is holding back too much else. Certainly not about computers."

"Have him try anyway. LaFoote may not know he knows. Where is Tommy?"

"Tommy went back to Paris to dump the information on the disk for us, and LaFoote stayed back in Aux Boix, where he lives. We had a CIA agent follow him back to his house. He was still there last time I checked. I told Tommy to get some rest. He's supposed to meet LaFoote at nine p.m. their time."

"All right. Let Tommy get some rest," said Rubens. "But when he checks in, have him try and move up his meeting with LaFoote."

"You don't want the CIA agent to get involved, right?"

Rubens gave her a withering look. "Do you feel he would succeed where Tommy wouldn't?"

"I just wanted to check. It does seem —"

"Like a random pattern that doesn't actually cohere?"

"I was going to say wild-goose chase."

Rubens got up from the console. "What is Johnny Bib doing?"

"His team has the servers under surveillance," said Telach. "They're trying to trace anyone who accesses these pages."

"Let me know if they come up with anything. I'll be upstairs."

At the very moment Rubens was asking about him, Johnny Bib was hovering over the shoulder of a cryptologist who'd been shanghaied into serving as a computer operator, trying to track the different queries onto the Web site they thought was being used to send codes through the terrorist network. The tracing work was done by a small program the techies called Spider Goblin 3. It was an extremely sophisticated version of the so-called spy programs used by commercial Web sites to track interested visitors to their Web sites. Spider Goblin 3 spat out a list of different nodes on the net showing where requests for the information had come from; this list was then compared to earlier captures of information to see if there were any matches.

There were literally thousands, as a typical request for a Web site might pass through twelve or more "nodes" on the World Wide Web network as it made its way to and back from the place where the information was kept. The difficulty wasn't that all this information was impossible to obtain — it was there for the taking. The question was what significance it had. Working on the theory that a computer used for one bad purpose might be used for another — as if it were a car owned by a gang who robbed banks and gas stations — Johnny Bib decided to look at the contents of the computers used in accessing the site. The trick was choosing which ones to examine.

Fortunately, this could be placed in the hands of a complicated mathematical formula, which Johnny and his team had compiled the day before. It had involved a great deal of probability work, and thus much of it had been designed by the team's statisticians — a fault, Johnny Bib believed, since statisticians were by nature imprecise and even messy. They were willing to live with errors in their work, which they classified as "inevitable." For Johnny Bib, nothing was inevitable. Unknown, perhaps, but not inevitable.

But even a mathematician sometimes had to compromise by rounding off. Numbers existed in the real world, after all.

"Yo, Johnny Bib, Johnny Bib," said Tristan Young. "Looky, looky, looky."

Johnny Bib practically hopped across the room to the console where Tristan was working. Twenty-three years old, Tristan's real calling was string theory and "real" cryptography, but he had been pressed into service in the computer area by a personnel shortage.

"Look at this," said Young. "Looky, looky, looky." He pointed to a solid screen of alpha numerals.

Johnny stared for a few seconds but could not discern a pattern. "Assembler code?" he guessed.

"No, no," said Tristan. "French and German car registrations. Watch."

Tristan hit a few keys and the wall of digits transformed itself into a list, punctuated at regular intervals by gibberish.

"Wonderful work," said Johnny Bib. "And where is the computer?"

"A dentist's office in a town near Marseilles, France."

"It accessed the Web site after it was changed?"

"Right before."

"Before?"

"Then again, like, oops, my clock is a little fast. Heh, heh, heh."

Johnny Bib straightened and considered this.

"The phone number for that bulletin board that was called from the pay phone in Morocco was in this same town," added Tristan.

"Very good," said Johnny Bib. "Very, very good."

"Looks like the dentist's computer has been hijacked," added Tristan. "We think there are other computers, spread out across the country, that are used for various chores. There are several Internet accounts associated with the owner of the phone that was called, which of course turns out to be a name we cannot find in any other record."

Johnny Bib looked at the registration numbers. Not one on the first page was prime.

Interesting. A coincidence probably, but interesting. A sign, definitely, that they were on the right track.

"We're checking the registrations and

tracing the other computers one by one. The whole nine yards, heh, heh, heh," added Tristan.

"Why is it nine yards?" asked Johnny.

"Don't know."

"A significant mystery," said Johnny, nodding. "Keep me informed."

47

They caught the last possible plane to Paris that night, an old Boeing 737 operated by a Spanish airline Dean had not only never heard of but which also apparently operated only one aircraft — this one.

The plane sat at the gate for nearly an hour after they boarded. Dean took out the World War I book he'd "borrowed" from the British and read about a wounded German calling to the Marine for help in the dark. The author wondered whether he should put the German out of his misery or take him prisoner. Doing either involved great risk, since he'd be exposing himself to anyone hiding nearby, as well as to the man himself, who might have a concealed weapon. The writer spoke honestly and simply of his uncertainty.

Something similar had happened to Dean in Vietnam: he'd come across a North Vietnamese soldier lying in the brush, stomach full of blood. The man babbled something in Vietnamese; Dean thought he was begging to be killed.

Dean's job was to kill the enemy. He wasn't squeamish about it. He'd taken down a Vietcong officer (or at least someone suspected of being one) just a few hours before. But for some reason he couldn't bring himself to kill this man.

What had stopped him? To this day he couldn't say.

Did war stay the same, or did men?

Lia curled her body tight against the corner of the seat, wedging herself next to the window.

All I need to do is sleep, she told herself. *Sleep will cure this.*

It didn't, though. The few hours' dozing on the plane left her restless and stiff, and every bit as confused and scared and unsure as she'd been before.

Lia had trouble finding the ATM at Charles de Gaulle Airport, even though she'd been at the airport dozens of times just in the past two years. It turned out to be only a few yards from the gate where she exited. Then she couldn't remember the PIN on the ATM card she was carrying, even though the support team always set the PINs on her cards to the same sequence. It took a monstrous amount of effort not to start kicking the machine, to calm down, to ask the Art Room for help.

She found Dean on the taxi line.

"You look tired," he told her.

"As if you don't," she snapped.

He didn't say anything else.

"Concorde Lazare," she told the taxi driver when they got in. The man started telling them in French what a nice place it was. *"Oui,"* she said. Then she switched to English. "Just drive there, though, OK?"

Dean turned and gave her a dirty look. "Excuse us," he said in English. "My friend has not had much sleep. I apologize for her."

Lia thought she, too, should apologize, but it was much easier not to say anything at all.

48

Many people say they would like to die in their sleep, but wasn't that a bit of unexamined foolishness? To die in one's sleep meant to have no chance to set one's affairs straight — to have no chance, really, to rage against the coming of the darkness, to hold out, to gasp a few breaths, to resolve to be brave one final time: to meet the ultimate fate with courage, the only real asset one took into old age.

To die in one's sleep meant to slip into the next life as a passive victim, and Denis LaFoote had never been in his whole life a passive victim. Something deep inside him rebelled at the whisper of death. He found himself struggling as if under deep water and pushed himself toward the surface. He was dreaming and then he was not dreaming — strong hands pushed against him, weighty arms that belonged to a man of flesh and blood, not some nightmare summoned from the dark places of his past. LaFoote pushed upward, calling on the muscles of his once-athletic shoulders and arms to help. The seventy-one-year-old man pushed and shoved toward the light above. He could feel himself choking, but he did not give in; he wasn't tempted by the sweet warmth he began to feel around his eyes, the lull of more sleep.

"Non!" he shouted. *"Non."*

He did not give up, to the bitter end.

Patrick Donohue sat at the edge of the bed after it was over. It had been some time since he had chosen to kill a man so personally, and he needed a moment to adjust.

Not to get over it, simply to adjust.

The old man had proven stronger than he would have guessed, but there were many benefits to having killed him with no weapon other than the pillow. For one, it was possible that a country coroner might completely miss the fact that his death was a homicide. The struggle had dimmed that possibility, as he'd had to push down heavily on the man's arms and chest with his body, which would leave telltale marks. But the chance had been worth taking.

Given that the coroner was likely to see the obvious, Donohue decided to supply a motive. He went to the old man's dresser, looking for his wallet. There were only thirty euros in the wallet; he took them. Then he rifled through the drawers quickly, finding nothing of any worth. In the living room, there was a strongbox with old franc notes — a considerable sum, well over two hundred thousand, which would translate roughly into forty thousand euros if taken to a bank. Donohue scattered a few around to make it clear that he had stolen them, then stuffed the rest in his pockets.

He made his exit from the house carefully. There was a policeman or some sort of official watching from a car up the block, who could only be avoided by using the windows at the back of the house. He'd seen the man arrive shortly after LaFoote, which added interest though not particular trouble to the job.

A half hour later, just outside of Paris, he called one of the numbers Mussa had given for reporting on the job.

"Done," he said.

49

When Tommy Karr woke up in the Paris safe house, he discovered two messages on the telephone number he had given Deidre. Both had been left the day before. One asked if he was "up to anything" the next day, and the other said that she would be outside the Picasso museum at 11:00 a.m., adding that she wouldn't mind continuing their tour. The museum wasn't that far from her residence, and she made it sound as if it was a casual idea, but Karr suspected a more elaborate plot.

Which he wholeheartedly approved of.

But duty came first.

The Art Room wanted him to try pushing up the meeting with LaFoote, who according to his CIA shadow had returned home and not stirred since. Karr called the retired French agent but didn't get an answer.

"You sure he's inside?" Karr asked Telach.

"Our CIA friend hasn't seen him leave,"

she answered. "It's still early. Maybe he's sleeping."

"It's also possible he gave Sherlock the slip," said Karr.

"Should I have him knock on the door?"

Karr thought about this for a moment. He didn't want LaFoote to think he didn't trust him. If he was home and wasn't answering the phone, obviously he'd draw that conclusion, no matter how the CIA officer tried to cover his appearance at the door.

And if he'd slipped away?

Well, good for the old codger then. Sending the CIA agent to play vacuum-cleaner salesman wasn't going to help.

"Nah. Just have him hang out. I'll check back later."

Karr caught some coffee — the French seemed to insist on far too much milk — then paid a visit to some of his CIA friends to get their opinions of Ponclare and his department.

Overworked and underpaid.

Which made the fact that he had a very nice apartment in the Marais area of Paris — the ultra-chic section, not the old Jewish quarter — more than a little interesting.

Karr did a little more checking. Ponclare's family had once been very well off but had lost nearly everything by the time of World

War II; the war finished off whatever small assets they had. As Rockman had told him, Ponclare's father had been a renowned French citizen, honors all around — but few francs in the bank, or at least so it seemed. Ponclare more or less had followed in his father's footsteps.

But over the last four or five years — since coming to Paris — Ponclare had managed not only to buy the expensive apartment but also to repurchase two of the family's estates. The French themselves had been interested in this, according to a rumor the CIA hands told Karr, but it wasn't clear if there had been a formal investigation.

The Desk Three op then ventured over to the Marais area to look up a retired American intelligence officer who had known Ponclare's father, but the retiree added little beyond the press clippings Karr had already seen. When LaFoote still didn't answer his phone, Karr decided to get an early lunch. Coincidentally, he happened to be only a few blocks from the Picasso museum. Karr swung over in that direction and arrived outside the walls just as Deidre herself was arriving.

"Fancy meeting you here," he told her.

"What a coincidence," she said,

kissing him on the cheek.

Karr tried taking the kiss in stride, though he felt himself blush.

They went inside the stone courtyard, Deidre explaining the history of the building as they walked toward the entrance. The collector of the salt tax had built it with money he'd skimmed from the tax, she said; unfortunately, the King figured out what was going on and the property was soon sold to pay for what he'd skimmed. Penniless and out of a job, the salt collector lived the rest of his life around the corner as a janitor.

"There's a more complicated version," said Deidre. "But that gets the highlights."

Inside, Karr found that there was an advantage to walking around an art museum with an art student: Deidre had interesting stories to go with each painting. Karr had never exactly been an art lover and wasn't one when they left the building an hour later — but he was definitely in love with Deidre.

Or at least, very serious *like*.

He led Deidre to a nice and inexpensive café a few blocks away that she claimed not to know. He excused himself and hit the men's room, first trying LaFoote — no answer — and then connecting with the Art Room.

"We have nothing new for you," Telach told him.

"I keep trying to get ahold of LaFoote, but there's no answer," said Karr. "What's our spook say?"

"Hasn't seen anything."

"Maybe I'll just shoot out there after lunch," said Karr. He actually doubted that LaFoote was there, but it would give him a chance to look over the town — and maybe see who the priest was whom he trusted. "Unless you have something else."

"No, I was going to suggest that myself."

"What's up with Charlie and Lia?"

"They're in Paris resting."

"Yeah?"

"They just got in. I told them to sleep. So how's Deidre?"

"Jeez, Marie, you sound like my mom."

"Just making conversation," said the Art Room supervisor. "Word is, I'm going to have to read you directive one-oh-three-seventeen-b soon."

"I'm guessing that's about fraternization with ambassadors' daughters." Karr laughed. "Did you make that up, or is that a real directive?"

"It may be real by the time you get back, Tommy. Check in when you're on the train."

50

"The Eiffel Tower in meters."

Rubens looked at the number on the small bundle of papers that Johnny Bib and his assistant Tristan Young had brought with them to his office. He had no doubt that Johnny Bib was correct — Johnny was never wrong about a number — but was it significant?

"As you can see on the next page," continued Johnny, "it is part of a formula regarding the integrity of the structure — and, by implication, how to bring it down."

Rubens flipped over to the next page as Johnny Bib continued, launching into a discussion of cosines and engineering formulas that Rubens couldn't decipher. The page he was looking at showed a series of hexadecimal numbers captured from the hard drive of a computer, the remains of a file that had been erased and partially filled with other data. The file had been deleted and then overwritten, but NSA analysts had extracted some of its remains —

they were outlined by yellow highlighter —
and supplied the missing contents.

Or what they *thought* were the missing
contents. More than 50 percent of the file
was gone.

The computer was located in a French
library and had apparently been "hijacked"
for use, the idea being to eliminate the possibility that any incriminating evidence
would be found on a local hard drive. It
was an elaborate precaution but not one
without its own risks, as the computers targeted could not be secured.

"What's on the rest of the drive?"
Rubens asked.

"That's my point. My point!" said
Johnny Bib. "There are files we can't access. We need the physical drive."

Rubens glanced at Tristan. He had an
embarrassed, almost guilty look on his
face. Whether that was good or bad
Rubens couldn't decide.

"Why can't we access the rest of the
files?" Rubens asked Tristan. "Is it encrypted?"

"No, sir. Physical errors. There are problems with the drive. Part of it is locked off
by the control program that runs at boot-
up and we can't access it without catching
it just as it boots. And they boot it physi-

cally, then connect to the drive. So we pretty much have to be there when it comes up, heh."

"You can't override the control program?" asked Rubens. "Delete it and restore it?"

"I can't without it being obvious that something's going on," said Tristan. "We're not one hundred percent sure we won't end up corrupting the drive worse. Physically having the drive is really the way to go here."

"The drive is a sixty-gigabyte drive," said Johnny Bib. "Only forty-three-point-three-six-seven-eight gigabytes are available. If we have it, worst-case scenario, even if it's written over, we can examine the flux and reconstruct it."

Rubens rubbed his forehead. The technique Johnny Bib referred to was a process that got around so-called "scrubber" or "shredding" programs, which overwrote data with specific patterns to obscure it. The technique depended on a series of high-powered electronic microscopes to physically examine the magnetic traces left as data was recorded and rerecorded. It was an extremely powerful if somewhat esoteric technique — and also expensive and time-consuming.

"You're sure that there's something there?" said Rubens.

"Not until we see it," said Tristan. "But the error log noted that the problem occurred at the same date and time the file was first overwritten — they mirror the directory and logs to another computer, where we, heh, found it."

"You're sure this malfunction isn't part of whatever hijacking program they installed?" asked Rubens.

"It's not part of the program," said Tristan. "But that is a possibility."

"If it is, it's a type we haven't seen," said Johnny Bib. "Which would be another reason to retrieve the disk drive."

"If the bad sectors occurred when the area was scrubbed, they would be easy to retrieve," said Tristan. "Kind of, heh, the reverse of what was intended."

"Where is it?" asked Rubens.

"We're working on the physical location now through trial and error," said the young man. "It's somewhere in a district that includes Paris, but there are a lot of libraries to query. We should have it within an hour, maybe a little less."

"You're sure there's no one in the library who knows?" asked Rubens.

"I don't think so," said Young. "The

whole idea of setting it up this way would be because you're worried about a physical search of your premises. And besides, the computer that led us here was in a dentist's office. It seems to have been used by a stolen car ring. First, we started looking at the patterns of when the computer was accessed —"

Rubens put up his hand. "I'm sure I would admire your technique as well as your fortitude, Mr. Young. Well done. But candidly, it's not relevant at the moment."

Rubens shifted the papers on his desk and took another printout, this one summarizing the data on the CD-ROM Tommy Karr had obtained. It had information about shaping plastic explosives, apparently from a secret French initiative undertaken a few years before. The files on the CD-ROM were all several years old and did not prove that the explosive was in the hands of terrorists. Nonetheless, the pattern was coming into sharper focus.

At least for Rubens.

"Johnny, would a carload of these explosives be able to destroy the Eiffel Tower? Could this explosive be fit into the equation you reconstructed?"

Johnny Bib blinked at him but didn't answer.

"That didn't occur to you?" said Rubens. "You didn't put these two things together?"

Johnny Bib blinked again.

Was it such an obvious question that the analysts had missed it?

Apparently, yes. Johnny Bib turned without saying anything and left the office.

Young blinked, unsure what to do.

"Find a similar disk drive in France and have it prepared so our ops can swap it," Rubens told him. "And please, find the library, or wherever this computer is. Call me — no, call the Art Room. I have to leave for the White House within the hour."

51

The trip on the train from Paris to Aux Boix took less than twenty minutes. Tommy Karr spent most of them staring out the window, thinking of Deidre. He'd never felt so distracted before, as if his mission were just a sideline job.

But of course it wasn't, and he snapped back in focus with the first step onto the railroad platform. LaFoote's house was an easy fifteen-minute stroll away; Karr made it in ten.

The CIA shadow sat in a rather conspicuous Renault at the end of the block. The CIA officer nearly jumped when Karr knocked on the window.

"He's still inside, huh?" asked Karr as he rolled down the window.

"Oh yeah."

"You can see the back from here?"

Karr leaned over the windshield, answering his own question. He did have a view of the backyard, but with a little care it would be possible to use the hedges at the side to crawl away without being seen.

"I can see. Nobody came or went," said the CIA officer testily.

"You do a lot of surveillance work?"

"No. He hasn't come out. Look — there's his car, right?"

"You sat here the whole time?"

"Of course. You just wanted him protected, right? Without knowing I was here. And no police, no DST, nobody."

"Yeah," said Karr.

"So?"

There *were* good CIA people, Karr thought to himself, plenty of them. But clearly this wasn't one.

"Can I go home now?" asked the CIA officer. "I haven't had any sleep."

"Hang out for just a little while longer," Karr said. "You talking to my people?"

"On a sat phone."

"Good."

Karr straightened, then strolled down toward LaFoote's house. As he suspected, there was no answer when he knocked at the front door. He looked in the window, saw nothing, then ducked around the side, looking for a back door.

"Looks like LaFoote ducked our CIA rental," Karr told Rockman.

"Figures," answered the runner.

There was no back door. Karr glanced through one of the windows, debating whether to go inside and search the house before LaFoote got back.

His hesitation vanished when he peeked through the window of what looked like a study and saw that papers were scattered on the floor of LaFoote's living room.

"I'm going inside," Karr told Rockman. "Make sure our lookout stays awake."

"What's up?"

"I don't know yet. But either the old guy is a lousy housekeeper or he's had guests."

Karr used his handheld computer to scan for a burglar alarm or booby trap, then opened the window and let himself in. The papers on the floor were franc notes, and there was an empty strongbox nearby.

He found LaFoote inside the bedroom, a grotesque look on his face. Even though he knew LaFoote was dead, Karr checked for a pulse. The body was on the cold side.

"Sucks," he said aloud.

"You want Knox to come inside?" prompted the Art Room supervisor, Chris Farlekas. Farlekas had just come on to spell Telach. "Your CIA guy?"

"Better keep him where he is or I may strangle him," said Karr, who for once in his life wasn't kidding. He corralled his anger and began searching the house for the other CDs.

"You have somebody coming up the walk toward the front door," warned Rockman about five minutes later.

"All right, thanks. I'll stay out of the front rooms. Tell Knox to warn me if he goes around the side."

Where would the old man keep the disks? As a veteran spy, he surely knew all the best hiding places — but he would also realize that all of the best spots could be found. Karr looked around the room, remembering LaFoote going through his friend's house. The walls were all plasterboard, completely intact and the paint years old. If the disks had been hidden in the strongbox they were gone.

The doorbell rang. Karr kept looking.

"Tommy, we just checked on the license plate," said Rockman. "That's a relative, same name, one of the nephews or something. Knox thinks he may have a key, because he's reaching into his pocket."

Karr looked around the room. The best place to leave CDs would be with other CDs. Since LaFoote didn't have a computer of his own, Karr looked for a stereo. But LaFoote didn't seem to have one of those, either. The op went back to the bedroom and bent to the mattress, sliding his hand underneath — he found a thin knife but no CDs.

LaFoote's lifeless eyes stared at him as he walked over to the bureau.

Nothing. He went back out into the living room, checking the bookcase. Nothing.

He walked into the kitchen, opened the oven on a hunch.

"Tommy, you *have* to get out of there," said Farlekas.

The door at the front of the house opened.

The oven was empty as well. Karr turned, then saw the large brown envelope on the counter, as if waiting to be mailed. It was addressed to a Father Brossard.

"Good thinking," said Karr, grabbing it.

"Denis?" said a male voice at the front of the house. "*Denis? Qu'est-ce-que c'est?*" The man started toward LaFoote's bedroom.

"Tommy!" Farlekas practically shouted.

"I'm out of here," he said, pulling himself out the window.

52

The national security adviser rubbed his hand across his forehead, as if he were trying to manipulate some part of his brain through the skin and skull. Then he leaned across the long table in the White House situation room, his voice reverberating against the paneled walls of the nearly empty conference room.

"What do we know for sure here?" Hadash asked Rubens. "You have a lot of guesses strung together."

"I agree," said Rubens. "But the information is provocative. I'm told that the stolen-car ring is run by a man named Mussa Duoar, who was born in Algeria. He's a Muslim, and apparently not a French citizen although he's lived in the country for at least ten years, if not more."

"Why isn't he a citizen?" asked President Marcke.

"I don't know," said Rubens. "Possibly a matter of choice. The family name seems to come up in connection with the

Algerian independence movement in the nineteen-sixties, but you could probably say that about half the population."

Marcke nodded. Though only Hadash, Rubens, Vice Admiral Brown, the President, and CIA Director Jake Namath were at the meeting, it was being held in the large room beneath the White House to facilitate easy communications with the Secretary of State, who had already left for Paris ahead of the President's scheduled visit. The Secretary of State's worried image filled a video screen nearby.

"The target would fit with other intercepts from the Middle East as a very high-value symbol," said Rubens. "This would be a grand slam for them, the equivalent in France of the World Trade Center. The impact in Europe would be immense. Immeasurable. And it makes sense given Arab and Muslim reaction to France's increased cooperation with the U.S. on security matters following their embarrassment over Iraq. They've been burning French flags in Egypt and Palestine for the past eight months. They'll go crazy with this."

"But how credible is the information?" asked Namath. "We're always getting this sort of background chatter."

"I think this goes beyond background

chatter," said Rubens. "There are gaps, certainly, but these things don't present themselves as complete pictures."

"There *are* major gaps here," said Hadash.

"Yes," conceded Rubens. "But the time factor is critical. If we interpret the date on the site as being significant."

"You have no idea if it has any significance at all," said Namath. "You told us that yourself. Is it saying this is the date we will strike? Or is it saying wait until the weather turns cloudy?"

Before Rubens could rebut him, Marcke cut in.

"We have to inform the French," said the President. "Think if the situation were reversed and this was the Statue of Liberty we were talking about — we'd want to know. Absolutely. And now. With as many details as we can provide."

"I doubt they'll believe us," said Namath.

"They may or they may not," agreed the President. "That's their call."

"They'll want specifics," said Lincoln.

"As would I," said Marcke.

Rubens had no problem sharing the eavesdropping information they had obtained from Morocco — it didn't involve sensitive technology, nor was the source on

French soil. The information about the computers was somewhat more delicate, but the work had been done from the United States and it provided a vital clue; there was no way it could be left out.

Telling them about the chemist, however, would make it clear that the Americans were running an operation on French soil. It was one thing for everyone to know that this sort of thing went on and quite another to admit it openly.

"Telling them about the French source would add a great deal of credibility," said the Secretary of State.

"That's letting them in too deeply," objected Brown. "And it may endanger our people."

"I doubt they'll assassinate your people," said the President drily.

"Agreed," said Rubens. "However, the Frenchman LaFoote believes the head of Paris security was involved."

"Unlikely," said Namath.

"Perhaps," said Brown. "But if he was, our people would definitely be at risk."

"They're at risk now," said Namath.

"The French don't know about our operation," said Rubens.

"I think any data we have we should share," said Lincoln.

But Rubens and Brown stuck to their position, and eventually Hadash backed them up; together they worked out an arrangement that would leave LaFoote and, more important, the Deep Black agents unmentioned. They would also leave out the fact that the explosives involved seemed to have been made by a chemist who had worked for the French government — but at the same time supply enough technical data about what they perceived the threat to be. The French would figure out what the explosives were, even though they would be given the impression that the Americans didn't know who had helped develop them.

"You think they would turn around and track the chemist, what's his name, on their own?" asked Namath.

"Vefoures," said Rubens. "They may. They're welcome to. We've tried. He's gone, almost surely killed. It's the car thief we need, Mussa Duoar," added Rubens. "He's connected to the computers. He's a devout Muslim. He has connections in the underworld. And to terrorists. He's in the middle of this."

"Car thieves don't blow up national monuments," said Namath.

"They also usually don't gather money

for terrorists," said Rubens. "Or have connections with radical Muslims."

"Connections that don't necessarily add up to anything except coincidences," said Namath.

"Granted, I'm making a leap," conceded Rubens.

"What about the warhead that's missing?" asked the President.

"Definitely still a concern," said Rubens. "Mussa was from Algeria."

"More connections," said Namath.

"Admittedly, it may be a coincidence. We have nothing tying him or any of this to the warhead. What we've seen so far are conventional explosives, the exact type that Vefoures was working on," said Rubens. He turned to Namath. "We have no indication that the warhead is involved and as far as I know it hasn't been located, unless you've found it."

Namath's frown made it clear that the CIA hadn't.

"The explosive could be used to fashion a triggering device for a nuke," said Hadash.

"Absolutely," said Rubens. "But it would be no easier with this explosive than with another. And quite frankly, such lenses are not easily constructed. You've seen all the trouble the Pakistanis have had."

"It would be easier to overengineer," said Hadash. "To compensate for the inferior lens."

"It would be a big bomb then," said Rubens.

"But that's what we're talking about."

Rubens conceded that he couldn't completely rule out the possibility that the warhead was involved, but even Namath had to admit that there wasn't any indication that it was. The discussion shifted over to other possible targets.

As the conversation continued, Rubens noticed that Hadash began glancing at his watch every few minutes. He obviously had a busy schedule today and even though it was still very early in the morning would want to push things along to wrap up quickly. Hadash and the President would be leaving Washington at 2:00 a.m. tomorrow, and Rubens knew from experience that the national security adviser would want to finish early and sneak home for a nap before boarding the plane. The President never bothered with such strategies; he seemed never to be affected by jet lag, either.

"What do you think the odds are that the French will believe us?" President

Marcke finally asked Rubens.

"Truthfully, I'm not sure."

"Admiral?"

"Not sure."

"Linc?"

"I don't know," said the Secretary of State.

The President turned to Hadash with the same question.

"About as much as if they told us the White House was being targeted," said the national security adviser.

I hope more than that, thought Rubens, though he didn't say it.

"How did the General's court hearing go?" asked Brown on the helicopter back to Crypto City.

"It was an informal meeting with the judge," said Rubens. He explained that the judge had appointed a lawyer to represent the General.

"Stay on top of it," said Brown.

"I'm trying," said Rubens. "There's a medical examination this afternoon."

"You'll be there?"

"I hope to be."

"You should try."

The secure phone buzzed in Ruben's briefcase; he was only too happy for the excuse to end the conversation.

"Rubens," he said, snapping the phone on.

"Johnny Bib says the explosives fit the Eiffel Tower program precisely," said Chris Farlekas. "They've located the library and he wants to go ahead and recover the hard drive."

"How difficult will it be?" Rubens asked Farlekas.

"Unknown until we get somebody in to look at the setup. But I'd think it'd be a piece of cake. It's a small library outside of Paris. The drive itself isn't anything special — you could replace it in a few minutes or so. There's a similar size one in the Paris safe house and we can upload the legitimate programs within an hour, maybe less. Whatever is on that locked-out section, of course, stays locked out."

On the one hand, the sectors had been locked out because of a physical error on the drive, then it would be unlikely that anyone would realize they had taken it. On the other hand, if the locked-out space wasn't really bad — if what Johnny Bib and his people thought was a malfunction turned out to be a clever masking program they had never encountered before — then whoever was using it would know they were on their trail.

In an ideal world, Rubens would have preferred leaving the drive in place for a few weeks and setting up some sort of trap to catch whoever accessed it. But this wasn't an ideal world; he was simply going to have to take a risk, and it seemed to him that the risk with the least amount of fore-seeable downside was in grabbing the drive.

"Can Tommy get it after he meets with LaFoote?"

"That may be difficult. There were com-plications."

"What sort?"

"LaFoote is dead. Looks like murder."

"I see."

A confirmation that they were on the trail to *something*, he thought, though be-yond that was all speculation.

"Get Dean over there right away," Rubens told Farlekas.

"Charlie Dean? Change a computer drive?"

"Good point," said Rubens. "Send Lia with him to do the actual swap."

53

Father Brossard proved not to be at home when Karr called, and wasn't expected back until the next morning. The priest's housekeeper was from Kenya, and her English turned out to be somewhat better than her French. She explained that the priest had many churches to cover and traveled constantly around the local diocese.

"You think I should break in?" Karr asked Farlekas as he walked back toward Knox and the Renault.

"I don't think Mr. Rubens would approve breaking into a church."

"Sure he would," said Karr.

"We want to see what's on the disks you got from LaFoote's house," said the Art Room supervisor. "I think that's more important right now. The account information may not yield anything."

"How many hiding places can a priest have?" asked Karr.

"Let me see if I can get ahold of Mr. Rubens again. Stand by."

Karr walked over to the car where Knox was slumped back in the seat. The CIA officer had been both apologetic and defensive since Karr had discovered LaFoote dead.

More the latter.

"I need you to create a diversion," Karr told him. "Keep the housekeeper occupied."

"How?"

"Just talk to her."

"But —"

Karr leaned against the car, which sagged heavily under his weight. "Do what I say, all right?"

"I'm sorry. Yeah."

The back door to the parish house was open, and Karr had no trouble sneaking inside and getting up to the priest's room while Knox pretended to be a parishioner in need of immediate counseling. The ruse wasn't particularly apt — the parish was small enough that even the housekeeper knew just about everyone who lived in the area — but it gave Karr enough time to check the room, which had no furniture besides the bed and clearly wasn't hiding anything. He nearly got caught in the kitchen when the housekeeper came back, but the telephone saved him.

"You were supposed to wait," said Farlekas when Karr got back to the car.

"Yeah, but I'm done now," said Karr. "He doesn't have it in his room and he doesn't seem to have a study here. According to the housekeeper he travels among several parishes."

"Mr. Rubens said that if you couldn't find it easily, bring the CDs back to Paris. We're looking for the account on our end in the meantime."

"Sure? Church doesn't look like it's locked."

"Tommy."

"I'll call you from the safe house in Paris."

54

"Wake up. We have to go steal a computer from a library."

Dean jerked out of bed with a start. Lia was standing over him, frowning.

"How the hell did you get into my room?" he asked her. "I had the dead bolt set."

"Oh, Charlie. You're so naive."

Dean pulled his clothes on and went to the bathroom to shave. Just as he finished he heard a knock on the door; thinking it was Lia, he yelled to her to come in. A French voice answered, informing him it was room service with his coffee.

Suspicious, Dean took a towel and covered his pistol, opening the door for the man. He was, in fact, from room service, and he did have a large pot of coffee. Dean blanked on the cover name used for the reservation, so he scrawled a signature that could have been anything from John Doe to Napoleon on the receipt. He was on his second cup when Lia returned.

"I got a car. Come on, let's go," she said.

He grabbed the small knapsack that had met them at the airport as part of their mission equipment. Besides some maps, his handheld computer, and a sweater, the knapsack had a spare satellite phone.

"Where are we going?" Dean asked in the car.

"A library."

"You said that."

"Why'd you ask again?"

"You going to be like this for the rest of your life, or just the rest of the day?"

"Like what, Charlie Dean?"

Her habit of saying his whole name grated on him, but he didn't give her the satisfaction of complaining about it, especially not now.

He wanted to talk to her, to *really* talk. He wanted to let her know . . .

What?

That he cared. That he loved her.

"Look," he started. "I know you're still . . ."

The words failed him. He wasn't sure exactly what he wanted to say — or he did, but he couldn't put it into words that sounded real. He wanted to hold her, protect her — he hadn't done that, had he?

"I'm still what, Charlie Dean?"

392

"I love you," he said.

But her frown only deepened.

The computer was located in a small library in a town on the eastern outskirts of Paris. Unfortunately, the Art Room had no way of narrowing down which of the two dozen computers the libraries owned; each one had to be checked. The process was simple — they could tell simply from the directory — but it would require trying each machine, including those that weren't in the public areas.

Farlekas suggested that the Art Room sabotage the library's network. Lia would then go in as a techie to fix it. But the library closed at 5:00, and by the time they got out to the town it was already 4:30. Dean and Lia decided it was very possible the librarians would decide dinner was more important than fixing the machines and put it all off for the morning. Besides, Dean's lack of French meant he'd have to stay in the background, difficult to do if he was supposed to be a technician. So they decided they would go in, look the place over, then break in after it closed.

Lia dropped Dean off and parked the car two blocks away before doubling back. She walked in the door expecting to see Dean at one of the public access machines, hunting and pecking. But instead he was talking in English with the librarian.

And quite animatedly. The woman, in her early forties, gestured with her hand and led him toward the back offices.

"What the hell is he doing?" Lia muttered.

"Looking for information on a World War One Marine who stayed in the village after the war," said Farlekas in her ear. "Good idea for a cover, huh? He says he got it from a book he's been reading."

Lia stifled her response and went over to the computers used for the library catalog, trying them one by one. Dean soon reappeared, listening to the woman as she told him he could find all of the information he wanted online. She led him to the computers and then offered a cup of coffee, which he accepted with a very mispronounced, *"Merci."*

"Well, he's got the dumb-American act down pat," Lia said under her breath.

The machines used for searching the catalog had only thirty-gigabyte local hard drives. Lia drifted through the library, noticing a room at the side that had two computers but was empty. She was just about to go in and check them out when Farlekas announced, "He found it."

"You're kidding," she said.

"If you're going to talk to yourself," said the Art Room supervisor, "better use French."

The computers were at the edge of the open reading area, and Lia could watch Dean easily by pretending to look through the nearby stacks. He sat at a small desktop unit whose monitor was on top of the case; there was no hope of opening it unseen.

With the computer spotted, the next step was to check the security arrangements and plan for the break-in. Lia drifted to the side of the room, examining the large windows. A simple contact burglar alarm was wired to the sill; she slipped a knife from her pocket and slit the wire covering open, then used a small clip to short-circuit the connection and defeat the alarm. Then she took a small Phillips-head screwdriver from her pocket and removed the screws in the lock at the top of the window, which would give way now as soon as it was pushed open.

She had just finished when she heard a commotion coming from Dean's direction. Lia went there and found him madly trying to stanch the flow of a full cup of coffee before it reached the computer case. The librarian who had helped him before was standing next to him, fretting.

"We need more towels," he told the librarian in English. Then he turned to Lia and said, "Can you help me take up the monitor? There's liquid in the case. It'll get ruined. Please. I don't want to harm this nice librarian's machine."

"*Je ne comprends pas,*" Lia said, looking at the librarian. "I understand not much."

The librarian told her in French that she had spilled the coffee and was afraid the machine would explode and could she please help. The woman seemed on the verge of tears. Lia told her to get some towels and not to worry.

"Where's the drive?" Dean asked as she picked up the monitor.

"In my bag."

He reached in and grabbed the small hard drive, which was about half the size of a paperback book. The case had a hinge and was opened by pressing two detents at the side; Dean had only just gotten it open when the librarian returned. But he handled the whole thing smoothly, grabbing the towels from her and somehow managing to swirl more coffee around while seeming to wipe it up.

The hard drive sat in a cage at the front of the machine, held by four screws as well as its cables. Lia, still holding the monitor, tried to think of a long enough diversion that would let Dean swap the drives. Before she could, the phone at the front desk rang and the librarian dashed over to get it.

"Bit of a ditz," Lia said. "Take the monitor."

"Seemed pretty nice to me."

"Right."

Lia slid around and unscrewed the drive. She was sliding the new one in when the woman put down the phone and started toward them. Dean managed to swing around and block her view temporarily; Lia fussed over the computer but couldn't quite get the wires back before the librarian returned.

"Saved," Lia said in French, standing up with a pile of paper towels and holding them out toward the woman. "Where is the garbage?"

"Here, come with me," said the librarian.

"You have to connect the cables," Lia whispered to Dean.

"Cables?"

"So the drive works. They just plug right

in. Get at least two screws in. Ask the Art Room if you need help. Go."

Lia followed the woman to the ladies' room. The librarian thanked her — then asked what she thought of the helpful American.

"Very . . . helpful," said Lia. She tried to stall, but the librarian turned quickly to go back.

A bell began to ring.

"Closing," said the librarian. "You have it back? Very good."

"Closing," said Dean, standing back. "I think we saved it. Maybe — is there a good place to eat?" he asked the librarian. "In town around here?"

The librarian frowned as if thinking, then named two or three restaurants. Dean asked if she could give him directions.

"I could take you there," offered the librarian.

"Would you really?"

"Dean couldn't get the power plug to go in before she came out," Farlekas told Lia from the Art Room. "You're going to have to get it working."

Lia stifled a curse and told Dean in what seemed like rusty English that she hoped all Americans were like him.

"You'll have to go back," said Farlekas.

"Oui," muttered Lia, heading toward the door.

"How'd she know I was American?" Dean asked the librarian as the woman shut down the rest of the machines and began locking up.

55

It was a little past 11:00 a.m. when Rubens returned to Crypto City from his meeting at the White House. He went directly to the Art Room, where Tommy Karr was just checking in from Paris.

"You're not making any jokes," said Rubens when Karr finished updating him.

"No? Maybe I'm tired," said Karr.

"Understandable. We haven't been able to locate the priest?"

Rubens looked at Rockman for the answer, but Karr supplied it.

"The Art Room has been checking. He did a mass this morning and was at some sort of counseling thing this afternoon. I'll be at the church first thing in the morning."

"You're sure Vefoures had another account?" said Rubens.

"I don't think LaFoote made it up."

"Very well. Go there first thing. We've prepared a report for the French Interior Ministry on some of what we know," added Rubens. "On the President's orders."

"Is it going to Ponclare, too?" Karr's animosity was obvious.

"That will be their call," said Rubens.

"Ponclare's the guy that screwed LaFoote," said Karr. "He may be a traitor. He may even have killed the old man."

"You don't usually jump to conclusions, Tommy."

"I'm not saying he's a traitor, just that we ought to be careful."

"We always endeavor to be careful."

Tommy laughed, it wasn't his usual hearty roar.

56

The restaurant the librarian recommended turned out to be right down the street. It also, not coincidentally, happened to be *the* one to which she was going. Since the hour was early — the French rarely ate before seven — she suggested a drink at the bar.

"Stall for as long as you can," Farlekas told Dean. "Lia's just getting into the library now."

It wasn't exactly the most difficult order he'd ever had to follow. The woman's English was very good, and the wine wasn't all that bad, either. She asked him about America; he told her about California and asked about France.

The woman seemed to suddenly realize that she hadn't told him her name. "Marie," she said, holding her hand out across the table. Dean shook the hand, its warmth tickling him for just a moment.

He thought of Lia and felt guilty, as if he were cheating on her somehow. The drinks turned into a light dinner. The woman ended up walking him to the Metro line two blocks away. They exchanged e-mail addresses — and a pair of kisses. The woman watched as Dean bought a ticket and went down to the platform.

Lia was standing there, arms folded. She didn't acknowledge him.

"Excuse me, mademoiselle," he said, walking up over to her. "Didn't we meet in the library?"

Lia gave him a death-wish glare.

"Sorry, guess I was wrong," said Dean. The train came in, its rumble light because of the rubber wheels the metro used. Dean got into the car, expecting Lia to follow, but she didn't.

"She's getting the car. She's OK," said the Art Room when he checked what was going on. "She's got the drive and is going to take it directly to the airport. We have a plane standing by."

He went back to the hotel and sat on one of the plush couches in the ornate lobby, staring up at the mirrored ceiling. It was more than an hour later when Lia arrived. She didn't acknowledge him, walking briskly past the doorman to the elevators at the side. Dean waited for a second and then got up to follow, entering the elevator just as the doors closed.

"Thanks for holding the door," he said.

"You made it."

"Look, I know —"

"What do you know, Charlie Dean? What do you know?"

"I don't see why you're mad at me."

Her face flushed. The elevator stopped at the second floor and two people got in, standing between them. Lia turned around, as if interested in the next day's forecast, which was posted on a small piece of paper at the back of the elevator car.

He wanted to tell her he loved her, but there was no way he could speak. They went to their separate rooms, Dean so angry with himself that he forgot to scan the room first with the personal computer. He flipped on the television, sat back on the bed, then remembered that he had to check the room for bugs.

He had just turned on the PDA when someone knocked on the door. He jerked around, surprised.

"*Oui?*" he said, pulling out his pistol. "Yes?"

"I'm going for a walk," said Lia.

Dean stared at the door for a moment, then looked down at the gun in his hand.

"Yeah, so am I," he told her, stuffing the

gun back beneath his shirt and grabbing his jacket.

They waited for the elevator silently. Inside the car, Dean hit the stop button.

"You're going to set off an alarm," said Lia as the car paused between floors. Her lip trembled.

"Look, I don't know what happened to you in Korea. I know you got beat up. I'm sorry. But I love you. I do love you." The words were choking, but he forced himself to continue. "Look, I'm not good at this. I get, whatever, tongue-tied. But I do love you. And if I can do something to help you, I will. Just let me."

Lia's eyes had puffed up and he could tell she was fighting back tears. He pulled her toward him, but she was stiff in his arms, still distant.

It's not like it is in the movies, he thought. *I can't make it better just because I wish it were.*

57

After he finished talking to Rubens, Karr went up to Montmarte to see the second cousin LaFoote had stayed with in Paris. It turned out to be a waste of time; the cousin wasn't around and there was no way to let himself into the small street-level apartment without being seen. He went over and asked one of the nosier neighbors watching him from a nearby window if he knew where the man had gone; the woman answered civilly but curtly, telling him that Monsieur Terre's uncle had died and he was most likely with the family.

"You see anybody else poking around?" Karr asked the woman in French.

"*Tâtonner?*" she answered, repeating the infinitive form of the verb *poke*.

Karr held his hands out and apologized for his poor French, first in French and then in English, claiming to be a Canadian from Montreal who knew the older Monsieur LaFoote and had hoped to find him with his second cousin. That got her to lighten up just a little, and she told him that Monsieur Terre kept mostly to himself, except for his very nice uncle — the age difference made him seem more an uncle than a cousin. It was the same uncle, LaFoote, who now was gone, to everyone's great sorrow.

Tommy thanked her and borrowed a piece of paper to leave a note. He scribbled something and then went over to the cousin's front door, slipping it into the crack — then placing a set of bugging devices on the sill so the Art Room would know if the place was broken into.

Tommy went back to the embassy to use the phones and see if any of the local intelligence guys had anything useful. After a few fruitless attempts to locate the priest, Tommy decided he would take a break and called Deidre. He got her answering machine and on the spur of the moment told her he'd be at the bar of the Ritz on the Champs Elysées at eleven if she wanted to have a drink. Karr had never been to the Ritz and didn't actually know for a fact that the famous hotel had a bar. But what the hey.

Then he called the sister of LaFoote's friend Vefoures, whom LaFoote had spoken to the other day in the car via cell phone.

"I'm a friend of Monsieur LaFoote," he told her in French when she picked up. "I'm afraid I have bad news. Very bad news."

When the woman didn't answer, Karr told her that LaFoote had died and the police were investigating. When he finished, the woman asked what sort of friend he was.

"A new one," said Karr, laughing — but only for a moment. "I admired Monsieur LaFoote very much. We were working together on something. I'd like to ask you some questions about it. And about your brother."

"I don't know much," she said. And before Karr could say anything else she burst out crying. Her wails continued for quite a while; finally she hung the phone up without saying anything else. Karr decided the best thing to do was let her be.

Shortly before nine, Karr went over to Gare du Nord, the train station where he was supposed to meet LaFoote. He took two Marines from the embassy detail with him in plainclothes, hoping that whoever had killed the old French agent would be looking for him. But if someone was, neither Karr nor the Marines could spot the person. The Art Room grumbled about the lousy French video system, which covered only a small portion of the station, but even before the train from Aux Boix came in it was clear to Karr that the station wasn't being watched.

The Marines liked the cloak-and-dagger stuff well enough to suggest he join them for a drink when they went off-duty. He took a rain check, heading back to the embassy to see how the French had reacted to the Desk Three briefing on the Eiffel Tower threat.

The reaction could be summed up in one word: *Impossible!*

Despite the detailed brief Desk Three had prepared, despite the high-level contacts and the comprehensive information, the French simply didn't believe that the threat was anything more than American imagination run amok. Plots against the Eiffel Tower were very popular among crackpots and terrorist wannabes, but no serious campaign against the tower had ever been undertaken. And besides, as far as the French were concerned, Middle Eastern terrorists had no beef with them — France was a vigorous defender of Arab rights. Yes, there might be some dissension of late as the French moved to work more closely with their American allies, but why would anyone want to destroy the Eiffel Tower?

Karr couldn't really blame the French for not taking the threat seriously. He didn't see all of the connections himself. Johnny Bib's team had developed a theory that a car thief named Mussa Duoar had been working on a plan to topple the Eiffel Tower with a massive bomb blast at the base of the monument. Duoar seemed an unlikely terrorist: the man made a tidy living selling stolen automobiles, a fact that everyone in France except for the police seemed to know. More than likely the police *did* know it but had been paid to keep quiet; in any event, Duoar had escaped prosecution even though he had been investigated several times. Perhaps it helped that many of his cars seemed to have been stolen in Germany and England and then transported to France; few Frenchmen were the actual victims of his crimes.

Even with the lightweight high-yield explosive Vefoures had been working on, the analysts calculated that it would take a medium-sized bus to carry what was needed to destroy one of the four legs of the tower. That was a *lot* of explosives.

However, some of the materials needed

to make the explosive had been purchased by a dummy corporation Duoar used in his stolen-car ring.

The CIA and State Department intelligence people at the embassy were divided about how real the threat was. Karr listened to them debate and tried to remain neutral, despite their prodding. Finally he just got up and left the embassy, walking out of the grounds and down the Champs Elysées toward the Ritz. He checked in with the Art Room as he walked.

"Nothing new," said Telach. "You'd better get to bed."

"Thanks, Mom."

He turned off the communications system before she could protest.

58

It was the most beautiful paint job Mussa Duoar had ever seen. The blue swept toward the front of the truck, a wave of the ocean captured on the steel. Above it, the yellow swirl brightened the dark interior of the garage; it was as if the truck glowed with an intense fire.

Appropriate, thought Mussa.

It was all moving together now, his many strings pulled from their different directions. Four men came around to the back of his pickup truck and took the heavy cart from the back. Mussa's heart jumped as they nearly dropped it onto the concrete — it was protected against accidental shocks and there was no way for it to detonate accidentally, but even so . . .

They walked the box to the back of the van. The box was twice as heavy as the case it was dummied up to look like. But except for the wheels, which were slightly bigger (and considerably sturdier) than the wheels on the cart it was replacing, the difference would not be noticeable to anyone who didn't try to push it.

Or open it.

"Careful, please," Mussa said, following along behind the case. "Careful now. This has traveled a long way over many months."

The men slid it into the specially prepared compartment at the back of the van. Mussa once again felt his heart thump as one of the carriers lost his grip. But the others held the case firmly, and it was soon in the back of the truck. Five other carts, these a bit lighter than the first but still a hundred or so pounds heavier than the carts they were to replace, were loaded in behind it. Mussa examined the vehicle as the rear door was closed and locked. The heavy-duty shocks and suspension kept it from sagging; it, too, looked like the genuine article.

Very good. Very, very good.

"Listen, all of you," he said loudly. "Gather around — I appreciate your work."

He set down the satchel he'd carried in, bending to unlatch it. Just as his fingers touched the clasp he stopped and straightened.

"Anyone smell gas?" he asked. "Natural gas? Is the line off?"

The workers looked around at one another. There was a gas line to the garage, but it was used exclusively for the heaters and hadn't been turned on for the winter season yet.

"Call the boiler people to check it," he told one of the workers. "Call now. Get them to come."

The man looked at Mussa as if he were crazy. It was nearly midnight.

"Perhaps I am being overly cautious, but I am always concerned about your welfare," said Mussa. "Well, make the call so you can all celebrate. Go ahead. Please. Put my nervous mind to rest."

He waited until the man had picked up the phone to bend back to the satchel.

"I promised extra consideration," Mussa said. "And I think you'll find I am as good as my word. Sommes," he added, calling over the foreman. "You divide this up as you see fit."

The satchel was filled with American twenty-dollar bills. They were counterfeit but good enough to fool these men and probably many others. Sommes took the satchel and began counting as the others gathered around.

Mussa went to the truck and started it up. He rolled down the window and called to the guards who were just outside. "Come. Get your bonuses. It's all right. Don't be left out. You deserve a reward as well. God bless you all."

The two men looked at each other and then trotted inside. Mussa took his foot off the brake, easing down the slight curb from the building into the driveway. Outside, he watched for a moment in his rear-view mirror, making sure that no one had left the building. When he had gone about one hundred meters, he reached into his jacket pocket and pressed the button on a small radio-controlled device, igniting the explosives he had planted beneath the floor before the project began.

59

"Does he have many good days?" asked the doctor.

"Every so often," said Rubens. He told himself it wasn't a lie — though it did beg the question of what a good day actually was.

The doctor nodded grimly.

"He's a genius of a man," Rubens said.

"Yes, I'm sure he was."

The past tense stung Rubens, but he couldn't really argue with it. The doctor glanced at the General's court-appointed attorney standing nearby and then continued the examination. The man called himself a gerontologist; it sounded like one of those baloney specialties, but apparently he was a medical doctor, since his card had "MD" after his name.

In Rubens' opinion, the examination was perfunctory at best. The doctor listened to the General's heart, looked at his eyes, asked him to cough, examined his ears, then read his medical chart for a second time. When he was finished, he sat down on the bed next to the General and asked how he was feeling.

Not much of a question, except that the General answered by talking about General Grant's campaign at the end of the Civil War. Even this was disjointed; the General stopped in the middle of a sentence and asked about Corey. The doctor glanced at Rubens, but Corey was a name even Rubens had never heard before.

He might have lied, but he couldn't come up with one quickly enough.

The doctor asked a few more questions — they ranged from details of the General's childhood to what he had just had for dinner — but the General remained silent, staring out the window. Finally, his lawyer suggested that perhaps it was time to go.

"They're working on new drugs, aren't they?" said Rubens as the three men walked down the hall.

"Difficult area," said the doctor.

"Yes. But there's hope."

"We have to fully understand the mechanism of the disease — and the underlying structures it affects. But someday, yes."

Rubens knew better than to ask if someday was in the General's lifetime.

"I'm sorry I'm late," said Rebecca, charging down the hall toward them. "Has the doctor come?" When she belatedly realized who Rubens was talking to, her face shaded red. "Doctor, I'm Rebecca Rosenberg, the General's daughter. I'm sorry I'm late. It couldn't be helped."

Rubens almost snickered when she called herself by her maiden name, instead of Stein. *That* was a new development — undoubtedly related to the trial.

What did she possibly hope to gain? Didn't she have enough money? How far did greed take a person these days?

"That's quite all right, Ms. Rosenberg," said the gerontologist. "Your father's lawyer and Dr. Rubens have been showing me around."

"Actually, it's *Mr.* Rubens," said Rubens, embarrassed at being mistaken.

"Billy does have two doctorates," said Rebecca. "Including one my father urged him to get."

"He always encouraged me," said Rubens, unsure why she had mentioned that.

Was this all about jealousy? Maybe it wasn't about money or making up with her father — maybe it was about getting back at Rubens for being close to her father.

"He was really an incredible man," Rubens told the doctor. "I owe him a great deal."

"I'm sure."

The attorney gave Rubens another of his forced smiles, then nudged the doctor forward down the hall, asking when his report would be ready. Rubens heard him reply that it would be ready by the morning.

"I'm not going to move him," Rebecca told Rubens. "Not to Mount Ina."

Rubens wasn't sure what to say.

"Mount Ina is a better facility," he admitted. "But the General would rather die than live where his cousin lives."

"I agree. Here." She reached into her pocket. "I just want you to know, that if you're concerned . . ." Her voice broke, but she continued. "We don't get along, I know. But you and Daddy do. Always. And . . . you care about him. When I started this, I wasn't sure that was true. I thought because the agency wanted to control him — I know that they do, so you don't have to deny it. But I don't think you do. So I just want you to know, that when we do get the decision, you can still visit. Here. No strings."

Rubens took the paper and began to read it. It was a letter on her lawyer's stationery, attesting that she believed Rubens was a good friend to her father and should be allowed visiting privileges similar to those he had enjoyed as custodian. It was signed and notarized.

He suspected a trick. He looked up after reading it, but Rebecca was gone.

60

Karr took the bottle of sparkling water and stepped away from the bar, forcing his eyes away from the doorway. It was 11:30. Deidre hadn't shown up.

The Ritz did have a bar, an expensive one called the *Bar Vendôme*.

Probably a great place to get stinking drunk, Karr thought. Too bad he couldn't do that while he was on an operation.

Too stinking bad.

61

Mussa backed the van into the garage, nudging the gas for just a moment after slapping the vehicle into park. It was an old habit, taught by his uncle when he'd learned to drive. He'd heard a dozen times that it was bad for the car — and certainly unwise in a garage — but the habit was difficult to break.

Mussa got out of the truck. A surge of paranoia crept over him as he locked the garage, and he walked around the outside of the rented house, carefully checking to make sure that no one was lurking in the shadows. Satisfied, he let himself in, then checked each room, including the closets and under the beds, scanning for bugs. Satisfied, he sat in the living room and turned on the AOL instant messaging device he had obtained specifically for tonight. There was one message waiting:

Yes.

It meant that the brothers were ready to proceed.

Tomorrow's itinerary was now set. Even if one element failed, the overall effect would be a masterpiece.

Mussa turned off the device and slid it into his pocket. He set three alarm clocks to wake him; one was a radio, another a CD player attached to a clock, the last a windup device that would go off even if the electricity failed. Little things could undo even the most elaborate plot, and Mussa did not intend to be undone.

Nostalgia replaced paranoia; he thought of the great difficulties he had overcome during the past few years and even the slights that would now be avenged.

The greatest was the murder of his father, but Mussa did not dwell on that. Nor, surprisingly, did he think about the sneers of the Frenchmen he met every day, the heathens who thought no believer could be their equal. He thought instead of the smirks he had gotten from the Saudis when he had first expressed his desire to prove his faith and earn his place in Paradise.

They saw him as a useful idiot, a man whose network might be used — or, to put it more honestly, a man whose greed might be convenient but whose courage and faith were lacking.

He would laugh at them tomorrow.

62

The earliest train from Paris to Aux Boix on Friday left at 4:50 a.m.; Karr was one of only a half-dozen people on it. He got into LaFoote's house through the back window and spent an hour looking around, without finding anything useful. Around 6:30 he snuck back out and walked to the village center, a short distance away. The mass Father Brossard was to celebrate wasn't until eight, and so Karr had breakfast in a *patisserie*, a small local bakery. The woman who ran it had just taken a batch of chocolate macaroons from the oven in back when Karr arrived; he bought one and after the first bite pulled a twenty-euro note from his pocket to grab the dozen that were left.

The owner refused to sell him more than five. He took those, along with two croissants, and sat at one of the two tables in the window. Neither susceptible to flattery nor particularly talkative, the woman failed to respond to Karr's attempt to make conversation. Finally he asked flat out if she knew LaFoote; she simply shrugged, then went to tend to her ovens.

There was a park near the center of town, cattycorner from the church. Karr imagined that retired people — like LaFoote, before he got involved in his crusade to find his friend — would spend at least part of the day on one of the three benches there. But if so, it was too early for them; Karr sat alone for a while, watching the light traffic. Around 7:45 an altar boy unlocked the front door of the church, peeked out briefly, then disappeared back inside. Karr got up and ambled over.

Deidre Clancy pulled on her robe as she got out of bed. Her stomach felt somewhat better than it had yesterday, but . . .

She lurched forward, barely making the bathroom in time. By now, her stomach was completely drained, and she managed to expel only a small bit of fluid as she hung over the ceramic bowl.

Bad snails? Or the flu?

She'd gotten sick yesterday immediately after lunch at a fancy reception and lecture on the Postimpressionists at the Musée d'Orsay. It served her right for blowing off the class she was supposed to attend.

Deidre got up slowly, ran some water on

her face, then walked shakily back to bed. The sun was up, but she was tired and there was no question of doing anything but sleeping for quite a while. She glanced at the blinking answering machine in the living room — she'd heard the phone ring several times but was in no condition to answer. She'd deal with it all later, or tomorrow, or next week, or never.

"Father Brossard?"

The priest, dressed in a simple black cassock, turned from the side altar where he had been fussing over some of the candles.

"*Oui?*"

"I was a friend of Monsieur LaFoote's," said Karr in French. "Can we talk?"

"You are the American?" said the priest in English.

"*Je suis Américain, oui,*" said Karr. "Yes, I'm an American."

"*The* American. Mr. Karr?"

"Yeah, that's me," Karr said. "LaFoote talked to you?"

The priest turned and began walking to the front. Karr got up and followed past the altar, entering the sacristy through a side door. Two altar boys were laughing about something as they came in; the boys immediately stiffened, standing at military attention as the priest cast a stern look in their direction. Karr smiled at them, but the boys remained stone-faced.

The priest continued to a narrow hallway and turned into a small, unlit room. He went to a file cabinet in the otherwise empty room and took out a brown envelope.

"Monsieur LaFoote gave me this a month ago," said the priest in English. "He left a message the other evening that they were to go to you, not the police. His funeral is tomorrow."

"He was a good man," said Karr as the priest handed him an envelope.

"He was a sinner."

"We all are, right?"

The priest didn't smile. He walked stiffly back out into the sacristy, no longer paying attention to Karr. He scolded the boys in French, telling them their souls had just gained more black marks for whispering in a holy place.

There were a few people in the church now, a dozen or so, scattered around. Karr took a seat; as the service began, a woman slid in at the far end — he turned and realized it was the baker, who made no sign that she recognized him.

There were three photocopies in the envelope. The top two were bank account statements for Vefoures from, as LaFoote had said, a small Austrian bank. There were regular wire deposits of two thousand euros a week, along with irregular withdrawals. The statements were several months old.

The third sheet was a copy of what looked like a signature card for another account at a different Austrian bank; rather than a full name the signature was a single letter: *P.* Instead of a name and address as contact information, there was a phone number. The account number matched the account the wired deposits had been made from.

Karr pulled out his PDA. He went online to the World Wide Web and tapped into a commercial Web site that had a reverse address lookup. The number wasn't listed. He tapped the screen lightly and got into the NSA's comprehensive address search engine.

It took nearly sixty seconds for the database to come back with an ID on the phone number: Jacques Ponclare.

63

Donohue turned right when he reached the top landing and walked down the hall to the second apartment. He paused, pulling on a set of latex gloves, then slipped the owner's key out of his pocket and placed it into the lock. The mechanism was old and the key worn; he had to jiggle it and lean forward to get it to work.

The apartment smelled musty, as if its owner had never once opened the windows in the fifty years she had lived there. The smell made Donohue gag slightly as he came in; he associated it with his own childhood in Londonderry, a place where every memory evoked disgust. He was soon over it, moving quickly to the closet where he had placed his weapon the day before.

The *Direction de la Surveillance du Territore*, or DST, had its official headquarters at 1 rue Nélaton, some blocks away. But for a variety of reasons, including security, low-key suboffices had been found in the city.

Ponclare, like some of the other section leaders and their teams, worked out of a bunkerized basement in the middle of what looked like an ordinary residential block. This made a mass attack on the DST difficult — but it presented certain advantages for anyone clever and bold, like Donohue.

Ponclare had only just arrived at work and typically would not leave his office for at least two hours — perhaps not for three or four — but the assassin had to be ready. His escape had already been complicated by the American President's plans to visit Paris later that day.

From what Donohue knew of Mussa Duoar, it was likely that the visit had been somehow factored into the assassination of the French official. Donohue believed that Mussa primarily acted as a conduit for orders from an organization outside of France, though he was enough of a snake that one could never be too sure. So long as his fee was paid, Donohue would not bother to inquire too deeply.

He began assembling the Barrett sniper rifle, a fifty-caliber American-made gun that fired a round capable of penetrating an engine block. The weapon was not his favorite, but it was necessary because of the distance and the fact that Ponclare might choose to drive one of the armored Peugeots available to him.

When Donohue finished setting up his rifle, he went to the bathroom. He avoided the shower where he had placed the body of the woman who had lived here after killing her yesterday. Despite the fact that he had wrapped her in plastic bags, there was already a distinct odor of decay; this, too, reminded him of the slums where he had grown up, and he flushed the toilet with disgust.

An hour and a half to go. He would wait.

64

As demanding as they were, his responsibilities as head of Desk Three were only part of William Rubens' job at the National Security Agency, and there was always a stack of paperwork waiting for him in his office. So when Marie Telach told him she wanted to update him in person on what Tommy Karr had found, he asked her to come up to his office. The few minutes he saved meant he could finish reviewing a half-dozen briefs, and by staying here he could initial a small stack of papers. Telach always looked a bit out of sorts when she came upstairs, blinking her eyes like a gopher pulled from her hole.

"Circumstantially at least, it looks bad for Ponclare," she told him when she arrived, detailing the money trail they had fleshed out from Karr's information. The chemist Vefoures had been paid from a bank account in Austria that seemed to belong to the French DST Paris security head, Ponclare. That fit with the story that Karr had been told by Vefoures' friend

LaFoote, that Vefoures had been brought back by the government for a secret project. The source of the money wasn't clear — it came from an Algerian bank whose owner could not, for the time being at least, be traced.

But was it really Ponclare's? The account had been set up only a few days before the first payment to Vefoures and had only been used to pay him. A preliminary search of the phone records showed that Ponclare had not called the bank from his office or the home number listed on the account. And there were no large transfers from any of Ponclare's accounts, nor any sudden transfer in for that matter.

"Perhaps he is extremely prudent," said Rubens.

"Or maybe it was set up to make it seem like a legitimate project to the chemist, and point suspicion at Ponclare if discovered," said Telach.

Rubens turned to the computer at the side of his desk and punched the keyboard, bringing Ponclare's résumé up in front of him. The man had worked for the French security service for three decades and had, at least according to his superiors, done a decent job. But he had no flashy results; he was clearly more bureaucrat than artist.

433

Ponclare had served briefly in Africa, where his service overlapped with LaFoote's. His job there seemed primarily to facilitate budget cutting; besides LaFoote, several dozen officers and foreign agents were let go during Ponclare's short tenure and no one replaced.

"Is there any connection with the car thief?" Rubens asked.

"Mussa Duoar? Not that we can see."

"Do they have accounts at the same banks?"

"No," replied Telach.

"The transfer from Morocco?"

"Duoar doesn't use any bank there."

"Nothing at all?"

"Neither there nor Algeria."

"What about Ponclare's father?"

"No. Duoar was just a child when Ponclare Senior went back to France. Duoar's father was active in the resistance movement against the French," she told him, "but he died after the country gained its independence."

"How?"

Telach shrugged. "Murky circumstances. Officially, an accident. Unofficially, it may have been something else. He was in police custody shortly before he died. We'd have to do quite a lot more checking to clarify what happened, and even then, I don't know that we'd get a true answer. Do you think it's relevant?"

Probably not, Rubens thought. He was grasping for connections, trying to see the whole pattern. "All right. The CD-ROMs that Tommy sent back last night?"

"Formula for a very potent bomb. Different ways of constructing large bombs and shaping them. Some of them are rather large — two hundred pounds, three hundred pounds. Various formulas the experts are analyzing."

"Has Johnny Bib's team examined the hard drive that Dean and Lia got from the library yet?"

"The drive just arrived. It'll take a while."

Rubens got up and began pacing, trying to ward off his fatigue; he hadn't slept now in quite some time.

The information about the account transfers added little, if anything, to what they already had — unless Ponclare had some theory on why he was used.

Someone would have to ask him about it. In person, to catch his reaction.

There was a chance that Ponclare was involved with the terrorists. Rubens couldn't disregard that. He needed someone he could trust to put this to him, perhaps catch him off-guard with it. And it had to be done directly, without going through channels.

The French, of course, would raise a stink. So would he, if the situation were reversed.

"Where's Tommy?" Rubens asked Telach.

"On a train back to Paris," she said. "He should be there in about twenty minutes."

Twenty minutes — and then another twenty or thirty in traffic to get over to the DST headquarters.

Karr wasn't the best person for this job — he was clearly prejudiced.

Dean was the man he wanted. He trusted his judgment.

"Send Mr. Dean over. Tell him to go to Ponclare and talk to him personally. Tell him what we've found. Dean can offer to have the information faxed to him as he's speaking. We're looking for a reason he would be used — someone he's wronged, revenge, something like that. Tell Mr. Dean that I'm going to be very interested in his personal assessment of Ponclare's reaction. Have Lia go with him."

Rubens paused.

"Yes, it is a long shot, Marie," he added. "But we have to fill in the blanks somehow."

65

The Eiffel Tower stood a short block from the Seine River, its legs spread over a large concrete and stone plaza. On the other side of the tower sat a long park called the Champ de Mars. The French had blocked off the side streets around the park with concrete barriers. Two large dump trucks had been placed on the street behind the tower, closing it off. Another truck and some wooden barricades had been placed on the river side of the tower. Hidden from view were two military vehicles with antitank weapons aimed at the approaches. Dean had his doubts that the weapons could be brought to bear in time, but it was obvious that the French hadn't completely dismissed the Americans' warning, contrary to what the Art Room had told him.

Despite the extra security, the tower was open for business. A long line snaked out from the chute in front of the north pillar as tourists waited to buy their tickets and then take the double-decker elevator up to the first or second observation deck. Once they reached the second level, or *étage,* as the French called it, they could board a smaller elevator and ride to the top.

"How do you think these guys manage to sell miniature towers for one euro when they're three in the souvenir shop over there?" asked Lia.

"They don't have the same overhead," Dean told her.

Lia frowned and turned to look across the road. "Big bus could jump this barrier pretty easily," she said, putting her hand on the metal rail that separated the tower platform from the road. "Go right through this pipe."

"Maybe you shouldn't stand there then."

"You won't save me if something goes wrong?" she said sarcastically.

Dean frowned. He wasn't sure if her sarcasm was a good or bad sign.

"They have enough gendarmes here," added Lia, referring to the military policemen, who were dressed in battle gear and carried automatic rifles. "You'd think they'd be able to do something about the souvenir sellers."

"The guys on the bikes are the ones who look after them," said Dean. There were two policemen who used mountain bikes to chase after the sellers when they got particularly obnoxious, but their efforts seemed halfhearted at best; the souvenir sellers would retreat, sometimes all the way across the river, only to return a few minutes later.

"Some security," grumbled Lia.

"You want them to close the tower?"

"If they're serious, yes."

"Life just can't come to a stop."

"You're either serious or you're not," said Lia.

"Maybe we should go up," suggested Dean. "Play tourist."

"Why?"

"I'd like to see what it's like," said Dean.

"Be my guest."

Before he could answer her, Rockman's voice echoed in his ear. "Charlie, Mr. Rubens has something he needs you to do right away. Find a taxi and we'll tell you what's going on while you're en route."

66

Mussa tapped his foot on the brake impatiently as the traffic showed no sign of letting up. He had given himself nearly an hour's extra time, and still he was going to end up being very close.

He would make it. He knew he would make it. He had to relax. He settled his hands on the steering wheel, tapping out an impatient beat. He thought of listening to the radio and reached in that direction — only to be startled by a sharp rap on the window. He pushed upright, angry — then saw that a policeman was standing there.

Slowly Mussa put his left hand on the button to lower the window. He had no weapon; they were liabilities now.

"Yes?" he asked.

"This is your truck?" said the officer.

"My company's, yes."

"Where are you going?"

"To Gare du Nord," Mussa said. "The train station. I have a delivery to the Eurostar and I'm running late. I was just —"

The policeman frowned at him, then took a step back from the window. "Take that road there to the left," he said, pointing. "We're blocking off traffic because of the American President's visit. Go now, before the road is completely closed."

"Thank you," managed Mussa, putting the van in gear and cranking the wheel to turn into the opposite lane.

67

Was there any number as perfect as 3?

Indivisible. Prime. Essential. Mystic in its many applications. Mysterious.

Very mysterious. Unfortunately.

Johnny Bib looked at the three blank pieces of paper on the large table in the center of the lab room. The pages represented the blank spots of a larger file that his team was trying to extract from the hard drive that Dean and Lia had taken from the French library. The drive had been corrupted by a power spike. It seemed to have happened as the drive was being overwritten, which was a bit of a break for the analysts, making it much easier to recover data. However, the scrubber program had succeeded in laying down its pattern more than three times over several areas — probably during an earlier session — and at least some of the files they wanted had been erased.

The recovery process in those areas was excruciatingly slow. The team used a device that looked at the magnetic recordings on the drive that were left by the very slight misalignment of the heads. These fluxes — Johnny saw them as tiny yes or no checks written on pieces of sand on a vast beach — were run through a series of programs that attempted to tease logic from them, looking for patterns that corresponded to computer language. This part wasn't necessarily as difficult as it sounded; it was another way of thinking about encryption, after all. But the way that the computer stored files added another level of complexity, and in any event the flux reading was painfully slow.

Three large blank spots, unlikely to yield their secrets.

Three. The ultimate prime, the ultimate number.

Was that a sign that they would succeed or fail?

"Johnny, look at this," said Blondie Jones, one of the computer geeks working on the project.

Blondie had earned her nickname a year before, when she'd come to work with her black hair dyed yellow. Her hair had since returned to its natural color, but her nickname had become permanent.

"This other set of calculations mimics

the simulation we found earlier, but on a slightly smaller scale. The tower blowup. Some of the values are similar, but the impact area is closer and smaller. It wasn't completely overwritten."

Johnny Bib walked over to the console where Blondie was working.

"You're sure it's not just a small-scale model they tried first, to control the variables and get the concept down?" he suggested.

"Look at the dates. And there's an access correlation here, when the library computer was taken over. See? We traced everything back and we found the computer used to initiate the connection. It's part of a network, like a commercial thing or something. I think the queries originated there, but we may not know until we download everything off those drives. Right now we're looking around. There's a hidden file structure similar to what we've seen on the others. It'll take a few minutes. Three or four."

"Better three than four," he said automatically. "Three is a much better number."

He looked at the data. A smaller explosion, a smaller effect, but the result was —

Oh.

Oh!

The upper stage of the tower — an easier target.

"Excuse me. I have to talk to Mr. Rubens. Find out what else is on that computer."

68

Donohue watched as the door to the building opened. The first man out was a plainclothes officer, a bodyguard of some type. He walked to the end of the block and got into a car. As soon as he pulled away from the curb, two more men emerged from the building, followed by a third dressed in a brown suit — Ponclare, his target.

Donohue bent slightly. His joints tightened. His eyes narrowed their focus.

Now.

He squeezed the trigger; in the scope he saw Ponclare's head burst as if it were a water balloon.

The sniper held the gun ready until the body crumpled. Then he got up and walked calmly to the door, savoring the satisfaction of a job well done.

69

The driver stopped, waiting to turn. Dean had glanced down at the handheld computer to look at the download of the bank statement when he heard the crack of a gunshot a block away. It was a sharp, loud bang, and Dean, a former sniper, realized instantly that they were too late.

"Pay the driver!" he yelled to Lia, jumping for the car.

Ponclare's office was down the block and around the corner. As Dean started to run, a man came around the corner, walking casually, as if nothing had happened. He wore an American-style baseball cap and had a camera around his neck and seemed oblivious to what was going on around him.

Dean got a glimpse of the man's face as he went past. Something poked at him in that moment, but he didn't realize it for a step or two, not until he reached the corner.

Two men with pistols drawn were running down the block toward a man who lay sprawled on the sidewalk. They were yelling for their boss: *"Monsieur Ponclare! Monsieur Ponclare!"*

Dean turned around to get another look at the man he'd just passed. Lia, done with the cab, ran up to him, asking what had happened.

Rather than answering, Dean started to cross the street. The taxi driver had picked up another fare — the man in the baseball cap. Dean stopped to let the taxi pass; as it did, he slipped a small tracking device from his shirt pocket and slapped it against the car's rear fender. Another taxi was coming down from the cross street; Dean ran out halfway into traffic to flag it down.

"What are you doing?" asked Lia, catching up to him.

"We have to follow him," said Dean.

"Why?"

"Because this is the second time I nearly ran into him. The first was in London when we went to check out the room Kensworth had stayed in."

70

Tommy Karr stared at the small metro ticket, momentarily unable to remember which way it was supposed to be fed into the machine so the magnetic strip could be read. He finally decided strip-down; the reader grabbed the ticket from him, whisking it through its mechanism and spitting it out at the other side. The green light on the panel flashed as he grabbed the ticket and walked through, wending his way through the tile-lined tunnels down to the platform. A train trundled in just as he arrived; he joined what looked like the smallest triangle queuing for the doors.

The doors began to close as he got in. Two men jumped in behind him, pulling a large black case; in the half second or so it took Karr to grab the pole and turn around they had snapped the top of the case open to reveal an amplifier, CD setup, and microphone. As the train began to move, one of the men produced a small and silvery alto sax. The subway car exploded with a jaunty blare of music that was part rap, part American blues, part rock.

Karr caught the glance of an elderly woman sitting nearby; she rolled her eyes but then dug into her purse for a few coins to toss into their cup. The two men sang a decent harmony — or at least it might have been decent had it not been distorted by the amplifier. Their words were a French-Croatian-English patois; rather than translate them directly, Karr's brain began supplying its own version of the song:

> *She's a gorgeous girl*
> *Too pretty for you*
> *Gone now.*
> *The bird flew, flew, flew.*

Whether the words had really come from the performers or not, Karr couldn't say.

The tune stayed with him as he changed trains, remaining in his head even when he ascended the steps at Champ de Mars near the Eiffel Tower. A policeman frowned at him as he stepped near the curb at the middle of the block; Karr smiled and then walked over toward the corner, joining a small knot of people as the light turned green.

"So, Rockman, what's going on?" he asked his runner as he crossed toward the tower. "They have more dump trucks here than a construction site."

"Marie's going to update you in a second," replied Rockman. "We're in the video system. We can see what's going on in the elevators and have limited views on each of the floors."

"*Étage*," said Karr, letting the French word roll off his tongue. "Where are Dean and Lia?"

"Marie'll give you the low-down," said the runner. "It's complicated."

A black man with a ring of Eiffel Tower souvenirs came up to Karr as he reached the curb. The man jangled the metal towers as if they were keys and said, "One euro," indicating the price. Three or four other souvenir sellers came up behind him; when Karr shook his head and walked past the first a second approached and gave him the same pitch, then a third and a fourth. The sellers wouldn't compete with one another directly, but each felt entitled to try his own selling techniques where another failed.

"Ponclare was assassinated," said Rubens over the com system.

"Hey, Chief," said Karr. "Who killed him?"

"We're not sure yet. Dean saw someone leaving the area who looked like a man he saw in the hotel in England. He and Lia are following him."

"You want me to help?"

"I don't believe that will be necessary," said Rubens. "In any event, we're still trying to piece together what's going on. The French don't know themselves. Continue where you are," added Rubens. "We're working on new information and we may need you to communicate it directly to the commander in charge at the tower scene. His name is Georges Cunard."

"Should I introduce myself now?"

"I'd prefer you didn't break cover unless necessary," said Rubens. "Not until we understand what's going on."

"Ducky."

Rubens didn't get the pun — *cunard* was "duck" in French — a fact Karr found even funnier than the joke itself.

Karr glanced at the massive concrete pillar that anchored the tower. Blow it up? No way. It seemed to him that if you had a bus of explosives, it would be much easier to park near a big department store over by the Opera district. A bus loaded with explosives would demolish Au Printemps, the fancy department store; people would be afraid to shop anywhere, not just in France. But then again, he wasn't a terrorist — he didn't quite get the symbolic value involved in hitting a place like the Eiffel Tower. He understood, obviously, that it was important, but he didn't really think like a madman.

Karr walked across the plaza, studying the line to the tower entrance at the north pier. There were several policemen as well as military gendarmes near the entrance, checking backpacks and handbags. They weren't what made the line so long, however; the double-decker elevator inside the pier could only hold a few dozen people at a time.

The south pier, however, had no line.

It had no elevator, either. If you went in there you had to climb the stairs.

"If I were a terrorist," Karr said aloud, "I'd walk up to where the beams weren't quite so thick."

"What are you talking about?" asked Rockman.

"Nothing much," Karr told him, digging in his pocket for some euros. "Frenchies got the ground covered. I'm going to take a look upstairs."

71

Mussa backed the truck to the loading dock and checked his watch. He had arrived ten minutes late.

Not enough to be fatal, fortunately, but things were now very tight. The rolling chests must be placed aboard the train before passengers were boarded; there were only a few minutes to do so.

He took a breath, then pulled open the driver's side door and slid out of the truck. There was a security guard a few paces away; the man returned Mussa's nod, then turned his gaze elsewhere. Mussa had taken the precaution of showing up here a few times over the course of the last several weeks, not just to understand the layout and procedures but also to make his face somewhat more familiar and thus part of the background.

He moved slowly toward the rear of the truck. As he did, he saw one of his men approaching.

Ahmed, very good.

Mussa unlocked the door and opened the rear compartment. The six large wheeled chests just barely fit in the back of the truck.

"A problem," said Ahmed, speaking in Arabic.

Mussa shot him a ferocious look — anything but French here would be immediately suspect.

Ahmed blinked, but when he spoke again, he still used Arabic. "Arno did not show up. Bomani and Heru are also gone."

Mussa tried to take this information in stride, but it was impossible. Arno's disappearance was especially troubling, as he was the only one besides himself who knew exactly how the chests were to be put together.

Could he do it by himself?

He glanced to the left, toward the policeman. A security official had joined him; they were speaking quietly.

Trouble?

If Arno wasn't here, where was he? With the authorities?

Impossible.

Fate was testing him. He had to move ahead.

"The others?" he asked.

"They have places in coach ten. Their

weapons are hidden. Yours as well. Your ticket is ready?"

Mussa nodded.

If Arno did not show up, would the train be delayed? It normally carried only a four-man crew, including the head conductor, or "chief of the train." Mussa had already arranged for one of the crew members to get sick at the last moment, limiting the crew to three and making the train easier to take over.

They wouldn't replace one person, but they undoubtedly would find another steward if two were absent. Mussa would have to take Arno's place. Fortunately, they were about the same size.

But the casks were heavy and difficult to manage for two people until they were on their rollers. *Even then.*

Once they were in the train, it wouldn't matter.

The operation had been designed from the start with seven men in mind. Now there would be only four.

Muhammad and Kelvin would subdue the passengers and the policemen, if they were unlucky enough to be in their half of the train when it decoupled. Allah would provide, after all.

Mussa glanced at his watch. He had five

minutes to get the chests aboard. As he looked up, he saw a small wedge of wood a few feet away. It looked as if it would just fit at the back of the truck, providing a ramp to ease the casks down.

"Get that piece of wood, quickly. Then find me Arno's work clothes. No, get that piece of wood first!" Mussa yelled as Ahmed reached to pull the first chest from the van. "They are heavier than they seem."

72

Donohue trotted up the steps to the Eurostar check-in area at Gare du Nord, trying to move quickly without seeming to be too much in a hurry. Passengers had to check in before departure or risk not being cleared through passport control and security. His first-class ticket allowed him a little leeway but not all that much. The next train was not for another hour. By that time Ponclare's assassination would be general knowledge, and the authorities would surely be at the station, watching.

A man and a woman had seen him get into a cab near the block when leaving the flat. Donohue had looked away quickly, but it seemed to him that the man had shot him an odd look. Had he heard the gun?

Had he recognized him?

Donohue thought the man looked familiar, but he couldn't place him. Or rather, he could place him in a dozen different situations — the hit at the park in London, the assassination of the Italian colonel in Naples, the strike on the Russian intelligence agent who had stolen money from the Russian *mafya*.

A dozen faces jumbled together; surely it was just paranoia.

It was definitely time to retire.

But he had the money.

It was inconvenient that someone had seen him but not fatal; by the time the man made any sort of report that could be processed and acted upon, Donohue would be across the English Channel. He had nothing to do now but follow his carefully drawn plan — Eurostar to London Waterloo Station, tube to Paddington and then Heathrow, from there to any of three locations, tickets already secured. A friend from the IRA days would meet him with a fresh, clean passport at Heathrow, along with a bag. He had nothing to do but follow the plan.

A red sign over the check-in area declared that passports must be ready for inspection. Donohue reached for his — it was a phony one, of course — and slipped out his ticket at the same time. The woman at the check-in gate smiled pleasantly and examined the ticket briefly before waving him on to the Frenchman at the passport desk a few feet away. The customs official squinted at his passport and passed him to the Brits behind him.

"And why are you going to England?" asked the officer.

"Live there, mate," said Donohue.

"Yes, of course," said the man, nodding and handing him back the passport.

73

Rubens stepped away from the Art Room consoles, walking to the side where a fresh pot of coffee was being brewed in the machine. He poured himself a cup, not so much because he wanted it but because he wanted to do something that would force him to pause, to physically step away from the situation.

Nothing was going on at the Eiffel Tower. Had that been a blind to divert attention from the plot to kill Ponclare?

If so, Deep Black had played an unfortunate role.

Surely not. A random pattern, unconnected.

Air Force One was just touching down at Charles de Gaulle Airport with the President and national security adviser aboard. Rubens had already told Hadash and President Marcke about Ponclare's murder and that they were following a possible suspect.

With an emphasis on *"possible."* Dean had acted on a hunch; so far the man hadn't gone anywhere they could see him. Even so, the President had decided to inform the French President personally. Marcke would suggest that the French have the man arrested as a material witness, or whatever the equivalent was in France.

A hunch, just a hunch. But Rubens did trust Dean's judgment.

A large clock sat on the wall above the coffee machine. It was going on 10:00 a.m. The judge in the General's competency case had called McGovern to tell her he would hold a hearing at eleven and announce his verdict shortly thereafter.

"I told you he was quick. One of a kind," she'd said on the voice-mail message.

She hadn't used the word *verdict*, actually, but it felt like one.

Rubens wanted to be there. Rebecca surely would.

"Boss, the man Dean and Lia have been following is in Gare du Nord, the train station," said Rockman.

As he walked to the runner's console with his coffee, Rubens pushed the General out of his mind. He had to concentrate on the here and now — he needed to watch out for his people. That was his priority. The General would have used those exact words.

"Where do the trains go?" Rubens asked.

"All over. There's a metro stop, commuter trains, high-speed, uh, what do they call them, TVG, I think — those bullet trains that go all over the place. They also have Eurostar there, the train that takes the Chunnel to London."

Dean had seen the man in London.

"Get the Eurostar passenger list right away," said Rubens. "Where are Dean and Lia?"

"Just going in."

"We're breaking into their video surveillance system," said Telach, coming over. "It'll be a few seconds. Listen, Johnny Bib is demanding to talk to you. He says he has new information."

"He can wait."

"He says it's about the Eiffel Tower. Something they just discovered."

"Very well," said Rubens. "Have Dean and Lia follow their man wherever he goes. Hopefully it will be someplace easy, like the Eurostar. Which line is Johnny Bib on?"

74

Lia turned left as she came into the large
hallway at the far end of the terminal,
walking down along the area of shops and
ticket windows. Dean's description of the
man they were following was less than complete — tall, dark hair, wearing jeans and a
gray windbreaker.

A pair of smoke-colored globes hung
down from the ceiling nearby — surveillance cameras. Lia put her hand to her
mouth as if covering her face while
yawning. "Rockman, they have a surveillance system. See if you can get in it and
look for Dean's suspect."

"We're already working on it, Lia, thank
you. All right, we have him: gray windbreaker going into Eurostar. No baseball
cap. Upstairs."

"You sure?"

"Go there. Charlie, look at this download on your PDA and make sure we have
it right."

Lia spun around and threaded her way

toward the stairway, which was about midway in the platform. She watched from the escalator as Dean sidled up to one of the large metal posts that held the shed roof up and took out his PDA.

"It's him," he said.

"Good," answered Rockman. "He's going aboard the Eurostar. A good break for us. I'll have his ID in a second. Go ahead and get aboard."

Lia walked toward the ticket window, where a customer was thanking a clerk for getting him a spot on the train.

"Not a problem, monsieur," said the clerk in French. "A lot of last-minute cancellations. The charge is ninety euros for first class."

"Ninety euros," muttered Lia. "I don't have that much cash. What card should I use?"

"Don't worry about it," said Rockman. "Your tickets will be in the system. Just show your passport. Real names; it's OK. Go."

Dean came up to the Eurostar level as the other customer fished out his wallet to pay.

"Dump your weapons before you go inside," continued Rockman. "Duck into those restrooms on the right after you get your tickets. There are no garbage cans inside the waiting area."

"You want us to go to London?" asked Dean. "Why don't you just have him arrested?"

"Charlie, we don't have an ID on him yet," said Rockman. "And to be blunt, the fact that you may have recognized him from England may not impress the French. It's their call."

"You're going to let him get away," said Dean, as if he were muttering to himself.

"No. Once he's on the train he can't go anywhere. The train can be met in England by the police. He won't be able to carry a weapon onto the train. You'll see; the security is tight."

"If you're going to have someone meet the train, why should we get on?" asked Dean.

"Things are a little fluid right now, Charlie. Stick with the program, OK? If he gets on the train we'll be able to deal with it pretty easily. Just follow. There's a lot of stuff going on here."

"Art Room knows best," said Lia sarcastically, reaching into the security belt beneath her jeans for her passport.

75

Donohue walked through the boarding area where the second-class passengers were already queued up. He continued past the small shops that sold refreshments, making his way to the restroom. It was a small crowd for a Eurostar, he thought, maybe a quarter of the normal size, which seemed odd, because the trains were normally much more crowded. He paused at a sink, washing his face and making sure that the stalls were clear. An American tourist was helping his young son at a stall nearby, dad watching over the unlocked door. Otherwise the place was empty.

The assassin turned and walked into a stall on the opposite end, sitting down on the commode.

When he heard the child flush, Donohue took off his windbreaker and unzipped the lining, turning it around so that the jacket was now bright yellow nylon, very different from what he had worn to the station. From his wallet he unfolded a small mustache, applying glue from the center of a roll of Life Savers. Mustache applied, he took out his passport and smeared the rest of the glue on the photo, daubing a tiny amount at the edges as well. Then he removed a replacement page from his pocket, unrolling it carefully and feeding it down carefully. The page was clear except for a new photo, but it had to be put down carefully to preserve the anticounterfeiting impressions. Mucking this up would mean having to pull off the mustache, fairly painful after the thirty seconds it took for the glue to set. But he got it perfectly.

He held the passport page at an angle, making sure there were no flaws.

Passport prepared, he removed a small envelope from behind the license in his wallet. Inside the envelope were two tinted contact lenses to change his eye color. He had trouble getting the first in; the second felt as if he'd jabbed his eye but slipped right into place. In his experience, few people checked the eye color entered on passports — as his experience at the gate proved, since the eye color entered on the document matched the tinted brown effect, not his real eye color, which was a nearly opaque blue. But it was the sort of detail that Donohue insisted on getting right, just in case.

He reached down to his pants and pulled them off, turning them inside out also so that they now appeared to be black sports pants rather than jeans. Psychologically, it was his most vulnerable moment, far worse in his mind than if he'd been caught monkeying with the passport. But this passed as soon as the waist was snapped. He finished his transformation by placing two lift blocks into his shoes, adding another inch and a half to his height. As a last stroke he ran his fingers through his hair, rubbing a bit of coloring cream into the sides. The cream dappled his black a touch gray; he stroked at the side, then took out a comb and straightened it.

He went out and studied the effect in the mirror.

Distinguished.

The loudspeaker announced that the train for London was now boarding. Donohue nodded at the mirror and left the restroom a new man.

76

Mussa felt the sweat pouring from his brow as he finished putting the last cart in place. The perspiration was not from fear; the carts were difficult to maneuver in the confined space at the back of the last first-class coach. He took two real carts and lined them up in front.

This was not what he had planned. He was supposed to be a passenger, sipping complimentary champagne, toasting the death of Ponclare and his father's ultimate revenge.

Mussa had posted a set of Ponclare's bank account documents to the Interior Ministry, along with additional information that would make it appear he had hired Vefoures and had LaFoote killed. A small amount of the explosive had been deposited in a warehouse that the police should have no difficulty finding. Ponclare would appear to have been a traitor, profiting by selling explosives to terrorists; the police should have no trouble linking him to the operation at the Eiffel Tower.

And, of course, he would be dead.

Since determining what had happened to his father three years before, Mussa had considered killing the Frenchman himself. Twice Mussa had actually constructed a plan. But simply killing Ponclare had not seemed satisfying enough. Even now, to be honest, he felt cheated — it was Ponclare's father he truly wished to have revenge on. Killing the son lacked the thrill.

Especially now, sweating like a dog.

Shaming Ponclare would make up for that, somewhat. For if the son was a traitor to France, what did that say about the father?

By extension, Mussa's father would get the recognition he deserved. He was nearly forgotten now, but as stories of Mussa's triumph circulated, a few old-timers would resurrect his father's memory. The family would gain great honor. Exactly as they deserved.

And Mussa would join him in Paradise, basking in the glory of God.

"What are you doing?" barked a voice behind him.

Mussa turned. The train's master — the person in charge of the serving crew, in this case a woman — stood before him.

"The new man," he said, bowing his head slightly.

Ahmed rushed up behind her. "Have you finished what I told you?" she demanded.

"Yes, ma'am."

"He's the substitute I told you about," Ahmed told the woman.

"I was told to report," said Mussa.

"By who?"

"Stephens, the Englishman," said Ahmed quickly.

"Where is your card?" asked the train master, referring to Mussa's railroad identity card. It was carried, not displayed on the uniform. Mussa did not have one.

"In my jacket," he said.

"Well, get it. Quickly," said the woman.

He nodded but did not move.

"Well?"

He pointed toward the next car.

"Be quick. We have to board passengers," said the woman. "If we are late we will hear about it."

She turned and walked out the nearby door, where passengers' tickets were being checked to make sure they got the right seats.

"Give me your card," he told Ahmed.

"My picture is on it," said Ahmed.

"Don't worry," said Mussa. "Give it to me."

Ahmed reached into his pocket and re-trieved the card. The expression on his face made it clear that he thought Mussa was crazy. But the trick was an old one that never failed: he placed his thumb over Ahmed's picture, then waited at the door for the right moment.

On the platform, the train master was just helping an old woman with her ticket and carry-on luggage when Mussa made his appearance.

"Here," he said, flashing the card in his hand. As he went to give it to the train master, he saw that the old woman was struggling with her bag. "Oh, ma'am, please, let me help you," he said, swooping in and grabbing the suitcase from her hand as if she were about to drop it.

"Seat twenty-four B," the train master told Mussa, her tone slightly less severe. "Help our passenger get situated."

"Yes, ma'am," said Mussa, sliding the identity card back into his pocket.

77

The security person at the entrance glanced at Karr but said nothing, barely watching as he walked through the small hallway to the metal steps. Three hundred and sixty steps encased in a well-painted but utilitarian steel enclosure led to the first level of the tower. Climbing them felt more like ascending the steps in an industrial building than a world monument.

The first thing that greeted him when he came out on the first level was a large souvenir shop; it was empty and even seemed a little forgotten, tucked into a corner of the plaza away from most of the tourists. He walked around the platform, trying not to remember his visit the other day with Deidre. It was difficult; he'd had a lot of fun and wished she were here now.

Assuming, of course, no one tried to blow the tower up.

Karr paused to look at the *Invalides*, the large military building nearby originally built as a veterans' hospital and nursing home and now Napoleon's final resting place. Tourists filtered across the plaza behind him, checking out the sights and occasionally reading the placards. Any one of them could be carrying a weapon — Karr hadn't been frisked or put through a metal detector — but the threat that Deep Black had detected was on a much larger scale. One or two gunmen might kill a dozen or even two dozen people, but they didn't strike terror on the grand scale. An event had to be massive to live in people's memories.

Why? Anything that happened here would be terrible, wouldn't it?

A French military helicopter, an Aerospatiale SA 342 Gazelle, passed about three-quarters of a mile away. The small attack helicopter was equipped with anti-tank weapons, more than enough to stop a bus or truck loaded with explosives. A second helicopter hovered in the distance. Local air traffic had been brought to a virtual halt for the U.S. President's visit; even outgoing flights at de Gaulle had been canceled for a while.

Karr continued around the plaza, heading back for the steps. He was probably the most suspicious-looking person here.

The second level was another 359 steps away. The girders got thinner and the space between them seemed more open; Karr had more of a sense that he was climbing well above the city.

As he neared the second *étage,* the Deep Black op noticed a figure dressed in coveralls dangling over the side. For a second he thought the man was going to jump; then Karr realized he was a painter. It wasn't until he was nearly level with the man that he saw the figure wasn't real at all but a mannequin, part of a display about how important it was to paint the tower. According to the sign, the process continued every year. The job was done by hand, with old-fashioned paintbrushes rather than spray cans or fancier devices. A picture showed some of the men testing safety ropes.

Sure enough, there were several men nearby dressed in coveralls climbing upward in the grid work toward the third level, using one of the utility ladders to ascend into the weblike structure that held up the third level and its antenna mast.

So where were their paint cans and safety ropes?

78

"What do you mean, you lost him?"

"We're not omniscient, Charlie," sputtered Telach.

"How could you lose him?" Dean was standing in the far waiting room at the Gare du Nord Eurostar station, usually reserved for passengers in the forward cars. The train was boarding and the place was empty.

"The cameras don't catch most of the waiting areas. Look in the men's room. That's the only place he could have gone." Telach's voice, normally understated, seemed strained and high-pitched.

"I just looked," said Dean, but he went in again. He glanced at the sinks and then opened each of the stalls. All were empty. He looked up at the ceiling. The vents were too small for anyone to get through.

The loudspeaker announced that the train to London was now in its final boarding. Dean hurried out, kicking one of the boxes placed on the floor for trash —

security protocol here did not allow containers where a bomb might be hidden.

"Where?" he asked Telach.

"We're looking."

He turned right, heading toward the exit down to the tracks. There were refreshment counters, small stores like those found in American shopping malls, on either side of the short hallway.

"Did you see a tall man?" he asked one of the women at the register on the right. "He had a gray windbreaker. He might have gone in the back."

The woman answered in indecipherable French. Dean didn't wait to hear the translation from the Art Room — he leaned over the side, getting a good view of the back. There were no back entrances; even supplies came through the small opening at the side.

The snack counter on the other side was even smaller, with no place for anyone to hide.

Dean continued to the boarding entrance. There were two officials there, just closing the door.

"Wait," he said. *"S'il vous plaît."*

"Charlie, where are you going?" asked Rockman. "Lia will take the train. You stay in the station."

Dean walked through the door and across to what looked like an escalator down to the train. It turned out to be a moving ramp and it took a moment for him to get his bearings.

"Mr. Dean, where are you going?" said Telach.

"I'm not letting Lia go alone. He's not here."

"She'll be all right."

That's what you said about Korea, he thought, but he said nothing, continuing toward the train.

Lia sat in car eleven, a first-class car near the middle of the eighteen-coach train. The Eurostar seemed less than half-full, if that. There were only three other passengers in the car — an elderly woman two seats away and a pair of twenty-something lovers who'd been whispering in German when Lia came in.

She hadn't seen anyone with a gray jacket on the platform, and she'd made sure she was one of the first passengers down and one of the last in. Probably he'd taken off his coat; the Art Room had downloaded a blurry picture of the suspect that she could use to check out the passengers more thoroughly once the train started. She would also put the camera attachment on the satellite phone to beam images back to the Art Room, so the computers could go over the faces as well.

They had two tentative names — Patrick McCormack and Horace Clark. The name was bound to be an alias, assuming the Art Room had matched it to the right passenger. But they were checking the names against various watch lists anyway.

The doors closed; the train began to lurch forward — and Dean appeared around the corner of the car.

"This isn't your car," Lia said as he sat down across from her. The first-class seats faced each other across a table, two spots on the right side of the coach and singles on the other.

"Why? Somebody sitting here?" Dean pushed back in the seat, spreading his arms across the back and taking it over. He had that sort of air about him, as if he owned everything he touched.

"Telach wanted you to stay in the station," Lia told him.

"That would have been dumb. If he got out, they would have seen him. He must have put on a disguise somewhere. Besides, I couldn't have gotten out of the waiting area without blowing my cover. Which I'm not supposed to do. Right?"

"Maybe there's an exit from the waiting area the Art Room doesn't know about," said Lia. "Rockman thinks every schematic he looks at is accurate just because he got it off a computer. I can't tell you how many doors I've gone through that the Art Room said didn't exist."

"If our John Doe got out, then he's long gone," said Dean.

A pair of French border policemen walked through the car toward the back.

"Do they always put policemen on the train?" Dean asked.

"Are you talking to me or the Art Room?"

"You. Marie said they're busy back there."

"They're always busy," Lia said. "Especially when you need them."

Lia realized how bitter her words sounded — and that the Art Room would inevitably have heard them, since her communications system was on. But the words were out and she couldn't take them back.

She had every right to be bitter — they'd let her down when she needed them the most.

No, they hadn't let her down. They hadn't been able to help, not immediately. They hadn't abandoned her — they'd sent the Russians, made phone calls, got

Fashona in place. Rubens would have sent the Marines if he needed to.

It wasn't the Art Room's fault or Rubens', or hers or anyone's. It was the nature of the job. All this high-tech garbage didn't save you from being alone, truly alone, when the volcano erupted.

You were always alone. Always.

Dean reached his hand across the small table toward hers. Lia pulled back.

"You going to be angry for the rest of your life?" asked Dean.

How do I answer that? she wondered. *Be sarcastic?* "If I'm lucky." *Be poignant?* "Maybe." *Be truthful?* "I have no idea."

She pulled out the phone and put the camera attachment on it. "I'm going to take a walk. Rockman, stand by to download live video of our companions on the train."

79

Rubens found it more difficult than normal to wait patiently for Johnny Bib to get to the point. He knew from experience that it would do absolutely no good to tell Johnny Bib to get to the point — if anything, it might make him take twice as long — but Rubens needed to get back to Hadash and the President as soon as possible.

"Six units of thirty-two-point-seventy-three pounds apiece," Johnny was saying on the phone line. "Of course the original formulas were configured in kilograms and I've converted."

Telach, standing over Rockman at the computer console a few feet away, waved at him.

"Johnny, what exactly are the units?" said Rubens, holding up his finger to tell Telach to wait.

Johnny was several stories above the bunkered Art Room, but Rubens could almost see him standing back from his desk in surprise at the question. He found it baffling that anyone couldn't follow his convoluted logic through its myriad twists and turns.

"Explosive value similar to the yield of the original equation," said the team leader. "But in small bits — in the formula they look like variables, but I asked myself, Why would the variables be just of certain sizes? And of course, if they were packages or packets that you had to carry a certain way, say if you sewed up vests full of explosive, OK? Vests a man could wear, then remove and set at the proper position. That's the way this formula is constructed, to figure out how many packets you need and where to put it. Now, if we substitute —"

"Johnny, tell me clearly: Are you saying that this formula is related to another attack on the Eiffel Tower or not?"

"The formula includes calculations for the tensile value of steel similar to the characteristics of the girder structure between the second and third *étage* of the Eiffel Tower," said Johnny Bib. "*Étage* means 'floor' in French."

"I remember my French, thank you very much," said Rubens, snapping his underling on hold. He pressed the button on the communications selector on his belt, connecting himself with Hadash in Air Force One. "George, there's a new development."

80

The stairwell that extended upward from the second floor of the Eiffel Tower was far more exposed than the ones below, and Karr could feel the wind whipping at him as he trotted up the steps. There were five or six men above him, across the opposite pier. A pair of elevator shafts ran through the center of the structure to the top, but only one was being operated. Its car rose slowly past the cluster of painters.

Or supposed painters. Karr still hadn't seen any paint cans or brushes or other equipment. Just coveralls that could hide quite a bit.

"Stand by for Mr. Rubens," said Rockman.

"You sound out of breath," Karr told him as he climbed. "If I didn't know any better, I'd think you were the one climbing the stairs."

"Tommy, I'm on the line with the national security adviser."

"Hello," said Karr. He quickened his

pace as he turned the corner, trying to keep the painters in sight. There were roughly a thousand steps to the top; Karr had gone up about a third of them. The men were two-thirds of the way to the third *étage*.

It looked to him as if one was taking off his coverall.

"What's going on?" asked Hadash.

"We've just found a formula to damage the top part of the Eiffel Tower using six bombs placed together on one of the main girders," said Rubens. "We're going to alert the French authorities. I'd like you to —"

Karr cut him off. "You'd better do it quick," he said, running up the stairway. "They're wearing explosive vests under their coveralls. That's how they got the explosives in."

81

Mussa checked his watch as the train passed Charles de Gaulle Airport and began to pick up speed. It took roughly an hour to reach the Chunnel from Paris; they had a little over forty-five minutes to go.

Forty-five minutes to be caught.

The brothers would be at the Eiffel Tower by now. Those two were maniacs — imbeciles, to put it more accurately. They would have others just like them to help.

Forty-four minutes to go. Forty-four chances to be caught.

Was he losing his resolve? Had he suddenly become a coward?

Hardly.

"The dragon lady is in a terrible mood," said Ahmed, coming back from the other car. "She thinks there was some foul-up with the ticket system and she will somehow be held accountable. The train was supposed to be sold out."

Mussa suppressed a laugh. To expedite the plan, they had filed a large number of phony reservations, aiming to keep the train nearly empty. Even the second-class cars, normally overflowing, were less than half-full. He had planned the attack for this run because there were few "walk-ups," or last-minute ticket buyers. Fewer passengers meant less chance at interference.

"You have to bring one of the carts forward with the drinks," said Ahmed. "It has to go to car nine."

Mussa selected the cart and backed it out of the holding area. It bumped sharply on the metal furring between the rug and aluminum flooring. The jerk shocked him, and for a millisecond he thought that he had taken the wrong cart and had somehow set off the explosives. This was impossible, yet for the tiny space of time he thought, he felt, he knew it had happened. Even when the shock of the moment passed, he found it difficult to breathe properly.

I am not a coward. I am a believer, and a great man. My father was a great man, and I am his son.

God is great.

Mussa pushed the cart into the passenger area of the train car. The clear plastic of the overhead rack caught his face in its reflections: a deep, worried frown. He forced himself to smile, or at least try to smile, and pushed forward, wheeling the cart to the end of the car. There were five people: an old woman, two young people in their twenties, a woman, and an older man in his fifties. The older man's stare swept into Mussa's face. Mussa felt himself wincing, as if the glance were a physical thing.

I can do this easily. I have built an empire and braved much greater dangers. I am a soldier of God, the one, true God.

He made his way between the cars, pushing the cart forward. The other steward, an Englishwoman, met him in car twelve and went with him to car nine. She had him help her set the trays in the vestibule at the end of the car. As he helped, someone came to use the nearby restroom.

Mussa glanced up as the man came through the door. As the man turned to go into the restroom, Mussa swore it was Donohue, the Irish assassin.

Impossible! He's in Paris, killing Ponclare.

Mussa stared after him for a moment, then realized that the man had a mustache. His hair had also begun to gray. And now that he thought of it, wasn't he a little taller than the former IRA man and thinner?

I cannot let my imagination run away with me, Mussa told himself, turning to help the other attendant.

82

Karr was about twenty feet below the nearest man when one of the others pulled an MP-5 submachine gun from beneath his coverall. Tommy started to duck down but lost his balance and slid down the stairway.

Bullets ripped against the metal. Slugs ricocheted everywhere.

Karr's chin slapped against one of the treads so hard he thought he'd been nailed by a bullet. He was surprised to find his face intact when he finally stopped sliding.

He jumped up, then ducked away as another burst bounced through the iron rafters.

"Get the French here, now!" he shouted. "And get the people down off the tower."

Piped over the Art Room's loudspeakers, the bullets sounded like a drummer's rim shots off the side of a snare. Rubens gritted his teeth and turned to Telach.

"Why aren't the French moving?" he asked her.

"We're working on it."

"Work faster, Marie."

"We're hearing shots at the Eiffel Tower?" asked Hadash over the line to Air Force One.

"Yes," said Rubens.

"The French President is just coming up," said Hadash. "I'll leave the line open."

"Of course," said Rubens.

Karr, pinned down, guessed he was still two hundred feet below the third floor of the tower, with the terrorists twenty or so feet above him. Except for the one firing at him, they were moving upward.

From what Rubens had said, the plan would be to put all of the explosive charges together. Which meant there was a little bit of time to stop them.

Easy enough if he had a gun.

The gunfire had stopped; the man had started climbing again.

Karr jumped up and took the steps two at a time, reaching the next flight before a fresh fusillade of bullets rattled around him. As he crouched down, he saw a ladder welded against some of the supports; if he could get to it, he'd be out of the gunman's line of sight.

After a long burst from the submachine

gun, Karr pushed through the steps, jumping up and swinging across to the ladder. His hand slipped as he transferred his weight, and for a moment he hung suspended between the stairwell and the beam.

Then gravity took over, and he began to fall.

83

Donohue could not believe that Mussa was on the train with him — and in the uniform of a train porter. But surely it had been Mussa — he could see the look of recognition in his eyes.

Or was this simply more paranoia?

Donohue bent to the faucet to run some water over his face. He rubbed his eyes and cheeks but kept his fingers away from his mustache.

It had definitely been Mussa.

Was he following him?

Or making his own escape?

Whatever, someone knew where he was or at least the direction he was taking to escape. That was not good.

Donohue's anger suddenly flared. He tightened his fists, trying to control it, trying to control himself. His plan was a good one — he was safe, surely.

Unless Mussa was following him to order his death.

He stared at the door. He had no

weapon but his hands.

He would kill Mussa if he had to. Mussa and whoever he sent. Kill them gladly with his bare hands.

Nearly trembling with his anger, Donohue punched the large square button next to the door to let himself out.

84

Tommy Karr saw colors and then brown, felt nothing and then fierce pain. His head snapped forward and he twisted, broken in half.

The moment pushed outward and then collapsed, time bending and twisting in three different directions at once.

He wasn't falling anymore.

He was across a beam, and the world was on a slant.

He'd fallen onto the grid work. The fall had knocked the wind out of him and battered his body, but considering the alternative, he was in *great* shape.

Gradually, Karr recovered his breath. He'd fallen only a few feet, slipping down to one of the cross members, landing like a noodle across it. His head had jammed against a metal screen. His left leg hung free, but his right rested on one of the tower lights, twisted in thick cable that connected the light to the others nearby.

"OK," he said aloud, "let's get this show

on the road." But he couldn't move.

He couldn't find his hands. They seemed to be severed from his body. Finally he managed to turn his head and see his fingers gripping the meshwork near his face. Karr moved them slowly, then pushed his head back against the stabs and jolts at his neck.

"Go, let's go," he told himself. "Go, go, go. Come on, Tommy!"

He forced himself to start climbing.

The screen ran up the side of one of the girders near the elevator. While the rectangular holes were too narrow for footholds he found he could push his toes against the metal for traction.

The terrorists were clustered above, no longer paying attention to him. He pushed himself to move faster, but his head spun and he had to stop for a moment, rest.

The elevator began moving downward. Two of the terrorists swung down from above the girder where the others were working — they'd been on the top floor, which probably explained why the police hadn't tried to get down from above.

Karr watched impotently as the two men began firing at the elevator. The machine continued downward as the bullets sprayed through it. He saw the face of a woman screaming and blood splattered against the glass doorway as the gondola disappeared below.

Kill them. Throw them off the tower. Now!

He started moving again.

The air around him exploded as the helicopters swooped in, one raking the side of the tower with its 7.62mm machine gun. Karr gripped the wire, the structure reverberating with the torrent of bullets the wash from the rotor.

A voice told Karr to leave, to get out of there now. It took a moment for him to realize it was the Art Room.

"There's a helicopter firing on them!" he shouted.

"Get down!" yelled Rockman. "Get out of there. Go!"

Yeah, right, Karr thought. *Move and I'm dead. I don't even know why I'm not dead now.*

The terrorists began firing back. Between the forest of iron grids and the buffeting winds, the helicopters had a hard time getting their bullets close to the terrorists. Finally one of the terrorists above slumped against the beam.

Two figures came down from farther up, down on the stairs. They were policemen.

"Tell the cops they're almost directly

above the terrorists," said Karr.

"What cops?" said Rockman. "There are no policemen on the third level."

"Are you talking to the French or what? There are two cops or gendarmes or whatever . . ."

One of the men had a case in his hand. White smoke flared from the stairs and there was a huge explosion — the man had fired an antiair missile point-blank into the fuselage of one of the helicopters. The craft pitched hard to the right, then disappeared.

85

Johnny Bib admired his boss — William Rubens was, he had to admit, one of the few people in the organization who truly appreciated the worth of a prime number. Still, Johnny had long ago concluded that Rubens was not a "people person." Johnny was willing to dismiss his rude behavior as a result of the pressure of the present operation. Still, Rubens irked him so much that he lost his entire train of thought. So when Blondie ran into the room waving a computer DVD-R disk in her hand, Johnny Bib had no idea what she was talking about.

"The computer that accessed the library. It's part of a network in a printing plant. They back up their drives several times a day on RAID-5 disk arrays," she said.

"What do you mean?" asked Johnny.

"The computer system that was used to access the library: it had a backup system that wrote files to two disks at once. They uploaded the formulas, probably because they had to work them at times the library computers weren't up. There were copies on the drive. They must have erased the originals, but I have some copies of deleted backups. They didn't erase them all, Johnny. They did it on some sort of schedule, but they didn't get parts of the temporary backups. There is a whole set of files they never erased."

Blondie put the disk into a nearby computer. The drive began to whirl.

"This is the most interesting, this series. Look — it's another set of formulas, an explosion simulation. It's almost the whole thing! It's like the Eiffel Tower, but one of much greater power. Look at all these formulas and the size of these numbers."

"What's being modeled?" he asked.

"A three-dimensional area affected by an explosion," said Blondie. "These values are so high — I think it's an earthquake of six-point-oh magnitude. Maybe it was to shake down the concept behind the formula, get the process right. They must have started here, figured out how to get the program to work, then revised it for the Eiffel Tower. Can we find somebody to try and re-create what's missing?"

"Wait," said Johnny Bib. "I've seen this before."

Johnny Bib stared at his screen. The

numbers of some of the equations would produce a Fibonacci series.

No, not precisely; no, he was wrong.

It was a progression, though. And one he'd seen recently.

It was a wave amplification.

He'd seen a similar model on the computer the French had compromised a few months before, the one the terrorists had stopped using.

"Hmmm."

"Part of this is just like the Eiffel Tower with the modular thing," added Blondie. "Where they had a routine to add the explosions together. But look, it's like weird, because there are these waves being focused and stuff? I don't get it."

Another equation with waves, but this clearly wasn't designed to calculate or demonstrate the effects of a tsunami. It looked more like a three-dimensional compression of some sort.

Numbers were strewn across the screen. Johnny Bib's brain pulled them into a coherent shape — focused wave formulas.

What would you want to compress with an explosion?

"Those variables are a multiple of the values from the explosives that are used in the Eiffel Tower simulation?" asked

Johnny, pointing at the screen.

"I think yes," answered Blondie.

"They wouldn't yield that large an explosion."

"No way. I mean, I'd have to work through the math, but I would just about —"

"Bring the team here quickly," said Johnny Bib, jumping up. "Bring everyone — everyone. And someone from the history department. Two people from history! Someone from special weapons — whoever worked on the French warhead that's missing from Algeria. Hurry!"

86

Karr tried to push upward while the terrorists were still distracted by the helicopters. But his arms wouldn't move.

The second helicopter roared toward the tower from behind him. Karr closed his eyes, sensing that he was being targeted this time. Flares shot into the air, and then gunfire. The world shook violently.

The helicopter wasn't firing at him but at the stairway above, where the missile-wielding terrorists were. Another missile shot away from the tower and the chopper wheeled away.

A dozen smells began to choke him. The helicopter buzzed back.

A body toppled past, rebounding in the grid work until it wedged against a pair of V-shaped cross members.

More gunfire.

Another terrorist slid down the steps until Karr couldn't see him anymore, something clattering with him.

A gun?

Karr had no idea, but he decided it was a gun and that he was going to get it.

"Rockman, if you can tell the helicopter not to shoot me, I'd appreciate it," he said, starting to claw his way back around the mesh to the stairwell.

"Tommy, get out of there!"

A rocket-propelled grenade whipped from the cluster of terrorists working with the explosions and vests. It exploded right beneath the helicopter's chin, and the aircraft seemed to rear up and then nose down, plunging to the earth after rebounding against the side of the tower.

Karr closed his eyes and snaked his way through the metal, diving back toward the steps in a tumble. As he was stunned, it took a moment before he could start crawling upward.

As he turned the corner onto the fourth set of steps, a large pole shot through the grid work a few feet from his head. He ducked belatedly, then turned to see where the pole had gone. It was only when he saw the object explode in the sky a hundred yards away that he realized it was a missile, launched by another helicopter.

"Tell the helicopter not to do the job for them!" Karr yelled to the Art Room.

"Tommy, get out of there. Get down!" said Telach.

"Yeah," he muttered. "I'm working on that."

Two eyes stared down at him as he turned the next corner: the dead terrorist lay across the stairwell, head and body at different angles.

His body lay atop something. A gun.

Karr crawled to the man as fast as he could. The only thing he thought of, the only thing he saw, was the gun.

Except it wasn't a gun. It was an empty launching tube for a rocket-propelled grenade. He pounded the dead man's body in his rage, pounded and pounded, felt something hard against his fist.

He clawed at the man, pulling away his clothes.

A pistol.

He grabbed it, made sure it was ready to fire, and turned in the direction of the white coveralls a few feet away.

87

Lia pulled a bag of chips from the rack at the refreshment counter, then realized she had only a twenty-euro bill. The attendant sighed but dug into the register dutifully. Lia took the money and walked toward the end of the car opposite the one she'd come in through, as if she were an absentminded passenger who'd lost her bearings. She'd already been through the train once without finding their quarry, but there was little to do now until they reached England, which wouldn't be for more than an hour; they were still a good ten or fifteen minutes or so from the entrance to the Chunnel.

Most likely, the suspect had found some other entrance at the Eurostar terminal to sneak out of. Dean had blown it when he decided to come on the train.

About time he messed *something* up. Maybe he wouldn't be so high-and-mighty, Mr. Perfect Ex-Marine.

She was angry at him for no good reason, just to be angry.

And she loved him.

Lia forced herself to concentrate on the job, scanning the faces in the seats as she walked through the cars. She continued through to the end, attracting a few odd stares as she pretended to hunt for her seat. As she turned around, she overheard one of the male passengers whispering to his companion something about a nice piece of meat.

She spun and unleashed a flood of French curse words at him. The man turned white and managed a meek apology as she spun away.

"What was that about?" asked Sandy Chafetz, popping onto the communications line. She'd just taken over for Rockman.

"Called me a sweet meal," said Lia.

"You sure he meant you, not his lunch?"

"Does it matter?" snapped Lia, passing between cars.

Dean shifted in the seat, staring at the door at the end of the coach. If the suspect — now tentatively ID'd as a Mr. McCormack, birth location and place unknown — had gotten onto the train, he must have disguised himself somehow. The easiest way to do that was by changing clothes, but he must have done more or Dean would have found him by now.

"Charlie, this is Sandy Chafetz. I've come in to help out. I'm going to run your end of the mission. There's a lot going on in Paris right now."

Dean turned toward the window, cupping his hand over his face so the fact that he was talking to himself wouldn't be so conspicuous. "Like what?"

"The Eiffel Tower is being attacked. And the President is still at de Gaulle."

"Is he the target?"

"We don't think so."

"Where's Tommy Karr?"

"He's all right. We want you to keep focused on your mission. We have a list of the passengers who checked in. Your subject was in a second-class car, seat number —"

"I went through this with Rockman," Dean told her. "There's a kid in that seat about nine years old. I even looked at her ticket."

He had pretended to be confused about the seat. The girl's mother, sitting next to her, showed the proper ticket. It was possible that she'd switched with someone, but the woman didn't seem to understand his question when he asked. In any event, McCormack was no longer nearby.

"We're using a pattern recognition program to review the images we captured from the security cameras in the station and compare them with the ones Lia took earlier," said Chafetz. "The first pass hasn't shown any hits, but we're widening the parameters. We're going to ask the British authorities to meet the train and quarantine it. They may have to do that outside the station; we're not sure yet. We don't have to make a decision for a while; the train actually goes pretty slowly once it comes out of the Chunnel."

"How good is your program?"

"Still experimental," Chafetz admitted. "But if we get a straight-on shot or a decent profile, we can match. Once we get beyond the first pass, things get a little more problematic. We're also looking at it ourselves."

"You can't just match up person for person?"

"We're trying, Charlie. The problem is we didn't start with a good shot in the first place and we didn't have direct coverage inside the waiting area. The French video surveillance system is not what you would call cutting-edge, and it wasn't set up to watch the Eurostar area. They obviously figured the security at the gates would suffice. So we have to enhance images from cameras on the far platform, and it's not quite a piece of cake. At the same time, your subject obviously changed his appearance. Since we don't know who he is, we have to work backward — we're matching the people who haven't changed. The computer program was not designed to do what we're trying to do, so even if we had good images to start with, it wouldn't be easy. It doesn't mean that we won't get it. Just that it'll take a few minutes. OK?"

"OK. I appreciate the explanation."

Lia came into the car and sat down across from him.

"The Eiffel Tower is under attack," he told her.

"Where's Tommy?"

"They won't say."

"Then he's in the middle of it."

There was a tone on the loudspeaker. The train master spoke, repeating the same message in French and English:

"Ladies and gentlemen, we are approaching the English Channel. We will be in the Chunnel for a short ride."

"Ahead of schedule," said Lia.

"We have six possibilities," said Chafetz. "We'll be able to download them to you in about three minutes. See if you can check each one out, get any additional information."

"Can you transmit when we're in the Chunnel?" asked Dean.

"Uh, no. All right, I'm sorry — the train is ahead of schedule. We may have to wait until you're out. We won't be able to transmit while you're in the tunnel. But it won't be long. It only takes ten minutes or so. You're not going anywhere."

"Just to the restroom," said Dean, getting up.

88

"French television is just getting images of the battle at the Eiffel Tower," Telach told Rubens.

"The surveillance network we tapped into?"

"That went out when the terrorists blew up the stairs and the elevator on the north and south legs. The news feed is all we can get."

"Put the French news feed on the screen," he told her.

A blurred blue image filled the screen, too shaky and distant for Rubens to make out. Then the Eiffel Tower came into view, the old grid work stark against the backdrop of the sky. Smoke curled from the side and top.

Rubens knew from Tommy's description that the terrorists were clustered around a girder about twenty feet below the third level. There wasn't enough detail for Rubens to make out what was going on, but he assumed that they were stitching their bomb vests together. They'd be almost done now.

"Tell the French not to let them put their bomb packs together," Rubens told Telach.

"We already have."

"Tell them again."

Johnny Bib burst through the door at the side of the room, two of his analysts behind him.

"Johnny, things are chaotic here," warned Rubens.

"I know where the old French atomic warhead is," said Johnny Bib. "We found another simulation, this one involving a nuclear device."

89

The first shot missed high.

The next took down the terrorist who was kneeling above the others on the girder.

After that, Karr lost track, emptying the pistol into the men perched in the grid work less than three yards away. Someone began firing back, but Karr kept shooting until he ran out of bullets. Then he slid back to the dead terrorist, hoping he'd missed another magazine of bullets before.

Two more helicopters buzzed nearby. The structure shuddered as slugs from the 12.7mm weapons hit the girders. Tommy looked up from the body and saw one of the terrorists fall. There were two men huddled on the girder across from him, working on what looked like a pile of small potatoes stacked against the X-shaped strut work.

Part of the bomb.

If the empty missile launcher had been a gun or if the dead man next to him had

had more bullets, Karr could have easily picked the two men off.

He grabbed the empty tube and ran up the steps another flight, thinking there might be another rocket-propelled grenade somewhere. But there was nothing there and not on the next one, either.

Something exploded below him. The French gendarmes had gotten ropes and were climbing up from the second floor; one of the terrorists had dropped a grenade on them.

Just give me a gun, Karr thought. Then, desperate to do something, he threw the empty grenade launcher at the terrorists. He missed by a mile.

Out of other options, he flung his body onto the grid work and began climbing down in their direction.

90

Mussa waited for the passenger to pass through the doorway before locking down the wheels to the serving cart and pulling open the cabinet so he could remove the two bombs. They were Semtex, more sensitive to shock than the material in the molded cases. How much more sensitive he wasn't sure, but he made sure not to drop them.

Unlike conventional trains, all but two of the coaches on the high-speed Eurostar shared what trainmen called a common truck, the large wheel assembly below the base of the car. These cars were essentially welded together; separating them while the Eurostar was moving without completely destroying the train was probably impossible. But for safety reasons there was one spot where a more conventional coupler was used. This allowed the train to be separated in an emergency inside the Chunnel, with either half able to proceed, thanks to the fact that there was a power car at either end. The device, called a

Scharfenberg coupler device, was located between cars nine and ten; it was invisible to anyone walking between the cars, since it was located below the floor.

Mussa had to place his two bombs in precise locations so that the coupler would be obliterated without damaging the cars enough to derail the train. Neither bomb was all that small, of course; they'd still kill anyone within a few yards of the burst — including Mussa if he was not careful.

He measured the location of the first bomb using the package itself — exactly ten bomb lengths from the sidewall at the center and then over four lengths toward the front of the train. Mussa dropped to his knees and turned the package over and over, only to find the spot blocked by the metal bulkhead of the car's inner door.

Had there been a mistake?

He slid the bomb as close as he could to the proper spot, then placed the other package. He rammed his fingers into the triggering devices — a simple poke hole at the top of each bomb — then began running into coach ten, grabbing his submachine gun from the cart as he went.

91

The bullet caught the top of Karr's shoulder and made him lose his grip. He tried to swing himself forward so that he would land on the man who had shot at him, but instead he bounced against the edge of the metal fence and rebounded to the left, tumbling over but somehow managing to fall into the V of two girders right next to the man with the gun.

Karr saw the weapon, a Beretta pistol; the next thing he knew he was falling against the man, struggling against the thick girder.

There were two other men nearby in a steel-piped cage, and there were wires around Karr's hand. The men didn't have the coveralls the others had. Karr thought for a second that they were policemen, but then something cracked, loudly, and he felt pain in his skull.

Something hard smacked his head again. A boot — one of the men was kicking him.

I'm dead, Karr thought, but he fought on.

Karr rolled and then saw that he was against the stack of bomb material — six large pieces of molded plastic strapped together with wire against the metal girder. He started tearing at them, felt something stabbing at him — he twirled and slammed his arm, throwing his assailant off.

The man fell, shrieking as he bounced off the ironwork.

Karr saw the wire for the bombs wrapped around the post. He grabbed at the wire, pulling but unable to get it off.

"Off!" he yelled. "Off! Off! Off!"

"The packages have to go off together," said Rockman in his ear. "Pull them apart."

Yeah, no kidding.

The helicopter loomed above.

"Get the helicopter away!" Karr shouted as the air around him began to explode.

92

Dean was just punching the lock button on the bathroom door when he heard the explosion. He slapped his hand against the open button, but the door didn't respond. He slammed the large button again, harder this time. The door hissed open as the train shuddered, wheels and brakes screeching ferociously. People in the car screamed, throwing themselves down — Dean ran through the coach toward the back as the lights flickered. The back end of coach nine had been blackened and some of the metal twisted; an old man lay white-faced on the floor, arm severed just above the elbow. He looked at Dean for a split second, horror in his eyes.

There were voices behind him, shouts. Dean pushed into the vestibule at the back of the train, now a jagged and misshapen envelope of metal. Sparks flew upward; the train rocked violently from side to side, still moving at a good pace.

The train had been severed; the other

half was behind them but a good distance away, with the gap growing even as the brakes were applied. The gap was five, then ten meters. There was another explosion, more sparks, screams from behind him.

Lia was in the other half of the train.

Dean waited a few more seconds as the gap grew wider, then he leaped into the darkness.

93

Rubens pushed the button on the com device, selecting the direct line back to Air Force One, and in the meantime strode toward Sandy Chafetz's console.

"George, we have more information for the French — and the British. The Chunnel may be a target," Rubens told the national security adviser. "The computer that accessed the one where the formulas for damaging the Eiffel Tower were discovered had another formula for blowing up the Chunnel. We're still trying to pull the scenario together, but it looks as if it's intended to trigger a tsunami across the English Channel. It may involve the French warhead."

"That's impossible," said Hadash. "Even if the tunnel were to collapse."

"Actually, the simulation shows it's *not* impossible," said Rubens. He stopped in front of Chafetz. "The shock wave would have considerable force, at least that of a large earthquake. We haven't been able to verify the calculations on our side yet, but these simulations anticipate waves reaching over fifty feet, which would flood much of the Netherlands, not to mention the ports along the coast. But even if they are wrong and just the Chunnel itself is destroyed, it would be a massive terrorist strike. The impact in Europe would be incredible."

Hadash didn't reply.

"We have to shut down traffic through it, at least until we have more information," said Rubens.

"Agreed," said Hadash. "I have the President of France here. I'm going to put him on the line, with the President's permission."

As he waited, Rubens glanced down at Chafetz.

"Where are Dean and Lia?" he asked.

"They're in the Chunnel. Something's going on there — one of the transmission stations just recorded a wild power fluctuation."

94

Dean's first thought as he rolled onto the track was that he hoped he didn't hit the third rail and fry to death. Then as he rebounded he realized the back half of the train was still moving in his direction at a very good pace and very likely to run him over. He felt the rumble and sensed the air closing in on him — he pushed to what he thought was the middle of the track, squeezing himself down as a tornado engulfed him.

Lia jumped from her seat when she heard the explosion. But as she got up, a man came into the car firing a submachine gun. She threw herself down between the seat and the table, rolling on the floor as the car exploded around her.

Charlie, Charlie, Charlie — are you OK?

The gunfire continued, the man and then another passing through the car. There were screams and then another explosion.

Lia wondered why she was still alive, why the gunman hadn't shot her.

She was in the interrogation room in Korea, rolling and fighting them off, attacked.

I'll kill them. I'll kill them.

But she couldn't. For the first time in her life she couldn't win, no matter how hard she fought.

The wind stopped. Dean remained prone against the ballast segment at the base of the tracks, the scent of burnt metal thick in his nose, his lungs choked with dust and smoke. He could feel his heart pounding in his chest and at his temple. The train had seemed to scrape along the top of his back, but he didn't think he'd been injured.

When his heart stopped pounding he pushed to get up. He slammed his head so hard that he fell down immediately, stunned; it was only then that he realized the train had stopped over him.

Finally he began to push forward, but he got only a few feet before his way was blocked; the rear power car was too low to the tracks for him to get under. There was no way around it. He tried to turn, but there was no room, and so he had to back up, working out slowly.

Lia's alive, he thought to himself. *And I'm going to go get her out.*

95

Karr pushed at the plastic lump, then felt his balance give way. He groped wildly in the air; before he could grab onto anything he smacked hard against a metal bar and began to fall in the other direction. But the cord he'd twisted around his arm pulled taut and held him.

Only for a moment. He slipped down two feet as the light it was attached to pulled away from the structure, socket and all. Tommy grabbed a cross member but lost his grip, swinging against one of the other girders and smacking his head. Blood ran down the side of his face. Dizzy but still managing to hold on, he realized the wire was now taut again. He gave it a gingerly tug, then a much stronger one, and pulled upward. He got his head even with the bomb sacks, but as he reached for them he slipped or the wire slipped and he spun into a thin ladder used by workmen when replacing the lights and doing other work. He grabbed at it, so disoriented that even with the solid foot- and handholds he thought he was falling.

The explosive packs were a few feet away to his left. When the world stopped spinning a little, Karr reached toward them, lost his balance, and slipped off the ladder. He became a disembodied head and unconnected arms, grabbing at wires and the air, pulling and punching and screaming.

One of the explosive vests flew downward, bounced off a post, and then sailed below, where it exploded. Tommy Karr saw the explosion in slow motion, gray and black particles steaming up toward him. He thought he was flying, then realized he was on the beam with the bombs. He took another package and this one he was able to heave, sending it far into space toward the gold dome. It disappeared there, and then there was another explosion from the ground, far away and yet close enough to shake him so violently he thought he was flying through the tangled steel.

The next vest sailed down but failed to explode for what seemed like hours. He grappled with a fourth and flung it, and somehow this one looked as if it exploded nearly in his hands.

Had it? The pain that had pulsated through his body left him. He felt a tickle in his neck, the light touch of a girl's fingers stroking him — Deidre, he thought. For a moment he thought of nothing and saw nothing and felt nothing.

The moment stretched into an hour and then collapsed back on itself. When he managed to clear his head he saw he was upside down, his legs jammed against the ladder, the last explosive pack on the girder above him, just out of reach. He grabbed it on his second try and flung it as far as he could.

It burst open into a cloud of dust.

His head weighed five hundred pounds. His heart thumped like the heavy whoop of a helicopter blade.

A helicopter was five or ten yards away, hovering there.

Somebody yelled at him in French.

He vaguely understood that they were telling him not to move.

96

Mussa permitted himself a moment to gather his breath after the train had been successfully stopped by Ahmed, who had slipped into the rear power car before the bombs went off. Running through the cars with their submachine guns, Muhammad and Kelvin had killed the passengers. Mussa himself had shot the French border policeman who'd had the bad luck to be on the back half of the train.

The man had turned to Mussa at the last moment, as the blood burst in a cloud from the side of his head. The look bothered Mussa — it was the expression of a man not ready to die.

Undoubtedly he'd seen that expression often, certainly in his early days. But he could not remember it bothering him as much as now.

A test from Allah of his resolution.

The floor shuddered and a hiss rose from beneath him. Ahmed was unhooking the power car from the rest of the train. He would drive it down the track about thirty yards, providing a barrier to anyone who happened to pursue. The engine would also have a very minor role in helping to deflect the explosive blast upward, in case the yield of the weapon was less than calculated. The track communication system, which used the tracks to convey signal and other information, would be jammed from the car with an electrical interference device.

God was great.

"We are done," said Kelvin, entering coach eighteen with Muhammad.

"The carts will be set up here. Come."

Lia's mind retreated as the punches landed against her. She stepped back, cowering.

Had she always been a weakling? Had she simply fooled herself into believing she was strong?

So many times she'd been faced with danger — in the Army as well as working with Deep Black — and she'd never felt fear like this, never been paralyzed.

All her life she'd lived by the belief that cowards died. She felt herself melting toward the darkness, a trapped mouse waiting to be exterminated.

Muhammad and Kelvin slammed the carts over the transom as they pulled them from the storage area where he had hidden them.

"Careful!" Mussa yelled. "Careful! One at a time. Both of you. Use caution!"

Assuming the calculations on his stopwatch were correct, they were roughly eight and a third miles from the French side of the tunnel, perfect — or as close to perfect as possible. All he had to do was set up the device.

The emergency lighting system bathed the coach a fitful reddish yellow. Mussa had night-vision glasses but opted not to use them; they were clumsy and there was more than enough light to see what he had to do. He directed the others to bring the first cart forward. One of the women they had shot lay in a pool of blood at the middle of the car, the point where the engineer had calculated the bomb should be placed. Mussa stepped over her and then guided the cabinet against her prone body before twisting it around. The cabinets had to form a tight box around the device.

Mussa removed the painted aluminum cover and false drawers and hinges from the cabinet, then reached to the bottom to clear out the connecting tabs. The final move was the most difficult — the explosive box sat on a wheeled tray that had to be pushed out toward him while the explosives unit remained in place. The dead body behind the cabinet helped the process; it gave them something to steady the cabinet against and then ease it to the floor. With the tray in place, he removed the plastic panel at the top, removed the wheels, and cleared the circuit units that connected it to the others and the timing circuitry.

Perspiration beaded down the side of his face as he finished. Kelvin approached with the second cart, which had to be lowered and wedged precisely against the first. This was a problem not only because it weighed nearly two hundred pounds but also because of the narrow squeeze in the aisles where it had to be placed.

Kelvin had begun huffing as they stopped. Grunting, he started to tip it and then lost his grip; for a moment Muhammad held it balanced precariously on two wheels. Mussa threw his own hands out to grab it, pushing at the top to send it back the other way, but it was too heavy — the chest fell backward toward the floor as Mussa felt the air vanish from his lungs.

Mussa stared at the space before him,

sensing that he was about to be vaporized but unable to act. And then he felt himself falling straight backward, the sensation of horror mixing with weightlessness.

Donohue leaped out of his seat, forcing himself upright against the force of the train's braking. He couldn't decipher what had happened. There'd been an explosion, several explosions — Mussa undoubtedly was behind this, the demented slime. Donohue would strangle him with his bare hands.

The police would be all over this.

One of the train workers was sprawled across the aisle, knocked out but breathing. Donohue pushed the woman aside and strode to the rear of the compartment. The train had been traveling at something over one hundred miles an hour when the explosion occurred; the automated emergency braking system had not kicked in and the engineer had hesitated at first to apply full brakes, unsure what was going on. They were rolling to a stop but still moving at a decent pace.

Donohue passed through the next car and then the next and the next; a policeman shouted at him, but Donohue didn't pay any attention, driven as much by his curiosity and his anger at Mussa.

When Donohue reached car nine, he saw that the vestibule at the back of the car over the coupling area had been blown off and the rest of the train left behind. The train remained on the tracks.

He guessed that Mussa would be back with the other cars.

With luck he'd blown himself up.

That would do Donohue little good now. The police would swarm over the train, collect everyone's passport — then check the identities thoroughly. Donohue had no doubt he could get past a cursory screening, but if his fingerprints were taken it would be a different story.

And they were sure to take fingerprints, weren't they?

"You, who are you?" barked a policeman behind him.

Donohue's anger sprang out of control. He moved without thinking, spinning and striking the policeman so quickly that the man did not manage to say a word before he fell to the ground. The assassin spun and, despite the fact that the train was still moving at a pace of twenty miles an hour or so, jumped out onto the tracks.

As Dean sensed he was nearing the end of the train the cars above him started to move. He froze, then realized that if he didn't get away, whatever he'd bumped up against going forward would eventually reach him. He pushed back, scraping both sides of his body.

The cars stopped in a second or two. The power car had nudged them against their set brakes as it uncoupled. It was now moving away at a slow pace.

Dean kept moving. When he finally reached the end of the train he pulled himself out. His arm scraped against the jagged end of the mangled coupler assembly as he got up. The pain took him by surprise and he cursed loudly, unable to stop himself.

Unwise, but too late to do anything about it.

He stuffed the collar of his shirt into his teeth against the pain and climbed up onto the car, whose door had been blown open by the explosion. The emergency lights turned the coach a very dull yellow, as if Dean were wearing sepia glasses.

Bodies were scattered across the seats, blood everywhere. He looked at each one only long enough to make sure that it wasn't Lia, then continued through to the car where she'd been sitting.

★ ★ ★

All her life she'd fought. Losing one battle — losing *this* one — didn't make her a coward.

Lia pushed to get away from the black cloud that sucked at her. She pushed and fought and clawed. She would not give up. Lose, maybe, but not give up.

"Where are you, Charlie? Where are you when I need you?" she mumbled.

"Here."

Lia turned her head to the left, then to the right. The darkness moved away like a cloud of mist clearing a lake. Dean was leaning over her.

"Are you OK?" he asked her.

"No," she said, managing to pull herself up into a half-sitting, half-leaning position.

She forced herself to examine her wounds. One of the bullets from the submachine gun or perhaps just a piece of metal from the floor had ricocheted and lodged in her calf. The bleeding had already slowed to an oozing trickle. Another bullet had hit her midsection, but it had only grazed her side, leaving a large red welt that hurt to touch but was otherwise not painful.

Bullets had riddled the table between the

seat, along with the cushions nearby. Lia had been saved, at least temporarily, by the configuration of the coach, as well the inexperience of the terrorists.

And luck. Never forget luck.

"Can you walk?" Dean asked.

"Maybe."

"They unhooked the power car and took it away."

"Why?" she asked.

"Maybe they're going to ram into the next train. Or maybe they're going to use it somehow to escape."

Someone moaned at the other end of the car.

"There's a light on the side of the tunnel about fifty yards that way," said Dean, pointing toward what had been the front of the train. "I think it's one of the crossover points to the service tunnel in the middle. Maybe there's a phone there. We can get help and warn them."

"Shouldn't we pull these people out?"

"Let's see if we can get help first."

"All right," she said, rising and testing her leg gingerly. It wouldn't take much weight, but she could probably hobble.

She *would* hobble.

"All right," she said. "Lead the way, Charlie Dean."

★ ★ ★

The cabinet took forever to hit the ground. Mussa tried to close his eyes but could not.

He felt the vibration, felt the shock, knew the horror of death. But he didn't die. The explosives had not gone off. As the chemist had said, the material was exceedingly stable.

By the time Mussa realized it hadn't exploded, he had already reached to pull it into the proper position. Now time began to speed up, and he found that his hands and legs couldn't move quickly enough. Kelvin recovered from his own shock and helped move the unit into place. Mussa pulled the panel off, then barked at the others to get the next units in. The next one was placed without a mishap.

Now the device itself had to be placed. Again the cart had to be tipped, but this time they were ready. Despite the weight and Mussa's trembling hands, it snapped into place. Surely God was helping him now. There was no longer a question of failure — there had never been a question of failure. He climbed over the seats to guide the last steps, confident, even awed. The greatness of what he was to accomplish pushed him on. The next units snapped down — there were two left now, two — and then he had merely to punch the buttons and wait.

But as he waited for the last cabinet, something made a thud behind him. He turned and saw a man crawl out from the seats. Mussa reached desperately to his belt, grabbing for his pistol, but it wasn't there; he'd put it down when he started to move the cabinets.

Mussa ran and kicked the man in the back, stopping him. He stepped to the man's side and launched another kick to the back of his head, then another and another and another, dashing the man's skull against the floor of the train. Rage welled in him, and he screamed at the man, asking who he was to try to prevent his triumph.

"Satan? Are you Satan?" he yelled.

Finally, he saw that the man was dead and stopped kicking.

The others were staring at him from behind the half-assembled bomb.

"You were to kill everyone in the train," he told them. "Everyone."

"We did."

"You will go back and make sure. For the glory of God! *Now!*"

97

When Deidre Clancy finally managed to get out of bed, her chest begin to shake. She felt as if all the blood had rushed from her head and refused to come back.

She went to the bathroom and ran water on her face, then saw the pile of towels she'd left on the floor. Her stomach turned, but this time the urge to vomit was gone; the worst of her illness had passed.

Deidre turned on the bath and took off her robe and got in, spraying herself with the wand as the tub filled up. When she was finished, she threw the soiled towels into the tub and filled it with water again, poking them a bit before letting it drain; she had no washing machine in the small apartment and couldn't face the idea of going to the Laundromat today, and maybe not tomorrow, either. After a few rinses the towels were clean enough to be hung on the rail and ledge outside the window. That done, she cleaned the tub and took a proper bath, the water as hot as she could stand it.

A half hour later, she got out, wrapped herself in a thick terry-cloth robe — she was now out of bath towels — and walked to the tiny kitchenette to measure out coffee for the ancient pot. When it was ready she poured herself a cup without her usual cream and went to the small living room, intending to veg out until her senses recovered sufficiently for her to come up with a plan for the rest of the day.

After a few minutes, she turned on the television, expecting to flip absent-mindedly through the offerings.

The first image she saw looked like something from a James Bond movie or maybe Schwarzenegger — helicopters buzzing in the air, circling a tower of smoke.

The Eiffel Tower, she realized.

A very good model, she thought. She punched the button for the next channel, but the image remained.

She glanced down at the remote, making sure she had pressed the proper button. The image remained.

It was the *real* Eiffel Tower.

Two more presses brought her to CNN. She watched the screen as a breathless correspondent based in London announced:

"These are live pictures from Paris, where a group of terrorists has attempted an attack on the Eiffel Tower. Police and local military units are battling them now. The American President landed at Charles de Gaulle Airport just a few minutes prior to the attack, and sources close to the French police say that American intelligence agents provided a last-second warning against the terrorist strike. As you can see, the operation is ongoing. . . ."

Deidre watched as one of the news helicopters zoomed its camera in on the grid work of the tower. A man was hanging upside down near the side, his leg caught in a cable. Two French policemen were climbing up from below; another was trying to get to him from above.

The large man didn't look like a terrorist. He had blond hair and was in jeans and —

Deidre dropped the remote as the man's face briefly came into focus.

It was Tommy Karr. And he was smiling.

98

"Are you sure about this?" demanded Hadash. He was essentially translating what the French President had just asked Rubens.

"*Oui*," said Rubens, speaking French so there would be no doubt in the foreign leader's mind. "*L'Eurostar.* They've found some way of getting the bomb on board the train. We believe they've fashioned something similar to C-4 to use as a kind of explosive lens and detonate the atomic warhead. We don't have all of the data, but I guarantee that they've done this, and that at a minimum an attempt will be made. Our best guess from the power fluctuations we've detected on the system is that it's already under way. Their models for the impact of the explosion predict a tidal wave that will engulf the low-lying areas along the Channel. We're still trying to interpret the data, but you must stop traffic through the Chunnel and get response teams in. I assure you, even if they fail, they will make an attempt."

The French President replied in French that what Rubens was saying seemed incredible and beyond belief. Rubens agreed but added that until an hour ago the same might have been said about an attack on the Eiffel Tower, and here he was watching a feed from French television showing it in broad daylight.

"A great tragedy for the world had it succeeded," added Rubens, who, despite his disdain for the French, meant it.

President Marcke came on the line, asking Rubens if he had any other information. Rubens told him that he had summarized the relevant findings and would share whatever details were needed with the French intelligence and military.

"Do it," said Marcke.

Rubens looked up at the screen. While the Eiffel Tower had not been completely secured, all of the terrorists near the bomb were either dead or severely wounded. Tommy had disabled all of the explosive packs, apparently made into vests that the terrorists had worn and then attempted to assemble on the structure.

French gendarmes had finally reached Karr, who was suspended above the iron latticework by one of the power cables from the lighting. Tommy seemed to be smiling, undoubtedly making one of his irreverent wisecracks to his rescuers.

Thank God.

Hopefully it wasn't X-rated. The French television crew aboard the helicopter caught the entire sequence before being warned away by one of the military aircraft. Undoubtedly a lip-reader back in the studio was already trying to work out what Karr had said. Knowing the French, it would be inscribed at the base of the tower by morning.

Several dozen people had lost their lives, and the structure had surely been damaged. But compared to what *might* have happened, the cost had been relatively minor.

One disaster staved off. And a much greater one looming.

"There is one other thing I should mention," Rubens told President Marcke. "Two of my people were aboard the train that is currently in the Chunnel. They were following a man we think might have been involved in the assassination of Monsieur Ponclare, the security chief. We haven't heard from them since the train entered the tunnel."

"I'm sorry to hear that," said the President. "We'll stay on the line."

"Yes, sir."

"The upstairs operator has a woman named Ellen McGovern on hold," Telach told Rubens as he turned from the screen. "She's an attorney. She said that you would want to speak to her, and that the operator was to mention her name."

Rubens realized that she had news about the General.

"I'll get back to her," he said.

99

Dean's eyes took a few seconds to adjust to the darkness as he climbed out of the yellowish coaches; even when they had, the tracks remained a muddy gray beneath an even darker black. A fluorescent light flickered at the side of the tunnel in the dimness ahead. It marked the doorway to the service tunnel that ran between the two railroad tubes. As Dean stared he made out small green arrows on the side of the tunnel wall in the direction of the door.

"That's the service tunnel back there," he told Lia. "Come on."

The air smelled damp and metallic. He'd taken off part of his shirt to tie around her injured leg, and he felt so cold he began to shiver.

"Let me help you; come on," he told her as she lagged behind.

"I'm fine."

"Can't admit you need help?"

"I'm fine, I said."

"We have to watch for the third rail."

"The train uses an overhead wire," said Lia. "Didn't you see it at the station?"

A stuttering crack snapped through the air: a muffled gunshot.

"They're still in the train," said Lia, stopping. "Look."

Dean turned and looked at the train as the crackle reverberated again. Shadows moved against the wall toward the back of the gray hulk.

"Go see if you can find a phone," Dean told her, starting toward the train.

"Charlie!"

"Do it," he snapped. "If you really are OK, just go do it."

100

Mussa wheeled the last cart out, then slipped around it and climbed on the seat nearby, walking the cart into place.

He expected a sharp snap as he pushed it into place. Instead, it barely clicked. Thinking he had failed to get it in properly, he pushed against it, but it refused to budge. Mussa leaned over, examining the seam at the top. It was tight; he couldn't get his fingernail inside.

He climbed up and pushed from every direction, just to make sure it was locked. It didn't budge.

One more task — the timer. He pulled the top panel off, revealing an oval inset.

"I devote myself to the one true God," he said, beginning one last prayer before setting the weapon. He pulled off his watch as he prayed and pried it from its band, then took off the face and the back.

Something moved at the end of the car. He glanced up and saw a submachine gun entering the car. The timer, which initiated and controlled the internal firing mechanism, dropped from his hand and bounded to the floor.

Mussa saw only the gun.

Ahmed, returning.

Cursing, Mussa hopped off the seat and dropped to the floor, hunting the watch piece.

"Where are the others?" asked Ahmed.

"Finishing their work," said Mussa. He put the clock piece in and twisted. The bomb was now set; it could not be stopped. But either when he dropped it or when he set it in, the switch at the side that selected the timer mode had slipped from nine seconds to nine hundred — the device's default, a hundred times longer than intended.

It began draining off, the seconds kicking down to oblivion.

"Is it ready?" Ahmed asked.

"Yes," said Mussa. He smiled at the other man.

"Let's go then."

Mussa looked at him in surprise. Where did he want to go?

"Aren't we going to take the engine?" asked Ahmed. "Arno said that was the plan. That's why I was to detach it and move up the tracks."

Arno had told him that?

Mussa stared at Ahmed incredulously. How could he believe that they would be spared? Why would he even want to be spared?

"You don't want to taste the joy of Paradise?" asked Mussa.

"Arno said we were to leave."

That was like Arno: he told everyone what he thought they wanted to hear.

Including him?

Ahmed pointed the gun at him haphazardly. At this point, Mussa wasn't afraid of being shot, but he worried that the bomb, despite the guarantees of the engineers, would somehow be damaged if the idiot fired.

Should he explain that the engine was only to block others and help deflect the blast upward if it was not to specifications?

"Aren't we leaving?" asked Ahmed.

"Yes, of course," said Mussa. As he began climbing over the seats, he heard more gunfire from a distant coach.

"The timer is running. We'd better hurry," said Ahmed.

"There's time. We can wait for the others," said Mussa.

"No, we should leave now. Let them fend for themselves. They can leave through the access tunnels. The engine will take us out."

Mussa thought it wise to humor Ahmed until he could wrestle the gun away. What was the worst that could happen? The bomb would explode now, no matter what.

"Lead the way," he told Ahmed.

101

Rubens hovered over Chafetz's shoulder, staring at her screen. The Eurostars received signal information through a special system that used the train tracks. The NSA had just been given access to the system and was looking at what had been recorded since the train had entered the Chunnel. There was a burst of gibberish, followed by a clearing signal that indicated there was no problem and then a series of what were being interpreted as shorts in the system.

The French and British engineers in charge of the signals had never seen such a sequence before. They believed at least part of the train was moving forward at a much reduced speed. They did not have direct communications with the train's engineer.

"Tell them to get out if you can," said Rubens. "Find a way to get them out."

Special military response teams assigned to the Chunnel had been activated on both shores. They would be ready to enter the tunnel in a few minutes. Traffic through the other tube had been stopped and the few workers in the service tunnel between the train lines were being evacuated. Emergency procedures were being started in the coastal areas, though Rubens doubted there would be time to even get out an alert, let alone do anything constructive to deal with the danger.

People were scurrying. But it was too late, wasn't it? His people, unaware of the plot, were probably already gone.

As originally composed, the NSA did not have an "action" side. Jobs such as planting bugs were farmed out, generally to the CIA, though the military services were also used. They were contractors in a way, specialists in their tasks and removed from the NSA hierarchy. It made it easier when something went wrong.

The General had pointed that out to Rubens long ago. He had chafed at the lack of an "action side," but there was that plus.

Rubens knew he had made the right decisions. While he regretted that the analysts hadn't been able to come up with the information more expeditiously, he did not regret the decisions that had placed his people in jeopardy and, in all likelihood, cost them their lives; these were the decisions he had to make. But he did feel the loss. It pressed its fingers against his skull. And the ache was amplified by the fact that they were impotent, observers only.

Do *something*, rather than nothing. That had been the General's motto.

Ruben turned to Telach. "Have we prepared a plan to disable the weapon?"

"We don't have information on how it might be armed or configured or anything," said Telach.

"Let's at least have theories ready," said Rubens. "And bring Johnny Bib down here. As crazy as he is, he's bound to have an inspiration."

102

Dean stared at the far wall of the tunnel, trying to decide if what he saw there were real shadows of the gunmen moving inside the train or flickers of his imagination.

They had to be gunmen — he could hear the muffled sound of the submachine guns again.

They were moving toward the back of the train, in his direction. Each coach had doors at the side, but they appeared to be all locked closed. The only way in or out of the train was the passage at the end of the decoupled car.

If they came out he could surprise them, jump down on them from the top of the train.

But how many were there? One? Two? More?

Dean moved along the walkway next to the tracks, stooping and then crawling toward what had been the rear of the train. He couldn't quite see in the windows, but as he came parallel to the middle car he saw two shadows prominently one car away. He slid down, flattening himself against the car at a space where there were no windows. He waited, taking the long, slow breaths he'd learned to take more than thirty years before, the calm, quiet breaths of a Marine sniper hunting his prey.

He heard the *clack-clack* of automatic weapons fire behind him, then beyond him. As the shadows moved through the car he had just passed, he started walking again, going as quickly as he could while remaining low, aware that there might be someone else in the train.

A voice echoed in the tunnel, distorted by an eerie echo.

Dean dropped to his stomach. The voice continued to speak — it was in French, he thought, and even if it had been in English it would have been difficult to understand because of the distortion of the tunnel.

The tone seemed unhurried. It was a matter-of-fact conversation, not a harsh bark of orders or worried alerts.

It was coming from the front of the train — from the tracks.

Dean crawled ahead to the last coach, the one that had been attached to the rear power car. He could hear footsteps and then saw a faint flashlight.

The engine had been pulled down the tracks thirty yards or so. The person with the flashlight was moving toward it, with another person, just one other person.

So at least two still in the train and two there, going to the engine. Maybe more in the power car itself.

The two figures climbed up onto the power car and disappeared. Dean slid around to the back of the coach. The doorway at the end was open, dim yellow light washing out. He waited, eyes sifting for shadows, ears perked to hear anything that would tell him someone else was aboard.

Nothing.

He moved back around to the side and peered in the window. Boxes sat in the aisle roughly in the middle of the car. Otherwise, it was empty.

Except for the dead.

He slid around the coach and pulled himself up onto the decking of the vestibule at the end of the car. People liked to talk about athletes who grew old and lost a step, saying they'd gotten wiser in the process and could use their intelligence to make up for the loss. But it didn't feel that way to Dean. Fifty-some years dogged every movement, leaning hard against him, pulling him away from the train. He'd been a kid in Vietnam, and he'd trade anything to have that kid take over his body right now.

Or maybe just one of the kid's weapons.

Dean craned his head upward just enough so he could see into the car through the door. He saw nothing — but his view was blocked by the boxes as well as his angle. There was no way to look in without going in — pushing his body across the space and exposing himself to whatever and whoever was there.

And so he did.

103

Lia grew more cautious as she came to the doorway, aware not just that there could be something lurking in the darkness but also knowing that the odd echoes of sound and the constant rush of air and sound filtered away soft noises, including her own footsteps. She had a tiny light on her key chain but didn't want to use it; it would show anyone else in the Chunnel where she was. She assumed anyone else here would be her enemy, and whether that was a fair assumption or not — there had been policemen aboard the train — it was not something she questioned. As she reached the door to the access tunnel she stopped, hearing something behind her.

Lia froze.

Then she realized that she would be framed by the fluorescent light above the door. She took a step back into the passage.

Someone grabbed her from behind and threw her down. In the weightless second as she fell she was transported back to Korea, back to the instant when she was overpowered in the airport terminal. She fought, biting the hand — the déjà vu sensation disappeared and she was completely in the present, thrashing and wrestling and biting and rolling and lunging and not surrendering, never surrendering, because that wasn't who she was.

104

Car eighteen had only dead bodies, some scattered luggage, and the large boxes blocking the aisle.

Dean took another step inside, trying to see around the boxes. They looked like the carts that the servers used as they brought refreshments to the first-class passengers; the carts had clearly been arranged like this on purpose, though Dean had no idea why. He tried to push one out of the way, but it wouldn't budge; they were all linked together somehow. He had to hop over two sets of seats nearby to get around the boxes.

A man lay in a pool of blood near the end of the car. His skull had been battered so badly it looked as if it had been made of sawdust and blood.

Dean moved on. The doorway to the next car was around a bend; he dropped to his knees and looked around the corner.

The doorway was open. The next car was empty.

He went in, stopping every few feet to listen. If someone came, he would hide in the seats, preferably next to one of the dead people, and spring out as the person moved past.

He didn't hear any more gunfire. They'd have finished their work and would be returning.

Dean moved through two more coaches. In coach fourteen he spotted a briefcase made of metal in the overhead rack. Thinking he could use it as a weapon, he stretched up to grab it. As he did, he realized he was exposed to the outside window and casting a shadow, just as the gunmen had. He took the briefcase down and dropped to the floor, crouching his way to the end.

So where were the gunmen?

Maybe they'd gone outside the coach and were checking along the sides or top of the train.

Or maybe they'd gone after Lia.

Dean heard voices approaching as he moved toward the end of the car. He slid into the last seat, hunkering against the window, the briefcase ready.

Two voices.

Another? Were there three?

He twisted his head, let his hand hang down, playing dead.

He saw the side of a man passing, sub-machine gun hanging lazily in front of him.

Wait for the second?

Yes. Here he was.

Was there a third? No, he'd seen two shadows. And he couldn't afford to, not if there were only two — they'd be too far away.

Go!

Dean leaped up, aluminum briefcase held out before him like the battering ram at the prow of an ancient galley. The man closest to him began to turn. The edge of the briefcase caught him on the chin; the gun began to fire.

Dean threw himself forward and they were rolling and there was more gunfire.

Dean pushed and punched, barely able to aim his blows. He could taste blood and heard bullets rumbling, but he had no sense of the fight beyond what his fists and head felt. The terrorist slammed and kicked, tried to wrestle the gun from under his body, tried to writhe away. Dean gripped him and pushed down, slamming at his head, wrestling and finding his enemy's head in his hands.

Finally, there was no more fight left in the other man. Dean had no sense of whether he'd killed him or merely stunned him. He threw himself forward toward the gun that had fallen. He scooped it up, aiming down the car, but the other terrorist had fled.

Just as well. The submachine gun, an H&K MP-5, was empty.

105

The woman kicked and bit and punched at him. Donohue struggled, but her ferocity had caught him off-guard; he tripped and fell backward, managing only to push her away. He leaped backward, took two, three steps, and set himself for her attack.

Fortunately, she didn't follow.

"Who are you?" the woman hissed between breaths. The accent was American.

"Who are *you?*" he answered.

"Why did you blow up the train?"

"I didn't," he said, surprised. "You're not one of the terrorists?"

She was silent.

"Were you a passenger?" he asked.

"Yes. Are you one of the policemen?" she asked.

He considered how to answer the question. A policeman would have more authority, certainly, and pretending to be one now was tempting. But it might be difficult to explain later.

If it mattered.

"No. I'm just a passenger. I jumped off the train," he said. "Terrorists blew it apart."

"I know," said the woman. "Why did you attack me?"

"I thought you were one of them," he said. He wasn't lying. "I didn't see you until you were just about on me — I didn't think anyone could be alive."

"We have to get to help," she said.

"How?" Donohue asked.

"Maybe there's something inside this tunnel. Through the passage. There's a service tunnel in the middle of the two tubes."

"What about the people who blew up the train?" he said.

"They unhooked the engine. I think they left."

"They left?" Donohue felt his anger flare, then drain away — Mussa had managed to escape.

Escape!

Better than he would do, unless he figured something out.

"Come on," said the woman. "Let's see if this entrance goes anywhere."

"You're hurt," he said, noticing that she was limping.

"I'm all right."

There were probably dozens of ways out of the service tunnel. If he lived, he would get Mussa. For that he would trade his life. He would strangle the bloody bastard with his bare hands. Oh, that would be delicious.

Who would blame him? He'd be a national hero. The Queen might even knight him . . . before throwing him in prison for the rest of his life.

"I'm sorry I hit you," he said.

"You almost killed me," said the woman, moving ahead in the passage. "I have a penlight on my key chain. Come on."

106

Dean found a magazine for the submachine gun in the terrorist's belt.

The man was still breathing; a quick kiss of the trigger took care of that.

Dean stepped over the body, moving in the direction the other man had gone.

Had he fled in fear? Or was he out of bullets, without even a spare like his friend?

Dean stopped at the vestibule, listening. When he thought he heard a creak in the next car, he threw himself inside, firing a burst from the gun as something flicked at the edge of his peripheral vision. In the same motion he dove to the ground, rolled, ready, waiting.

But there was nothing.

Dean got to his hands and knees and moved forward slowly. He paused about midway, listening. When he started again the front of the car lit up with gunfire. Diving into the nearby seats, he could almost feel the bullets zipping overhead.

The burst was long; Dean suspected it was covering an advance and got ready. When it stopped he made a feint with the gun toward the aisle and drew more fire. This time the burst was much briefer. When it ended he held the gun up and fired a few rounds toward the back of the car, then burst out into the aisle, gun blazing, throwing himself across to the other side.

As he landed on the floor he realized the terrorist had retreated. Dean jumped up and ran to the end, breath shallow, blood spurting from his head. He spun himself around the bend to the floor, ready to fire but not shooting this time. He had to conserve his bullets.

He waited a breath, two breaths, then began moving forward again.

Maybe the other man was out of bullets.

Why was he still in the train? And what were the boxes there for?

Another bomb.

Maybe the man was running to set it off.

As Dean reached the end of the coach he threw himself around the passage, diving headfirst into the other car. Dean began to run, racing through the coach. But as he sprang into car seventeen the air around him exploded with ricochets and shrapnel. He fired down the aisle of the car, the MP-5 shaking and then stuttering as he dove straight down to the floor, rolling and crawling and pushing behind the seats.

He was out of bullets.

Dean waited. When the terrorist didn't come, he slid toward the aisle, gun-first. A fresh fusillade drove him back.

Sure that the man would be coming for him, he pushed against the bottom of the seat cushion, coiling his body, ready to spring out.

He'd use the gun as a battering ram, hope that he'd be lucky, or lucky enough not to be killed.

When the man didn't appear, Dean told himself to wait — then changed his mind and slid the gun forward.

More rounds spat through the car, ricocheting and slapping around him. The seats were thick and the gunman had no angle, but the fact that Dean hadn't been shot yet was due largely to the gunman's inexperience — if the terrorist had been trained better, he would have held his fire and closed the angle down patiently, relentlessly, seat by seat.

Dean glanced across the aisle at the acrylic shelving. He could see a reflection — the terrorist, lying at the end of the car, gun poised.

Why was he on the floor out in the middle of the aisle?

Dean slid his gun forward into the aisle. Another few rounds, poorly aimed.

There was only one reason he'd be on the floor — he'd been wounded so severely he couldn't move.

But he had Dean pinned.

There were several bodies blocking anything but a shot from the aisle.

Dean climbed up into the seat, hunkering and gathering his breath. With a sudden heave he threw himself over the top of the chair, flying into the next row. The gunman didn't catch on until Dean hit the cushion on the other side.

More gunfire — and then nothing, a click, the gun empty, a curse.

Had he heard that? Or did he want to hear that?

Dean jumped to his feet.

107

The gangway of the power car was claustrophobic and smelled like a burnt transformer. Ahmed sat in the engineer's plush velvet seat and pushed the levers. The transformers behind them began to hum.

It was theoretically possible to escape at least the blast — they had less than ten miles to go and just over ten minutes to do it. They'd have to clear the tunnel by a good margin to escape the blast, but it was possible.

Did he want to live?

Allah was offering him a choice. If he escaped he might have other triumphs.

Or he might be captured. More likely the latter.

The train stuttered forward.

God wasn't offering him the choice; the devil was. Mussa reached toward the red brake switch on the left. As his fingers reached it, he threw his body against Ahmed's head and arms, grabbing for the gun with his other hand.

108

Rubens jerked around as the voice came through the loudspeaker.

Lia, talking to the British authorities via the emergency phone system in the maintenance section of the Chunnel.

"They've split the train in half and separated the engine from the back half. There were at least two of them. Everyone in the back half of the train is dead. Cut the power. Stop them from getting away."

"Can we talk to her?" Rubens asked.

"We should be able to cut right in," said Telach. "Lia?"

A British operator asked who was interfering — then the line clicked and he was gone, his voice erased by the Art Room's computers.

"Lia?" repeated Telach.

"Marie, are you on the line?" answered Lia, her voice fainter than it had been before.

Rubens punched his mike button. "Lia, this is Rubens. The terrorists have assembled a nuclear bomb on the train. I want you to talk to one of our experts on how to defuse it."

"Are you serious?"

"I assure you I am very serious."

109

Dean took three steps and then dove as the man brought up a pistol from his side. The gun went off close to Dean's head. He grabbed for it, managing to push it to the side as it fired again. Something burned the right side of his thigh, the pain so intense Dean yelped.

He waited for the next shot. Paralyzed by pain.

It didn't come. Dean hadn't been hit by the bullet but rather fragments of the man's skull, shattered as the 9mm shell entered his head.

Blood dripped down his pants as he stood. He bent back down and grabbed the pistol, then began making his way to the car where he'd seen the carts clustered together.

110

Lia listened as the weapons expert explained how he thought the bomb would work — a set of conventional explosives would force the nuclear material together, creating a critical mass and triggering the atomic chain reaction. It was essentially the way early nuclear bombs worked, or at least one type of them, ever since "Fat Man" had been detonated over Nagasaki.

"Depending on the design, the warhead may not be in the exact center of the assembly. From the formula I saw, they had to compensate for the lack of proximity to the plutonium by layering the explosions, probably because they couldn't be sure of handling the material in a way —"

"Just tell me how to disarm it," Lia told him.

"We won't know until you can describe what the mechanism is like."

"What am I supposed to do, run back and forth?" she snapped.

"If you could disrupt the explosive assembly around the core of the weapon," said Johnny Bib, who was listening in on the line, "then it stands to reason that the explosion would not work as designed. The formula has a set of variables that I believe describe modules. Removing one module will alter the result exponentially."

"In English!"

"Take one of the explosive modules away," said Johnny Bib. "There'll still be an explosion, a huge one, but it won't compress the nuclear material. No boom."

"Look, there's someone with me. Have him talk to the British police or whoever I was talking to and describe what happened." She turned and held the phone out for the man who'd surprised her in the tunnel. "Talk to them. I'm going back on the train."

He grabbed at her arm. Lia jerked back out of the way. If her leg had been all right she would have tossed him over her shoulder.

"You can't go back," said the man, his Irish brogue thick now. "It's suicide."

"I have to go back. Just tell them what happened." Lia hobbled toward the entrance. Her leg muscles loosened as she moved and she was able to walk more normally, making decent progress.

"Listen," said the man, coming after her. "You have to get out of here. Come on."

"Don't worry about me."

"Don't worry?"

"Look, I'm a professional. Just take care of yourself," she said finally, heading back for the Chunnel tube.

Donohue watched the woman leave. She must be some sort of undercover police officer — but she had an American accent.

CIA?

Or a British MI5 agent undercover. If that was the case, it would be dicey dealing with her.

Not with that accent. Clearly American. And an American would be an asset.

She was *something*. She'd nearly flattened him in the tunnel earlier.

Help her and she'd vouch for him when they got out. No one would even question him.

Donohue decided he had nothing to lose by following along and finding out. He gave her enough time to get out of the service tunnel and back into the train tube, then began following as quietly as he could.

111

Dean examined the boxes more carefully this time. They were definitely different units, but they were locked together somehow. The surface seemed to be a plastic material painted to look like metal at first glance. At the top of one of the boxes a small watch face had been inserted in an octagonal cutout; as Dean watched, time slipped away: 424, 423, 422 . . .

He tried to pry the clock up and out of the indentation with his fingers, but it wouldn't budge.

He could break it, probably, by slamming something into it. But would that stop the timer or merely cause the bomb to explode prematurely?

Where was the stinking Art Room when he needed them?

Dean climbed up over the seats and squirreled around to the back of the car. He saw the dim outline of the power car down the tracks; it sounded like it had been started up again.

Whoever was in it would be waiting for the gunmen.

He stepped back, thinking there must be a way to close the door manually. But it wasn't obvious, and after a moment searching he decided he was better off trying to figure out how to defuse the bomb.

There were now a little more than 350 seconds left — less than six minutes.

He could break the timer as a last resort.

He began hunting for another switch, looking at each side of the device. When he didn't find one, he thought it might be possible to pry the watch out and reset it. He reached into his pockets, looking for his keys, only to remember that he didn't have any. He bent to the dead woman whose body rested against the bombs. Her pocketbook was on the floor near her seat. He opened it and fished around. There was a small nail file at the bottom.

As he started back he heard a sound at the end of the car. He pulled the pistol from his belt as he ducked behind the seat back.

"You going to shoot me?"

"Lia."

"That thing there's a nuke," she said, limping toward it. "Johnny Bib says it's put together like building blocks. We have to pull one of the blocks away."

"You're kidding."

"Oh yeah, I made it up."

She reached forward and put her fingers on the crack at the side, pulling. It didn't budge.

"We have to pull it apart? It won't explode?"

"I have no idea, Charlie Dean. Just help me."

"Wait," said Dean. He ran to where he'd dropped the MP-5, thinking they might be able to use it as a pry bar.

"What happened to your leg?" Lia asked, pointing to the bloodstain.

"I bit a ricochet. How's your calf?"

"Still here. Johnny Bib's a nut, you know."

Dean couldn't get the muzzle of the weapon into the razor-thin opening between the boxes. He started using the gun like an ice pick, hammering away. Nothing moved.

"This back one, here," said Lia. "Look, there's more of a crack. Give me that nail file."

She took the file and began wiggling it in. It hit something about an inch in.

"Slam the file down," she said. "I think I

hit a lock or something. Come on."

As Dean positioned himself, he saw the time draining — they were in the two hundreds now.

"Here, come on, come on," said Lia. She grabbed the gun and together they slammed it down on the file. It broke, but the box moved about a quarter of an inch away from the others, just enough to slide the gun in.

They pushed together, once, twice — and the third time was the charm. The box moved perhaps an inch away.

"More!" Lia yelled.

Dean got up on the seat back and kicked at the gun, forgetting that he had hurt his leg. The knee twisted and the pain was so bad he felt his whole body go weak and then numb.

But the box moved about six inches.

"Again, come on," said Lia, and she twisted around to help him. He put the pistol down and they pushed, once, twice, three times, a fourth, a fifth — the snaps at the bottom finally gave way and the box tumbled down with a heavy crash.

So did they, rolling into the seats and then onto the floor, Lia barely avoiding getting crushed.

As Dean looked up, a shadow came

around the corner at the back of the train. He dove for his pistol.

Mussa heard something as he climbed onto the train. What were Muhammad and Kelvin up to?

He checked the machine gun he had taken from Ahmed. He'd have to kill them, too. There were only a few minutes left, no sense keeping them alive now.

As he turned the corner, the bomb seemed to explode. His first thought was that Allah had permitted him the sublime ecstasy of seeing his weapon erupt.

And then he realized he was very wrong. Someone was trying to take it apart. He was so shocked it took a moment before he could lift his weapon.

Donohue crouched at the back of the car, trying to decipher what was going on from the others' conversation.

The woman had found a man, on either the train or the tracks. They were American agents. They were talking about a bomb. A nuclear bomb.

Had Mussa stolen a nuclear device?

Donohue ran into the car, starting to say that he would help. As he did, he saw not the woman or the man she'd found somehow, but Mussa, standing at the far end.

There was a submachine gun in his hand.

Lia's head slammed hard on the floor and the box crashed alongside her, a half inch from her face.

She was in Korea, in the terminal. There was a man at the door, yelling.

The old man who'd been with her before the other plane arrived. He was in charge of the terminal or something, some sort of civilian official.

He stood in the doorway. The officer whirled back in anger, pulling out his pistol, but the old man remained there, a solemn look on his face, shaming him.

He said something.

The officer started to raise his gun, but the old man gave no ground.

Silently the officer waved at the others. They left, and so did he.

Why had she forgotten that? Why had her brain pushed it away? The old man had saved her.

God bless him for his courage.

Mussa couldn't believe it: Donohue stood at the end of the car.

Donohue!

He turned his submachine gun toward him and began to fire.

Dean heard the submachine gun rattle as he grabbed the pistol. He twisted upward. The shadow lurched forward — the man with the submachine gun was firing at the far end of the carriage, ignoring him.

Dean's first bullet struck the side of the man's head. It seemed as if it had no effect. With the second shot, the head disappeared backward, blood flying in a thick spray everywhere.

"Come on! Come on!" Dean yelled, scrambling to get up. "Let's get out. Come on."

Lia lay on her stomach on the floor between the seats and the piece of bomb that they had moved. Tears were flowing from her closed eyes and her whole body heaved with sobs. Dean grabbed her, pulling her past the man he'd just shot, a light-skinned Arab dressed in the uniform of the train crew. He half-carried, half-dragged her to the end of the car. He let go of her, thinking he would jump down to the tracks and reach back for her. But when he got to the ground she had already clambered down.

"I can do it on my own, Charlie Dean,"

she said as he tried to help her.

"For once in your life, accept some help, damn it," he told her. "Just shut up and be thankful."

"I am thankful," she whispered as he hoisted her over his shoulder. "And not for once, either."

112

Rubens paced back and forth in the Art Room. The French response team had just gone into the service tunnel that ran down the middle of the Chunnel. It would take several minutes before they reached the area Lia had called from.

In the meantime, all he could do was wait. This was the worst thing in life, wasn't it? Simply standing — or rather pacing — doing nothing.

It was how he felt with the General, really. Unable to help.

Perhaps Rebecca felt that way as well. Maybe she fought simply because doing something was better than nothing.

The front half of the train was now safely in England. The power in the lines that fed the train through the pantograph at the top of the train had just been cut, in case this was being used to power the bomb somehow — though it was probably a futile gesture.

But you had to do something, didn't you?

"Jesus!" said Telach.

Rubens turned and saw a puff of smoke blowing from the feed of the British side of the Chunnel entrance.

"Oh, God," said Telach.

Rubens walked to her and squeezed her elbow. "Steady now," he said. "Just steady."

"Earthquake data," said Chafetz. "Incomplete. Incomplete. P waves are — hold it . . ."

Rubens waited. Seismologists generally divided the shock from an earthquake — or an underground explosion — into two types of waves, P waves and S waves. More familiarly, the blast could be measured on the Richter scale commonly used for earthquakes. In theory, a sixty-kiloton explosion would register into the sixes on the Richter scale, though the exact force would depend on the circumstances. (Actual nuclear devices that yielded sixty kilotons often registered considerably less on the Richter scale — though the force of their impact was hardly negligible.)

Rubens crossed his arms in front of his chest, waiting.

"What's going on?" asked Hadash from Air Force One.

"Mr. President, there's been an explosion in the Chunnel," Rubens said.

Marcke came on the line. "They detonated the nuke?"

"We're still looking for data, sir."

"Three — we don't have numbers here," said Chafetz.

Rubens turned at her. One of the analysts in the back section stood up and yelled, "Less than three-point-two. Less! Not a nuke."

A *huge* explosion nonetheless.

But not a nuke.

Someone started to clap. Several other people started to say something else.

"Please," said Rubens, raising his arms. "We have much more to do. And two people in the Chunnel."

The room went silent.

"Mr. President," said Rubens. "It appears their explosion failed to detonate the warhead, if they had it."

"Thank God," said Marcke.

"Yes, sir."

113

They'd gotten no more than three or four hundred yards from the power car when the tunnel behind them exploded. Dean, with Lia still on his back, flew down face-first into the tracks, slamming so hard he blacked out. When he came to, Lia was clawing at him, pulling him forward.

"Come on," she said. "Come on."

"Wait."

"No!"

A roar filled his ears. His face was wet and he thought he'd cut himself.

Then he realized his pants and shirt were wet as well.

"Come on!" Lia screamed. "Water's flooding the tracks. The access tunnel is there. Go! Come on!"

Dean got up, then stumbled as a wave of water pushed at him from the back.

"Come on!" Lia yelled, pulling at him.

Water was everywhere. By the time they managed the twenty or thirty yards to the access doorway it was to his knees.

Lights were flashing in the service area. Alarms were sounding, but above it all Dean could hear the rush of water.

"This way," said Lia. "Toward France."

"It's miles."

"You want to wait for the water to reach us? Go! Go!"

Dean started after her. She tripped over something and, unable to stop himself, he tripped over her. They tumbled down against the concrete, sprawling.

"I don't think I can go any further," he said.

"You have to," she hissed, pushing up.

"Stay where you are," said a voice in French.

Dean looked up to see a French FAMAS assault rifle in his face. He'd never been so happy to have a gun pointed at him in his life.

114

Rubens waited until he heard Lia's voice for himself before finally allowing himself to believe his people were all right.

"They had this bomb cobbled together from a bunch of carts or crates that looked like the things they use to give out meals from," she told him.

She and Dean had been taken to a hospital in Calais. Rubens had no idea how good the medical facilities were; all he knew was that it had no video hookup, so he could only talk to his two ops.

"You'd have thought the French would have figured it out," she added. "They're so obsessed with food."

"I'm glad to hear you're still your cynical self," said Rubens.

"I'm not cynical," she said.

"Sarcastic. Excuse me."

"I have a lot to be sarcastic about," she said. "And thankful for."

The last remark was so completely out of character for Lia that Rubens found it impossible to say anything else until Dean came on the line.

"Mr. Dean, I hope your injuries are not too severe," he told him.

"I've had worse."

"Our understanding is that the north-bound tube of the Chunnel is completely flooded," Rubens told him. He was looking at a video image from the French side — several feet of water surrounded the closed access doors.

"Everyone on our half of the train is dead," said Dean. "What happened to the other side?"

"The front part of the train was able to make it out before the explosion," Rubens told him. "It followed its protocol for a de-coupling at speed. It could have been much worse. Much, much worse."

The other train tube was intact. Divers with special protective gear would be sent to inspect the flooded tube — and recover the warhead's plutonium, assuming it could be found and recovered safely. Eventually, the Chunnel would be repaired.

Eventually being many, many years in the future.

"So what happened at the Eiffel Tower?" asked Dean. "Was that a diversion?"

"On the contrary. It appears to have

been a related attack, and very real. Monsieur Duoar was quite a planner. He wanted to see a crescendo of terror. The tower plot was foiled with the help of Mr. Karr," continued Rubens. "I'm surprised you haven't seen the video of him hanging upside down from the third *étage*. French television has been playing it nonstop for the past four hours."

"You kidding?"

"I do not kid, Charlie. I leave that for others." Rubens broke the connection.

He was in his office when the attorney, Ms. McGovern, finally returned his call back to her.

"Mr. Rubens, good time?"

"It is," he said.

"You sound tired."

"A little."

"That attack in France, and the Chunnel — it sounds incredible."

"Oh? I haven't had a chance to check the news."

"Terrorists attacked the Eiffel Tower and the Chunnel," she told him. "It sounds terrible."

"I'm sure." He turned away from the desk, looking toward the chair that sat in the corner of his office. It was a leather club chair that had once belonged to the General.

"The judge made his decision," said McGovern. "I told you he would move quickly."

Rubens waited, but instead of telling him what the decision was, she changed the subject.

"You have Rebecca's letter?" she asked.

"Yes," said Rubens.

He'd lost. So be it.

"That's a good sign, don't you think?" said McGovern. "She does love her father. She's just concerned about him."

"Yes," said Rubens.

"The judge saw no reason to go against the General's wishes," she told him. "You were appointed."

Oddly, it didn't feel like much of a victory.

115

Karr knew there was someone in the room with him, but it seemed to take forever to open his eyes. When he finally did, he saw not a person but an angel floating at the side of the bed: Deidre Clancy.

"Hey," he said.

"Hey yourself."

"Hey," he said again, sliding up on his elbows. "Whoa, that hurts."

"It shouldn't. Your blood's fifty percent Demerol."

"See, that's where the doctors always get it wrong," said Karr, easing back down. "Give me a good pint of Guinness stout and nothing would bother me."

"Take more than a pint."

"Probably."

"You're a national hero, you know. The French are calling you the American Golden Bear."

"Yeah?"

"You and your friends in the Chunnel."

"Which?"

Karr listened as Deidre told him about Lia and Dean, who had been pulled out after foiling a plot to explode a nuclear device in the Chunnel.

"The French President claims it wouldn't have exploded anyway," added Deidre. "But that sounds pretty political. And French. Want me to move the bed? You have a lift thing in the back."

He grimaced as the bed moved, but it did feel better.

"They have guards on your door to keep the media away," she told him.

"Really?"

"I'm not kidding. I think they have orders to shoot to kill."

"So how'd you get in? Your dad?"

"I tried that, but it didn't work. So I told a little white lie."

"Like?"

"I said I was your fiancée."

Karr started to laugh. His ribs had been broken and he started to wheeze and cough — and laugh even harder.

"You don't have one, do you?" she asked.

"Well, maybe now."

116

In the dream, she was back in Korea. She was powerless to do anything, completely unable to resist. He and his henchmen dragged her to the little room. She began to scream, but no one came and the men began to pummel her.

"Hey."

Lia shook herself awake, practically jumping out of the seat. She was in an airplane with Charlie Dean — an Air Force VIP jet that had been used to take the Secretary of State to France. It had been detailed to take them home at the President's direct order.

"Bad dream?" asked Dean, sitting across from her.

A dream? Yes. A nightmare. And more.

She'd gotten past it. Whether that was good or not — what that really meant — she didn't know.

"Hey, did you have a dream or what?" Dean asked again.

"None of your business, Charlie Dean."

He grabbed her arm. "You are my business," he said.

She frowned but then said softly, "Just a dream."